I0727900

Once Upon a Crown

DEMELZA CARLTON

Three tales in the Romance a Medieval Fairy Tale series

Embellish:
Brave Little Tailor
Retold

DEMELZA CARLTON

A tale in the Romance a Medieval Fairy Tale series

One

The one thing George loved most in all the world was dragons. At least, he had until a few minutes ago, when the biggest, grumpiest dragon to ever crawl out of a cave had disarmed him and knocked him down with a single swipe of its mighty tail. Now he didn't feel particularly fond of dragons at all.

George raised his head slightly, wondering why he wasn't dead like the charred, armoured corpse beside him. Perhaps the dragon's eyesight was so bad that he thought George was already dead. As soon as George moved, though, the dragon would realise its mistake. And rectify it.

George suppressed a sigh. He didn't lack for courage – he'd challenged the dragon, after all, and he intended to defeat it. But standing before a dragon while the damn dragon held his sword under one claw would only turn him into a piece of toast before the fire, for in one gout of flame, he would be dead, George had no doubt.

Cowardice wasn't his problem. It was common sense, and the ability to see consequences no one else could. The other boys in town would boast of how long other knights had stood while the dragon roasted them with its fiery breath, but George had little admiration for such men. There was honour in defeat if you learned enough from it to ensure victory in the future. What honour was there in taking ten seconds to burn to death before your armour collapsed with your charred bones inside? Even George didn't remember the name of the knight whose body lay beside him. A century from now, no one else would remember him, either. But they would remember the man who slayed the dragon. Even if George wasn't the man to do it today.

The dragon headed down the hill toward the river, distracted by something more interesting than the boy whose sword he'd stolen. George recognised opportunity when he saw it. He leaped to his feet, and sprinted toward the city gates.

His heart hammered in his chest, but he didn't dare stop to look back. All he could focus on was his booted feet pounding the road ever upwards to the safety of the city walls. Fifty yards more. No, forty. Thirty. Twenty-five. Twenty. Fifteen. Ten.

Eight, seven, six…

His fleet feet ate up the distance faster than he stuffed down dumplings at the dinner table.

Three, two, one…

SAFE.

Laughter and applause greeted George as he slowed to enter the city gates.

"Dragon too big for you, boy?"

"No one ever wrote a ballad about a hero running away from a dragon!"

"Leave dragon slaying to men who know how to fight, boy. Go home to your father."

"The girl put on a better show than he did!"

George did his best to ignore the ribbing, but the last comment hit home. In his battle lust, he'd forgotten about his fairy godmother, Lady Zoraida, who'd graciously agreed to be the maiden bait who tempted the dragon out of its cave. If she'd been injured by the dragon, he'd never forgive himself.

"Where's the girl? What happened to her?" George blurted out, finally allowing himself to peer back down the hill to where the dragon's cave lay.

"Held up her end of the fight better'n you, boy. Threw some of the dragon's own fire back at him, she did. He didn't like that, neither. He tried to eat her, but she drew a big purple circle in the air and disappeared. Don't know why. She was holding her own against the dread beast, and no mistake. Maybe she didn't want to be a hero. I mean, who ever heard of a maiden who defeated a dragon?"

George opened his mouth to say that his saintly namesake had needed the help of a maiden to defeat his dragon, but he closed it again. The city guardsmen didn't want to hear stories about how other dragons had died – they wanted to witness the death of this one, which had terrorised their town for too long.

Instead, George said, "If you do, I want to meet her."

He'd apologise to Lady Zoraida when he saw her next, George promised himself, though it would probably be a while before he did. She hadn't been happy about helping him with the dragon, and he'd lost the enchanted sword she'd given him, too.

He had no luck with women or dragons.

Sighing deeply, George trudged home.

Seeing as he was still alive and there were a few hours of daylight left, he should help his father in the shop. More monster slaying could wait until the morrow.

Two

Melitta would never forget the day she decided she would become a hero. It was the holy day of St John, and the entire court was present in the Great Hall for the feast.

"Your Majesties, may I present to you, the renowned knight from far off lands, the hero of countless battles, the mighty Sir Chase!" the herald bellowed.

From her place at the high table, two seats away from Queen Margareta, Melitta had an ideal view of the knight who strode into the

Great Hall, haloed by the rosy rays of the sinking sun behind him. His armour caught the candlelight from all directions, bathing him in gold. Gasps rose from the long tables on either side of him. Only the king and his knights could afford so much metal, while most of them wore leather. To wear such glorious armour, for surely it could not be real gold, this travelling knight must be rich indeed. And if it was real gold…why, he must be the best knight in all the lands, and a true hero.

The kind she wished to be.

King Erik called for a place to be set for the knight, before announcing grandly that there should be a tourney on the morrow, so that his own men could test their skill against such a legendary hero.

Cheers erupted around the hall and men raised their cups to toast the king's health.

Melitta didn't need to read the men's minds to know they all shared the same thought: every man present wanted to beat the newcomer in a fair fight, for honour won in battle, even a mock battle, was more precious than life itself.

"Fools," Queen Margareta muttered to Mother, loud enough for Melitta to hear. Whether she included her husband in that, Melitta didn't know.

As if the knight had heard, Sir Chase bowed his head and removed his helmet.

Now it was Melitta's turn to gasp.

Sir Chase was the handsomest man she had ever seen. Dark hair warred with light coloured eyes, and yet the outcome of the battle was…mesmerising. No wrinkle or a scar marked his face, beneath a thatch that bore not even a single white hair. He appeared younger than even their ever-youthful queen. Too young to be a hero, yet here he was.

Sir Chase bowed low before the dais. "Your Majesty King Erik, I am honoured by your hospitality. I wish only to serve."

This was when he would whip out his sword and lay it at the king's feet, Melitta knew, as he pledged his fealty and honour to the king's service. She'd seen enough knights sworn in to know the way of it.

Yet Sir Chase's sword remained firmly in its scabbard.

"I eagerly await tomorrow's tourney, for what better way to show a man's fighting prowess? Yet there is more to a knight than his sword."

Queen Margareta's musical laughter rang out across the hall, silencing all conversation. "Pray continue, Sir Knight."

"As you wish, most beautiful queen. A true hero must keep his wits as sharp as his blade. His honour must shine as bright as his armour, and never be allowed to tarnish. So that if his liege or his lady is plagued by the most enormous monster or the tiniest gnat, he can dispatch it forthwith."

Gnats? In summertime, they had more problems with flies, Melitta thought, shooing several of the buzzing nuisances away from her meat. How did they manage to seek her out so fast? She'd been so focussed on Sir Chase she hadn't seen them appear.

"Allow me, Your Majesty," Sir Chase said.

He reached behind him for his bow, notched an arrow to the string and let it fly. His arrow lodged in one of the tapestries high above Melitta's head.

What was he doing? In her momentary distraction, Melitta must have missed something Sir Chase had said.

Melitta bit her lip, and concentrated on his thoughts.

His gaze centred on a fly buzzing above the queen's head as he drew another arrow. The point followed the insect until he had a clear shot, when the knight released. His arrow arced up, skewering the insect before embedding itself in the wax encrusting a lit candelabra at the back of the dais. The candles wobbled for a moment, but did not fall, to the knight's relief.

Evidently deciding that Melitta's meal was a far safer target than the queen's, a fly zoomed past Melitta's face.

For a single, heart-stopping moment, Sir Chase's eyes met Melitta's. His eyelid drooped in what was definitely a wink.

She clearly heard him say, "Fear not, young maiden. A knight's duty is to save every lady, not just the queen."

His arrow point followed the fly as it finally left her alone and bumbled toward Mother.

Melitta felt a burst of satisfaction from the knight as he released the third arrow. It would meet its target, the queen would be impressed, he would have a place at court, he…

Queen Margareta leaped to her feet. "Guards!"

Melitta stared. A thin line of blood trickled down the queen's fingers to where the arrow had lodged in the table before her. A shimmery wing was all that remained of the fly, now squashed under the weight of the arrow point. The knight had shot the bug, all right, but he'd been so intent on his target that he'd unwittingly hurt the queen.

Sir Chase was too stunned to resist as two

of the king's trusted men seized his arms, and a third reached for his sword. "Your Majesty, I meant…I meant to rid you of a pest, not…" Sir Chase stammered.

"Silence!" Queen Margareta thundered.

At her side, King Erik rose. "Anyone who seeks to harm my queen commits treason. Such a heinous crime is punishable by death."

Sir Chase's thoughts were a jumbled mess of panic as he found he could not speak. Yet rising through it all was a scream of horror that he had not meant to harm the queen. Melitta believed him.

But the queen did not.

"He's telling the truth!" Melitta was surprised to hear her own high voice echo across the hall. Somehow, she'd risen from her seat, and now her knees wanted to wilt so that she could sink under the table and hide from what seemed like every eye turned toward her. Yet Sir Chase's talk of honour and heroes emboldened her, and she forced herself to stand tall. Maidens could be heroes, too. "He shot a fly. Look!" She pointed at the arrow with a hand that shook.

Mother shoved her back into her seat, telling her to hush, but it was too late. The queen had heard every word.

Glittering dark eyes seemed to survey Melitta's soul. Melitta stared back defiantly. Until, miracle of miracles, the queen inclined her head and yielded.

Queen Margareta turned to the knight. "Get out," she said softly. "This once, you may leave with your life. Set foot in this kingdom again and you will not be so lucky."

Melitta slid out of the knight's mind as easily as she'd ventured into it. He bowed one last time toward the dais before making a hasty exit. And while Sir Chase vanished from her world, he never really left her thoughts.

Only it wasn't his handsome face, or his shiny armour that stayed with her. No, it was his words. And the dead flies.

And the hope, one day, of being a hero once more.

Three

George's father looked up from the boot he was piecing together. "Dragon watching again, hmm?"

Not wanting to talk about his horrible failure any more, George simply nodded. He considered helping his father with the boot's fellow, but he was too weary for the kind of precision it required. Instead, he spread a piece of leather out on the cutting table. Destruction was more his style today. George reached for a pair of shears and set to work cutting out soles for shoes.

"Who was today's challenger?" Father asked.

It was too much to ask that Father had been too busy working to hear the dragon roaring.

George snipped savagely. "No one of consequence."

Father nodded sagely as the boot took a distinct curve in his hands. George would always envy the nimbleness of his father's fingers, forming such beautifully shaped shoes from a flat piece of leather. "So your dragon is alive and well, then? How about the would-be slayer?"

"Alive," George bit out as he snipped the sole free. "He ran away." Because he was outmatched, George snarled inwardly. Better to run away and fight properly another day.

"A smart slayer. Will wonders never cease?" Father lifted a needle to his eye and threaded it in one smooth stroke. "That's who will rid us of that nuisance. Not some mighty hero with a stout sword and shiny armour, but a man with a powerful mind. Dragons are cunning creatures, and fighting one will always be a battle of wits."

"I wish more people listened to your good advice, Father," George said, wishing he had. When his father found out his own son had been today's idiot, George intended to make himself scarce. "I don't think I'll watch the next challenger fight the dragon. I'll stay here and help you instead. There's a lot of orders here. Will we get them done in time?"

Father held up a finished upper, ready to stitch to the sole George had cut. "Together, I'm sure we will. Your mother would be proud."

George winced. If his mother was still alive, his father wouldn't need him in the shop so much. And she would have forbidden him from going anywhere near the dragon, let alone attempting to fight it. Even his fairy godmother had tried to talk him out of it, but he'd been too stupid to listen.

George snipped around another sole. Zoraida had been better at battling the dragon than he had, and his mother had had more wits than any man alive, or so his father said. Perhaps that was how his namesake had defeated that long-ago dragon. The stories all said he'd saved the virgin princess from the beast, but maybe she'd defeated the dragon and all he'd done was offer her his cloak to cover her singed clothes. The townspeople had proclaimed him a hero and not believed a girl could beat the beast.

For who had ever heard of a maiden hero? Not George. He'd like to meet one, though. Such a paragon might be able to tell him what he was doing wrong.

He sighed and set down his shears. No, she probably wouldn't even notice some lowly shoemaker's son. She'd be inundated by marriage proposals from every prince, knight and nobleman for miles around. For a woman who could best a dragon would also bear brave sons.

Or so they said.

If only he'd inherited his mother's wits.

Then he'd know how to best a dragon in battle…

Four

After St John's Day, Melitta resolved to spend more time on archery. She dusted off her bow, took a few minutes to remember how to string it, then headed to the field reserved for the archery butts. It appeared that everyone else shared her passion for archery practice, for the normally deserted butts now had queues of men and boys waiting their turn.

Everyone in the training grounds seemed to want to best Sir Chase at his fly-shooting, even if the knight himself had departed in accordance with the queen's command. While they were waiting, a bunch of boys Melitta's age had climbed the fence into the next field and were shooting at a pile of horse dung.

"I got that one!" one boy cried excitedly.

"No, you didn't," another boy snapped, looking like a smaller version of the boy he'd contradicted. Brothers, Melitta assumed. "It just flew away and you didn't see it."

"Watch where you're shooting!" cried a third boy, as horse dung splattered his shoes.

"You're aiming too low," Melitta said, jerking her chin at the boy who'd caused the splatter. "When they notice movement, they fly up and off. So you need to aim higher, for where they're going to be."

The boy she'd tried to help glared at her. "What would a girl know about archery?"

His friends joined in.

"Yeah, what would a girl know?"

"Girls can't be knights!"

"Girls don't belong in the practice yard."

"Shouldn't you be in some chamber

somewhere, practising your sewing?"

Melitta regarded the boys coolly. "I'm already better at sewing than you are at archery. Maybe you all would be better off inside sewing."

"What's going on here?" The deeper voice of a man cut through the boys' enraged protests. The master-at-arms, Sir Faris. "Shouldn't you boys be practising, instead of flirting with girls?"

More shouting ensued, until Sir Faris waved the boys into silence.

"What are you doing here?" the knight asked Melitta.

She lifted her bow. "Waiting for my turn to practice."

Sir Faris' eyebrows rose. "Is King Erik's army so weak we need girls to man the walls? I see more fighting men here than any other kingdom in the world can boast. We would be in dire straits indeed if we had to rely on girls to protect the castle."

"Queen Margareta once protected the king

from a dozen men," Melitta returned. She had heard the tale many times.

"Is that the tale your mother tells you? I heard the queen distracted the men with her womanly charms so that the king could slay them and lay their bodies at her feet for daring to attack her." Sir Faris' gaze held pity. "Girls on the practice field or the battlefield are little more than a distraction. Go home to your mother, child."

Melitta met his gaze. "My mother is with the queen, and she shall hear of this. After I have had my turn at the butts. I have as much right as any man here."

Any pity Sir Faris had shown vanished. "Then pick a queue, girl, and be prepared to wait a while. My men have been here since dawn, when a little lady like yourself was fast asleep in her bed." He stalked away, cupping his hands to his mouth to shout instructions to a man sighting on the furthest target.

Melitta surveyed the field. At this rate, it would be several hours before the men tired of archery and let her anywhere near the butts. In the meantime, she could stand around, watching, or she could join the boys in shooting shit. Neither appealed to her. Sure, she could carry out her threat and tell the queen what had transpired, but she knew her mother was working on a dress for the young princess's betrothal ceremony, and if Melitta joined them, she'd soon find her hands full of pins and silk. So much for her hopes of being a hero.

Melitta marched to the armoury, resolving to put her bow away until later in the evening, when the men were gone. She wasn't giving up, she told herself. Merely postponing practice.

The armour-master was nowhere to be seen, but Melitta heard a clatter from the darkness at the back of the cavernous cellar that housed King Erik's armoury. "Sir Bruno?" Melitta ventured.

"What is it, boy?" a gruff voice demanded. Sir Bruno, the armour-master, emerged from the darkness carrying a pile of shields almost as high as his head. "Who are you?"

"Lady Melitta, Lady Penelope's daughter," Melitta replied. From girl to child to boy, Melitta had had enough of diminutives for one day.

Sir Bruno scratched his bald pate. "What can I do for you, my lady?" Before she could respond, the stack of shields unbalanced and clattered to the floor. Sir Bruno growled out a string of colourful curses, only half of which Melitta understood.

One of the shields rolled, hit the wall and toppled over at her feet. Melitta reached down to pick it up and was struck with the design on the round shield. Concentric circles, much like the archery targets outside. A dark stain marred the design. "What are you doing with these?" she asked.

"Throwing them out, milady. Some of these are centuries old, captured from Viking raiders, and no use to anyone. Even if they weren't mouldy like the one you hold, lady." Sir Bruno reached for the offending item.

Melitta clutched it to her chest. "So if I wanted to use it for an archery target, no one would mind?"

Sir Bruno laughed. "If you were to throw it in the fire, not even the king himself would object, my lady."

"Good." Melitta surveyed the mess. "May I have another?"

"You may have them all. As many as you can carry." Sir Bruno laughed.

Oh, so he thought a girl couldn't lift a shield or two? Melitta fumed. Bolts of silk might not seem like much until you had to carry them halfway across the castle to the queen's chambers, up and down stairs until your arms ached. She selected two more and hefted all three in her arms. Heavy, yes, but no heavier than an armload of silks for her mother. "Thank you," she said sweetly, hitching her quiver higher on her shoulder as she turned to go.

"Any time, my lady," Sir Bruno called after her.

Five

Melitta set up her practice range in the corridor outside her mother's apartments. She wedged her shield target in the window, then stood back to take aim. Her first arrow hit the wall and clattered to the stone floor with a sound reminiscent of mocking applause.

Practice, Melitta told herself. The more practice she got, the better she'd become.

By the end of the morning, she could at least hit the target on every shot. She hadn't forgotten how to shoot, at least. She kept at it until she managed to hit the white circle in the centre three times in a row. Only then did she set down her bow to massage her aching fingers. It wasn't enough. She'd have to soak them.

Melitta headed inside her chamber, intent on finding a jug of water. She immersed her whole hand in the one on the table, beside the dinner a maid had delivered for her hours ago. Only now did she realise how hungry she was.

As she devoured her dinner, Melitta mused that there must be a simpler way to heroism than hours of archery practice. Her fingers would be a mess of callouses before the week was out – she wouldn't be able to sew a stitch. Her mother would not be happy.

Too bad. Lady Penelope had made her own choices in life. Melitta was old enough to marry, which meant she got to make choices, too. If she chose not to spend her whole life at a loom like her mother, it was her choice.

Melitta tore off a piece of bread and dipped it into the dish of honey. The movement set off a small swarm of flies that she hadn't seen until now.

Dropping her bread in disgust, Melitta reached for her quiver. At this distance, she could stab the flies with the point of her arrow – no bow required. Yet her fingers closed on the strap that held the quiver to her shoulder. There was a faster way to swat flies that didn't require a bow or arrow.

Carefully, she raised the strap. The flies buzzed on, oblivious. One or two even settled on the surface of the honey once more.

Melitta took a deep breath, then struck. The strap slapped against the table, making her tray jump before it landed with a clatter. For all the noise, it didn't look like she'd caught a single one. Chagrined, Melitta flipped over the strap to see if she'd perhaps caught a particularly slow fly.

She counted. Then counted again. No, surely not. After a third count, the strap dropped from her nerveless fingers. "A dozen," she breathed in disbelief. "A dozen dead with a single blow. Take that, Sir Faris and anyone else who says a girl has no place in battle. Sir Chase killed them one at a time, yet I can take a dozen in a single stroke!"

Seizing the strip of leather, she took the steps two at a time to the practice range. Most of the men had gone, but the boys were still there, taking their turn on the butts.

"You're wasting your time!" she called, flapping the strap. "You're using the wrong weapon! Look, I killed a dozen in a single blow!"

"Let me see that, girl." Sir Faris seized the strap. "A dozen currants? Deadly foes, indeed!" He laughed, and the boys joined in.

"They are not currants, or any kind of fruit," Melitta snapped. "They're flies, the same as the ones they've been trying to shoot all morning. I killed a dozen with one blow. More than even the great knight yesterday managed to do!"

"The one the queen threw out of the kingdom? He wasn't so great," one of the boys mocked to more laughter.

Melitta folded her arms across her chest. "So you say, yet all of you are out here, working on your bow skills so you can do better than him. Well, you've been bested by a girl. How many of you can kill a dozen with one blow?"

The boys howled with laughter.

Sir Faris laid a hand on her shoulder. "They have the right of it, girl. Catching flies will never win a battle, and a knight who thinks so is little more than entertainment at a feast. Forget your dozen and do something more suited to your station."

Melitta shrugged off his hand and stalked away. Sir Faris was wrong, she swore to herself, and one day she would prove it to him, and the world.

Six

"Are you sure you aren't coming? This could make our fortunes, you know," Father said, hefting another chest into the already full cart.

And make shoes for the rest of his life? George shook his head. "I'm sure, Father. I want a chance at adventure. If I fail…well, I will know where to find you, to ask for a job."

Father patted the horse as he passed. "Of course you will. This Shoetown is where the forest meets the desert, far to the south. In a land where the court ladies dance through a pair of slippers each and every night. A land where a shoemaker might fancy himself a king."

George laughed. "Where you will make yourself as rich as a king, you mean. The rest of it – the business of ruling a kingdom and keeping the neighbouring kingdoms from invading – is more trouble than it's worth, I'm sure."

Father rested his hands on George's shoulders. It rankled that George wasn't as tall as his father yet, and might never be. "Some might say the same of an adventurer's life. Slaying monsters is more trouble than it's worth, as you've already learned."

George's heart sank. His father had been strangely silent about his battle with the dragon, though he had to have heard about his crushing failure. The whole city and surrounding countryside knew. Still, George summoned a smile. "What is it you and Mother used to tell me when I was small and learning to make shoes in the workshop? Your first attempt will fail. Yet I had to keep trying until I succeeded. No matter how many times I failed. Because it's about learning to do it right, so you don't fail any more."

Father's smile looked just as forced. "Just as long as you live long enough to keep trying until you succeed. Shoes are not as dangerous as dragons."

"I know." George met his father's gaze without flinching. His resolve didn't waver, despite the ache in his heart at having to farewell his father.

Father climbed onto the cart. "When you have slayed the beast, come and find me. I promise to make you boots from the beast's hide."

If the dragon didn't make a meal of his own hide instead. A lump formed in George's throat. His father had more confidence in him than George had for himself. "You can count on it," George said.

They exchanged a long look, where not a word was said. Least of all the fateful farewell.

It only ended when Father tapped the horse with his whip, urging it forward. The moment shattered, and they parted ways, perhaps for the last time.

Despite Melitta's best efforts, tales of her fly-killing achievements reached every corner of the castle within a day. She could not set foot outside her mother's apartments without someone mentioning a dozen with one blow, before they dissolved into laughter. So she shut herself in with her sewing.

"Ooh, is that a new gown for the queen?" an excited voice asked.

Melitta glanced up to find Inga, one of the maids, staring avidly at her. Given she was working on blue silk, which only the queen wore, on any normal occasion, the question would have been quite a silly one. However, under the circumstances…

"No," Melitta replied. "This is the princess's betrothal gown. The king wants her to wear white, but the queen insists the gown be blue. Mother had some blue silk so pale it almost looks white, which met with Queen Margareta's approval, so I get to make it while Mother makes the queen's gown."

Inga nodded. "Lady Penelope makes the most beautiful gowns."

Melitta couldn't disagree. Her mother could take cloth and thread and turn it into something magical. Moreover, Mother seemed to actually enjoy creating clothing.

She'd once travelled the world with her husband, Sir Godfrey, until Melitta's father had nobly sacrificed his life to save a convent from a bunch of barbarians, or so Mother said when she told the tale. He'd earned himself sainthood as a result, for thanks to his sacrifice, none of the novices were harmed by the barbarians, when a miracle turned them into birds and they flew away.

It was such a far-fetched tale, Melitta wouldn't have believed it, if the nuns in the convent where she'd spent her earliest years hadn't sworn to its veracity. Some had even been witnesses to the events of that day, and Melitta had seen it in their thoughts. Not that she was the sort of witch who could turn men into birds – oh, no. Mind reading was the questionable gift she had inherited from her mother, though she rarely used it.

Without Melitta having to tell her, Queen Margareta heard the tale of Sir Faris' remarks on the training ground, and her response was everything Melitta could have hoped for.

Though the queen never so much as touched a sword, it was well known that she was as deadly as the king. She had summoned Sir Faris to the throne room to answer why he had not allowed a girl to enter the practice fields. She'd insisted that in ancient times, women had trained just as rigorously as men, for women were as likely to die at the point of a blade as any man, so they had a right to learn to use any weapon they could handle. When he began to protest that having women present would distract the men, an excuse quickly picked up and seconded by some of the other noblemen present, she'd shaken her head that her king's troops were so weak. Why, all an enemy army had to do was bring a woman with them and they would be undone, which simply would not do.

Then she'd sweetly offered to stand on the training ground herself until men learned not to be distracted. And she'd do it naked.

Silence had descended on the court for a long moment. Melitta didn't need to read the men's minds to see the lust burning in their eyes. The queen's beauty was enough to halt an army in its tracks, even without taking into account her magical powers.

At that point, King Erik had waded into the fray in her support. Most said it was to protect the queen's modesty, or some such noble thought, but Mother had muttered that it was more about keeping his men alive. Men lost their minds over the queen in ways they never would for Melitta.

So Melitta spent her mornings in the practice yard, ignoring the laughter as she learned how to hold a sword without dropping it. By the end of a week, she considered herself a passable swordswoman who could manage an occasional bout against one of the young squires without falling on her backside. She'd even won a few, amid grumbling from the boys.

Sure, she might not be a hero yet, but she intended to do everything in her power to be ready when the opportunity came. She would not spend a lifetime sewing clothes for a court who didn't care a jot about her. At least, not until she'd had her fair share of adventure, like her mother had.

Eight

When George set out from his father's house, he had a fool-proof plan, or so he thought. Unless he was a fool for thinking it up, which was always possible.

Somewhere, there were other would-be heroes. Others who wished to slay dragons. He would journey to another town where no one had heard of his defeat, and make it known that he wished to engage an apprentice. An apprentice hero, if there were such a thing. Perhaps even several, if he could find enough suitable boys. He didn't dare hope for a girl like his fairy godmother, and yet…he'd seen dozens of men challenge the dragon, but he alone among them had survived by running away. And he'd managed that only because Zoraida battled the dragon alone, distracting the beast.

He'd take up residence in the best inn in town, and pay the town crier to shout his news to all who would hear it for a few days. Then, he'd have applicants lining up across the town square, he was certain of it.

He'd even made up some signs he would nail to the outside of the inn, for those who could read. After all, if his father was right and a man needed more brain than brawn to beat a dragon, then an educated apprentice would be a wise choice.

He unrolled the signs on the table, surveying the top one with a critical eye. He hoped it would be enticing enough. He'd drawn the dragon himself, and his drawing skills had never been the best.

Heroes wanted, the poster read, for monster slaying of all kinds. Apply within.

"Are you looking for a hero, boy?"

George looked up. The man who met his gaze looked like one of the knights who'd died trying to defeat the dragon. A hero, in other words.

A hero who would claim all the glory, if they were to team up to kill the beast, George's traitorous mind added.

"Where's the dragon and what's the reward?" the man asked, turning the poster so the writing was right way up.

"Kasmirus, between the city and the river," George admitted. "But I don't know the reward. Every time it kills another knight, the king increases it."

"How big is the beast, and does it breathe fire?"

George swallowed. "It would scarcely fit in the square outside, and its fiery breath is so hot, it has been known to melt a man's armour."

The man considered the scroll for a long moment, then rolled it up. "Which means it's impossible to kill."

"Not impossible," George countered. "All creatures must die some time."

The man grinned. "Even us. But there's nothing heroic about being roasted alive. I'm Sir Chase." He held out his hand.

"George," he said, clasping the knight's arm briefly before letting go.

Sir Chase gestured to the innkeeper. "Two more ales for me and my friend here!" When the innkeeper nodded, Chase turned back to George. "Where are you headed?"

"Aros," George said. It was the nearest large town to Kasmirus, though hopefully far enough for no one to have heard of him before.

Sir Chase started, his eyes widening in horror for a moment before his expression relaxed into a smile again. "Not a good city for heroes, Aros. Their queen isn't fond of adventurers."

George raised his eyebrows. "That's not what I heard. When they hold tourneys, the queen richly rewards the victor. She holds heroes in high regard, or so it is said." And a kingdom where its queen held so much power was the most likely place to find a girl who would answer his call for a hero, George thought but did not say.

Sir Chase choked on his ale. Wiping his mouth with the back of his hand, he said, "Aye, I heard the same. Until I met the woman. Beautiful as the day is long, but cold as ice. Looking into her eyes is enough to freeze your soul, and no mistake."

George paused for a moment, considering. Was he wrong to head for Aros? Perhaps he should travel further to another city.

No, he decided. What was a queen to him? He wanted to recruit some of her subjects, not meet the woman or even set foot in her court. "Then I'll be sure to avoid her," George said finally.

"Wise choice." Sir Chase raised his ale. "And

I will avoid your dragon. I heard about a pack of troublesome wolves in the north. I might go see to those instead."

George clunked his cup against the knight's. "To both our good health, and long lives," he said gravely, and drank.

As he drained his drink, George prayed that he wasn't making the wrong decision in heading for Aros. Only time would tell.

Nine

Every squire in the bailey was talking or thinking about the apprenticeship, Melitta was certain of it. She'd even ventured to read some thoughts to confirm it. The hero would have a hundred applicants before the week was out, and every single one of them bigger, stronger and better with a sword than she was, or would ever be. The only thing she was better at was…sewing, not a talent in high regard among heroes.

Unless she could sew herself a heroic

reputation in the next few days, Melitta didn't stand a chance.

On the morrow, the line stretched from the tavern to the city gates, as every likely lad vied for the chance to be a hero's apprentice. Some wore little more than rags, but for once, they shared something with the simply dressed tradesmen's sons and the noble boys in their leather armour, mail and emblazoned silk surcoats: their eyes were filled with hope.

Any hope Melitta had harboured died at the sight. She hadn't any chance of being chosen. It wasn't like she even knew what their family emblem was to embroider it on a surcoat.

"What is our family crest?" Melitta asked her mother.

Mother's loom continued its steady pace. "We have none. My family came from a court where we had no need of such things – a name was enough. And your father…to tell you the truth, I cannot remember. He wore the sign of a cross for the holy crusade he was on, so I never saw any other symbol on him."

"But we should have one. Maybe it wasn't the done thing where you came from, but everyone else at court has their heraldry," Melitta pressed.

Mother laughed. "Why? Are you thinking of fighting in a tourney and wearing your own colours? Tell me you're not as silly as all those boys lined up outside."

"Being a hero is not silly. Some people would say making pretty clothes is silly," Melitta retorted. The moment the words left her lips, she regretted them, but it was too late.

Mother's loom clicked into ominous silence. "We are ladies of the court. We set the tone for fashion and dress amongst the highest in the land. The courts of other kingdoms look to us for what to wear. For new ways to fashion fur and fabric. If you find all your silk dresses so silly, perhaps you should wear a sack instead."

Now Melitta felt even worse. "I didn't mean — "

"Or is it armour you want? After killing a

dozen with one blow, you feel your hands are better employed with something sharper than a needle? Do you want to join those boys out there, wishing for something that will only get them killed like your father was?" A tear stood bright on Mother's cheek.

"I'm sorry, Mother," Melitta said quietly. "I'm not as reckless as that. I just wish for more to life than clothes and maybe marriage."

Mother wiped her tears away. "I know you aren't your father, but you're all I have left. And sometimes you remind me of him so much…when you don't remind me of me." She sniffed with what Melitta thought sounded like finality. "When I was a girl, I wanted to be an assassin, like one of the Sultan's daughters. Then my mother gave me this awful gown that I couldn't stand, so I unstitched it, dyed it anew and remade that gown until I could bear to wear it. My own mother didn't recognise it. And then I met your father…and found a new passion." She sighed. "I know you don't share my passion for creating cloth and clothing. I had hoped you might find something else you enjoyed. Heaven knows you've sneaked into enough places in the palace to have tried everything that you could."

"But not slaying monsters," Melitta said.

Mother laughed weakly. "I'm not sure there are any monsters left in the world to slay. All the monsters I've met have been human, and you aren't an assassin any more than I am. Could you kill a man, Melitta?"

Melitta herself didn't know the answer to that. "If I had to, I suppose," she said. Remembering the flies, she perked up. "I did kill a dozen with one blow. That knight who came to the feast would say it shows the mark of a true warrior."

"Then I shall make you a surcoat with new colours, that says what a hero you already are. And on the morrow you can walk past those hordes of boys, putting them to shame," Mother said.

Now Melitta's eyes threatened tears. "Even after what happened to Father, you would let me apprentice myself to a hero as a slayer of monsters?"

Mother's smile seemed forced, but her words rang true. "If your passion is for monsters, I cannot stop you from pursuing it. My parents never wanted me to marry your father, but I gave them no choice in the matter." She rose and headed for the chest where she kept her best silks. "So, what colours would you like to wear, my young warrior?"

Melitta thought for a moment. "What do we have that is closest to honey?"

Ten

When he saw the queue outside the tavern in the morning, George thanked his lucky stars. He would have an apprentice to help him in no time – that dragon was as good as dead. Aros had been the right place to go, after all.

Yet as each boy walked into the private room he'd rented in the tavern, he began to have doubts.

"Wrong room."

"You're no hero!"

"Why, you're younger than me, and smaller

to boot!"

It seemed tales of his failure at home had indeed spread to this city, too. At this rate, he'd have to try another town even further away to find someone who hadn't heard of his disastrous dragon battle.

As the light through the window turned rosy, George prepared to pack up and move on. The line that had held such hopes for him this morning was non-existent. The last boy had crushed his hopes under his hobnailed boots.

"Excuse me?"

George looked up at the distinctly feminine voice.

"I heard there was a place for an apprentice hero?" The girl – or perhaps a particularly skinny boy, George thought, though he doubted it – sidled into the room. She'd cut her hair like a pageboy, but she looked old enough to be a squire. Clad in a tunic and hose that were too well-made to belong to a peasant, she wore them like they were her own, and not borrowed from one of her brothers. Practical clothing, suitable for fighting in a practice yard. The only bit of finery she wore was a flame-coloured surcoat, embroidered with words George couldn't quite make out.

Then she turned, and it came clear. "A dozen at one blow," he read. He eyed the girl, whose slender arms couldn't have wielded anything larger than a dagger in her life. "I don't believe it."

She set her hands on her hips. "Ask anyone in town. One blow and I had a dozen dead. Just like that." For a moment, it seemed like fire burned in her eyes.

George was mesmerised. She reminded him of his fairy godmother. Only closer to his age.

He shook himself. This girl couldn't help him defeat the dragon. He needed a better warrior than he was.

"Innkeep!" George shouted.

The innkeeper stuck his head in the room. "More ale?"

"Yes," he said. "But first...have you ever heard of anyone who can kill a dozen with a single blow?"

The innkeeper grinned broadly. "You mean Melitta here? How can a hero as big as you not hear of such things? You'd better not show any disrespect, or you'll be number thirteen!" He left, laughing.

The girl looked incensed. "Do you believe me now?"

She didn't look like a killer, but then, Zoraida hadn't looked like a fairy godmother, either. Especially not while battling a dragon. And Zoraida had held her own against the beast.

"Are you afraid of dragons?" George demanded.

"I'm not afraid of anything," she insisted.

"Have you ever met a dragon?" he pressed.

Doubt flickered over her features.

The answer to his question was no.

"Have you ever run away from a fight?" George asked.

She snorted. "Of course not."

Unmanned by a girl. George dismissed the thought as quickly as it had come.

"Can you handle a sword?" he asked.

"Tolerably in the practice yard," she said. "I'm better with a bow and I can ride."

George was in love. Standing before him was the perfect woman.

"And I think you should choose me for your apprentice," she finished. She eyed him. "But I'm not going to sleep with you."

Apprentice? All George's dreams of getting her into bed sputtered and died. Had she read his thoughts?

"Yes," she replied. "A minor inconvenience I inherited from my mother. That and a fairy godmother."

The wheels in George's mind started turning. The two of them, plus two fairy godmothers. Between the four of them, they might be able to best that dragon.

"You're hired," he said.

Eleven

Melitta's feet felt like they were floating all the way back to her mother's apartments. Out of all the would-be heroes, boys who were far better with a bow and a sword, he had picked her! She couldn't wait to start her training. Wondering what kind of monster Sir George would test her with first, Melitta dreamed of dragons as she packed her things. Her dresses would stay, of course – silk skirts would only get in the way in a fight.

Melitta thought to fill a chest with her

things, but by the time she had assembled all of her suitable fighting clothes, they took up scarcely a quarter of the space in the smallest chest her mother owned. She would be better served with a sack, or a saddlebag. Perhaps...

"So, the rumours are true? The whole castle is buzzing with the news that the hero chose a girl as his apprentice. And not just any girl...you." Mother loomed in the doorway, her hands on her hips as though she planned to block her daughter's exit.

Melitta couldn't keep the pride out of her voice. "Yes, he did," she said. "And he believes I can kill a dragon. I saw it in his thoughts."

Mother's frightening figure seemed to shrink as she sank onto a chair. "I don't believe it," she said weakly. "All those boys, squires, knights in training...and he chose you?"

"Yes, Mother." Melitta wondered where she might find a suitable sack. Perhaps in the kitchens.

"He must think you are a doxy, a whore who will leap into his bed the moment he commands it," Mother declared. "You must send word to his lodgings that you are no such thing, and as a lady of the court, you will have no further dealings with such a dishonourable man."

Melitta grinned. "He did think about me naked for a moment, but when I told him I would never sleep with him, he seemed resigned to it. He truly offered me the apprenticeship because he believes I have the makings of a hero."

Mother let out a sigh, deflating in defeat. "But are you sure this is what you want? I had plenty of adventures in my youth, particularly after I met your father. But never once did I have to take up a sword, or fight a monster who was stronger than a man. Even then..." Mother swallowed. She continued, "I thought you wanted to meet this hero because, well...you are of marriageable age. I saw how you looked at the knight the queen banished, and it made me realise... I was about your age when I met your father. Your age when I chose my husband. It is plain that no man at court has caught your eye, but a newcomer with an eye for adventure…Why, were I younger, I would find him difficult to resist." She laughed, blushing.

Marriage? Melitta recoiled at the very idea. "No," she said decidedly. "I am not in love with Sir George. Or Sir Chase, though I admit he was a handsome fellow."

"I could speak to the queen," Mother began eagerly. "Perhaps you will know of a suitable man. Not someone at court, but perhaps one of King Eric's bannermen…"

Melitta curled her lip. "And have her marry me off to some chubby cheeked prince where I will be forced to pop out babies, in between weaving and sewing until my womb and hands no longer work? No, thank you. I wish to live a little before I am chained to a birthing bed."

"Perhaps a widower who already has children. Enough heirs that you need not breed at all," Mother suggested, but Melitta didn't need to read her mind to know that her own mother didn't even believe she could do such a thing.

"I am not ready for marriage." Even as the words left her lips Melitta knew they were true. She wasn't. She might never be.

Mother bowed her head. "I know," she admitted. She took a deep breath. "Which is why, though it breaks my heart to do it, I shall allow you to go with my blessing. And a warning. Whatever monsters you choose to kill, never attempt to cross a mermaid."

Melitta managed a smile. As a mind reader, she knew the queen's secret as well as her mother did. "For Queen Margareta will never forgive me."

Little more of consequence passed between her and her mother until her departure on the morrow. Melitta and her mother packed her things, and it seemed like no time at all before Melitta mounted her gelding and said farewell.

Farewell to the life she had lived, as she rode through the gates on the first step of her journey to become a legendary hero.

Or so she hoped.

Twelve

After a week of travelling, staying in a different inn every night, Melitta finally worked up the courage to ask George, "So where is this dragon we're going to kill?"

George took his time putting down his dagger and swallowing his mouthful of pork, before he answered, "We're not killing the dragon yet."

Melitta opened her mouth to ask why, but George cut her off.

"I've seen you practising on the targets in

the inn yards," he said. "You can handle a bow, though your marksmanship could do with some work. And you say you have killed a dozen, but I have not seen it. First, we should test your skills against something smaller. More manageable."

Melitta's heart sank. Killing flies was one thing, but something bigger, living, breathing... She swallowed. Melitta wasn't sure she could do it.

George pulled a crumpled piece of parchment from his saddlebag and unrolled it on the table. "There is a town two days' ride from here which has a wild boar problem. One beast in particular has a price on his head. So your first quest in training to be a hero will be to kill this pig and claim the reward." He sat back, lifting his tankard to his lips.

Melitta's blood ran cold. "A boar? A wild boar? A beast that looks like a pig on the outside, and may taste like one when it's dead and roasted, but while it lives, it is the receptacle of the devil's rage that few would stand against?"

"Are you afraid of a pig?"

Desperately, Melitta wanted to say no. But if she did, she knew it would be a lie. As one of the ladies of the court, she had often been allowed to accompany hunting parties. When the court hunted deer, fox, or the frequent hawking expeditions that the queen was so fond of. Melitta could watch the queen's falcon in flight all day, so graceful was the bird. But when King Erik had caught wind of a monstrous boar that he wished to hunt, Mother had forbidden it. Melitta had stood at the window, watching the hunting party leave without her, bitterness festering in her breast. There had been few ladies in that party, and all the men had carried spears instead of bows. It wasn't till much later, when the weary hunting party returned victorious, that Melitta realised why.

The beast had gored three knights - one fatally - before it had succumbed to the spear piercing its heart. By all accounts, the dead knight had saved King Erik's life, by leaping in front of the beast. When the queen had heard this, she forbade any future boar hunts. It might be King Erik's kingdom, but none disobeyed the queen.

Melitta swallowed. "We will need to be prepared," she said carefully. "We will need stout spears, for arrows will not be enough. I have never handled a spear, and I fear I may not have the strength to strike true before the beast is upon me."

George's eyes widened, as though she had surprised him. Good. "You've fought a boar before?"

"They are hunted by the king and his court," Melitta replied, pressing her lips together before he could make her spill the truth.

Sir George shook his head and appeared to regain his composure. "Then you have two days until we arrive in the town of Sanglier in which to formulate a plan for how you will kill the beast."

Two days? Two years would not be enough.

Melitta began to wish she had never left
home in the first place.

67

Thirteen

During the two days' ride to Sanglier, Melitta scarcely uttered a word. Countless times, George had opened his mouth to comment on the weather, or ask her about herself, but he hadn't been able to make his tongue cooperate. He'd never met a girl who could incapacitate him so.

The one time he'd managed to hold a conversation with her, he'd told her about the Sanglier boar. He'd expected her to be afraid – Lord knew he was! – but she'd been as calm as still water as she described the best way to kill a boar.

With a spear. George didn't own a spear, and despite her admission that she had never fought with one, at least she'd seen one and knew what to do with it.

On reflection, he probably shouldn't have told her killing the beast would be up to her. Yet she'd sounded so knowledgeable, he'd been scared to tell her his plan, lest she scoff and call him a fool. He was the master and she was the apprentice, or at least that's the way it was supposed to be. There might be more to Melitta than he realised – and not just her fairy godmother, either.

Even if she was bluffing, which he doubted, if she got into trouble, she had but to call for her fairy godmother and she would have a powerful witch to save her. George knew his own fairy godmother was as likely to let him die as she was to save him, so he knew he couldn't count on any help from Zoraida. Not yet.

So as he sat down to the afternoon meal with Melitta, George ventured, "So what is your plan?"

Melitta glanced up at him, then directed her gaze at her bowl of stew. Haltingly at first, she began to tell him what had occupied her thoughts for the last two days.

George let out a low whistle. "That's not a bad plan at all. Let's see how it goes tonight."

Melitta paled. "Tonight?"

George didn't dare admit it to her, but staying at inns every night had taken all of his coin. If they didn't kill the boar tonight and claim its reward, he could not afford so much as a loaf of bread to break their fast in the morning.

He nodded gravely. "Tonight."

$\mathcal{F}$ourteen

Looking down from her tree branch perch into the darkness below, Melitta repeated Sir George's words in her head. It wasn't a bad plan. It wasn't.

Then why did she feel like there were snakes writhing in her belly?

She shifted again, searching in vain for a comfortable spot on the hard tree branch. There was the trap, made of timber hastily nailed together this afternoon. It was barely visible in the moonlight now. The earthy smell of truffles and mushrooms filled the air, hopefully enough to entice the boar into the trap. If that bait wasn't enough, it sat at the foot of an oak tree, amid the remains of a century's worth of acorns.

Even Sir George had said the bait should be sufficient, but after several hours of sitting out here in the cold dark, Melitta wondered if perhaps they should have taken the advice of a man they met in the tavern. He had insisted that the only way to lure a pig was with the scent of fermented apples. Melitta had been on the verge of agreeing to include some apples in the bait, when the man had promptly offered to sell her a barrel of cider for a price higher than her mother would pay for a bale of silk. Yet now she was tempted to climb down from her tree, and venture to the tavern to see if she could acquire some of the overpriced cider. Anything to end her vigil.

Wait, was that movement?

Melitta squinted down the road. No, it was just the baker. He'd opened a window to set the rising bread dough on the windowsill. If he was baking already, then dawn would soon follow. The end of the night with no sign of their bloody boar, or sleep for her, either.

But wait...was that?

Yes!

A hulking shadow, low to the ground, passed in front of the bakery, ambling at a pace that showed the boar was in no hurry. Then it stopped and lifted its head so that its snout and tusks were clearly outlined against the light coming from the baker's window. Melitta's stomach lurched. Tusks like that could gut a man. She didn't even want to think of what it would do to her.

If he gored her, would the tusks go all the way through and come out her back?

She shut down that thought as quickly as it had come. Pigs couldn't climb trees, so she was safe up on her perch. She just had to wait for the animal to enter the trap, so that she could spring it, and the deed would be done.

She held her breath as the boar approached.

Still in no hurry, it paused to sniff the ground before taking a few steps and lowering its snout to the soil once more. Slowly, slowly fate was closing in on the beast. It was a good plan, just like Sir George had said.

Moonlight shimmered on the dew-dropped l eaves below her, before it abruptly winked out. The boar stood at the very entrance of their trap. Four steps would carry it all the way in, she decided, and then it would be trapped. No more terrorising the town for this pig.

Two steps. A long moment of snuffling, disturbing the moonlit leaves. Another step.

Melitta's lungs screamed for air, but she didn't dare inhale. Just one more, she begged the beast.

The beast trotted forward and buried its snout in a pile of mushrooms.

Melitta wanted to cheer, but she knew she couldn't. Not until the gate was closed. Now she tugged on the rope fastened to the gate below. It wasn't till she heard the latch click shut that she finally let herself breathe again. It was done. They'd captured the boar.

Sir George clambered down from his tree. Though he had said killing the boar was her task, in the end he had agreed to wield the spear that killed it.

So the knight took up a spear, hefting it in his hand as he approached the gate. The pig did not hear him at first, for it was too busy feasting on the bait. But he must've made some noise that alerted it, for the pig started, turned, and faced him.

Instead of throwing the spear directly into the pig's chest, as the beast presented him with the perfect target, George hesitated.

The pig did not. It charged at the gate. Which, to Melitta's horror, swung open. Somehow, it hadn't closed properly, and now the boar was no longer trapped, but it most certainly was enraged.

With a spear in his hand, George still stood in the perfect position to kill the beast. Melitta watched in awe, waiting.

George had other ideas. He took to his

heels and fled, with the boar not far behind.

Sir George was a coward? Melitta couldn't believe it, yet the evidence was right there before her eyes.

George headed for the only sanctuary either of them could see – the lit bakery. He wrenched open the door, and flung himself inside, but he didn't get a chance to shut the door before the boar followed him in.

A great commotion arose from the bakery, culminating in the door slamming shut. Which might have been good except both George and the boar was still inside.

Melitta crept down from her tree. She wasn't sure what to do, but she couldn't just sit there and do nothing. She snatched up the spare spears, and carried them to the bakery. She was George's assistant, after all, and if he needed more weapons, it was her job to provide them. And she might learn something from watching the battle, she told herself. She crept toward the lit window, the volume of the clatterings and crashes increasing with every step. Finally she was close enough to peer through the open shutters. She raised her head for scarcely a moment, before she had to duck to avoid being hit by the body flying out the window.

Sir George rolled, crouched, then clambered to his feet. He dusted himself off before he seized the spear from Melitta.

"That beast is going to die," he said through gritted teeth, advancing on the window.

But the boar, rampaging through the wrecked bakery, was hard to sight between the overturned tables and smashed furniture. Then it tore into a bag of flour and powder filled the air, making it even harder to see.

The beast shook its head, scattering flour everywhere, but it was unable to dislodge the bag from its tusks. It ran around madly, trampling everything in its path, until the bag finally flew off and landed in the fire. The empty flour sack began to smoke.

"There!" George hissed, loosing a spear. He caught the boar in the chest, but that didn't seem to slow the beast any. If anything, the pain only goaded it into greater action. It stampeded around the house, until it managed to dislodge the spear. Blood droplets dotted the floury floor as the pig's eyes seemed to grow red in the firelight. Lowering its tusks, the boar charged at George, only to be stopped by the wall beneath the window. George readied another spear but he only managed to jab at the pig before it darted away with an angry squeal. Melitta couldn't even tell if he'd wounded it this time.

What followed, Melitta could only call a battle of wills between Sir George and the beast. The beast would charge George, George would attempt to stab it with a spear, sometimes successfully, sometimes not. Then the beast would retreat, only to charge George again. Minutes passed, or maybe it was hours. Melitta could not be sure. Finally she was left holding the last spear. The others lay splintered inside the bakery, except for the one George still held his hand. The boar disappeared into the fog of smoke and flour, so that this time when it charged, it surprised Melitta. Yet something in her refused to just sit and watch this time. With George square in front of the window, she couldn't line up a perfect shot with the beast's chest, but she could at least do some damage, she decided.

Tightening her grip on the spear, she offered up a prayer to anyone who was listening: Let this battle end now.

George's spear struck it in the chest, and the boar lifted its head to let out a screech of pain.

Melitta took her chance, burying the point of her spear in the soft flesh at its throat. The boar backed up, tearing the spear from its flesh even as it ripped the weapon out of her hand. A gout of blood erupted into a crimson waterfall that turned the white flour into red mud. The beast tottered for a moment, as if drunk on the cider Melitta had denied it, before it collapsed for the final time.

"We did it," she said, surprised at how shaky her voice sounded. Heroes should have steadier voices, so she tried again. "We did it." There, that was better.

"I'd say that you have," a deep voice said behind her.

Melitta whirled. Somehow, while the battle had raged, the entire town had assembled behind them, and the dawn lit up their distinctly unfriendly faces.

"You destroyed the only bakery in town, and my house," the baker continued.

George drew himself up. "Your boar did that, not us," he said. "If we hadn't stopped him, he might've rampaged through your town. Who knows how much more damage he would have caused?"

A hard-eyed woman stepped forward. "That beast never attacked buildings, just people. And where will I get my bread tomorrow, now? All the dough was trampled in the dirt." She pointed at George's feet.

Only now did Melitta realise that George must have swept the bread dough off the windowsill when he dived out of the bakery.

"We'll pay for the bread out of our reward," George began.

The baker turned red. "Your reward won't even pay for half of the flour that beast destroyed. Seems to me you should be paying the town for the damage you caused. You're worse than any pig."

Melitta bit her lip, knowing before she did what she would read in the minds of the townsfolk. They had to get out of there, and fast.

"We should go," she murmured to George, tugging urgently at his arm.

He glanced at her, then said, "We'll just get out things and our horses and be on our way then." He made as if to march through the crowd to the inn.

The townspeople were having none of it. They close ranks, barring his way, and it all went downhill from there.

Fifteen

"Run!" Melitta screamed.

George's feet weren't stupid – they obeyed. His head took a moment to catch up, by which time he'd drawn level with Melitta. "We should get our things, and our horses," he gasped out.

She shook her head. "They wanted to lynch us. My horse and a few clothes aren't worth dying for."

George opened his mouth to ask how she knew that. They'd seemed like reasonable townspeople. Surely, he could talk them around to giving them at least some of the reward they'd promised…

"No. That baker is the most influential man in the village, the one putting up most of the reward, and he wanted us quartered. He'd seen it done once to a traitor when he was a boy, and he longed to see it done again. His memories are quite gruesome, and his imagination…even more so. Especially when he was imagining me getting quartered." Melitta screwed up her face, then tapped her head. "Mind-reader, remember? For my sins."

George swallowed, then accelerated. Being roasted by a dragon was one thing, but dying at the hands of a mob? That was no fitting end for a hero.

They ran until every breath burned in George's chest, but he didn't stop. He didn't dare look behind him, either, for he knew it would only slow him down.

He started to feel lightheaded, and he nearly cried when Melitta said, "They're gone. No one's close enough to hear any more. We can...stop."

She sank to her knees, her chest heaving as she gasped for breath.

George slowed, his eyes fixed on her breasts. Would they heave like that if he kissed her?

Melitta drew a dagger from her belt and waved it in his direction. "Touch me and I'll cut you."

Right. Mind-reader. How could he forget? George swallowed and fought to turn his thoughts to more practical matters. Like where he could lie down and not move for a few hours, without being disturbed.

He stumbled along the road a way, before he found what he wanted — a trail that led to a small clearing, with the remains of a long-dead fire in the middle. "We'll camp here for the night," he called.

Melitta staggered through the trees. "I'm camping here for the day. You might have slept last night, but I didn't." She settled herself on a patch of pine needles, wrapped her cloak around her, and dropped almost immediately into slumber.

George's reasonable mind reminded him that someone should stay awake to keep watch, but he was too tired to care. If he was truly in trouble, his fairy godmother would save him. Or if Lady Zoraida wouldn't, then Melitta's godmother would come.

He found a patch of grass that was reasonably flat, stretched out and prayed that things would look better when he awoke.

Hunger woke Melitta. She stretched, stiff from sleeping on the ground, but she'd been too tired to care. Judging by the light, it was mid-afternoon – she'd slept half the day. Not nearly long enough, but she was too hungry to stay asleep. What she wouldn't give for a plate of stew like she'd eaten last night. Or a chunk of roasted boar…

She'd killed the beast. King Erik had always made a point of offering the first morsel of meat to the hunter who landed the killing blow at hunt feasts. Those townspeople owed her that much. Ungrateful peasants.

"Sir George," she called, softly at first, then a little louder, until the cloak-shrouded form on the grass shifted.

"Mmph?"

"Sir George, perhaps we should seek out an inn, for a bed and a meal. Where are we headed next?"

George sat up and glared at her. "And pay for it with what? Do you have any money on you to pay for room and board? Mine is in my saddlebags, in the stable with the horse you insisted we leave behind."

Melitta's mouth dropped open. No money? No…meal?

"But they were going to kill us," she said.

George snorted. "So you say. But what do I have except your word for it? If you read minds so well, what am I thinking about now?" He closed his eyes and bared his teeth.

Melitta swallowed, then bit her lip to read his thoughts. "You're…you're thinking it's my fault we're out here with no money and no horses. If I'd trapped the boar properly, none of this would have happened." For a moment, her heart constricted in her chest. He was right. If the boar had stayed in the trap instead of escaping...

She'd heard the latch click shut.

Melitta jumped to her feet. "I shut that gate. You must have opened it when you leaned on it to throw your spear. Or the pig burst it open when it charged. At you. This isn't my fault. This is yours. And what kind of hero runs away, anyway? If you hadn't run, it wouldn't have chased you. You're a coward, Sir George. You don't deserve to be a knight!"

George winced. "I'm not."

"You are a coward! I saw you! I killed the beast, not you! You couldn't even stab it properly when you had it penned in the bakery!"

George rose. "I'm not a knight."

Melitta couldn't seem to find the words to respond. Finally, she managed to say, "What are you, then?"

"A hero who wants to slay a dragon."

Her mind whirled. "You mean you've never slayed a dragon before? What did you do, run away from that, too?"

George bowed his head. Melitta didn't need to read his mind to know what that meant.

"Coward! Lying, cheating coward! You said you wanted to train me to be a hero, when you wouldn't know a hero if one danced naked before you. I'm more of a hero than you'll ever be. At least I slayed that boar!"

"And a dozen with one blow before that, in case I forget," George muttered.

The taunt barely stung, coming from him.

"I demand you take me home," Melitta insisted.

George spread his arms wide. "I'm not stopping you."

Melitta set her hands on her hips. "A lady must have an escort. An armed escort. You might not be a knight, but I am the daughter of one. The daughter of a knight and his lady, and a lady of Queen Margareta's court, no less."

George's breath hissed out through his teeth. "A lady? Are you serious? A lady who ran away from court to chase dragons? I'm surprised we made it this far without your knightly father coming to drag you back home. He should be along before nightfall, if we're lucky."

"He's dead. He died defending the convent where I was born. He's a saint now," Melitta said.

George sketched a sweeping bow. "My condolences, then."

"My lady." Melitta said through gritted teeth.

"What?"

"My lady. You might not be a knight, or any kind of nobility, but you will address me properly," Melitta replied.

George unfastened a pouch from his belt and tossed it to her. "Well, then, my lady, how about you start a fire and start making us something to eat, while I go get some more firewood for tonight. Because if your saintly father isn't going to come riding in here on his heavenly steed, this is where we're camping. In case you didn't notice, we took the south road out of town, and no one else has passed this way all day. Unusual, given it's usually such a busy trade route between the town and the sea. The next inn is a day's ride, or several days on foot, but that's the least of our worries. This road is rumoured to be home to a particularly nasty band of bandits with considerable bounties on their heads. They may or may not be giants, according to some of the stories."

"Giants." Melitta couldn't keep the disbelief out of her tone. "Everyone knows there's no such thing as giants."

"People say the same about dragons. Do you believe in those?"

Suddenly, Melitta wasn't sure. If George had lied about being a hero who could teach her things, had he lied about the dragon, too?

"Maybe?" she ventured.

He nodded slowly. "That's fair. Until I saw the beast with my own eyes, even I couldn't be sure. I may not be a knight, or any kind of hero of reknown, but I swear I will kill that dragon. And if you stick with me, I'll show the beast to you."

Melitta curled her lip in disgust. "Why would I stick with you at all?"

George's smile was grim. "Bandits, remember? Even if they aren't giants, two against a band is better odds than one girl with a dagger."

Despite herself, Melitta shivered. She didn't want to admit it, but he was right. "Fine."

"I'll be back soon, then," he said, striding through the trees.

"Wait, where are you going?"

He stopped. "To get firewood, of course. While you start a fire and make a start on the evening meal. Can you handle that, my lady? Or will you need servants to do it for you?"

"I was raised in a convent before my mother and I came to court. We all had chores to do.

I'm not some useless princess, you know. In case you forgot, I killed that boar."

George inclined his head. "So you did. Maybe you can use your skills to catch us something smaller for supper." And with that, he vanished into the forest.

Melitta swallowed. Even if there were bandits on this road, it wasn't like they had anything to steal, she consoled herself as she set about finding some kindling for the fire.

Seventeen

She was a lady. A court lady, no less. So far out of his reach she might as well be a princess, George fumed as he marched down the road. A lady with a fairy godmother, even. He should have guessed from the cut of her clothes when they first met. But he'd been so mesmerised by the thought of a woman warrior, a girl with the courage he lacked, he hadn't noticed…

She'd dealt the death blow to that boar, and no mistake. She hadn't hesitated at all — one stroke, one shot, and the deed was done. For all his fumblings with the other spears, she'd made him look like a callow boy. She'd hunted with royalty – that pig couldn't have been her first kill.

He was so stupid!

What he should be thinking about was how to find firewood in a forest. Oh, sure, there was wood aplenty, but it was all part of trees that would need several well-placed blows with an axe George did not have before they'd part with anything resembling firewood. Perhaps a tree or branch that had fallen...

But this patch of forest seemed far too clean, even for George's town-bred eyes. Surely there should be more branches on the ground, yet there were none. Almost as though the undergrowth had been picked clean of fire fuel by too many travellers, or a nearby town or...a large band of bandits.

George almost laughed at himself. He'd only heard about the bandits because there was a reward for their heads, but the descriptions of them varied so much, it was hard to know what to believe. A large band, or giants…evidently they'd attacked some knight or other who'd spread the story of them being such a formidable foe. It was probably one man with a crossbow.

Finally, he spotted what he sought – a freshly fallen tree, lying across the road. Better yet, embedded in the stump was an axe. Uttering a grateful prayer of thanks, George wrapped his fingers around the haft and tugged on the weapon. It didn't budge.

Deep, booming laughter echoed through the trees, and George's heart sank. A man clad in shaggy furs that blended in with the bark of the tree behind him unfolded to a height George had to admit made him quite the giant.

Perhaps the rumours were true, he thought uneasily, before he banished that thought.

"You're not strong enough, boy," the man said, prying the axe from the stump with one hand. "See? Takes a proper man to wield such a weapon."

George's feet wanted to run, and he was ready to let them do as they pleased, but he had nowhere to run except back to Melitta. A lady who would be quite the prize to a bandit like this one. George's blood ran cold. Would he sell her as a slave, or use her as one? Or both?

He might not be a knight, but he was all the protector she had. He couldn't lead this man to her.

George forced himself to shrug and feign nonchalance. "I prefer a sword or a spear, mostly. Better for slaying dragons and other such beasts. Trees don't exactly put up much of a fight, do they? Less of a challenge."

The man tossed the axe at George's feet, where it stuck in the earth, inches from his toes. "Go ahead, boy. If you can cut through the trunk, you can have a seat at my fire tonight."

George thought quickly. "Why cut it up here? Why not just take the whole tree to your fire and cut it close to where you need it? I'll help you carry it instead. It seems only fair if I share your fire." And it would keep the man far from Melitta.

"You think you can carry half of this, boy?" The man grunted as he hefted the trunk onto his shoulder.

George eyed the tree. "Sure. The branches and leaves are much bigger than the trunk, after all. But you'll have to lift your end a little higher, or the branches will drag on the ground and slow us both down. I'm plenty strong, though I'm not as tall as you."

With what looked like considerable effort, the man tilted the tree so the branches cleared the ground. George buried his hands in the branches without taking any of the tree's weight. "Great, that's great. Lead the way!"

The giant glanced back, but most of George was hidden behind the tree, so there wasn't much for the man to see. With another grunt, he set off down the road. Away from Melitta.

With his hands full of leaves, George followed in the man's wake. He prayed fervently that he was doing the right thing, because he was damned if he knew what that was right now.

Eighteen

In nearly no time at all, Melitta had a small fire burning in the clearing. Supper, however, would be another matter. When she dug into the pouch George had given her, she found nothing but a few crumbs and a piece of cheese that looked like it had seen better days.

Like he'd said, if she wanted supper, she'd have to catch it herself.

Armed with only a dagger, she doubted she'd catch anything worth eating, if she even knew where to look.

She thought hard, remembering the times she'd gone hunting with the queen. The hunt she'd enjoyed most had been at a large lake where the river curved, and many birds congregated in the winter time. They'd shot so many, the whole court had feasted on goose for weeks. Queen Margareta had commented that hunting on the water hardly seemed fair, for every animal must drink and the hunters had so many advantages.

Melitta must find water, then, she decided. Both to drink, and to hunt. And water ran downhill, so all she had to do was head down, and she should find some. Satisfied with her logic, she set off in search of a stream.

Twice she considered turning back, but the second time, she thought she heard running water. Instead of stopping, this spurred her on, until Melitta splashed into a tiny stream. The rivulet was scarcely large enough to do more than wet her boots, but she followed it until she came to its end in what at first appeared to be little more than a puddle. Melitta parted the bushes and found herself ankle deep in a lake that stretched more than a hundred yards across. And on the edges, standing in the shallows, was a veritable badelynge of ducks.

Her heart soared, then sank to the very depths of the lake as she realised she had no way of catching any of them. Short of leaping on top of one and cutting its throat, which would surely frighten them all off. She'd end up covered in mud for the price of one bird, if she even managed to catch it.

No, there must be a better way.

The boys in the town outside the convent had occasionally brought birds to sell. Without shoes or weapons, she'd wondered how they managed to catch them. When she'd asked, one boy had showed her his slingshot. They'd thrown stones at the birds eating the grain in the fields, Melitta remembered now. The sisters had always bought the birds and baked them into big pies, sometimes even for the Harvest Feast.

The ducks were bigger than the boys' birds,

but they should still fall to a well-placed stone. Melitta hunted along the lakeshore for suitable stones, tucking them into the pouch at her waist. When she had filled the pouch, Melitta crouched behind a bush, trying to decide which duck to target first.

That one. It looked plumper than the others – if she scared the rest away when she killed it, that one duck alone would make a suitable meal.

She grasped a stone and drew her hand back, ready to throw.

Without warning, the entire flock took flight, quacking and flapping in panic for no reason Melitta could see.

Melitta swore. Then she glimpsed movement out of the corner of her eye, and slowly turned.

The source of the panic stood calmly on the branch of a dead tree at the water's edge, clutching its dinner in one talon. The falcon might have been the twin of Queen Margareta's favourite hunting bird, but this magnificent creature wore no jesses. It was as free as the sky above, and judging from the tilt of its proud head, sovereign of all it surveyed.

"You cost me my dinner, bird," she muttered, sending the rock in his direction instead. Her missile fell woefully short, splashing into the water three yards from the tree.

Melitta tried again, and again. Each time she got closer, until finally one stone hit the branch beside the falcon. It spread its wings and took off, letting its prey fall as it flew away.

Without thinking, Melitta ran for the creature the falcon had caught, hoping it would be something suitable for her own dinner. She picked up the tiny bird, so small it fitted into her hand, and almost laughed. She'd seen bigger mice in the castle at home.

But as she scooped the bird up, she felt the thrumming of its terrified heart. It was still alive.

She lifted it higher so that she might inspect it, and the bird lay still as the dead on her palm, frozen in fright.

"So you frightened away my dinner!" a voice boomed over the water as a man strode into view. "Maybe I'll eat you instead." He laughed.

Melitta tucked the bird into her now-empty pouch, and planted her feet firmly. She was tired, she probably looked like she'd been sleeping in the woods, and she was hungrier than ever, but she'd be damned before she showed fear to a man who looked wilder than she. Why, his bramble-bush beard looked like it hadn't been trimmed in months, if at all, and his clothes looked they'd last been worn by a bear. But he had a bow and a quiver full of arrows, not to mention the huge sword sheathed at his side.

"It wasn't me," she returned, tossing her head. "A falcon made the ducks take fright. He stole my dinner as much as he stole yours."

He scooped up a stone and advanced on her. "I saw you throwing rocks, girl. Do you know what I do to those who defy me? I crush them, like this." To Melitta's horrified fascination, he squeezed his fist and when he opened it, nothing but dust flew out.

Melitta gulped. She reached into her pouch, but found nothing except the bird and the piece of cheese. Clutching the cheese in her hand, she fought to keep her voice calm as she said, "Dust? That's nothing. Anyone can turn a stone to dust. I can make them weep." She clenched her fist and liquid dripped through her fingers to the ground.

This made the man hesitate. "You some kind of sorceress or something?"

"Yes, I am," Melitta said truthfully.

"How far can you and your magic throw a stone, then?" he challenged, seizing another rock which he skipped across the lake.

"Further than you," Melitta returned, uttering a silent prayer as she drew the bird from her pouch, hiding it as best she could from his watchful eyes as she launched it into the air. Either someone had heard her prayer or the bird had recovered, for once it was airborne, the bird kept flying, far away. "See?"

she said triumphantly. "I can throw a stone so far it never comes down!" She pointed to where she could barely make out the bird as a speck in the sky.

"I don't see it." The man's voice was alarmingly close. Too close.

While Melitta had been distracted, watching the bird's flight, he'd crept up behind her. She reached for her dagger, but didn't have time to pull it out before something hard crashed into the back of her head and everything went dark.

Nineteen

The first thing Melitta was aware of was the lecherous thoughts of a group of nearby men. That was hardly a surprise, though the vague inclusion of herself in those thoughts was worrying. More worrying still was the realisation that if she was reading their minds, she must have shed some of her blood. Only then did she recollect the blow to her head, which now throbbed faintly. She had been unconscious for several hours, then, she decided.

Melitta attempted to reach for the back of her head, to assess the damage, but she found that she could not. Her hands were tightly bound behind her with coarse rope. A normal girl might've panicked, but as the daughter of a master weaver who was as experienced at untangling knots as she was at breathing, Melitta simply set to work. In a moment her nimble fingers had set her free.

She sent her thoughts out to those of the unpleasant men. There were six of them, she found. All clad in fur and leather, like the clothes of raiders from the North. The man who had attacked her was among them, and she burned with anger and the desire for revenge on the man who had hit her and evidently carried her off to this place. He would pay for his disrespect. The others… Their thoughts marked them as little better than him, given what they wanted to do to her. They sat in the middle of a sort of longhouse, lounging around a fire. Though none of them was actually looking at her, she skipped through their thoughts until she found a man who was at least looking vaguely in her direction. She lay on a straw pallet in the shadows at the far end of the longhouse. She was far enough away that if she chose to, and no one saw her, she could sneak out of the place and escape. However, that left the matter of revenge.

She took a deep breath, then wished she hadn't, for the straw she lay on was far from clean. Other captives like herself had been dragged here, she realised, and forced to endure the attention of these horrible men as they slaked their lust. That hadn't been the end for the poor girls, either – after the men were done raping them, they sold the girls into slavery. Melitta's anger blazed within her. This ended here and now. They had taken their last slave.

Conversation around the fire shifted and she was surprised to see George in their thoughts. They had shared a meal with the man sometime earlier – Melitta's stomach rumbled at the thought of the meal she had missed – and he had since fallen asleep on a bed not far from where she lay.

Melitta suppressed a smile as she realised their thoughts of him were tinged with fear. Had he fooled them into thinking he was a hero of some sort, too? They seemed to think he was uncommonly strong, carrying a whole tree to their camp, when keeping up with him had almost killed one of their number. The man in question ventured that it would be safest to kill George before he woke. Several of his companions agreed.

Slowly, Melitta opened her eyes. George was indeed asleep, just where they'd thought he was, and if she kept to the shadows, she might be able to reach him without any of them seeing. He might be a charlatan and no hero at all, but he was the only ally she had against them. And he might not be a hero but he was correct when he'd said that two against a band of brigands was better than her against all six. Besides, she might not like him, but it didn't seem honourable to let these men slaughter him in his sleep.

The men began to argue loudly. Some wanted George dead, and some feared to do the deed. Those whose voices roared the loudest had minds petrified by fear. While they struggled to decide whether it was more dangerous to attempt to kill George or to let him live, Melitta took her chance. Keeping close to the wooden walls of the longhouse, she made her way to the alcove where George lay. Remembering a trick the young squires in the castle played on one another, she pinched George's nostrils shut with one hand while clapping her other hand over his mouth. He woke with a start, just as the boys had. She released his nose but kept her hand over his mouth as she whispered in his ear, "They are planning to kill you. Quickly, bundle up your bedding so that it looks like you are still here asleep, and come with me." George did as she asked, then followed her to the darkest end of the longhouse. Melitta was delighted to discover that they'd ended up in the bandits' storeroom. Now, she could finally satisfy her hunger. The two-day-old bread she sank her teeth into tasted like ambrosia. And the first flagon of wine she uncorked... even better still. She stopped after a few sips, though. It would not do to dull her wits. She would need them as sharp as possible to achieve her ends before the night was over. She glanced back the way they had come to find the men's argument had erupted into blows. They could not reach agreement on whether George should live or die. What the others did not know, though, was that one man had already made up his mind. No matter what the others decided, he would make sure George didn't live to see morning.

After some time, the fighting ceased. Two of them headed off, muttering, even as they bundled themselves into bed. The remaining four sat drinking around the fire, until one by one, they succumbed to the potent brew.

All but one — the man who had vowed

George would die. He drank sparingly, and his companions were too drunk to notice. When he was certain the others were asleep, he took his axe and stumbled toward George's bed. His head was a jumble of thoughts, the uppermost of which was anger at some trick George had played on him. A trick he suspected but did not quite understand. Disliking what he didn't understand, the man took courage from this and hefted his axe.

With one terrible blow, he cleaved the bed in two. Not content with this, he chopped at the bedclothes several more times, as if to sever George's head, feet and manhood. Then, somewhat satisfied, the would-be butcher headed for his own bed, where he curled up beside his axe like a normal man might cuddle up to a lover.

When Melitta was certain they were all asleep, she whispered to George, "We should burn this place down around them while they sleep."

"No man deserves to be burned alive!" he

whispered back, his eyes wide with horror.

"They rape and kill for fun," she hissed back. "If the king's men caught them, they'd be strung up and slaughtered, like the beasts they are."

"How do you..." George swallowed, falling silent as he remembered. "Mind-reader. Right. We should take some of the food out of here first, and then barricade the doors so that they can't escape when the fire takes hold."

Melitta nodded in satisfaction. Two against six would be more than enough for this night's work.

Twenty

George and Melitta dragged barrels and bales from the longhouse, stacking them up in the clearing outside. He couldn't help darting worried glances at the bandits each time they were in view, but the thunderous snoring was oddly reassuring.

Then Melitta came out of the door, carrying a burning brand.

"We could just leave," George suggested. "Let the king's men catch up with them and administer justice."

"I won't let them rape another woman," Melitta insisted.

His blood ran cold. "Did they…?" he began, staring at her.

She glared back. "No. And if we kill them before they wake, they won't." She hefted her makeshift torch.

"You can't burn the building. It's sod. The best it will do is smoulder," George told her. He felt oddly relieved by the admission. She would have worked it out on her own, he reasoned.

She kicked a nearby crate in frustration. "Then how are we supposed to kill them and claim the bounty on their heads?"

The bounty? George felt lightheaded. They didn't stand a chance against six men, each of them easily twice his size.

Melitta wasn't paying attention to him. Instead, she fished about inside the crate she'd kicked. "Perfect," she breathed. "We'll shoot them."

"What?"

Melitta straightened, holding a crossbow in each hand. "There's a dozen of these, and quarrels, too. Load them and stack them –" she surveyed the clearing "– beside those two trees. They give a good view of the door to the longhouse. When they emerge, we'll shoot them. No need to reload if all the bows are ready to go."

George's stomach roiled. Shooting a man from an ambush hardly seemed more honourable than killing one in his sleep. "We don't need the bounty," he lied weakly.

Melitta shoved the crossbows at him. "Load them, I said. You owe me a horse. I'm not walking home," she said. She grabbed another armload of weapons and began winding the first one up. When she'd finished, she dropped the rest at his feet. "I'll light up the roof." She advanced with her brand again, touching it to the longhouse. The sod began to smoulder in places, flaring into flame where dried grass had taken root.

"It won't be enough. The smoke it outside,

not in," George told her. Though his heart rebelled against it, urging him to run, he continued loading the crossbows in accordance with her command.

Melitta frowned at the roof. "Then I'll have to go inside and light the place up. Starting with that smelly pallet." Before George could stop her or call a warning to be careful, Melitta marched back into the longhouse with murder in her eyes.

For a long moment, he waited, listening to the click of each crossbow before he set it in readiness beside its fellows. Seconds ticked by and his heart sank at the thought of having to go in after Melitta to save her. Would he be too late?

Shouldering the final crossbow, George took a step toward the door.

Melitta erupted from the longhouse, sprinting toward him. "Fire!" she cried, pointing behind her.

So she'd lit it, George thought, until he realised that wasn't what she meant at all. An angry giant of a man burst out of the door after her. George fired the crossbow. The bolt caught the man in the throat, and he collapsed on the ground with a gurgle before he lay still.

"One down, five to go," Melitta said, pointing a bow at the dark doorway. She had a smudge of soot on her cheek, but her eyes blazed with fire.

Once again, George fell in love.

"Get him!"

Melitta fired before George could even aim. Her bolt caught the man in the belly. She swore, picked up another bow, and fired again. This one penetrated his forehead, felling him like the tree George had pretended to help him carry here.

He didn't have time to reflect on it, though, for two men fought to get out of the doorway next, and they both had to choose their targets. His first shot missed both of them, to George's dismay, but the second one plunged into his quarry's thigh. Before George could fire again, Melitta's quarrel found his chest.

"Four!" she cried, reaching down for another weapon.

The fifth man charged out of the door, straight at her, bellowing, "Witch!"

Melitta dropped her bow in surprise.

Thank the heavens the man hadn't seen George, for George had scarcely a moment to bring his bow up to fire at the man before the giant reached Melitta. He wasn't fast enough to stop him, either – the man crashed into Melitta, throwing her to the ground. She managed to tug out her dagger and plunged it into his side before either of them realised he'd stopped moving. The fletching of George's bolt stuck out behind the man's ear.

Melitta rolled the man off her with difficulty. George moved to help, but she hissed, "Watch the door. There's still one left!"

The sixth man had already made it out the doorway, but instead of heading for them, he took off at a run. George didn't think. He paused only to snatch up a second bow before he was off after the man, trying to get a clear shot as the giant weaved through the trees.

As if by magic, a crossbow quarrel sprouted from the man's back, and he keeled over, face first. When George reached him, he wasn't sure if the man was alive or dead. He prodded the man's shoulder with his bow. "Get up," he said.

The man rolled, seizing George's bow in one hand and bringing a blade up with the other.

A bolt pierced the man's eye, and the knife dropped from his fingers as he fell back to the ground, lifeless.

George turned.

Melitta stood a dozen yards away, crossbow clutched to her side, with a look of grim satisfaction on her face. "He didn't deserve a quick death. None of his victims got one."

George looked askance at her, not trusting his voice. She'd killed a man. No, she'd killed four. He'd killed two. For all his talk of heroism and honour, he'd never killed a man before today.

"Not all the girls these men took were sold as slaves. This one liked to torture them, sticking knives into them so they bled to death while he raped them. He wanted to do the same to me." Melitta kicked the corpse.

George drew in a shaky breath. If she was right, these men deserved to die. Bandits, with bounties on their heads, he reminded himself. A bounty they could use to replace what they lost in Sanglier.

"See if you can find some sacks," George found himself saying.

Melitta frowned at him. "What for?"

George dropped to his knees and reached for the dead man's blade. "We'll need to put these heads in something so we can carry them to town to claim the bounty."

Now it was Melitta's turn to look sick. "Right. All right. I'll see what I can find."

Twenty-One

A tentative knock sounded at the door. Melitta crossed the inn's best chamber to open it. "Yes?" she asked.

The chambermaid dropped a curtsy. "Beg pardon, milady. I thought this was the knight's chamber."

"George's across the hall, in what I understand is your second best chamber," Melitta said, pointing. "He said that a lady deserves the best, and a knight will make do with whatever else is available."

"Aw, he's a gallant one, isn't he? All chivalry and courtly love." She sighed blissfully. "So romantic. When will you be married, milady?"

Married? Melitta's eyebrows rose so high she suspected they vanished into her hair. Hopefully never, she thought but didn't say. Instead, she replied, "When a man demonstrates he truly deserves me, and asks for my hand."

At the sound of a male voice clearing his throat, the maid turned bright red. The girl spun on the spot. "Your armour has arrived, good Sir Knight," she mumbled. She bobbed a curtsy, holding out the box. She waited only long enough for George to take it from her hands before she hurried off downstairs.

George's eyes met Melitta's. His expression was unreadable. "So do we open it in your chamber or mine? After all, one set of this armour belongs to you."

Now it was Melitta's turn to blush. If she was going home to court, she truly didn't need armour. But after killing that boar and then the giants… People looked at her differently. Well, they looked at George mostly, for he was the hero who had claimed the bounty on the bandits. But he'd split the money with her immediately, instead of taking the lion's share for himself, as Melitta would have expected. Though she might have killed more of the men, she was still just an apprentice hero.

"Mine is larger," Melitta said opening the door wider to allow George in.

He set the box on the table and pulled out the first piece of armour. Holding it up to his chest, he said, "I believe this is yours."

He was right. The leather curved in ways that no man's armour should, or needed to. Melitta felt the urge to buckle it on immediately, though there was no enemy here. She still occasionally remembered the gory mess George had made hacking off the six giants' heads, for she had been unable to hold down her gorge long enough to help. George had not complained, nor even mentioned it, for which she was grateful. She thought she should feel something, after killing those men, but if anything she was glad. Proud to have been the one who stopped them from hurting anyone else. Was this what George had first seen in her on the day they met? The makings of a true hero?

She watched him buckle his own armour over his tunic, as eager as she was to see how well it fit. He'd chosen leather, like her, despite the reward being enough for them to afford steel. Not to mention all the goods the bandits had stolen, which by right of conquest had belonged to both of them after the men were dead. She knew George still carried some of the jewels in the bottom of his saddlebags – insurance against the day when he might need to sell them. For a gold necklace could buy a fine horse and enough food to keep a hero going until his next quest. He'd offered some to her, but she had refused. When would she ever wear them? She'd left all her jewels back in her mother's apartments in the castle. She had no need for more.

"I took the liberty of ordering you new boots as well," George said, pulling a pair out of the box. "Yours appear to have been damaged by water at some point."

Though it seemed such a long time ago now, Melitta remembered the exact moment when it happened. She'd gotten her feet wet collecting stones to catch birds for their dinner on the lake, and all the trouble of being captured by giants and fighting her way free, she hadn't noticed they were ruined until too late. "Thank you," she said.

He cleared his throat. "If you'll allow me, I have a special potion of my own design, that when rubbed on shoes properly can make them entirely waterproof. I can do it tonight, and then you never need worry about getting your feet wet, ever again." He shuffled his own feet on the floor boards, keeping his head down and not meeting her eyes.

"I would be very grateful," Melitta said truthfully. "Wherever did you find such a magical potion?"

George laughed. "In my father's workshop. He was a shoemaker, and until I chose a different path, so was I. His creations were much sought after at court, as were my mother's. Her embellishments were so beautiful, she made boots for the king and queen themselves. My work… was of a more practical bent. I was never as good as my father, or my mother. So I made shoes for the rest of the town, while my mother and father made shoes for those who could afford the best."

Melitta touched the leather. "So did you make these, or someone else?" They were as fine as any she'd worn at home, but her knowledge was all about cloth, not leather.

George smiled sadly. "Not me. You deserve the best, so a better shoemaker than me made them. Perhaps not as fine as my mother's work, but she had a rare gift, may God rest her soul." He spread his hands wide. "May I help you put them on, to see if they fit?"

Melitta couldn't say no. She perched on the

edge of a chair and George knelt before her. She held out one booted foot, which George clasped reverently. He pulled off her ruined shoe, then cupped her heel in his hand before sliding the new boot on in its place.

"Perfect," he breathed, reaching for her other foot.

He took longer with the second one, pausing to smooth her wrinkled hose.

His stroking fingers seemed to set her heart racing as Melitta's breath caught in her throat. True, no man had ever touched her feet before, but her body reacted as if this was more than just a touch. Melitta prayed he didn't notice the strange effect he had on her.

He slid the second boot on as easily as the first, then urged her to stand and walk. She obeyed, marvelling at the softness of the leather around her foot, though the sole was thicker than she was used to. More practical than what she'd worn around the castle, though of no less quality. George might not have made these boots, but he had commissioned them, and he was a good enough shoemaker to know what was best. Yes, the fit was perfect.

"Thank you," she said again, trying to emphasise how much she meant it.

"My pleasure, my lady." George clambered to his feet. "Shall I help you with your armour, too, to make sure that fits as well?"

Melitta wanted to protest that she was perfectly capable of dressing herself, but she'd never donned armour before, and George had been so familiar with his own. So, she nodded.

Together, they lifted the surprisingly heavy garment over her head and settled it around her hips. He smoothed the leather across her back as she cinched the buckle around her waist. A little too tight, she realised, as she tried and failed to reach for the shoulder straps. Melitta hurried to loosen the belt.

George's breath was warm on the back of her neck. "Allow me, my lady."

She suppressed a shiver at the sound. She wasn't cold, she wasn't afraid...so why was she reacting so strangely?

George's hands smoothed the straps over her shoulders, then, one by one, he fastened the buckles on either side of her collarbone to keep the armour in place.

"George..." Her voice sounded so breathless Melitta barely recognised it. Was it just her, or did his hands linger on her for just a moment? It was hard to tell beneath the layers of wool and leather. Perhaps it was the memory of his touch that lingered.

"Yes, my lady?" He stepped around her, then stood before her, his eyes taking in every detail. From the curve of his lips, she believed he either liked what he saw or he was trying not to laugh.

Melitta longed for a mirror, but even the best room in the inn had no such luxury. So, she did as she always had on such occasions — she bit her lip and slipped into someone else's eyes to see what she looked like.

Warmth engulfed her, as passionate as a lover's embrace. "A true goddess, a goddess of war," George's voice rumbled, though his lips never moved. In that moment, Melitta felt like the most beautiful woman she'd ever seen, and loved like...like the way King Erik worshipped his queen.

Gasping, Melitta withdrew back into her own head, grasping the table to stop herself from stumbling over her own feet. Some goddess, she thought angrily. "What do you think?" she asked George.

Adoration still warmed his eyes, but his tone was more businesslike than his thoughts. "It fits," he said. "What does it feel like?"

Like she wanted to throw her arms around him and kiss him, Melitta thought. No, those were his thoughts, not hers, she scolded herself. "It feels fine," she said.

His expression softened, as though he could read her mind and the stray thoughts she struggled to suppress. "You look very fine."

Melitta's mouth was dry as she once again found it hard to breathe. The armour, her fuzzy mind told her. It must still be fastened too tight. If she unbuckled it, then she wouldn't feel so lightheaded. Or hot. Yes, she was too hot in all these clothes. They must come off.

Her mind slipped effortlessly into George's head, and his thoughts echoed hers. Clothes. Off. Certainly…

Twenty-Two

George couldn't tear his eyes away from her. Every fibre in his body wanted him to dart forward and take Melitta in his arms. He couldn't be imagining the invitation in her eyes.

Except…his brain refused to let him. She was Lady Melitta, companion to a queen, and he was…little more than a cobbler. Which meant he must be daydreaming.

"Milady? Sir Knight?" A maidservant dropped a deep curtsey in the doorway.

"There's a young priest downstairs, seeking the hero who killed them robbers on the coast road. He's fair wild about it, too. Says he won't eat or drink or rest until he's spoken to you." She looked at George.

He wanted to tell her she had the wrong person, and it was Milady the priest wanted, for the most he'd done was butcher the robbers' bodies for their heads and then collect the bounty for his bag of grisly remains, but he needed to escape from her chamber before temptation won him over and he did something stupid.

The lady who'd killed a dozen with one blow would end him just as easily as any of the giants. She truly was some ancient goddess of war, come to earth to…well, what she'd come for, he wasn't sure. But she'd already conquered his heart, and many men would follow.

George nodded, then followed the maid downstairs. A woman's light tread behind him told him Melitta had followed, and why not?

George could no more stop her than he could prevent the sun from rising.

The priest was a beanpole of a man who didn't look much older than George himself, yet his slumped shoulders and cavernous eyes spoke of troubles he'd endured that no many should be subject to.

"What troubles you, Father?" George asked.

The priest's eyes drank him in like a thirsty man's first gulp of water, before spitting him out again as he realised his saviour was a mirage. "Nothing and no one can help me," the priest said. "Unless I can find a man who slays monsters no one else can touch."

"Valiant Sir George here slayed a dozen giants. Cut their heads off with his sword," the maid said proudly, as though she had witnessed this remarkable feat. "He's the man you want, Father."

The priest's eyes widened. "You?"

George couldn't blame him. He knew he hardly looked like a hero. The sort of knight a lady like Melitta might look on with love. He sighed. "Two. I killed two giants. Not twelve." And, as honesty had truly taken hold of him, he added, "And I took their heads off with a knife. Severing a spine is dull work for a sword."

The priest's jaw dropped. "You killed two giants with only a knife?" He swallowed, still staring at George. "Perhaps you are the hero I seek."

George inclined his head, waiting. He could hear Melitta behind him, but she didn't say a word. Probably wanting to hear what the priest had to say before deciding whether to offer her help. George wished he'd been as cautious.

"Deep in the forest, beside a lake to the west of here, there is a holy well whose water works miracles. When the Grand Master of my order heard of it, he insisted we must build an abbey to protect such a holy site. For two years, we have waited to hear tidings that the new monastery has been built, but we received no word. Finally, my superior sent me to discover what is causing the delay.

"I journeyed for days, then took ship for the coast. From there, I headed south along the coast road. Many people told me cautionary tales about giants or robbers who preyed on travellers on the coast road, but I could not turn back. I reasoned that a solo traveller under a vow of poverty would not attract the attention of robbers, and I was relieved to find I was right. I saw not a single soul on the road until I reached the road to the lake." The priest nodded his thanks as a tavern girl handed him a cup.

He drank deeply before he continued, "The lake road showed signs of recent traffic, but I followed it all the way to the water before I found a camp of men making clay bricks for the abbey. They set them out in their moulds in the sun for some time, before firing them in an oven so they are hard enough to build with. Remarkable, really. Making their own rocks, when there is not enough stone with which to build."

George waved his hand, urging the priest to

continue.

"Bricks were piled up everywhere – enough to build an abbey to rival the one where our Grand Master resides. I explained to the men who I was, and how I would like to see how their construction fared. They conferred among themselves for a moment, before one of the men drew me down to the lake's edge. He pointed across the water and told me the well was on a particular hill overlooking the lake, and that's where they'd started to build the abbey. If I wanted, I could walk around the lake to the hill and look for myself. They had bricks to make while daylight lasted, he said."

The priest sat down heavily and drained his cup. "I followed the path around the lake. The first thing I saw was more piles of bricks. More than enough to finish an abbey, so why did they need more? Still, I ascended the hill. The builders had cut into the side of the hill to dig a huge cellar – enough to hold supplies for a large community. Perhaps the Grand Master planned to move to this abbey, I thought, which was why he wanted such a grand building. The idea stayed with me until I reached the crown of the hill, where I stopped. For there was no abbey. No church, no monastery…nothing, but that cavernous cellar on one side and, half hidden in the summer grass, a low stone well on the other."

The priest shook his head, as if reliving the moment and still not believing it. "It was a hot day, and I had quite a thirst. While I may not be as holy as some, I'd like to think I am a godly man, and I was there in obedience to the wishes of my order. So I approached the well, intending to drink those most holy waters."

Melitta made an impatient sound in her throat.

The priest hung his head. "I know, mistress. I am human, and I was tempted. I will pay my penance for such presumption, I promise. I pulled up a bucket of water, and the moment the liquid touched my lips…" Here the priest's voice seemed to fail him. He swiped a hand across his brow. "I am sorry. I…"

Twenty-Three

The priest's fear was so thick Melitta could almost taste it. Cloying and bitter, yet he drank the draught because it was his duty to do so. He lived and would die for the vows he'd made to his order.

"From the trees there erupted a creature I can only describe as the wrath of God made flesh. It shone as bright as the sun, fearsome to look at, and moved nigh as fast as that very orb's rays. The thunder of its hooves would have shaken the very heavens above as it charged toward me." The priest swallowed. "I think it would have impaled me and tossed me into the well, as a warning to others who dare to take what they do not deserve. I suspect I would have deserved my fate, but I had not the faith to accept it. Weak as I was, I ran around the well and into the forest, as fast as I could, back to the brickmakers' camp. It was only when I reached the other men that I realised the beast had not followed me, and I was safe."

Even though Melitta had seen the image in the man's mind, she didn't believe it. Such creatures couldn't exist.

And if they did, what he wanted them to do sat squarely in the realms of sacrilege.

George folded his arms across his chest. Melitta had to admit that the new breastplate made him look more muscled than was actually the case. "So you want us to go to this building site of yours, and slay a beast."

The priest nodded fervently. "Oh, yes. If you will do that, I can promise you a rich reward. Not just in heaven, but here on earth, as well. My superiors gave me enough gold to hire more labourers, if that was the problem, or material if it is missing, but no amount of coin will convince workmen to build the abbey as long as it is guarded by a fearsome beast."

"We'll take the job," George said promptly before Melitta could stop him. "Will you take us to the construction camp on the morrow?"

"Of course, Sir George," the priest said warmly, sagging with relief against the bench. He glanced at Melitta. "Are you taking the lady with you, sir?"

Dread twisted in Melitta's belly. This was a bad idea, and she needed to tell George that before he committed himself, and maybe even her, to this folly.

"Of course," George said. "It's a little known piece of lore that having a virgin present can calm even the most savage beast. She is my secret weapon." He deliberately avoided meeting Melitta's gaze.

Wait until he sees what his secret weapon

will do to him the moment no one's looking, Melitta fumed. She wanted no part in this.

The priest, who had recovered his spirits remarkably quickly, called for food and drink to celebrate the bargain he and George had made.

Try as she might, Melitta couldn't seem to get George's attention long enough to warn him about what the priest wanted. After a frustrating hour, she gave up and headed upstairs to her chamber to get some sleep. She'd tell him in the morning, she decided — right before she rode off in the opposite direction. She'd had her fill of heroes and those who hired them. She'd head home and, if she still wanted to, slay monsters there.

Twenty-Four

George plied the priest with far more drink than was good for him, but even deep in his cups, the man didn't drop so much as another hint about the beast they faced, or the best way to kill it. Which was unusual in itself, he had to admit. What man was so afraid of something he refused to talk about it at all? Didn't he want it dead?

He turned to ask Melitta, for with her mind-reading magic it was possible that she had caught more from the man than he had, but he was disappointed to discover that she'd disappeared. Back to her chamber, he assumed, resting before tomorrow's journey.

Sure enough, when he'd managed to roll out of bed the following morning and drink enough to dispel his lingering hangover, he found Melitta at breakfast in the common room downstairs, wearing her breastplate and a grim expression.

"Good morning, my lady," he wished her warmly.

Melitta eyed him over her cup, drinking deeply before she replied, "No morning is good when the day must end in killing a unicorn."

George spat out a mouthful of water. "You're killing a unicorn? But those things are purity itself. Killing one would condemn you to hell for eternity. Don't do it, my lady, I beg you."

Melitta slammed her cup down on the table. "I never said I'd do it. You did, though. You promised the priest that you'd kill his unicorn.

And virgin or not, I won't help you do it. You're on your own for this one." She rose and made to leave.

If she left, he stood no chance against the dragon. Ever.

George grasped her wrist. "My lady – Melitta – please. Don't go. I need you."

Melitta wrenched free. "I'm not killing a unicorn, George."

Possibilities spiralled through his mind. Slowly, he began, "What if we don't have to? What if we just trapped it, like we did with the boar?"

Melitta snorted. "Like that worked. Or don't you remember being run out of town without our things? And I killed the beast, in case you've forgotten."

George waved away her worries. "This isn't the same thing. I'll speak to the priest before we set out. I know all he needs is to get the beast away from the building site, so it's safe to build the abbey. If we trap it, then he can do what he likes with it. We can earn our money and be on our way to fight something more deserving of death, like a dragon."

He'd sparked her interest, he knew, but he wasn't sure if it was enough.

"Imagine the tales they'll tell about us if we not only killed a dozen giants, but captured a unicorn, too," George added.

"Six, not a dozen," Melitta replied. "And you only killed two of them."

"But a unicorn…" he wheedled. "Have you ever seen a unicorn?"

She sighed. "No. If I hadn't seen one in the priest's memories yesterday, I still wouldn't believe the creature exists. And I certainly couldn't bring myself to kill one."

"A lady who has killed a dozen with one blow, and a wild boar that was terrorising a town, and four giants…my lady, if you decide something must die, may God help anyone who stands in your way." George meant every word, but he wasn't sure Melitta believed him.

A slight smile curved at her lips. "Flatterer. You make me sound so frightening, yet I suspect I will be little more than virgin bait for the beast, if anything."

George placed his hand over his heart. "I swear by my own life that I find you terrifying, my lady."

She seemed to measure him with her eyes for a long moment, before she gave a nod. He hoped he had passed her inspection. "You promised to put your magic potion on my new boots," she said.

He bowed his head. "Indeed I did. In all the excitement last night, I forgot. I will remedy that tonight, if you allow me to."

"Before we must face the unicorn, or after?"

"Before, of course. When you meet your first unicorn, you must wear your best boots."

Melitta laughed. "I must be mad, listening to you. And yet, your words have untold power. My first unicorn. I like the sound of that too much to refuse. We will go with this priest, see his unicorn, and if he still insists the beast must be killed…then we will decline the task and be on our way."

She made it sound so easy. Yet for her, it would be, George was sure of it. He swallowed his last mouthful of breakfast. "We ride."

An hour later, ride they did – but without the priest, who had claimed illness after drinking too much the previous night. He gave them directions to the lake campsite and promised he would catch up to them. Melitta waited until she was out of his earshot before expressing her doubts that he'd arrive before they'd dealt with the beast, and George had to agree.

Still, he rode to battle alongside a veritable goddess of war whose eager enthusiasm was more contagious than any plague. Oh, but what a pleasurable plague. George felt his own courage rising every time he glanced at her.

Yes, it was his courage. Nothing else, for nothing could happen between them. Fairytales were for knights and ladies and royalty. Shoemakers were never the hero who won the heart of a fair lady. One day some prince would ask for her hand and she would be someone else's lady. Never his.

George knew his place, and counted himself fortunate that today it was at her side. What more could he ask for, except victory?

Twenty-Five

By the time the lake came into view between the trees, Melitta had to admit they had a good plan. The priest had not put in an appearance, so they'd decided to trap the beast and wait for the priest to come. When he did, they would demand payment, or release the unicorn.

The brickmakers' camp was just as the priest had described it, and the men there were only too happy to direct them to the well. Melitta was tempted to walk around the lake right away, but she agreed with George that it was best to wait a day or two for the priest to catch up to them. Surely he couldn't be more than a day behind.

On the morrow, George told the men, he would save them from the unicorn. Cheers erupted and the labourers broke out a barrel of mead they'd been saving for a special occasion. Melitta didn't tell George they believed it would be his last night alive, for they'd seen the unicorn kill several of their number before they'd retreated to the other side of the lake. Much like the boar, when it attacked, it lowered its head and charged with its horn first, attempting to impale or gore its target.

For the first time, Melitta wondered if their plan could work. She'd counted on the unicorn being a sort of skittish horse, not some fully armed, more deadly version of one of King Erik's war destriers. If one attacked her, she would most certainly fight back to protect her own life, purity be damned. How pure could a murderous beast be, anyhow?

Something to worry about in the morning,

she told herself, as she rolled herself in her cloak by the fire. The men had offered them space in the hut they shared, but Melitta had declined the offer. With that many men in a confined space all night, the smell would be unbearable.

George slept on the other side of the fire, apparently not bothered at all by what awaited them on the morrow. He was a strange man, confident as the finest knight at one moment, and as humble as the lowest servant the next.

"You should rest, my lady," he said softly.

So he wasn't asleep after all.

Melitta squinted at him through the flames. "How did you know I wasn't asleep yet?"

He chuckled. "The lining of your cloak is silk, and it rustles when you move. When you are restless, it sounds like wind rustling through the leaves above. Sleep, my lady. Tomorrow will come whether you are awake to greet it or not, and our fate is already written. You won't change the outcome of tomorrow's battle by worrying over it."

"You're not worried about dying tomorrow? If we do something wrong?"

"Tomorrow, anything could happen. We could live or die. Take a wound, catch the plague, step on a snake, be crushed by a horse, be hit by a falling tree…and die. Life is short but precious. Tomorrow, your day will end in you seeing a unicorn for the first time. Whatever else happens…is already ordained."

Melitta frowned. "I don't believe that. We have free will. We can make our own fate. I left the castle. You left your shoemaking shop. You can't know what will happen tomorrow, or what choices we will make."

"Worrying about it won't change that."

"You'd make a good court philosopher, George. Have you ever considered that?"

George snorted. "Me, at court? Surely you jest. That's your place, my lady, not mine." He sounded so sad as he said it, too. Almost as though he wished…

"Good night, George," she said.

"And sweet dreams to you, my lady."

My lady. There was something in those words, and the way he said it. Part mockery, part respect, and a lot of longing.

She'd miss that when they parted ways. But not yet. They had a unicorn to face on the morrow, and all else paled into insignificance before it.

Twenty-Six

The men making bricks wished them luck as George and Melitta set off around the lake for the construction site. Melitta was unusually quiet, her eyes darting around as though searching for something. Perhaps she expected the unicorn to pop out of the trees to surprise her.

Did she know something about unicorns that he did not?

Probably. She seemed to know a lot about a lot of things, which constantly surprised him.

He'd thought that court ladies spent all of their time drinking, talking, and perhaps sewing. Certainly nothing particularly useful. Maybe Melitta was different, or maybe he'd just been wrong. Yet if she had fit in so well in court, what was she doing out here with him? Unless the goddess of war was lying about running away from a marriage that her parents had arranged for her, she was here because she wanted to be.

Because she wanted to be with him, a tiny voice inside his head taunted him..

Impossible. Georgie knew the score. It was a unicorn she wanted, not him. After all, she was by his side, not sparing him a glance, whilst she strained her eyes searching for the elusive beast.

The abbey was almost exactly as the priest had described it. A brick cellar carved into the cleared hillside, with the hill itself crowned by a circlet of stone that George took to be the well fed by a miraculous spring, or whatever it was. Magical, miraculous, blessed by a saint...the priest hadn't been too clear about that. All he had said was that the well had the power to heal the sick.

Now, George believed in miracles as much as the next man, but most wells that worked miracles that he had heard of worked their magic through the cleanliness of the water. No more magic required. In a city, clean water might be in short supply. Yet here, with such a large lake on their doorstep, why one would go to the trouble of digging a well for water…perhaps there was something to the stories, after all.

Not that George had any intention of needing the healing waters from the well. Together, he and Melitta would trap the unicorn, then return to camp and claim the reward when the priest arrived.

When Melitta reached the crown of the hill, she stopped. Turning around to look back the way that she'd come, a smile lit her face as she took in the view. "It's so beautiful," she breathed. "The view across the lake and over the forest... Though I would never join a religious community, I could live here."

"Why not? Are you not pious enough?" George teased.

Melitta closed her eyes and shook her head. "I grew up in a convent, remember? I know what life in the cloister is like. Reporting to the chapter house every morning for your chores, and then again every evening to report that they were done. It is all work and prayer and drudgery. Some found joy in it, but not I. Being closed within walls like that, even if you could see out... It was like being in a prison, or a tomb. I wish to live in the world, not separate from it."

"So this is what the unicorn is fighting to protect? The freedom of this hill in the forest? A domain without walls?" George asked.

Melitta shrugged. "I do not know. If the unicorn were here, perhaps I could read its mind. But as it is not, its motivation shall remain a mystery."

No unicorn? Now it was George's turn to

scan their surroundings. Of course, she was right. There was no sign of the beast. Merely the grassy rise, and the big brick pit.

"Can you do that? Read the minds of animals, I mean?" George asked.

"Sometimes. When they use natural instinct, often there are no thoughts to read. A hunting beast usually only knows hunger, and a hunted beast only knows fear. They do not wonder, 'What if?'" Melitta managed a small smile. "Perhaps they all subscribe to the philosophy you described last night. They do not worry, and so they sleep better for it."

George peered into the cellar. It certainly looked big enough for their needs. But it was deeper than he'd thought. The fall from the top might kill a man, or a beast...

"Do you think our plan will work?" George asked abruptly. A sudden thought struck him, and he glanced around again, worried. "Perhaps we'd best not talk of it. After all, a unicorn is a kind of horse and horses understand what we say. So if the beast heard us, and knew our plan, it might also be smart enough to avoid it."

"The beast is not close enough to hear us," Melitta stated with all the confidence of a woman who knew she was talking about. "Perhaps there is something we must do to summon it. What did the priest do? Drink the water from the well?" She moved toward the well, her head darting around like a bird's at every step.

George's heart rose into his throat. He would not place her in danger. Not again. "No, I should do that," he said. "I did not mean that bit about you being virgin bait. I know you're a better marksman than me, so if anyone should be the bait, it is myself." He managed a sickly smile. "If you save me from the beast, I will make shoes for you for the rest of your life."

Melitta tilted her head to the side, as if considering his offer. "Very well," she said slowly. "You draw some water. I shall stand back, and we shall see whether there is any truth to this nonsense about unicorns preferring virgins."

Her eyes glinted with mischief, and for the first time George doubted. He'd believed her to be a virtuous lady, but he'd heard talk of something called courtly love. He'd dismissed it as mere wind – sonnets and other words and such, expressing ideas and ideals that had little to do with the reality of marriage.

Another thought struck him. What if that was what Melitta had run away from? A man at court who had forced her against her will, dishonoured her, and that was why she had been so adamant that the giants must die. Anger burned in his breast. When he escorted her home, he would ask the name of the vile wretch. George might not be a knight, but he had honour, and her honour would not be satisfied until the man had breathed his last.

Melitta was laughing softly. "I meant you, you fool. No man would dare touch one of the ladies of Queen Margareta's court without the lady's permission. The queen would castrate him, before subjecting him to a slow and painful death that he justly deserved. I am as chaste as I choose to be. If the beast does not attack you, then we shall know that unicorns have a fondness for virgins. For you are one, are you not?"

Oh, by all that was holy… George's cheeks grew hot as he blushed like a maiden. Though he longed to tell her she was correct, he refused to lie to her. "I am not," he said shortly. "So the beast will react to me as savagely as he did to the priest. May your purity keep you safe."

He unhooked the bucket from the side of the well, check to make sure it was firmly tied to the coiled rope, then flung the pail into the depths. A splash sounded deep below, and George grasped the rope to haul it up once more.

Melitta's voice was scarcely more than a whisper. "George."

He continued hauling up the bucket, but his eyes were no longer on the dark depths. It seemed just a shimmer between the trees, but it rippled, moving faster than anything he'd seen. Then the horse stepped out of the trees, and George could only stare. The rope fell from his fingers, as he took in the legendary steed.

He had never seen a finer piece of horse flesh. This beast belonged in a king's stable, at the very least. Or an emperor's, perhaps. Yet when the animal raised his head, and with it the wickedly sharp horn that was easily the length of George's forearm, George knew this beast belonged in no stable in heaven or on earth.

The unicorn tossed its head in apparent agreement, before it pawed the ground.

George tensed. Now he would live, or he would die. He prayed that the plan would work. Or that Melitta would succeed when he…

The beast started forward and George bolted. He darted this way, and then that, knowing that to run in a straight line would be to court death. Death by impalement. He circled the well. Once. Twice. On the third time, he broke and ran, heading downhill in the way they'd decided.

The unicorn's hooves thundered behind him. So close. But if George turned to see how close, he would die.

Five more steps. Four. Three. George uttered a prayer. A wordless cry that this would work. Two. One.

George closed his eyes and leaped into nothingness.

Twenty-Seven

Melitta's breath caught in her throat as George jumped into the cellar. She was so certain he'd fall to his death but he managed to catch onto the opposite wall, sliding down it to the earth floor, apparently unharmed.

Melitta breathed again.

The unicorn reached the edge of the pit and it appeared to hesitate, perhaps sharing Melitta's doubts that it would survive the jump. Then it reached the same conclusion Melitta had – if the man could walk around after jumping in there, then he would be fine.

The beast backed up a few paces, then bunched its muscles and leaped.

Right at George.

Melitta screamed out a warning.

He scrambled up the wall like a monkey, digging his hands into the mortar like his life depended on it. Which perhaps it did, for if the unicorn charged at him in the confined space of the cellar, it could still kill him.

Without thinking, Melitta knelt by the lip of the hole, reaching down to help him up. Together, they dragged him over the edge and lay on the grass, gasping.

Below, the unicorn let out an angry scream like no horse Melitta had ever heard before.

George rose to his knees. "It worked," he marvelled. "The beast is trapped, just like we planned it." He beamed at her, eyes shining with relief. "And I'm still alive!"

Confident one moment, as humble as dirt the next, Melitta reminded herself. No, she'd never met a man like George before, and she probably never would again.

He leaped to his feet. "I should go and see if the priest has arrived. And tell him his abbey is safe." He offered Melitta his hand.

She declined. "I'll stay here and make sure the unicorn doesn't escape." And as she watched, she would fix every detail in her mind for later, because she doubted she'd ever see another unicorn.

George hesitated for a moment, before he came to a decision. "All right. If the priest doesn't arrive before the midday meal, I'll return with some food for you."

"Wait." Melitta held up her hand, bit her lip, and reached with her mind. She found the brick makers on the very edge of her awareness, on the other side of the lake. Most of their minds were intent on the clay they worked with, or irritated that some beast had stepped in the moulds before the clay was properly dry. But one mind bubbled with anticipation, half hoping and yet not daring to hope that George would succeed. The priest.

Melitta withdrew. It took a moment for her vision to clear, so she shook her head a few times before she said, "He's there. I can feel him."

George sighed in relief. "Then I will bring him and your midday meal."

Melitta nodded and waited for George to be on his way before she clambered to her feet. Sleeping on the ground was not the most comfortable thing she'd ever done, as her aching body chose to remind her. If she returned home after this, at least there would be soft beds every night.

But a night's discomfort was worth it to see a unicorn, Melitta reflected as she peered down at the beast. It hadn't moved from the spot where it had landed.

It raised its head and let out another horrible, almost human scream.

"I don't like walls, either," she told the animal, "but George will be back soon with that priest. He'll release you, one way or another. Just be patient."

The unicorn let out a huffy snort, just like any normal, impatient horse.

Melitta moved higher up the hill, so that she could lean against one of the few remaining trees that gave her a good vantage point from which she could watch the beast in the cellar. Of course, the view of the lake was beautiful, too, reflecting the blue sky above. Almost as pretty as the ocean at home on a clear day.

The sound of hoofs pounding on turf dragged her out of her daydream. Melitta watched in frozen horror as the unicorn, which had somehow miraculously escaped from the cellar, charged up the hill right for her.

Twenty-Eight

At first, when George told the priest they'd captured the unicorn, he'd been excited. Almost as eager as George to go back and get Melitta. But when George told him the tale of how he had trapped the beast, which was still alive, the priest's enthusiasm waned significantly.

First, he had to see to his horse: make sure the beast was fed and brushed and tethered so that it could not escape. Then he needed to change out of his travelling clothes, for such dusty garments were disrespectful to wear when visiting such a holy site. Then, he needed to relieve himself, which took an inordinately long amount of time, at least in George's opinion.

Finally, when the priest appeared to be ready, George told him of his promise to bring a midday meal for Melitta. The priest's eyes lit up at this, as he busied himself putting together a veritable feast for the three of them to share on the hilltop.

Privately wondering how they were supposed to carry so much food, let alone eat it, George set off around the lake again, with the priest staggering along behind him.

Urgency quickened George's steps, though he did not understand why. Melitta was more than capable of defending herself, and there was no way the unicorn could get out of the cellar. George himself had struggled to climb the wall. A beast with hooves and no hands stood no chance. Yet still he worried, and wondered why.

If the priest's far-off abbey knew of the miraculous properties of the well water, then plenty of others must know of it, too. At any time, a knight might come on the quest for the water and if such a man found Melitta at the well…who knew what might happen? The man might try to carry her off, or otherwise harm her. Worse, he might try to seduce her, or at least win her heart. George himself might have no chance of making an impression on her heart, but that didn't mean he wanted some noble knight to win it instead. George was a man, after all, and as subject to jealousy as anyone else.

George burst out of the trees at a run, and immediately knew something was wrong. Melitta was not by the side of the cellar where he'd left her, which could only mean something had happened to her.

George would never forgive himself.

Time seemed to slow down, for which Melitta was deeply grateful. She ducked out of the way, hearing her tunic tear as the unicorn's horn raked its way through it. Her skin burned, and she knew she been grazed by the beast, too. She ran to the only structure she could see – the well. Putting the stone circle between her and the beast, she dared to turn around to see how close it was. Only to discover that the unicorn still stood beside the tree where she had been standing, only moments earlier.

Melitta crept around the well, in order to get a better view of the beast. Her mouth dropped open in surprise.

In trying to impale her, the unicorn had in fact pinned itself to the tree with its own horn. Try as it might to yank itself free, the beast was stuck. Fearing that it might free itself once again, Melitta ran down the hill for the bag of belongings they'd brought with them. The length of rope they hadn't needed to get George out of the cellar was what she wanted now.

Melitta threw a coil of rope over the beast's neck, securing it with some difficulty as the beast struggled with the tree. Next, she tied the makeshift halter to the tree, looping the rope several times around the trunk before tying it with the strongest knot she knew. There. Let the beast try and break free from that.

Behind her, the horrible unicorn scream sounded again. Melitta whirled, but there was no other beast. Just the one before her. The unicorn tied to the tree let out a frustrated snort. An answering snort came from further down the hill.

They couldn't be two beasts. They couldn't be. And yet...

Melitta checked to make sure the unicorn was securely tied to the tree, then made her way down to the edge of the cellar. To her amazement, there was also a unicorn in the cellar. Looking from one beast to the other, Melitta marvelled. Two unicorns, not one. She would never forget this day.

The beast in the cellar let out another scream, then flopped over on its side, panting. Melitta might not be an expert on horses or unicorns, but she knew this wasn't a good sign. When the beast screamed again, the second one answered it.

For the first time, Melitta dared to slip inside a unicorn's mind. But all she met was a blaze of unbearable pain. Pain in her... arm? No, the pain was not hers. It belonged to the unicorn. He had broken its foreleg when it landed in the cellar, and it could neither walk nor escape.

The second beast had come to its rescue, she assumed. But what use was another unicorn to one trapped in the cellar with a broken leg?

"Melitta? Melitta!" George's shouts became increasingly urgent.

Melitta rose from a crouch and waved. He had the priest with him, she noted. Wonderful. The priest could put the poor animal out of its misery. Or perhaps he knew something about healing horses. She certainly didn't know enough to do anything for the animal.

"How did it get out?" George burst out, catching sight of the second unicorn.

Melitta wanted to sink back down to the ground, she suddenly felt so exhausted. But she didn't want to look weak in front of the priest, who was still the client, after all. "It didn't," she said, pointing. "The first beast is in the cellar. The second beast came to save it, I think." She peered into the cellar again. "Come here. I think it's broken its leg. We have to help it somehow."

"Two unicorns!" the priest breathed, so eager to see inside the cellar that he almost knocked Melitta over the edge.

"Are you going to put it out of its misery, Father?" she asked. "Or miraculously heal its leg?"

The priest's eyes shone, but he didn't seem to see her anymore. "Miracles. Miracles on such a holy site," he muttered. "That's what we must have. A miracle." Like a man possessed, he headed for the well.

"No, Father!" George shouted, running after the priest to hold him back.

But the priest would not be stopped. He drew a pail of water from the well, but he didn't stop to drink it this time. No third unicorn appeared to attack him, either.

With the bucket dangling from one arm, the priest climbed down the ladder Melitta hadn't seen before into the cellar with the injured unicorn.

"He will be killed," George said. "We must

stop him."

Melitta shook her head. "Wait. He said the water can work miracles. The unicorn is the guardian of the well. Surely the well would want to help him."

Down in the cellar, the priest blessed the bucket of water, before pouring it in a thin trickle over the beast's leg. When the bucket was empty, he tossed it up to the grass at Melitta's feet. "Fetch me more water," the priest commanded.

George hurried to obey.

The priest pulled the beast's leg straight, then poured the second bucket over it in the same manner. Five times he sent George back for more water, until the cellar floor was awash, but neither man or beast seem to care. When George brought up the empty bucket, Melitta filled it with grass instead and send him back to the priest with it. "Perhaps he is hungry," she said softly. "When a witch used powerful healing magic on me, I remember I woke absolutely starving."

The priest grabbed a handful of grass, which the unicorn happily lipped from his hand. "Remarkable," he said.

"Are you going to kill him?" Melitta demanded. From where she was standing, there was absolutely no doubt that the priest was tending to a male unicorn.

"Never," the priest replied, reaching out to stroke the unicorn's flank. He looked up at George and Melitta, standing on the edge above him, as if seeing them for the first time. "We must build steps to get him out of the cellar immediately."

"You do what you must," George said firmly. "We only came to catch a unicorn for you, and we caught two. It seems to me we have done our job, and it only remains for you to pay the sum that was promised, and we shall be on our way. Building is best left to those who know how to do it."

"An abbey with a holy well that works miracles, and two unicorn guardians. This will be the holiest place for miles around." The priest nodded. "You shall be richly rewarded."

And that, Melitta reflected, might be the first time a hero was ever paid for not slaughtering the beast he was contracted to kill. And the world would be a better place for it.

Thirty

Loaded with more coin than George thought fair for capturing what were little more than angry horses, he and Melitta set off that evening in search of an inn where they could spend the night.

Yet as the sun began to sink, the largest settlement they encountered was a cluster of houses with not enough people to support an inn. One of the farmers offered space in his barn, and George was of half a mind to accept, but Melitta shook her head slightly, so he declined the offer. Instead, they bought food supplies for several days' travel and continued on their way.

By nightfall, George was ready to set up camp in the first clearing they saw beside the road. Melitta looked just as tired, so when he saw a likely spot, he called a halt. This time, she didn't argue.

They soon had a fire going, and Melitta demonstrated she was quite the expert at toasting bread and cheese.

"Where did you learn to do that?" George demanded over his third golden-brown morsel.

Melitta laughed. "In the convent, when I was a little girl. Mother loved to weave and sometimes grew quite distracted by whatever project she was working on. One of the older nuns used to toast bread and cheese for me, but she'd died of a summer fever, so I took out a toasting fork and tried to do it myself. I got burned a lot to start with, but then I got better. By the time Mother noticed, I was so good at it, I was allowed to make hers, too." She glanced at the sack of food. "Is there pork? Slices of cold roast pork or a smoked leg of ham crisp up quite nicely over a hot fire."

George dug out a joint of meat he couldn't identify in the firelight, and sliced some off for her. "If it's as good as what you do with cheese, my belly is ready to worship you and your cooking skills forever."

Melitta let out a decidedly unladylike snort. "You should see what Queen Margareta's cooks create for feast days. I can cook well enough not to starve, but they can roast meat so that it fair melts in your mouth. They can make cabbage fit for kings, and their dumplings…I used to eat so many dumplings it's a wonder I wasn't sick. I used to have competitions with the little princesses, to see who could eat the most dumplings. I was bigger, so I always won, but when the little prince joined in, he ate too many and he was sick all night. The queen forbade any more contests after that."

George's blood ran cold. One moment she

was the girl of his dreams, and the next...so far out of reach his dreams were laughable. Melitta was raised with royalty, and she deserved a prince. Not him.

"It sounds so perfect," he said slowly, uncorking a skin of mead that had come with the food. He drank deeply, then passed it to Melitta. "If life in the castle was so good, why did you ever leave?"

She took a swig. "I think it was the princess's betrothal gown. She was to be betrothed to some neighbouring prince, and both of them younger than I am. I looked at the dress, and the court, and I realised that if I didn't do something, this was all my future would hold. Sewing dresses for the queen and her daughters. Watching them marry princes while I..." She sighed. "Mother offered to make a match for me. Any man I wanted at court, she said. Queen Margareta has always regarded me like one of her children, for she and Mother have been friends since I was a baby, so she would have made sure I married a man befitting my station. But when I looked at all the young noblemen, practising their archery or swordplay in the training grounds, I wanted none of them."

Melitta tipped the skin up, gulping down almost as much as George had. "It's the mind-reading, you see. It's a curse as much as it's a blessing. For all the couples who claim to be happily married, I know the truth. I know who is loved and who is not, who is terrible in the bedchamber and who is such a perfect lover anyone would swoon to be with them. I know everyone, inside and out, their secrets and their shames, and no one ever changes. I was trapped in a gilded cage from which I thought I should never get out…until that knight came. And then you, calling for those who wanted to be heroes. And you…you picked me. Out of all those boys who talked of nothing else for days, lining up to be considered for the apprenticeship…you picked me." She drank again, but spilled some of it down her tunic. Swearing, she tried to mop up the mess.

George couldn't tear his eyes away from the patch of skin showing at her belly. "What knight?" he asked, trying and failing to curb his jealousy.

"Sir...I think his name was Sir Chase. Highly skilled at archery. But not so skilled at diplomacy. He offended the queen and she banished him from her court. I never saw him but the once. It was what he said that stuck with me, though. He said a hero was more than a sword. More than his weapons and armour and skill on the battlefield. That his wit and honour were worth more than anything. And that to a true hero, every woman was equal to a queen when it came to who was worth saving."

Melitta tugged her tunic down and for the first time, George saw the dark stains across it. The cloth was torn, too, with the worst stains creeping from the ragged edges.

"Is that blood?" he demanded, reaching for the hem of her tunic.

Melitta glanced down. "Probably. I should

wash. I'd intended to order some hot water so that I might bathe properly once we reached an inn, but – "

"Is that your blood?"

"I imagine so. Neither of the unicorns was injured."

George jumped to his feet and paced around the fire. "We should have stopped at that hamlet, where you could have received aid. We should have used some of that holy water to heal you. If I'd known you were hurt…My lady, please forgive me. Let me see what I can do to help."

"There's no need," Melitta said, yanking up the hem of her tunic so that her belly was bared. "Look, the cuts have closed already. The graze is still a little raw, I'll allow, but by morning it will have healed, too."

George's mouth went dry. He shoved away the inappropriate thoughts that crowded into his head to really look at what she showed him. He traced the line that matched the rip across her tunic. How had she not been eviscerated?

"When did this happen?"

"Today, when the second unicorn charged me. I didn't move fast enough, so her horn scraped a little skin off on her way past." Melitta shrugged. "It hurt at first, but then I forgot about it. The other beast needed healing more than I did." Down went the soft wool, covering her belly.

"Today." George shook his head. It wasn't possible. "Normal people don't heal that fast."

Melitta managed a smile. "Mind-reading isn't normal, either. My gifts were never particularly useful in the castle. Now...I don't mind them so much."

"But...how?"

"When I was younger, I fell ill. So ill my mother thought I would die. The queen found a witch who specialises in healing, and she tried her magic on me. She cast a spell so powerful she fainted for days afterwards, Mother said. When I awoke, I was healed completely. The sickness was gone, and it has not returned. It wasn't until a few weeks later, when I tripped on the stairs and barked my shin, that I realised what else had changed. Within hours, my skin had healed itself, so even I could barely see the damage the next morning. I have never known a day of illness since, and all the times I pricked my fingers while sewing became little more than a momentary nuisance."

George laughed bitterly. "I wish my fairy godmother had given me gifts like yours. Instead, I think too much, so I am slow to act. But she gifted me with fleet feet, so that when I am in danger, they will take me far and fast to save me, like a coward. She gave me an enchanted sword, too, but I lost that the same day. To a dragon."

Melitta headed for her saddlebags and rifled through them until she found a fresh tunic. She turned her back on George and tugged off the torn one. He stared at the fine curves of her shoulders, her back, her hips as they framed her bottom, wishing, longing for what he couldn't have, before she smoothed a fresh tunic over all that temptation.

She flung her cloak around her shoulders and returned to the fire. She sat beside George, reaching over to pat his knee. "You're not a coward, you know. You stood at my side and shot those giants, showing no fear. Why, you even chased one down. If you hadn't run from the boar or the unicorn, both of them might have killed you. You're the bravest hero I've ever met, for you faced all of those things with a maiden at your side. I'm no hero, I know that, though I try. I couldn't kill the unicorn yesterday and when that giant tackled me to the ground, he would have killed me for certain, if you hadn't shot him first. You may not be a knight, but you have the wits and honour to be one, if you wished it." Her eyes seemed to burn into his as they reflected the flames. "Return with me to Queen Margareta's court at Aros. Once I tell her all the things you have done, she will knight you, I am sure of it."

Her hand was warm on his, but George

knew he could never accept what she offered. "I cannot. I ran from a dragon once, and my cowardice still haunts me. I will not rest until the dragon is dead, or I am."

Instead of turning away from him in disgust, Melitta's lovely eyes widened. "What happened?"

Swallowing back his shame, George told her. Every painful detail, from the first folly of wanting to face the dragon in the field to his final, ignominious defeat.

And when his voice died away, he found her head resting on his shoulder, for she was fast asleep.

Laughing quietly to himself, George gently laid her on the ground and wrapped her cloak around her. He supposed his story was boring to a girl who was the earthly embodiment of the goddess of war. He banked the fire and dug out his own cloak so that he might get some sleep, too.

Thirty-One

Melitta woke up warmer than she expected. When she opened her eyes, she realised why. Somehow during the night, she'd cuddled up to George, and she could feel the heat of him even through the thickness of her cloak.

She edged away from him, wishing that they had managed to find an inn to spend the night in. She almost wished they'd accepted the offer of that barn, but she wouldn't go that far.

That particular hamlet had been poor enough before the giants turned up, and when travel slowed along that particular road, the giants hadn't been averse to stealing from them. Now, with their best breeding stock long gone into the giants' bellies, and their women sent who knew where, some of those men had been desperate enough to consider robbing travellers for their own profit. Not wanting to be their first victim, Melitta had asked to buy supplies from the farmers. If she'd paid twice what the food was worth, no one had commented on it. She hoped that the return of travellers along their road, now the giants were gone, might help them more than turning bandit themselves.

Or it might do nothing. Melitta would never know, as she wasn't likely to travel this road again.

She sighed as she crouched down to stir up the fire, searching for a hot coal among the ashes. She soon had it burning merrily again, with flames hot enough to toast some of yesterday's bread. Even with the fire going, the brisk morning wasn't warm enough for her to want to take off her cloak. Not for the first time, she wished she hadn't cut off her hair as the breeze sent icy fingers tickling her neck. Melitta pulled up her hood.

"Are you cold, my lady?" George crouched down beside her and set another piece of wood on the fire. "From behind, you looked like a witch casting some sort of spell."

Melitta laughed. "There are those who say that my mind-reading gift makes me a sort of witch, if not the spellcasting kind. But seeing as you called my cooking magical last night, perhaps I am casting a spell over breakfast after all." She offered him the stick she'd used to skewer her toast.

Melitta rose and busied herself saddling her horse and fastening her saddlebags. She'd remembered George's story about the dragon last night, and, more importantly, she'd remembered her unanswered questions.

"You never did tell me. Where is the dragon we're supposed to face, and when will we do it?" she asked.

George dropped his food in the fire. "What?"

"You told me last night how you fought the dragon, and failed. I saw in your mind that you believe we can win, together. So when are we doing this? Or am I still not ready?" Much though she hated to admit it, Melitta didn't feel any more like a hero than when she'd first set out. Without her bow, her archery hadn't improved. Her sword skills were still rudimentary at best and she might have killed a few men, and the boar, before she helped trap two unicorns, but none of that felt particularly heroic.

Whereas a dragon…that was the sort of monster only a hero could conquer.

George uncorked the water skin and took a drink. "My lady, you were ready the very day I met you, and no mistake. If anyone can defeat a dragon, it is you. After all I've seen you do already, I have no doubt of that. It is me who may not be ready, and to tell the truth, I may never be. What if I run away again?"

Did he really believe that? Melitta's heart swelled in her chest. With pride, no less.

"I couldn't have done any of what I have without you. All of the monsters we've vanquished, we've done it together," she said warmly. "And with the assistance of your fleet feet, as you call them. A hero is more than his sword or armour. It takes cunning and honour and so much more to do what we have done. We shall find this dragon, face it, and we shall defeat it. And we'll do it without enchanted swords and other such silly things. We'll have what other knights won't. We'll have a plan."

For a moment, George raised his eyes to her, and they were filled with hope. "I want to believe you, but what if I run? I will never forgive myself if I leave you to face the beast alone."

Melitta smiled. "Last night, you told me of all the men who had faced the dragon before you. How they stood and fought, until they died. Whatever we do, and however we do this, there must be a way to put those fleet feet of yours to good use. They helped you outrun a dragon once. I bet you could do it again. We'll need a bigger cellar, though."

"Have you ever seen a dragon? They have wings. They can fly."

Melitta swallowed. "No, I've never seen one. But you have. Which is why I need your help. What do you say, George? Time to go kill a dragon?"

George bowed low. "Whatever my lady wishes."

Thirty-Two

Kasmirus had changed little since George left, he found, as they entered the gates. But the people of Kasmirus…they had altered considerably, and not for the better. An air of melancholy surrounded the town like some deadly miasma. Though it was Sunday, everyone wore dark, funereal colours.

George's blood ran cold. He stopped the first man he recognised, a baker he'd often bought bread from. "Please, tell me. What ails the city? Is it plague?" For nothing else could send a whole city into mourning, surely.

The baker shook off George's grasp. "By all that's holy, I hope not. Is a dragon not enough for our sins? When I think of those poor girls…I won't let my daughters leave the house now, for it is not safe. The sooner some knight dispatches the dragon, the happier we'll all be."

He got no more information from the next two people he asked, so George headed for an inn frequented by wealthy merchant visitors to the city. A more costly establishment than he might have chosen for himself, but he had a bag full of the abbey's coin and Melitta's comfort to think of.

Sure enough, when he showed he had the coin to pay for the room, the landlord lost interest in him, directing a chambermaid to take them to their rooms.

Melitta ordered hot water to be sent up so that she might wash, and George left her to her ablutions, promising to spend the time listening to gossip in the taproom downstairs.

The common room was nearly empty, and

the merchants George met knew little of the goings-on in the city, being but recently arrived themselves. Finally, in desperation, he asked the barman what he knew about the dragon.

"Only that the king has promised half the kingdom and a lordship to the man who slays the beast," the barman replied. "Many have tried, but none have succeeded." He squinted at George. "Are you thinking of trying your luck?"

"Perhaps," George replied defensively.

The barman laughed. "Take my advice, Sir Knight. Climb back on your horse and ride far away from here. That dragon brings death to anyone who goes near it, and none can withstand it. The only reason I stay in the city is that it is too dangerous to travel. The beast preys on travellers now, too, as his appetite grows. Soon, we may not have any trade at all, if the dragon develops a taste for merchants, too."

Talk turned to the current high prices of trade goods, which the merchants toasted with another round of wine, so George thanked the barman and headed back upstairs to share what he'd learned with Melitta.

A lordship and half the kingdom. That wouldn't turn him into a prince, but perhaps it would be enough for Melitta to consider allowing him to court her.

He fought down a laugh. All he had to do was defeat a dragon, and survive. Then he could beg the goddess of war for her hand.

He knocked on Melitta's door, but received no answer. He knocked a second time, before calling her name.

The door creaked ajar, revealing a red-eyed Melitta. A tear rolled down her cheek, and she wiped it away. "The vile beast must die," she said through gritted teeth.

George grinned. "On that, we agree."

Thirty-Three

Melitta could feel George's curiosity at her tears, but she couldn't seem to stop the flow. She'd opened her mind to the townspeople while she lay in the bath, and though she'd closed herself off from their thoughts since, their vast grief still roiled within her.

Those girls. Those poor girls…

"That vile beast must die."

George agreed wholeheartedly. How had she ever thought him a coward?

Haltingly, she began her tale. The tale of a

city in mourning.

The words came slowly, describing the images lifted from so many minds, but the gist was the same.

On the day the priests blessed the fleet in the name of Our Lady, they had led a great procession out of the city toward the river. In the forefront of the throng was a statue of the Blessed Virgin, carried by four virgin princesses dressed in white wool to match the robes on the statue.

The dragon had flown overhead, as it did so often that they took little notice of it. It flew across the countryside, stealing and devouring sheep in the fields, before retreating into its cave, only coming out when it hungered or some hero challenged it.

That day had been different. Perhaps because they wore white wool, or perhaps the dragon was simply curious. He shot a gout of flame before him, enveloping the girls and the statue in searing heat. While the girls screamed, the beast had devoured them, and the statue, too.

The people of the city had watched in horror before fleeing back inside the walls to hide from the dragon.

On the morrow, the king had offered to reward the dragonslayer with half his kingdom, but no one had claimed the reward.

Even now, Melitta could feel the beast stomping about in the caverns beneath the city where it lived. Waiting. Watching. For who would be next?

It was one thing for the beast to kill knights who challenged it, but another to kill and devour innocents. Those girls hadn't deserved to die.

Melitta made up her mind. "That dragon wouldn't understand honour if it climbed up its bottom. We're going to play dirty."

George looked intrigued. "How?"

"What do you know about killing dragons?"

He shrugged. "I know my namesake killed one with a sword, using a maiden for bait. I've always wondered about that."

Melitta's anger rose, not at George, but at his saintly namesake. "So it seems even saints have no honour when it comes to killing dragons. Fine. But no maidens. We'll use a sheep."

"A sheep."

Melitta took a deep breath and told George what she planned to do.

Thirty-Four

Feeling terribly exposed, George rolled the barrel to the mouth of the dragon's cave. He draped the sheepskin over it and prayed that it would be enough to fool the beast. Once the bait was in place, George took to his heels and fled. Not to the city, but to a high vantage point where Melitta waited.

Together, they crouched amid the leaves of an oak Melitta had chosen for its good view of the cave mouth.

They didn't have to wait long. The dragon

had heard George, and it emerged from the darkness, sniffing the air.

George gulped. If the beast could smell him, it would find them.

The beast lowered its snout and sniffed delicately at the woolly barrel. Then it opened its mouth, enveloping the barrel in searing flame.

"Oh, no," Melitta murmured.

While the barrel still burned, the dragon wrapped its tongue around it and tugged the whole thing into its mouth. Tipping its head back, the beast swallowed it whole.

"Yes!"

George didn't dare make a sound.

"Do you think we put enough arsenic in the barrel to kill a dragon?" she asked.

George shrugged. "We filled it to the brim. That much poison could kill an army. Surely it's enough for a dragon."

He didn't voice his biggest worry — how would they know if it was dead? If it was deep in the caves, he didn't want to go in after it only to discover the beast was alive and well.

Melitta tapped her head. "I can feel it. Dragons are magical beasts and their minds are…different. I don't even need to concentrate to hear its thoughts. I wish I could block it out. It's a vile creature. Like some humans, it enjoys killing."

Now the true wait began. George did his best not to doze off, but it was hard. Melitta stayed alert, and she'd wake him when she could no longer sense the beast, surely.

"It's coming out. The poison is working," she said eventually, excitement burning in her eyes.

A long moment later, George glimpsed movement inside the cave. The dragon staggered out, looking for all the world as if it had drunk too much ale.

George held his breath. He could almost taste victory, it was so close.

The dragon slumped to the ground, opening its mouth as if gasping for air.

Fighting for its last breath. Good, George

thought.

Then it vomited up a steaming mess. Once. Twice.

The dragon shook its head, coughed, then ambled back inside its cave.

"It's feeling better," Melitta whispered, sounding disappointed.

George wanted to rage at the heavens. The dragon deserved to die in agony, not survive an attempt to poison it.

"Perhaps it's immune to poison. We'll have to try something else," she said.

Thirty-Five

In the common room of the inn that night, Melitta threw her hands up in despair. "I don't know any more. I've never had to kill clever vermin before."

"Beg pardon, mistress." An elderly merchant rose from his seat and bowed in her direction. "Did I hear you say you need to kill rats that are too clever?"

Melitta opened her mouth to tell the man to mind his own business.

"Because one of my warehouses had a

terrible problem with rats, but my steward told me an old wives' tale he swore worked. See, poisoning works for a while, but then they grow wise to that, seeing their friends die when they eat poisoned food, until none will touch it. You may try a new poison, but they'll learn about that, too. My steward swore he knew a poison that they'd never suspect. He painted all the walls and containers with a white powder he called lime. Now, the stuff's not poisonous on its own. Oh, no. But it makes a body powerfully thirsty, because it's salty, see. So the beasts eat it and think they're safe. Then they go for water, drinking as much as they can hold. And that's what kills 'em, because the water works some magic on the lime and they explode. Poof!" He demonstrated with his hands.

Exploding rats. What would he come up with next? Melitta forced down the retort she wanted to make and tried to think of a way to thank him so that he'd go away.

"You know, that could work," George said,

nodding. He raised his tankard. "My thanks, sir." He signalled for the barman to get the man another drink.

"You're welcome." The man returned to his seat.

Melitta eyed George. "Are you serious? Or have you drunk too much wine?"

"He's right about lime. If you put throw a piece in a bucket of water, it bubbles and steams like it's boiling. If you put enough of that inside a dragon with a lot of water and whatever makes it breathe fire, you'd scald it from the inside out."

"Would a barrel be enough?"

George drained his tankard and smiled. "On the morrow, we shall see."

Thirty-Six

George rolled the barrel of lime to the mouth of the cave. This time, they'd smothered the sheepskin in mutton fat to disguise the smell. He prayed it would work as he jogged back to Melitta's treetop perch.

Once again, the dragon emerged and devoured the barrel disguised as a sheep before heading back into its cave.

They didn't have to wait long before the beast ambled out again, and headed for the river. George watched in satisfaction as it drank and drank. Surely when the water mixed with the lime, it would be enough.

The dragon turned and made its way back toward its lair, more slowly this time as if the mixture in its belly was affecting it.

Now George tasted victory. True victory.

"Hey, dragon!" a voice roared. "Come and fight me!"

A knight appeared, swaggering toward the beast with his sword held high.

The dragon peered at the armoured man, then staggered toward him.

"That idiot's going to steal our kill!" George protested, climbing down as fast as he could go. "Hey! You! That dragon's ours!" he shouted as he sprinted toward the beast.

Not fast enough. The dragon lowered its head and unleashed a gout of flame.

The armoured man screamed as flames enveloped him. Then the sound died, and the smell of burning flesh reached George.

The dragon turned its head, fixing one slitted eye on him. For a moment, George could have sworn recognition flared in that look. But it couldn't be. Dragons weren't that bright.

Then a thick, muscled tail came out of nowhere and knocked him flat. Again.

And the world went dark. Again.

Thirty-Seven

Melitta reached the ground a moment behind George, but she was no match for him when it came to sheer speed. She suspected no man could beat him, so powerful was his godmother's gift.

She wanted to shout after him, to warn him that the dragon wasn't weakened, that they couldn't have given it enough lime. But she could scarcely catch her breath as she ran.

The armoured knight became a human torch, and there was nothing she could do to stop it. Tears of frustration sprang to her eyes, but she didn't slow. The dragon had seen George, and it knew him. And remembered.

George was too busy looking at its head that he never saw the tail swing up, sending him flying. Then it lowered its head, drawing flame from deep in its belly to burn him to death, too.

"No you don't, you vile beast!" she screeched. Charred, armoured corpses littered the ground, along with their weapons. Melitta picked up a short sword that looked about her size, though its blade was burned black. "Over here! Let's see if you can get this maiden!" She flapped her woollen tunic.

With agonising slowness, the beast turned its head to regard her.

Curiosity washed over her, but nothing more. The dragon didn't see her as a threat.

Melitta reached down and picked up half a scorched steel breastplate that she slipped over her head. It was far too big, but that didn't matter. She clanged the sword against her armour. "I said over here!"

The dragon burped, releasing a fireball that scorched the ground for a dozen yards. Mercifully, it missed George.

"HERE!" she screamed. She broke into a clumsy run, clanking with every step as she charged at the dragon.

It lowered its head, breathing in deeply, before belching flame.

Her mind locked on the beast's, she read his intention in time, and darted out of its path.

The dragon bellowed, moving its ponderous bulk until it faced her again. Down went the head and Melitta felt the inrush of air as though it reached her own lungs.

Full to bursting. Couldn't…breathe…

It tried to flame, but nothing came out.

Again, it inhaled. And deep inside, something ruptured.

This time, it was the dragon that screamed.

Then all hell broke loose.

Thirty-Eight

George raised his head slightly, wondering why he wasn't dead like the charred, armoured corpse beside him. He felt strange, like this had all happened before.

He heard a scream, a sound so primal it couldn't have come from a human throat. And then the whole world was aflame.

He threw himself flat to the ground to allow the blast to pass over him, praying that he'd survive it, as he must have before. Then the heat passed, and he allowed himself to look.

Flames roared up into the sky from what looked like the carcass of a dragon, and out of the flame came a woman. No, a goddess, whose eyes burned like she'd harnessed hell itself.

"Melitta?" George croaked.

She smiled. "Oh, good, you're not dead." She stabbed a finger behind her. "That bastard is, though. And good riddance."

They'd killed the dragon. Well, she had, really, but had he ever doubted it?

Melitta tugged off her breastplate and let it clang to the ground. "We did it." Her smile was more radiant than the fireball behind her.

George laughed. "We did. You're a hero, my lady." He clambered to his feet and brushed himself off.

"So are you," she said. Then she threw her arms around his neck and kissed him.

George's world blazed white. This time he didn't want to wake up.

Thirty-Nine

With her lips pressed against George's mouth and his arms holding her like the most precious thing in the world, Melitta surrendered to the moment. There was nothing more she wanted than to be here, now, with him. The warmth of a fire at her back and the warmth of his love before her…

Melitta broke away from his kiss, gasping.

"Marry me," he said.

She blinked. Surely she hadn't heard correctly.

"I love you. Marry me, Lady Melitta. I could never love another woman the way I love you."

Perhaps she had.

Then his lips claimed hers again, and nothing else mattered. This was as mind-blowing as every kiss she had ever felt through someone else's thoughts, and yet it was so much more. Because she could feel it, burning within her. Hers. No one else's.

"We're perfect for each other," she said breathlessly. She flapped a hand at the bonfire behind her. "Together, we can do anything."

He laughed and scooped her up in his arms, spinning her around in a circle before heading toward the city.

Any other day, Melitta might have scolded him and told him to put her down. But today…all she wanted was to feel his arms around her.

"The sooner we get back to our lodgings, the better, my lady," he said softly in her ear.

Lodgings. Yes. Where there was a bed.

A cheer rose up as they entered the city gates.

"What's your name, sir?" a page in the king's livery asked.

"George."

"George, you are invited to a feast with the king, where he will grant you the reward you deserve for slaying the dragon," the page said, breathless with excitement.

George's arms tightened around Melitta. "Tomorrow, I will meet with the king. After I have been to my lodgings and changed into clothes more appropriate for the king's court."

But not before Melitta got him out of his clothes and kept him that way for some time, she thought dreamily.

Cheers and congratulations followed them all the way to the inn, until the door shut behind them. Still George didn't set Melitta down until he'd climbed the stairs and reached the door to her room.

She wound her arms around his neck and kissed him deeply. "I want a reward, too," she said, trying to tug him into her chamber.

"Tomorrow," George said.

"No, tonight," Melitta said. "I want you tonight."

George cupped her face in his hands. "My lady, your honour is as dear to me as my own. And I will not share your bed before the king grants us our rightful lands and titles. Only then will we have our true reward." He kissed her lips softly, a whisper of the passion they both felt. "Sleep well, my lady, and I will see you on the morrow."

She stared after him as he headed for his own chamber and closed the door.

Her lips still tingled from his kiss.

Today had been the best day of her life. She sighed in blissful anticipation. And tomorrow would be better still.

Forty

As they broke their fast the following morning, another messenger arrived in the king's livery.

He bowed low to George and said, "His most illustrious majesty King Boleslas invites you to the castle for a feast to celebrate your victory over the dragon. There, before all his court, he will give you all the honours he has promised. You will be named a lord of half the kingdom."

"We will be there," George replied.

The messenger glanced at Melitta. He

seemed lost for words for a moment, then added smoothly, "Of course, a seat will be found at one of the lower tables for your squire. I will see to it." The man hurried off.

Melitta burst out laughing. "I know the light is dim in here…but did he really think I was a boy?"

George smiled fondly. "How many maidens kill dragons? I'm sure in the light of day, he could not fail to recognise your beauty." He frowned. "But you should be at my side, not at one of the lower tables. You earned this as much as I have, if not more."

"I've spent a lifetime sitting at the high table, beside the queen. While a knight may wear what he will, a lady does not sit there without a fine gown. If I sat beside you like this, I would shame you," she told him. What she didn't tell him was that she'd tasted the thoughts of everyone in town last night, and they all believed he was the hero who had slayed their dragon, and that he had somehow saved her from the beast. Changing their minds and enlightening them with the truth would be harder than slaying the beast in the first place. A task Melitta would never be equal to, she feared. Let George receive the rewards and adulation. She would share them with him soon enough. "I am content. I will attend the feast as your squire. No fine gown required. And afterward, we will keep our promises to one another."

George rose. "My first feast at court. My father would not believe it." He took a seat beside the fire. "It's a good thing I have you here to tell me how to behave, or I fear I would make some grave mistake."

"I am sure you won't," Melitta said, sinking down by the fire. "I remember my first feast. I must have been five or six. Mother and Queen…no, she was just Lady Margareta then, had gone without me, and left me in the care of two of the sisters from the priory. I screamed that I wanted to go, and because the sisters were to attend the Harvest Feast, they brought me along to the shuttered balcony where they could share the celebration apart from the revellers.

"I could scarcely sit still. All I wanted was to peer through the shutters at everyone. There was the Harvest Queen, dressed all in gold, though she was a farm girl who only got to be queen for one night. I thought she was the most beautiful woman I'd ever seen, and I wanted to be her, though my mother said I was too high-born for that.

"Then Lady Margareta stood up with King Erik, who was only a prince then, but no less handsome, and joined the dance. Then I forgot the Harvest Queen and dinner and everything…all I wanted was to be a beautiful dancing lady with a prince of her own. I was a lady, the same as she, or so I thought, and that was what my future held.

"I dreamed of dancing and princes and romance for many nights after that. Oh, the dreams of a little girl. Like something out of a fairytale. Where all princes are heroic and handsome and terribly in love with the lady of their dreams."

Melitta peered into her empty cup, then tossed the dregs into the fire, where they hissed and spat.

"It wasn't until a much later feast, where I was wearing as much silk as my mother, that I realised maybe I didn't want a prince, or a husband at all."

George drank drained his cup without looking at her. "So it's not true what you told me in the forest? The real reason why you ran away from home? Because your father was going to force you to marry a prince?"

Melitta laughed so hard she nearly choked. "No, my father is dead. A saint, or so they tell me. And my mother will never force me into a marriage I do not want. She did want me to pick a husband, though."

"But you did run away."

Melitta frowned. "You make it sound like I sneaked away in the dead of night, instead of in the morning light with my mother there to say farewell. I left the life I had because it dawned on me that I wanted to be my own hero, instead of waiting for some knight to save me and fall at my feet. And tonight, I will feel like it is my first feast all over again. You will sit at the high table, and I will watch in anonymity from the lower tables. But this time, I won't envy the ladies sitting up there with you."

He bowed his head. "Very well, my lady. I find it difficult to believe that someone like you who was promised a prince could possibly choose a lowly shoemaker like me. If I were you, I would take the promised prince, for who can refuse royalty?"

Melitta just smiled. There was no point telling him that when you could see in the minds of everyone, there was very little difference between a prince and a peasant. All men had hopes and dreams and desires, and she wanted the man who shared hers, no matter what his title.

And tonight they would share…everything.

Forty-One

When George took his seat at the high table, he had to admit it was a heady experience. Never had he seen so many people crowded into one room before, and all of them so richly dressed. He glanced down at his own simple clothes, but Melitta had assured him they were good enough. The court wanted to see a fighter, a hero, the man who had slayed their dragon scourge. Still, it didn't help him to not feel self-conscious when everyone around him wore silks at bright as flowers while he wore wool.

Fine wool, for he could afford it, but wool nonetheless. And right now, it made him itch like the coarsest stuff imaginable with all those eyes on him. How did Melitta stand such scrutiny?

Only now did he understand why she didn't want to sit at the high table. So many people staring…

Then the food was served, and it wasn't so bad.

The king had seated him on the end, beside a girl in blue who said nothing and refused to look at him. How he would have preferred to have Melitta by his side. And when they were married, he would. Not even the king would refuse to give his lady all the honours that were accorded to him.

George scanned the crowded tables, looking for the only woman he wanted. Past the courtiers, knights and their ladies, the colours grew duller as the benches were filled with men-at-arms – no women there. Except

Melitta. She perched on the end of a bench near the window, nibbling at something on the point of her dagger. The men at the table – no, boys, all of them, he realised. Squires to the knights, most likely. The boys ignored her, talking among themselves and paying her no attention at all.

George raged at them. Didn't they realise they had a hero in their midst? A lady, no less, who had slayed a dragon?

Evidently not, for they all laughed at something one of the boys had said, while she sat there calmly.

The food was plentiful and the wine flowed freely, though George partook sparingly of both. He didn't want to make a fool of himself when the king called him up to receive his reward. What if he stumbled and fell? Or said something that offended the king?

By all that was holy, he needed Melitta by his side, helping him. He was nothing without her. And yet, she sat at the other end of the hall, oblivious to his eyes on her.

What if she'd changed her mind?

George fretted through the interminable feast, heartily wishing he never had to attend another. Maybe this was what Melitta meant about not missing such things. How much food and wine could a man consume? Surely they were all sated by now, he thought, but servants kept bringing out more platters and jugs.

Finally, King Boreslas rose to his unsteady feet. He'd had more to drink than most, George judged, watching him sway.

"My subjects!" the king cried. "Lord, ladies, knights, men! We are here to celebrate a great victory. Sir George has defeated the dragon that oppressed us for so long." He raised his cup in a toast. The whole hall cheered, and drank with him as he emptied his cup. "And he shall be rewarded!"

More cheers, even louder still.

"Kneel, Sir George!"

This was the part Melitta had explained to him in painstaking detail. He hoped he didn't forget anything.

George dropped to one knee before the king, then pulled his sword out of its scabbard. He laid the blade across his open palms and held the weapon out.

"I pledge my honour and obedience to you, Your Majesty. My life to your service, as God is my witness." George prayed he'd remembered the words right. Melitta had said it didn't matter if he made a mistake – no two men seemed to state their vow of service in the same way.

King Boreslas inclined his head and took the proffered sword. Wrapping both hands around the hilt, he muttered some words in Latin that George didn't understand. He finished with, "Rise, Lord George, and take up your blade in my service." He presented George's sword, hilt-first, back to him.

George slid the blade back into its scabbard, as Melitta had advised him. With his back to the hall, he couldn't see if she was smiling or shaking her head in mortification.

The hall erupted in more cheering, so he hoped he hadn't made too great a fool of himself.

"And as a final reward for his heroism, I have decided to bestow my only remaining daughter, Princess Sativa, on him in marriage, this very night. My personal confessor and priest will marry them in the castle chapel after the feast, and if I'm not mistaken, Lord George will have an heir on the way before the night is through!"

Laughter and cheering echoed through the hall as men toasted George's marriage and virility. Even the priest rose to his feet and he nearly fell over, he was so drunk.

King Boreslas ushered the girl in blue forward to kneel beside George. He spouted more Latin, then announced that he had blessed their union.

George's mouth was dry, and not in a good way.

He couldn't marry the princess. Couldn't accept her as a bride. It was Melitta he wanted, no one else. The princess beside him continued to ignore him, just as she had for the rest of the feast. He couldn't marry a girl who pretended he didn't exist, no matter how grateful her father was.

"And when God sees fit to end my reign, Lord George will ascend the throne in my place!"

George could have sworn his heart dropped right into his boots. Heir to a throne? No. Not him. This was preposterous. He was barely even a hero. He couldn't be a king.

"As my heir, you must sit at my right hand, Lord George!"

People shuffled along the benches at the high table to make space for George, who staggered to take his place beside the king.

"Now, who will be the first to declare their oath of loyalty to Lord George?" King Boreslas declared, his gaze sweeping the hall.

Courtiers rushed from their seats to be the first, crowding before the high table so that George couldn't see past them.

Melitta. What would she think of this? Being a lord was one thing, but one day a king…she didn't like court. She would never consent to be a queen. And then there was the matter of the princess he didn't want. But how could he tell a king that his daughter wasn't good enough to be his bride? George would be lucky to keep his head.

Melitta would know what to do. Melitta would help him deal with this mess. Unless she believed he had thrown her aside to marry the princess…

He rose onto his toes, straining to look past the crowd so that he might see her, catch her eye and beg for her help. But she was nowhere in sight.

George's world crumbled around him. Without her, he had nothing.

Forty-Two

As benches scraped and men rose to pay their respects to their new overlord, Melitta made her way to the back of the hall. She knew good manners decreed that she should congratulate George on his good fortune, and on his bride, but she wasn't sure that anything she said would be considered good manners tonight.

She climbed the stairs to her chamber, where she packed up the little she had, and decided to leave George a note. It would be hours before the dragonslaying lord would find it, by which time she would be well away, she was certain. What need did he have for her anyway? He had his bride, his lands, his lordship – everything he had ever wanted. Melitta fought down a sob. He didn't need and definitely didn't want her. After all, who'd choose a mere lady when he could have a princess? He'd said as much this morning. Even last night, he'd hinted that it wouldn't have been honourable to give in to their desires. She'd thought he meant delaying by a day, but evidently she'd misunderstood. Instead, he'd meant that today he would marry a princess, and she would have what? Permission to watch? Melitta wanted to give him a piece of her mind about that, too.

Yet when she faced the empty piece of parchment with a quill in hand, she still did not know what to say. She had to write something, she knew. Dipping her quill in the ink, Melitta forced herself to write what was right.

I congratulate you, Lord George, she wrote. My best wishes for your future health and happiness. Should you ever have need to hire a slayer of monsters, you will find me…

Here she stopped. For where would he find her? Her first thought was to return home, as she had promised her mother, but Melitta wasn't sure she could go back to her old life. She liked the adventure of the life she had led since she left home. She would not easily give up her leathers for silks once more.

Finally, she wrote: You will find me where I am needed most.

Vague but probably the best she could come up with at the time, she decided.

She sealed the scroll with a blob of wax and left it on the table in her room. It was all she left behind, for little remained of her childish dreams of love, marriage, and happiness.

Shouldering her saddlebags, Melitta headed down to the stables. She would saddle her horse and be gone before anyone thought to ask for her. By the time George read her message and thought to look for her, she would be safely asleep in an inn in the next town. Perhaps, if she was lucky, she would have already found information about her next quest. Unbidden, a smile sprang to her lips at the thought. The people of Kasimus might not believe a maiden could slay monsters, but she would show them. She was a dragonslayer now.

The stables were surprisingly quiet, for all that they were full of horses. Oh, the horses made plenty of noise, but there was no one about. Even the stable hands were off celebrating this night. After all, it wasn't every day someone slayed a dragon that had plagued your city. The whole city was celebrating.

Yet Melitta heard the clink of harness and was instantly on the alert. "Who's there?" she demanded, sliding her dagger from its sheath. "Show yourself!"

The clinking ceased, but no one appeared. Melitta was not fooled. Carefully, she bit her lip and sent her thoughts out, questing for the mind of what she suspected was a horse thief.

But the jumbled mind she touched was no

thief at all.

I will not be a prize, the distinctly feminine thoughts repeated to herself. I will not be handed over as a prize. I am a princess, not some bauble!

Melitta's horse thief could be none other than the Princess Sativa, George's intended bride. An unwilling bride, Melitta realised uneasily.

Forgetting her own hurry to leave, Melitta made her way to the stall where the princess hid behind a horse. "Princess?" Melitta ventured. "Why are you not at the feast, celebrating with everyone else?"

Melitta had to give the girl credit. The princess stepped out of hiding, her chin held high. "You shall not stop me," the girl insisted. "I am not a prize to be won. I will not be handed to that shoemaker in marriage like some pretty bauble."

Melitta balked at the girl's tone. "George is no mere shoemaker," she said, frowning. "True, he was once a master shoemaker. But he is also a hero, a slayer of monsters and giants. He has saved maidens and whole towns from monsters. And he slayed a dragon at the very gates to your city. Your father has seen fit to make him a lord and give him lands to match. Any girl would be lucky to be allowed to marry such a man." Melitta had to swallow hard against the lump in her throat as she said this. She would consider herself lucky to marry George, lordship and lands notwithstanding. This spoiled princess, royalty though she might be, did not deserve him.

"I will not be a prize," the princess repeated stubbornly.

Only then did Melitta realise that the clinking harness she had heard was the saddle and bridle the horse behind the princess now wore. The princess would rather flee than marry George.

"He does not love me," the princess continued. "Though I sat beside him, he scarcely even looked at me. He had eyes for only one person in the feasting hall." She glared at Melitta. "You. The one he calls his squire, but you are more than that, aren't you? You are his lover."

Melitta tried hard not to laugh. She loved him, she knew that. But she had never shared his bed, not in the way the princess meant, and now she never would. For he was to marry this girl and Melitta was nothing to him. "I am not his lover. I am his partner, in that we slayed the dragon together. We have slayed many beasts together, but I think his hero days are done."

"Lover or not, his heart belongs to you," the princess said bitterly. "You shall not stop me. I ride to the coast, and my betrothed. A man who loves me, or at least he did once."

Melitta's heart ached for the girl, for she saw herself in this proud princess. Both fled their homes in search of a better life they imagined lay outside the castle, though they sought very different things. Which was a sillier goal, though — love, or a dragon? Melitta couldn't suppress a smile. A dragon, of course, for she knew love existed.

So did Princess Sativa.

"Take only what you need with you," Melitta urged. "Food, water, weapons, and clothes that are suited for rough travel. Nothing that will mark you for what you are, because there are men on the roads who will take advantage of a lady. They will see you as even more of a prize." Melitta was tempted to tell the girl exactly what sort of prize those brigands had thought her, but she wasn't sure even that would make the princess change her mind. After all, Melitta had known, but she'd gone anyway. "You would be safer in your father's castle."

The princess drew herself up. "What would you know of it? A girl pretending to be a squire knows nothing of the cage that is a royal court."

Melitta laughed. "Forgive me, your royal highness, but I was raised in a royal court, a princess in all but name, alongside Queen Margareta's own children. And I could take my place at her side again tomorrow, if I wished. But I will not leave these walls without my armour, my weapons, and enough money and provisions for the journey, because I know there are monsters out there." She pulled a dagger from its ankle sheath and held it out to Princess Sativa. "Take it, princess, for I promise you will have need of it."

Sativa swept aside her cape, revealing two sheathed daggers strapped to her girdle. "I am not a fool."

Melitta sincerely hoped the girl was right. Still, she dug through her bag until she found a clean tunic and hose. "Then at least take these. Court dresses will be no use to you on your journey."

Sativa hesitated, then took the clothing. "I thank you. But I must repay you, and I will need all the coin I have for my journey, as you say. Wait." She disappeared back into the horse stall.

Melitta fought not to tap her foot in impatience.

Finally, the princess emerged, wearing Melitta's spare clothes. "They are finer than they look. Here, consider this a gift." She thrust a wad of silk at Melitta.

"I have no need for silk," Melitta replied, realising too late that she held the princess's feast gown. "Oh, no. I cannot wear this."

"Every priest in the city is so drunk they cannot tell the difference between one woman and another. Yet in an hour, my father will command one of them to conduct a wedding, marrying me to the shoemaker. If you wear this, they will think you are me. Marry the man, if that is your wish. By morning, it will be too late for anyone to do anything. I will be gone and you will be his wife." Sativa's eyes implored her. "Please."

"My lady? Are you here, or am I too late?" a male voice called. George.

The princess paled. "He cannot catch me here. He will stop me!"

A princess too proud to beg for help. Melitta made no attempt to hide her smile.

Rescuing maidens in distress was what heroes did, and she was every bit as much a hero as George.

Who had eyes for only one woman at the feast, hmm? Perhaps Melitta might stay after all, and marry such a man. And in so doing, save a princess.

Lifting her chin, Melitta marched out of the stables. "Lord George," she greeted him.

George sagged in relief. "Thank God. I thought you'd left. Melitta, I swear I didn't know about the princess. I must speak to the king, tell him I cannot…"

Melitta silenced him with a wave of her hand. "Ah, but you can. I have it on good authority that the princess will not attend your wedding. But I have a mind to. Give me a moment, for I must be properly dressed."

They found an empty chamber, and George guarded the door while Melitta changed into the princess's gown. The silk felt strange against her skin after so long in linen, leather and wool. And yet, when she laced up the overdress, it felt as familiar as anything she'd worn at home. She looked down at the shimmery blue silk embroidered with gold thread, reminiscent of one of Queen Margareta's gowns. A wedding dress fit for a queen, or a princess. Too much for a mere lady, a girl who chased dragons and unicorns.

Melitta swallowed, then pushed open the door. George turned slowly, his eyes taking her in.

"My lady." He bowed so low, his head nearly touched the ground. "Never have I seen a woman more lovely."

She heard the clop of a horse's hooves, trotting across the bailey and out the gate. For good or ill, Princess Sativa had left in search of love, or her destiny.

Far more sensible than searching for dragons, Melitta now knew.

Her eyes met George's and they shared the same thought, though George's inability to read minds made him voice it.

"There was a drunk priest I passed on my

way here. If you are willing, Lady Melitta..." he began.

"A drunk priest, you say? Then I am more than willing," Melitta replied warmly, linking her arm through George's and leading him back to the feasting hall.

They paused outside so that George could help her cover her hair with the princess's veil. When he was satisfied that it was straight, they stepped into the hall together.

In almost no time at all, Melitta knelt beside George in the castle chapel, trying to make sense of the priest's words as he slurred through the ceremony.

King Boreslas and his court crowded into the room, talking so loudly they made it almost impossible to hear the priest.

"Melitta?" George prompted.

"Oh, yes, I do," Melitta replied.

More mumbling as the priest wrapped his stole around their joined hands, before he uttered something that ended with the word "wife".

Melitta rose, dusting off her knees. She had saved the hero from the princess, just like something in a fairytale.

"Godspeed, princess," she said softly.

"What?" George asked.

"Oh, nothing. Let's head for your bedchamber, before this drunken rabble decide to follow us," Melitta said. "I want you all to myself tonight."

George grinned. "I was thinking the same thing, my lady."

Forty-Three

Melitta was breathless by the time they reached George's chamber. She didn't want to let go of his hand, but she reluctantly did so when she realised he needed both hands to properly bar the door against intruders.

For a moment, George put his back to the door and just drank her in.

Being stared at so intently while she wore another woman's dress that Melitta knew was too long for her was disconcerting, to say the least. "I have chests full of dresses like this back in my mother's apartments. Ones that fit me far better, for Mother and I made them for me. Once we decide where we shall live, I can send for them. Or we could go fetch them…"

Her voice trailed off into silence as George stepped forward to claim a kiss. And another one. And she soon forgot everything about clothing until he said, "My lady, I confess that while you look beautiful in it, the only desire I have for your gown is to extract you from it."

She laughed, and helped him undo the lacings. His hands were so warm through the thin silk, it was almost like wearing nothing at all, until she found she really did wear nothing at all. She'd never been naked before a man before. Melitta folded her arms across her breasts, suddenly shy.

George was too busy shucking off his own clothes to notice. His surcoat, his tunic and even his hose lay on the flagstones, on top of the puddle of silk she'd shed.

His strong arms lifted her, carrying her to the bed. "I've dreamed of this," he said.

Melitta swallowed. "I know."

He laughed ruefully. "Of course. So you know that I am no expert at loving a woman but I would like you to enjoy it." He reddened.

So did Melitta. "I'm…I am no expert either, as you know this is my first time. But I have touched the minds of many couples when they…couple…and I think I know what I might like, or at least, what I would like to try."

At first, she guided his hands over her breasts and between her thighs, letting out little gasps of pleasure as with each touch, he awoke desires in her she'd never felt before. It was one thing to taste another's desire, but something else entirely to be devoured by her own.

She began to moan as George's fingers found a rhythm inside her that built and built and built to a climax that made her cry out.

When Melitta descended from on high, she knew only one thing: she wanted more. More of him, more of him inside her, and more of the pleasures only he could give her.

"My lady," he began, looking concerned.

Melitta pressed a finger to his lips. "I'm not your lady yet. First, you must fill me with more than your fingers, and then, when you are all mine, only then, will I be yours."

"As my lady wishes," he replied with a mischievous glint in his eye. He grasped her hips, spreading her thighs wide.

Melitta closed her eyes. This would hurt for only a moment, she knew, and then…

George's tongue darted inside her, licking and sucking at tender flesh until she cried out anew.

"George!"

Slowly, he withdrew, wiping his mouth with his hand. "When you are all mine, I want to hear you call me your lord."

Melitta inclined her head. "We have an accord."

Her mouth was dry in anticipation, but Melitta had no desire to drink. She wanted George, and if he was willing… "Will you…lie on your back? I would like to try…something."

Something that had made other women scream with pleasure. Something their lovers had enjoyed, too.

"As you desire, my lady." George flopped onto the furs, folding his arms behind his head.

Now she could truly take in the man she had married, in all his naked glory. Oh, she knew he was all lean, hard muscle, but one in particular drew her attention more than the others right now. She ran her fingers down his length, gently stroking him as she'd seen herself do in his dreams.

He groaned a little, thrusting his pelvis into her willing hands. She could give him pleasure with nothing but her hands, she knew, but neither of them would be satisfied with that. Not tonight.

Shivering in anticipation at her own daring, she climbed atop him. If she stroked him and he thrust his hips again in the same manner, he would be inside her.

Melitta made up her mind and reached

down.

George laughed and grasped her hips as he thrust upward without warning. The tiniest sting – a mere needleprick, healed in a moment – was over before it had barely begun, and she could think only of the heat of him, the hardness of his length as he drove into her. Slowly, masterfully, in control of every moment as he watched her reaction.

Melitta closed her eyes, lost in his love and the sheer sensation of making love – and being made love to – for the first time.

Steadily, another climax built within her as she felt the same need for release radiating from George. She knew he was close when he drove into her that penultimate time, sending her soul careening out among the stars. Yet she squeezed him within her, and felt his mind fly up alongside hers. The joint sensation was so exquisite, it surpassed anything she imagined even heaven could offer.

"Oh God!" she cried as George groaned his pleasure aloud.

Then she heard him laugh. "No, not a god. Just your lord, my lady. As you are mine."

She squeezed him again, and was surprised to discover it shot a little bolt of pleasure through her own loins. "My lord," she repeated. "I hope you plan on more lovemaking tonight, and every other night, because as long as you are my lord, I will want you in my bed."

She winced as George withdrew and went to clean himself up. "I will grant your wish, my lady, but I have one wish of my own."

"Oh?" Melitta tried to keep her face blank as the thought of all the things men liked their lovers to do in bed. She hoped he wasn't about to ask her to –

"In the interests of remaining your lord for as long as possible, I have one question about the dozen who died by your single blow."

Melitta swallowed. Oh. That.

"What did they do to offend you so, that they needed to die?"

She wet her lips. "They tried to steal my

honey from me."

His eyebrows flew up. "Honey? God forbid I ever try to steal your honey. I shall devote the rest of my life to providing you with every kind of sweetness you might desire, and defending you from anyone who might try to steal from you. May you never need to land another blow again."

It was her turn to laugh. "Not even if we hear of another dragon that must be slain?"

"Dragons are different." He lay down beside her once more. "And while I have never seen a lady look more beautiful in silk than you did tonight, I cannot get the vision out of my head of you, yesterday. Slaying that dragon and striding out of the flames like a goddess. Why, just the memory is enough to reinvigorate me for another round or two, at least."

"Another…?" Melitta followed his gaze and blushed. "I wanted to throw you down on the ground outside that cave and have my way with you," she admitted.

"Then you must have been reading my

mind."

He entered her again, chuckling at her gasp of delight, and between his tender lovemaking and passionate kisses, Melitta didn't care whether the thoughts in her head were his or her own. She loved him, and if he was the prize for slaying a dragon, the rest of the dragons in the world could go on living, for she had the most perfect happy ending to her very own fairytale, without a prince or princess in sight.

Appease: Princess and the Pea Retold

DEMELZA CARLTON

A tale in the Romance a Medieval Fairy Tale series

One

To six-year-old Princess Sativa, betrothed seemed like such a strange word. Mother had told Sativa that it was a fancy word that meant promised. She was promised to the prince, and he was promised to her. When she'd asked what kind of promise, her mother had only smiled and said, "The unbreakable sort."

So now Sativa sat in the place of honour in her father's hall, beside her promised, Prince

Reidar. She wasn't sure what she wanted to do with him. Big boys like him usually spent all their time in the practice yard, sparring with swords and shooting arrows into targets. He had a sword strapped to his side, too, like one of her father's knights. It was smaller than their swords, though, for he was only a boy.

It certainly bothered his mother, though. Queen Regina looked like she'd drunk vinegar instead of wine every time he bumped her with his sheathed sword. More than once, Sativa had been forced to smother her laughter, or risk a quelling glance from her own mother.

Sativa yawned, remembering to cover her mouth before her mother saw. She wouldn't have been so excited about attending this feast if she'd known it was so boring. She'd eaten her fill of the food, and she wasn't allowed any wine, so why did she have to keep sitting there? Normally when she'd finished her dinner, she could go play with her little sisters, or the castle kittens, but her mother insisted she must spend the whole dull day with the prince. Her betrothed.

He'd arrived here on his horse yesterday, and he'd scarcely said a word to her since.

She eyed him carefully as he ate another piece of meat. He had a tongue and teeth, same as her, so he should be able to talk. While she watched, she caught him smothering a yawn. He was as bored as she was!

"Do you want to see my horse?" Sativa asked Prince Reidar.

Reidar turned to Regina. "Mother, may I?"

"Kings do not ask permission, they command," came the reply through Regina's gritted teeth. She eyed Sativa with distaste.

Reidar drew himself up. "Mother, I am going with my betrothed to see the horses," he announced grandly.

Regina nodded once.

"Mother," Sativa began.

"You may go. A feasting hall is no place for children, and it grows late," Mother said. She peered fearfully at the hall's high windows, where the afternoon sun slanted in.

Sativa forced a smile. Her mother had been afraid of the dark for as long as she could remember. Not for herself, but for her children. Apparently Sativa's fairy godmother, Dalia, had told her that her daughters would be stolen from her by evil that swooped out of the darkness. Queen Dorota had lived in nightly dread ever since. "Yes, Mother," Sativa said.

Sativa led the way out of the hall, hearing Reidar's heavier footsteps behind her.

"His name is Philip, and he's really only a pony. Father says I may have a proper sized horse when I am bigger." Sativa glanced back over her shoulder. "As big as you, I think."

"When you are my queen, you will need a proper horse to ride. How else will you go hunting?" Reidar said.

"Queens don't hunt, Mother says. Killing is a job for men."

Reidar laughed. "My mother hunts as well as any man, or so my father says. So do many of the ladies at my father's court. They call it sport, pitting oneself against a noble beast, then bringing its carcass home for the victory feast. When you come to my castle, I will make sure you learn to hunt."

Forbidden pleasures and a new horse. Maybe her betrothal wasn't such a bad thing.

"What else do you have in your castle?" Sativa asked. "Will I get to wear beautiful gowns like my mother does?"

"Fit for a queen, I am sure. You shall choose them," Reidar said.

Betrothal sounded better and better.

Sativa led the way out to the fields beside the castle, but there wasn't a horse to be seen. "Where are they?" she asked in dismay. She found a guardsman at the castle gate. "Where are the horses?" she demanded.

"This time of day, the horses are all in their stable, having dinner, young mistress," the guardsman said.

Sativa wasn't supposed to enter the stables, but with her mother and everyone else at the feast, no one but she and Reidar would ever know. "We must speak of this to no one," she said imperiously as she led the way.

Two

His mother was wrong, Reidar decided as he followed the little princess. Sativa would make quite a queen one day, if her six-year-old self was any indication. As long as no one did anything to dampen her fire between now and their wedding, which would be at least a decade away. She had her mother's fair colouring, so she'd probably grow up to look like her. Regal and feminine and fiery — everything his kingdom needed in a queen, for if the border wars continued, she would need to rule while he kept the neighbouring armies at bay like his father was doing right now.

She might not hunt yet, but she at least rode. That was good, and she knew her way to the stables well enough. His sisters would not be so sure, leading the way around his father's castle, but the princess of a bigger, more prosperous kingdom like this one, living in a castle surrounded by such a huge town, would need to be more assured than the girls at his father's seaside castle back home.

"This is Philip," Sativa announced, waving at a fat pony that looked very much like a hairy barrel with legs. A hairy barrel that snorted, blowing his mane up off one baleful eye that stared disdainfully at Reidar for a moment before it disappeared beneath the descending mane. "He likes apples." She fetched an armload of fruit from the apple barrel, her shoes scuffing through the straw.

Then her face screwed up, and she sneezed. And sneezed again. Reidar counted seven in all before he began to grow concerned for her health.

By the time the sneezing fit had subsided, her eyes and nose were running and Sativa needed to hold onto a post to stay on her feet.

Reidar's heart sank. Perhaps his mother was right, after all. He'd need a strong queen, not a weak one, and Sativa's health mattered. She wouldn't just have to rule the kingdom in his absence – she'd have to give him an heir or two to ensure the succession, too.

"Are you well?" he asked.

She sniffled loudly and wiped her nose on the back of her hand. Then she seemed to remember herself, and she pulled out a handkerchief to clean herself up in a more ladylike fashion.

"It's the straw," she said thickly. "It makes me sneeze something awful. My father found a physician who had seen something like this before, in a son of some sultan of a desert land far to the south. He called it rose fever, because the prince sneezes at flowers. Me, I sneeze at straw. Not all straw. Just the stuff we have here, which the farmers insist on growing as pasture because it makes our fields the most fertile in the region. Pea straw, they call it. He said I should go to the desert, where it is dry, or by the sea, where it is too salty for such straw to grow."

Reidar couldn't help it. He laughed. "No wonder your parents wanted us to be betrothed. My father's castle is on a cliff overlooking the sea. The salt breeze blows day and night, so that all you can smell is the sea. When you are my queen, I shall build you a tower, and the topmost room shall be your bower, so that you will never need to sneeze at straw again."

"It sounds like heaven," Sativa admitted. "A place with no straw, where I can breathe. Do you truly mean it?"

Reidar pulled a ring off his smallest finger and held it out to Sativa. "Take this as a symbol of my unbreakable promise. I swear that one day, when I am old enough, I will return to save you from this place, and carry you off to my castle to be my queen."

Sativa smiled. "Just like a hero in one of my nurse's fairytales." She slipped the ring onto her finger, and for a moment, the amber caught the sunset light, glinting gold as the silver setting glowed around it. "I will wait for you, my prince," she promised.

Three

Regina found Reidar, as she always did. "So you already know, then," she greeted him.

Reidar traced his finger around the jewels on his father's crown. His crown now. "Yes, I know. Father is dead of his wounds from some skirmish in the border lands, and they are bringing his body home for a proper burial at sea, as befits the King of Viken."

"You will need to find a wife, and have heirs as soon as possible." Regina continued, as though he hadn't spoken.

Reidar rose. "I shall. Have someone summon Rudolf home. He shall be my heir until someone more suitable is born. And send an envoy to Kasmirus, to bring me my bride."

"Rudolf? The boy was sent south for good reason. His claim to the throne is second only to yours, my son. Some might say his claim is stronger, if only because his father was the eldest son. Best to keep him where he is, or he will steal your throne out from under you before your father's ashes are cold." Regina nodded in satisfaction.

But Reidar would not be dissuaded. "You see conspiracies where there are none, Mother. Rudolf will be sent for, because his father is dead, too, and he must swear fealty to me as his new king. If he refuses, then that is something I must deal with. All the more reason to marry."

Regina's eyes blazed. "There are fertile girls aplenty at court. I will see that they are dressed in their best tomorrow, so that you may make your selection."

Reidar shook his head. "A queen must do more than breed. She must rule, and bring alliances and armies when I need them most. You must go to Kasmirus, and bring back my bride."

Regina laughed. "I am too old to travel, my son. Better for me stay here. Besides, I had heard that King Boreslas lost his daughters to a dragon. Your bride is in the belly of the beast, if I am not mistaken."

"That's the tale they tell at the docks, now? Sailors selling stories of dragons eating maidens in foreign lands? Sounds like a fairytale to me, Mother. All the more reason to send an envoy to Boreslas. He owes me a bride, or an answer." He surveyed the sea from the tower windows. He could see to the horizon from up here, though not the land where Sativa lived. If she still lived. "I give you leave to prepare for my father's funeral, and for my coronation. When my bride arrives, you may also plan my wedding. My father trusted you to rule while he was at war, and it was fitting. But now I am king…and I shall do things my way."

All colour drained from Regina's face. Had she truly thought she could control Reidar as she had his father? More fool her.

Reidar ignored her, and summoned a servant. He gave orders for the court to assemble for sad news, for he knew they must be told of his father's death.

For the king was dead. Long live the king.

Four

Princess Sativa played with her amber ring as she waited for her father to notice she'd arrived. For years now, it had been too small to fit on her fingers, so she wore it on a thong around her neck.

Her heart went out to her grey-haired father, for now he looked like an old man.

Her father had aged a lot since the dragon came. First the loss of her mother, then the dragon plaguing the city, and then the final blow of losing her sisters in one fell swoop, just as the seeress had predicted, though Queen Dorota had not lived to see the dragon devour her daughters.

Sativa's sneezing had kept her indoors, away from the parade where her sisters had died that day. It was bittersweet, to know her affliction had saved her from a fiery death. If the dragon had only torched the fields of straw instead, perhaps she would have seen some bright spot in the animal's advent, but no. It stole sheep and maidens, and only burned knights who tried to slay it.

Or it had until last night, when everyone within a hundred miles had learned of the dragon's death. How it had happened, no one knew – not even those watching from the city walls, for there'd been so much fire and smoke no one had been sure the dragon was dead until a man walked through the gates, carrying a maiden, and announced that he'd killed the beast.

And now her father wanted to hold a feast for the man? It was too much. They were still in mourning for her sisters. To host this sort of celebration when…

"Sativa, my dear! How go the preparations? Do you need a new gown to wear?" Her father was so cheerful it could only be a lie.

Yet she forced a smile that matched his. "The castle kitchens are cooking up the feast to end all feasts, they say, they are so happy the dragon is dead. But I thought, so soon after the loss of my sisters…something more sombre might suit…" She caught the look of horror on her father's face and lapsed into silence.

For a moment, she stared into eyes that mirrored hers. All the guilt and devastation at such a tragic loss, the wish that it had been her instead, and the complete and utter despair of having to live knowing the girls were gone, shone through his irises.

"Your sisters would have wanted a celebration. The biggest, grandest feast ever held in our halls to mark the death of that foul beast. They would want it to be remembered.

It is the end of mourning, for today we celebrate a triumph over the devil himself!" Father said fiercely. "You and all the court will wear your brightest raiment. We will commemorate this day! A thousand years from now, they will still talk about how the dragon was slayed!"

Sativa hoped that sometime in the next thousand years, someone found out how the dragon had been slayed. So far, the only part of it they'd found was its head.

"Yes, Father," she said dully. She would do as he asked, because he was the king, and if he gave in to the despair she knew filled his heart, they would all be lost.

Five

"I find that hard to believe, Sir George. You've slayed monsters that were more troublesome than a dragon?" Father asked.

The dragonslayer – a shoemaker, Sativa had been horrified to discover, who her father persisted in addressing as though he was a knight – looked down at his food, abashed. It took him a moment before he managed to say, "Your Majesty, every monster is troublesome. Your dragon is certainly the biggest beast that I've ever faced, but size is not all that matters.

Some of them are so cunning, or there are so many of them, or they are so intent on killing you…why, it's a wonder I'm still alive. There was this pair of unicorns up near your western border…"

Sativa beckoned a server over to refill her cup. She half-listened to the shoemaker's story, which seemed to include pigs, giants and his paragon of a squire, who had saved his bacon more times than he could count. Every time he mentioned his squire, his gaze swept the hall, settling on a table at the back, where the squires sat. Most of them squabbled over the food, focussed only on stuffing their faces with more meat than most of them had seen in months, judging by their ravenous appetites, but there was one on the end, smaller than the rest, who sat aloof from the fighting.

The small squire turned to look at the dais where Sativa sat, and she found herself staring back in the most unladylike way. The squire was no squire at all, but a woman, wearing leather armour that had clearly been made to accommodate her breasts.

She had saved the shoemaker's life?

Surely not. Had she been the maiden the shoemaker carried off the field yesterday? She must have been hurt fighting the dragon, yet she showed no signs of any injury now.

Sativa shivered. Something about the girl's eyes, even across the hall, chilled her very soul.

She began to pay attention to the shoemaker's story in earnest now, eager for details on what this woman had done.

"Truly, I couldn't have killed the dragon without her," the shoemaker concluded.

Father laughed. "You are too modest, Sir George. But the time has come to make you more than that." He rose to his feet, more unsteady than usual. He'd drunk more wine to maintain the cheer he insisted upon for this event.

"My subjects!" the King shouted. "Lords, ladies, knights, men! We are here to celebrate a great victory. Sir George has defeated the dragon that oppressed us for so long." He raised his cup in a toast, then drank. "And he shall be rewarded!"

The crowd cheered and drank with him, but Sativa merely bowed her head. With all eyes on her father, no one would notice that her cup stayed on the table where it belonged.

"Kneel, Sir George!"

The shoemaker stumbled a little and Sativa prayed that he would not embarrass her father by sprawling at his feet. Someone must have heard her prayer, for the shoemaker managed to regain his balance and make his way to her father without any further mishaps.

Now Sativa drank as the shoemaker droned his way through his vows of fealty to her father. Someone must have coached him, she suspected, because he didn't stumble over the words as he presented her father with his sword.

Her father made him more than a knight — when the shoemaker rose, he was a lord.

This seemed to make him even more nervous — it took him a couple of tries to get his sword back into his scabbard, so that when he succeeded, a cheer rose up from the hall for the newly minted lord.

Even Sativa managed a smile at this.

"And as a final reward for his heroism, I have decided to bestow my only remaining daughter, Princess Sativa, on him in marriage this very night. My personal confessor and priest will marry them in the castle chapel after the feast, and if I'm not mistaken, Lord George will have an heir on the way before the night is through!"

Sativa's smile died.

Six

Reidar sent his advisers away for the day, rubbing his temples. Wearing a crown was a heavier burden than he'd thought, even on the days when the gold circlet didn't sit on his head. Keeping the people of the borderlands safe while repelling invaders and dealing with a dozen attempts to steal his crown...and that was just this week.

He was sorely tempted to find some way to let the would-be usurpers wear the crown for a day, so that they might take on the cares that came with it. On the morrow, they could return to their normal lives with no desire to ever wear that treacherous circlet again.

But he couldn't, in conscience, do it. One man with too much power could wreak a lot of havoc in a day.

Or even one woman.

Reidar sighed. "Mother? I sent everyone away so that I might have some peace. Why are you still here?"

She stepped out of the shadows. The Queen Mother should not lurk so, but no one would have been brave enough to say such a thing to Regina. Not even her son.

"I have a matter of great importance to speak to you about. Alone," she said.

Reidar spread his hands wide in invitation. "Very well, Mother. Speak."

She glanced around. "Not here. There is something I must show you first." She beckoned imperiously, and stalked out of his solar.

Sighing, Reidar followed.

She led him to her own apartment. "Now, line up! Let him see you!" she ordered as she went in.

Reidar wanted to turn around and not follow her any more, but as the king, he could hardly admit to being afraid of what he might find in his mother's chambers. So he sighed again and stepped inside.

"Which one do you like best?" Mother demanded.

She'd lined up a bunch of children. Highborn, by the look of them, and all girls, though it was hard to tell at this age. They had no curves to them for they were all too young to be women yet.

"What for?" Reidar asked tiredly. "I don't need a cupbearer. If you want another lady-in-waiting, it would be better for you to make your own choice. I have no idea what to look for in a female companion."

That was a lie, but he managed to utter it with a straight face. He looked for the ship carrying Sativa every morning and every night, but there had been no sign of it yet. Still, he would ascend the tower again tonight, in the hope that he would see it.

"You like them pretty and young, yes? Well, pick which one you want!" Mother said impatiently. "You need an heir!"

The girls giggled at this, and some of them blushed. Maybe some of them were women, though just barely.

"I'm not marrying some girl scarcely out of the nursery so I can get her with child! Mother, I have a bride, who is on her way here now. Send these girls back to their mothers, where they belong. I will sire no bastards on the daughters of my sworn bannermen. There is no honour in such things. Better to hand the kingdom over to one of the usurpers across the border than fail in my duty as king. I promised to protect my people, not seduce their children!" Reidar glared at the girls, who quailed under his gaze. He softened his expression — it wasn't their fault they were here. They were good, obedient daughters who would one day make fine wives for other men of the court. "Girls, go home," he said.

He waited until they were gone before he rounded on his mother. This time, his voice was cold. "Mother, I am betrothed to Princess Sativa, and until I hear word from her father that she is dead, I shall keep my promise. But even were word to arrive at this very moment that she truly is in the belly of this dragon of which you speak, I still would not take a child to be my queen. We may have been children at our betrothal, but more than a dozen years have passed since then. I have no doubt she is a woman grown, and everything I could expect for my queen. She will not break her promise, and I will not dishonour her or myself in breaking mine." He stared at the doorway the girls had run through in their haste to escape. "Would you have my people think me a paedophile?"

She swelled indignantly. "I would have them think you are a king, seeing to his succession."

Reidar sighed. "As a queen yourself, I need

not remind you that these things take time. Nine months, at least, and sometimes longer. How long was it after your marriage that you gave birth to me?" He met her angry gaze for a moment before he turned on his heel and left.

He didn't need to hear her answer. It had been seven years. Seven years of trying, and giving birth to his sisters and all the other children who had not survived long enough to leave their cradle, before he had come along.

If his people had to wait seven years for his heir, then so be it. They had a young, strong king. They would have Rudolf, a man with enough royal blood to stand in the heir's place until then. Now, if their neighbours would just stop attacking them for no good reason, Reidar might be able to get his people a little peace. For he knew he should have no peace from his mother until he was wed. And maybe not even then.

Seven

In the flurry of activity around the new Lord Shoemaker, Sativa slipped away before her welling tears fell. The crown princess could not cry before the court.

She barely made it to the corridor before tears blurred her vision, but there was no one to see her distress as she fled to her chamber. A chamber she had once shared with her sisters, but was now cold and empty.

No one had lit a fire in here, and horror enveloped Sativa as she realised why. She was not meant to return here tonight – she was supposed to spend the night in her new husband's chamber. Crushed under the body of some shoemaker, as they consummated a marriage she did not want. Had not agreed to. Would never agree to, while she was betrothed to Prince Reidar of Viken.

Her fingers flew to the ring she wore on a thong about her throat, a solid reminder of the boy she had not seen since their betrothal. The prince would be a man grown now, strong enough to challenge the shoemaker for his rightful bride.

The thought of Reidar made her smile through her tears. He would ride up on his charger, wearing armour like the knights who'd come to fight the dragon. Only he would come to fight for her honour, and her love. He would make short work of the shoemaker, before lifting Sativa herself in his arms and carrying her off to his kingdom.

Her heart swelled at the thought. Yes, yes! Reidar would save her.

Sativa darted to the table and seized a quill, then searched for a clean piece of parchment. She would write him a letter, telling him about the dragon and the shoemaker and Reidar would come…

Too late.

Because her father would have her marry the shoemaker tonight. Tonight, the lowborn boy would take her maidenhead and make her miserable. Would Reidar even want someone so tainted when he arrived weeks later? What if she was carrying the shoemaker's child?

Sativa shuddered. She would not give her body to a man who did not deserve it. Who did not love her. Better to be devoured by a dragon, like her sisters had been, than that.

As long as she stayed in the castle, she would not escape this marriage. Her father would force her to it, for he could not go back on his word.

But Sativa refused to go back on her word. She'd promised to wed Reidar, and she would. She'd leave the castle tonight, and by the time her father realised she was missing, she would be far from his walls. There was no time for farewells, and who would listen, anyway? Her sisters were dead, and her father had given her away like some bauble. No, there was nothing for her here.

Down went the quill. Instead, she collected what coins she could find. Her sisters had no need for money now, and she had no idea what the price would be for passage to Reidar's kingdom, she told herself as she pawed through the chests containing her sisters' belongings. For if he could not come to her, she would go to him. With him, she would be safe.

She bundled together some spare clothes, then donned a cloak in the hope that it would hide her. Sativa paused for a moment to say a silent farewell to her sisters' spirits and the home she had known for all her life, before she turned her back on it forever.

Eight

Sativa had managed to saddle her mare, Salt, and fasten the saddlebags to the animal, when she heard approaching footsteps. Swearing silently, she slid into the stall with Salt, praying that the intruder would go away. She held her breath as she peered through the gaps in the stall wall.

Whoever it was did not respond to prayers, for they came into the stable. One of the squires, she thought at first, until the squire came into view.

Sativa almost swore again as she recognised the flaming hair of the woman the shoemaker had been staring at all night. The one who'd been so indispensable at slaying all those monsters. She would not let her lord's bride escape.

"Who's there?" the woman demanded, sliding her dagger from its sheath. "Show yourself!"

Sativa sidled deeper into the stall, hoping the woman wouldn't see her. She refused to be dragged back to the hall, to be a prize for the shoemaker. The straw shifted under her boots and Sativa nearly fell on her behind, but caught herself in time. Salt lifted her head from her dinner and snorted at Sativa, blowing fragments of straw everywhere.

Sativa gasped in horror, the worst thing she could possibly do.

The tickle started in her nose, building until it was unbearable, as if an angry bee had lodged up there and wanted out. Sativa couldn't stop it. She couldn't.

She sneezed.

Damned pea straw.

The door to the stall flew open, and the flame-haired woman stood in the breach, blocking Sativa's escape.

Sativa kept her head down, hoping the woman wouldn't recognise her, doing her best to keep the horse between them.

"Princess?"

Too late. The shoemaker's woman was an observant one.

"Why are you not at the feast, celebrating with everyone else?" she asked.

Because there was nothing to celebrate. Not any more. And this woman would not stop her. Sativa took a deep breath, fighting back another sneeze, and told the woman so.

Her dark eyes widened in surprise. And disbelief. For who could blame her? A princess's life must seem like paradise to a commoner.

Sativa continued, "I am not a prize to be won. I will not be handed to that shoemaker in marriage like some pretty bauble." She wanted to say that she would challenge anyone who tried to stop her, but Sativa was no fighter. This woman walked like a cat on the hunt – the way swordsmen stalked each other in the practice yard. So Sativa closed her mouth and glared instead.

The woman didn't seem to notice. "George is no mere shoemaker," she said slowly. Then she gave the tiniest smile. "True, he was once a master shoemaker. But he is also a hero, a slayer of monsters and giants. He has saved maidens and whole towns from monsters. And he slayed a dragon at the very gates to your city. Your father has seen fit to make him a lord and give him lands to match. Any girl would be lucky to be allowed to marry such a man." Her voice swelled with pride as her smile beamed across the stable.

This woman wanted to be the lucky girl, Sativa realised. She wanted to marry the shoemaker, and from the way her eyes flashed, she considered Sativa her rival.

Could they come to some sort of arrangement? If the woman let Sativa go free, then she would be free to marry the man she wanted.

"I will not be a prize," Sativa said. When the woman didn't seem to understand what she meant, Sativa continued, "He does not love me. Though I sat beside him, he scarcely even looked at me. He had eyes for only one person in the feasting hall. You. The one he calls his squire, but you are more than that, aren't you? You are his lover."

Any normal woman would blush at such bluntness – Sativa even felt her own cheeks grow hot – but this woman looked like she wanted to laugh.

Instead, she glanced around, before lowering her voice to say, "I am not his lover. I am his partner, in that we slayed the dragon together. We have slayed many beasts together, but I think his hero days are done."

"Lover or not, his heart belongs to you," Sativa stressed. Would the woman force Sativa to lower herself to her level and make a bargain with a commoner? Sativa tried again. "You shall not stop me. I ride to the coast, and my betrothed. A man who loves me, or at least he did once."

For who could know what Reidar thought of her now? She had not seen him since their betrothal.

A smile flickered across the woman's face so fast Sativa thought she had imagined it. Then her expression turned serious as she looked the princess up and down with a practiced eye.

"Take only what you need with you," the woman said. "Food, water, weapons, and clothes that are suited for rough travel. Nothing that will mark you for what you are, because there are men on the roads who will take advantage of a lady. They will see you as even more of a prize."

Sativa drew in a deep breath, wanting to shout at the woman that she was no one's prize.

The woman finished, "You would be safer

in your father's castle."

Sativa saw red. Safer married to a shoemaker? Forced to share his bed? "What would you know of it? A girl pretending to be a squire knows nothing of the cage that is a royal court."

This time, the woman laughed. A ladylike laugh, Sativa realised uneasily, just like her mother had taught her. And then she dropped the tiniest curtsey, as though she wore a gown and not a man's garb. The kind of curtsey a princess might offer her equal.

After a moment, the woman wiped her eyes. "Forgive me, Your Royal Highness, but I was raised in a royal court, a princess in all but name, alongside Queen Margareta's own children. And I could take my place at her side again tomorrow, if I wished. But I will not leave these walls without my armour, my weapons, and enough money and provisions for the journey, because I know there are monsters out there." She drew a dagger from its ankle sheath and held it out to Sativa. "Take it, Princess, for I promise you will have need of it."

Sativa swept aside her cape, revealing two sheathed daggers strapped to her girdle. "I am not a fool." Even if she now felt like one. How had she not noticed the woman's cultivated speech? And why would a woman so highborn want to marry a shoemaker?

The woman fumbled through her bag and pulled out a cloth bundle that she thrust at Sativa. "Then at least take these. Court dresses will be no use to you on your journey."

Sativa glanced down. She still wore her feast dress – how could she have been so stupid? She should have changed into something less showy. She should have bribed some other girl to wear her gown, to pretend to be her at the feast.

Here before her was another girl. But would she wear the gown?

Sativa took the clothing. "I thank you. But I must repay you, and I will need all the coin I have for my journey, as you say. Wait."

She worried that she was making a terrible mistake as she stripped off her silk dress and put on the other girl's clothes. They were made of cloth as fine as anything else Sativa wore, and hardly scratched at all. A blessing. But to dress as a man...Sativa had to force herself to leave the stall, stepping out into the strange woman's scrutiny.

"They are finer than they look," Sativa managed to say. She bundled up her gown and thrust it at the woman. "Here, consider this a gift."

"I have no need for silk," the woman replied, dismissing it as nothing more than an ill-fitting gown. She was a fine lady indeed in her homeland. "Oh, no. I cannot wear this."

Sativa was growing desperate. Every moment she delayed, she came closer to being caught. "Every priest in the city is so drunk they cannot tell the difference between one woman and another. Yet in an hour, my father will command one of them to conduct a wedding, marrying me to the shoemaker. If you wear this, they will think you are me. Marry the man, if that is your wish. By morning, it will be too late for anyone to do anything. I will be gone and you will be his wife." Sativa's eyes implored her. "Please."

"My lady? Are you here, or am I too late?" a male voice called.

The shoemaker.

Sativa's breath caught in her throat. He was looking for her. "He cannot catch me here. He will stop me!"

To her credit, the woman did not hesitate. She took the gown from Sativa's unresisting fingers, tucked it under her arm and winked at the princess. Then she marched out of the stables.

"Lord George," Sativa heard the woman say.

"Thank God," George said. "I thought you'd left. Melitta, I swear I didn't know about the princess. I must speak to the king, tell him I cannot..."

Sativa waited until their voices had died

away before she turned to fasten her saddlebags and check that she'd saddled her horse correctly. She rarely had to do it without the help of a groom, but needs must. Finally, she summoned the courage to leave the stables, leading Salt.

There was no one in sight as she swung onto the mare's back, but movement caught her eye and she stilled.

A door swung open, and a lady stepped out. A lady in a shimmery silk gown, with embroidery that drank the light of the torches in the courtyard, glowing gold as if by magic. It was Sativa's gown, but it was Melitta's now.

A man bowed low before her. The shoemaker. "My lady," he said throatily.

Sativa's breath caught in her throat. No man had ever spoken to her with such emotion in his voice. If Reidar loved her half that much, she would be a fool to delay. She wished the shoemaker and his lady well, but she could not stay to see more.

Sativa spurred her horse into a trot, not

daring to look back as she departed into the welcome darkness.

Nine

"Even if your girl hasn't been eaten by the dragon, the beast will take her from you all the same," Regina announced as she swept into Reidar's solar.

Reidar set down the report he'd been trying to read. "Explain yourself, Mother," he said, trying not to grit his teeth. He failed, naturally.

"Word has reached the city that he has increased the reward. Whoever slays the pesky dragon shall have half the kingdom and be named the highest lord in the land." Regina spread her hands wide. "Well, we all know what that means."

Reidar sighed. "No, I do not. Speak plainly."

Regina gave an exaggerated sigh, as if to demonstrate she'd been doing it for far longer than her son, and was far more skilled, too. "Half the kingdom is the usual dowry that comes with a princess's hand in marriage. If your girl lives, she's the other part of the prize."

"King Boreslas would not do something so dishonourable as to break the betrothal without offering me some sort of recompense. He would not offer my bride as a prize without consulting me." Reidar picked up his scroll and pretended to concentrate on it.

"Perhaps the letter has gotten lost. There are plenty of pirates on the sea between here and Kasmirus, my son. Six ships have not arrived in port, and there was no storm to delay them." Regina nodded in satisfaction, as though she was the siren who had lured these ships to their doom.

Reidar almost laughed at the image of his mother, sitting on a rock without her clothes, singing for ships full of common sailors.

"When our neighbours stop raiding our borders, and you stop wasting my time with tavern gossip, perhaps I shall have time to wipe out the pirates," Reidar snapped. "Perhaps you should take a ship out and fight the pirates yourself. I'm sure they would find you a formidable enemy." He didn't hide his fierce grin.

"You're as insolent as your father was," Regina snapped back.

Now Reidar truly did laugh. "It must be something that comes with kingship, for you've never told me that before. Now, leave me alone, Mother."

Regina marched out the door.

Insolent. Well, she'd called him worse. Only now did he let the rest of her words sink in, and Reidar began to worry.

Desperate times called for things no man would normally do. Breaking a betrothal was a small thing, when your whole kingdom was beset by a dragon as dangerous as Boreslas' one was reputed to be. A king who would offer half his kingdom to the slayer of such a fearsome beast was a desperate man indeed. Perhaps Reidar should offer Boreslas some of his own best warriors to assist him. He had lost many men fighting the dragon, and it was the mark of a good ally to help when needed. Perhaps when the winter snows set in, and his marauding neighbours decided to stay home, he would venture across the water with a band of warriors. He could defeat the dragon and claim his bride, who would look on him as her hero, for he would have saved her father's kingdom.

He laughed softly at himself. Why, he'd grown quite sentimental for a moment there. Almost as though he was in love with Princess Sativa, the woman he hadn't seen since she was a child. Was she comely, now, with the kind of curves a man wanted? Would she still have her childish fire, refined to something more queenly? Would she have turned from rebellious daughter to obedient wife? Somehow, Reidar doubted it. Oh, she might be beautiful enough to put the sun and moon to shame, and she was born to be a queen, but if she was to rule here she would need every spark of stubbornness she'd possessed as a child, stoked up to a roaring blaze. The women of Viken were as fierce as their men, and Sativa would lead by example as their queen.

Or he would have to give in to his mother's increasingly strident demands that he marry a Viken girl. And in choosing one, he would offend the families of all the girls he'd overlooked.

Not for the first time, he prayed that his envoy would bring his bride safely to him soon. Unharmed, uneaten, unmarried.

Then he returned to the report in his hands, because as long as a monarch lives, his job never ends.

Ten

Sativa watched the sailors loading up the ship, wincing as the captain bawled orders, before she summoned the courage to address the man.

"I seek passage to the sea, and onward to Viken," she announced.

The captain grunted, then turned to face her.

Sativa was tempted to turn away from his scrutiny, but what was this man to cow her? She stood firm and jingled her purse. "I can pay."

"We already have a passenger," he said. "What's your name, girl?"

Girl. Sativa longed to tell him who she was, but she wouldn't get far if she did. She glanced down at her borrowed clothes, then jerked her chin up. "Lady Melitta. I helped Lord George slay the dragon."

The captain's eyes widened. "If you don't mind sharing, mayhap we do have space. I'm Captain Ziemowit. You can call me Ziemo, my lady." He executed a stiff bow.

Praying that she wouldn't be called to slay anything, Sativa followed him aboard. At the back of the boat was a wooden cabin, not much larger than Salt's stall. Sativa had to duck her head to go inside.

"What is it, Captain?" a fretful female voice asked. "Will no one let me mourn in peace?"

"We have another passenger. An important lady. She avenged your husband, she did, and all those others the dragon took." Captain Ziemo cast Sativa an adoring look. "I watched the battle from this very deck. While the menfolk fell, she stood firm and faced that dragon to its death."

So Sativa's suspicions were true. The squire had been the true hero. Sativa wished she'd thanked the woman, but it was too late now.

"Very well," the woman said, rolling over in her bunk to squint at Sativa. "I have no maid, so the other bunk is free. It is no less comfortable than mine, for I have tried them both. I am Lady Nekane, or I was, before the dragon killed my husband, Sir Hurik. If he had but waited a day…" She sighed heavily. "Now I must go to my sister, for I have no one and nothing else. He spent all our funds on new armour to protect him against the dragon, but it was not enough."

Sativa inclined her head to the widow. "I am sorry for your loss. No doubt, your husband waits for you in heaven now, at peace with all the other lost heroes."

"Yes, yes!" Lady Nekane said, then dissolved into tears.

The captain shook his head and backed out of the cramped cabin. Sativa followed him.

She pulled out her purse. "How much do I owe you?"

Captain Ziemo waved away her coins. "Nothing, my lady. My ship is at your disposal. The least I can do for the dragonslayer. The honour of meeting you is enough. We have a full cargo, and she has paid for the cabin. If you do not mind the weeping. If you do, I could put her ashore and tell her to find passage on another ship."

Abandon a widow in such grief? Never. Sativa shook her head. "Fate has been cruel enough to her. Let her stay."

The captain bowed. "As you wish, my lady. I shall have your things brought aboard. Where are they?"

Sativa hefted the small sack she'd removed from her saddlebags. "This is all I have. I travel light, for I am going home." She prayed this would not be a lie. Reidar's castle would be her home. It had to be.

Eleven

By morning, Nekane's constant crying had nearly driven Sativa mad. Sativa wanted to scream at the woman that she'd lost all four of her sisters and almost been married off to a stranger because of the dragon. At least her late husband had chosen to fight the beast. But Sativa understood grief better than most, after losing so much more. Grief paid no heed to reason or sense, especially when it was so fresh. Why, Nekane had not been a widow for more than two days.

So Sativa spent most of her time on deck, staying out of the way of the crew as they occasionally adjusted the sails. There was less of this than she expected, for the current carried them seaward.

When the endless fields gave way to forest, Sativa wanted to cheer, because she wasn't sneezing any more. But it grew hot and still between the trees, with no breeze reaching the river, so the sailors rolled the sail up and tied it the beam at the top of the mast, and there they stayed.

Sativa approached the captain. "What are they doing?" she asked.

He shaded his eyes from the sun and looked up. "Catching the breeze, perhaps, or admiring the view. 'Tis cooler up there than on deck. I'd be up there myself, but someone must steer the ship."

There was a cool place on the ship? Sativa tugged her sweat-soaked tunic away from her skin for what felt like the dozenth time. She longed to be in the tower room she'd shared with her sisters, wearing little more than linen shifts in the heat. But there would be no such days again. Her sisters were dead, and she would never go back.

"They'll make space for you if you wish to join them, my lady," Captain Ziemo said, evidently mistaking the look of longing on her face. He cupped his hands to his mouth and shouted, "Move aside there. The lady is coming up!"

Sativa opened her mouth to protest. Surely it was too high and too dangerous. Her mother would have screamed aloud at the very thought. And her father...

No longer cared. He'd handed her over to the shoemaker.

Lady Melitta would do it, a sly thought whispered through her mind. It was true. Lady Melitta would be up the mast in no time. Why, the woman had defeated a dragon and who knew what else. The captain would think less of her if she did not.

Sativa swallowed and made her way to the

mast. It was just a dead tree, she told herself. She'd climbed plenty of trees as a child, until her sisters had tried to copy her and Viola had broken her arm in a bad fall. Then her mother had banned them all from such things. Since her mother died, Sativa had never felt the need to disobey her. Until now.

Someone had cut notches into the mast, which made it a much easier climb. Sativa had to stretch for some of them, for they'd evidently been cut with a man's longer limbs in mind, but she managed until she grasped the sail. That's when she made the mistake of looking down.

Sativa swore.

The men around her laughed. "I didn't know ladies knew words like that," one of them said.

Sativa felt her face grow hot. If she were still alive, her mother would be ashamed of her.

"Don't look down, lady," a boy who could not be more than ten years old told her. "Hook your elbows over the yard and hang onto the shroud." He demonstrated, and so did the others.

They all looked like men being crucified, Sativa thought uneasily, as she dug her fingers into the folded sail. But crucifixion took days to kill a man, and they wouldn't be up here that long, she told herself.

And there was a breeze up there, she was pleased to find, as it caressed her face. She was level with the treetops, and she could see the forest stretching for miles on either side of her.

"Ooh, an eagle! Look!" The man pointed.

Sativa's eyes followed his finger. Sure enough, the enormous bird wheeled above the forest, too intent on its prey below to pay any attention to a ship sailing along the river. Or perhaps the regal bird simply did not care.

She envied the animal its graceful calm as it glided across the sky. She would never be so free. And yet, for the moment, she soared above the river, thanks to the ship that carried her to her destiny.

Twelve

Sativa spent most of her time atop the mast, where one of the men had nailed a little platform for her feet to rest on. She only descended when she had to – for mealtimes, and at night, when she ventured into the cabin she shared with Nekane so that she might sleep.

Nekane never noticed if she was there or not, and Sativa was hardly the person to comfort a grieving widow. If her plans came to pass, she would soon be happily married to a man she had no intention of losing to a dragon. If there were any such beasts left in the world. Sativa certainly hoped not.

Sativa was aloft when she heard the cry, "Captain! There's a ship in trouble ahead!"

The lookout on her left pointed.

Ahead of them, the river curved around a bend, and it appeared that a ship had taken that bend so fast, it had tipped over. Perhaps that was to be expected in such a strange boat, which looked very little like the broad-beamed river boat Sativa travelled on. The craft lay on its side, looking for all the world like a bowl a giant had sat on, squashing the usually flat base until it folded into a ridge at the bottom, and forcing the sides up like a sort of funnel. If it weren't for the pointy bits at either end, and the mast in the middle, Sativa would be hard pressed to recognise it as a boat at all.

It had ropes tied to it in several places, which stretched across the water and the shore, where dozens of people were trying to right the stricken vessel.

"We'll anchor here for the night," Captain Ziemo shouted, pointing. "Surely that little fishing village has a tavern, eh?"

The men cheered, and Sativa had never seen them work so fast. Even Sam, the cabin boy, seemed excited to be going ashore.

Sativa considered going with them. After all, when would she ever have another opportunity to visit a fishing village, or a tavern?

Almost as though the captain had read her mind, he turned to her. "Lady Melitta," he said gravely, "Would you be kind enough to watch over my vessel while we're gone? We will be under way in the morning, I promise you, as soon as the way is clear once more." He gestured at the stricken ship.

Sativa didn't know what to say. She wasn't sure if Melitta was familiar with ships, but after listening to the shoemaker's stories of her, there was little the woman could not do. Finally, she said, "I...I am not a particularly experienced mariner, Captain Ziemo. But if the ship should sink while you are gone, I will be certain to swim to shore, so that I might point to where your vessel lies."

Ziemo's eyes widened in surprise, before he let out a roar of laughter. "A good jest indeed, my lady. But my *Wydra* is sound as a drum. The only water in her bilges is the sweat of the men who work aboard her, I promise you."

"Men you promised some shore leave, Captain!" one of the men shouted as they lowered the boats over the side. Within moments, they'd climbed down the side of the ship and into the two boats, stranding Sativa on the ship with Nekane.

Rather than sit in the cabin with the endlessly weeping widow, Sativa climbed to her perch atop the mast and watched the men trying to save their ship.

It had run aground in the shallows, she saw now, and while the ship might look strange to her eyes, it did not appear to be damaged. She expected splintered planks or some part of it to be stove in, but instead it just lay there, like a toy boat some giant child had discarded, waiting for the boy to return for it so that he might make more mischief in the duck pond.

After plenty of pulling and shouting that achieved nothing, the men stretched out on the shore, opened a barrel of something, and started to drink. Someone lit a fire, and it soon had a stewpot suspended above it. Though she could not smell it, Sativa imaged the stew would smell delicious around about now.

She sighed. Their ship's cook had gone ashore with everyone else, so she would have to see to her own dinner for once. Descending to the deck, she helped herself to the ship's provisions. As she ate, she prayed that Reidar kept a good cook. More often than not, the meals aboard the ship were so bad, they had almost made her wish she was home in her father's hall. Almost, but not quite. So she choked down enough food to keep hunger at bay, and waited for the day when her ordeal would be over.

When the sun started to sink, one of the

men on the other side of the river gave a shout. The others came to stand with him, staring at the grounded ship. Unable to hear what they were saying or see what captivated their attention, Sativa ascended the mast once more.

Waves lapped at the ship now, lifting it as all the assembled men had not managed to. Even as Sativa watched, it started to right itself. It was the tide coming in, she realised. She'd heard of such things, but never seen them until now.

She watched in fascination as the men worked with the tide to refloat their ship. Even she felt pride swell in her heart as the masts rose so high in the sky they were silhouetted against the rising moon. The ship was saved!

She felt the thump of booted feet on the deck below. The crew had returned early, perhaps to take advantage of the turning of the tide and the cleared channel. Best to stay aloft and out of their way as they readied the ship to sail, she decided. So Sativa watched the stars come out instead, some as faint as a whisper and others as bright as a trumpet blast in the sky. Movement caught her eye, and she watched in wonderment as a star shot across the sky like an arrow, then vanished.

What had her nurse said about such things? Were they a good omen, or bad? Sativa racked her brain until she found the answer. They were not omens at all, but wishes. The one who sees such a star must make a wish.

Quickly, she squeezed her eyes shut and wished with every spark in her soul that she would reach Reidar safely and soon.

"Please, oh please, leave me be!" a female voice begged.

Sativa glanced down at the deck. "Quiet, you," a rough male voice said, followed by the smack of skin against flesh.

Nekane cried out.

Sativa stiffened. What man would dare strike a lady? Not Captain Ziemo, certainly, or one of his crew. They were honourable men, or so she'd thought. She should do something.

But what? She was no match for most of them, except maybe young Sam, the cabin boy. She might pretend to be Melitta, but Sativa was no warrior. She'd been taught to command men with her voice alone, for what more did a queen need?

She wet her lips, wondering what to say. What if the man was too drunk to listen, and turned on her instead?

It did not matter. No man should strike a lady.

"Leave her alone," Sativa said, or tried to. Her firm tone came out as more of a squeak.

"Who's there?" the man growled, lifting a lantern high. His other hand tightened around Nekane's arm, until the woman whimpered. "Show yourself, boy!"

Boy? Sativa seethed.

"What's the matter, Karl?" another voice asked.

Nekane's captor jerked his chin upward. "There's a boy atop the mast, Captain."

"Come down, boy, or we'll shoot you

down!" the second voice boomed. It did not belong to Captain Ziemo.

Better to be obedient than dead, Sativa told herself as she descended. Her feet hadn't even touched the deck when a rough hand grabbed her arm and almost knocked her off her feet.

"What's your name, boy?" the hand's owner asked, bringing his hairy face so close to Sativa's that she could smell his breath. Not that she wanted to.

She coughed. "Sam," she said weakly.

"Want me to kill young Sam here, Captain?" Bad Breath asked. He shook Sativa until her teeth rattled.

The captain's hat cast a shadow over his face as his hulking shoulder loomed above Sativa. "Bring him along. We could do with a new cabin boy. Lost the last one, didn't we?"

The men laughed. Only now did Sativa realise there were more than three of them. There were at least a dozen — more than the crew of the *Wydra* — all carrying casks and chests from the ship's hold.

"You're pirates!" she cried, hating how her voice still squeaked with fear. No wonder they thought her a boy. "Stealing from Captain Ziemo – he won't stand for it!"

More laughter. "Your captain's drunk under a table, along with the rest of his crew. Strong brew they sell in the taverns hereabouts. Too strong for you. So what'll it be, boy? You can come with us or I'll cut your throat and throw you over the side. Plenty more boys who'd kill to be cabin boy on a pirate ship. More wealth than you'll ever see on a tub like this."

Pirates. So much for her wish for safety. Sativa swallowed. "I always wanted to be a pirate cabin boy," she whispered.

"Good choice. Now get them both to the boat, and see that they stay there." Someone gave Sativa a push, toward the side of the ship.

Peering over the gunwale, Sativa could just make out the boats lying in the *Wydra*'s shadow. Below her, a bulky shape swung away from the ship and landed in the boat. The man leaned forward and dropped a bundle on the bottom of the boat. The bundle yelped.

Nekane.

Sativa couldn't leave her alone with these pirates. Summoning what courage she had left, she swung her leg over the side and felt around for the rope ladder she knew had hung there in daylight. She'd never climbed down anything so frightening in her life. Slapping against the hull of the ship, splashed by waves, until hands grabbed her around the middle and hauled her aboard a boat. But not the boat that held Nekane – another one, full of chests that left her nowhere to sit but on top of one.

Sativa drew a deep, shaky breath. This would not end well.

Thirteen

Reidar paced the tower, unable to stay still. He could see several ships from the windows, but he knew none of them could be hers. Not yet. His envoy would have just arrived in Kasmirus, if he hadn't met with any delays. He probably hadn't even seen King Boreslas yet. So it was too much to hope that she might be aboard one of the vessels in view.

And yet…

Reidar sighed. He'd dreamed of her last night. She'd had golden hair as a girl, the same colour as the straw that made her sneeze, so the beauty in his dreams had been blonde, too. She'd stood in the crow's nest atop the mast, her hair streaming behind her like a pennant in the breeze. As eager to glimpse him as he was to see her. Then she'd slid down that mast as lithely as any sailor, her curves hugging the wood like he wished they'd mould to him. And she'd run across the dock, her boots hammering on the timber as she flew toward him, her arms outspread like wings…

And then he'd woken up to realise that the hammering was not in his head, but outside, as some fisherman felt the need to mend his boat below Reidar's window.

By then, his dream bride was gone, for dreams were no more than moonbeams, and he was alone in his bed, longing for a lady he barely knew with no idea of what she even looked like now.

What would his men say, if they knew? They'd think him a fool, to be so besotted with a woman. A woman he hadn't seen in years.

Did she think of him at all, or had she forgotten him entirely? He wanted to believe she'd kept her promise, and the ring he'd given her, but his gift was likely lost among dozens of others from her many suitors, men who might be wooing her even now, while he was far away. Oh, they might be betrothed, but a woman's heart was far stronger than any childhood promise. Especially one she'd likely forgotten. If only he could stand before her and remind her.

Curse this war! Why couldn't his neighbours be content with their borders, and let him sit on his throne in peace for just a little while? A few summer raids were one thing, little more than fun and friendly rivalry between his men and theirs. But this…trying to claim his throne as their own, and his lands as well? These northerners had no idea who they were dealing with. They must think him some weak boy, easily set aside. If he was to join the war against him, they would soon learn he was as much a warrior as his father.

Reidar clapped his hands and laughed aloud. Were there anyone in earshot, they would think him mad, but he didn't care. He knew the cure for worrying about a woman. He would go to war, as his ancestors had. In the heat of battle, he'd have no cravings for a woman's warmth. Just a sword and a shield, waiting to sing a song of victory over his fallen foes. With an army at his back, of course. He might be a fool when it came to women, but not when it came to war.

Fourteen

The boat carrying Nekane arrived at the ship first – the very same vessel that had lain on its side for most of the day, if Sativa was not mistaken. It bobbed about in the waves as though it had taken no damage from its stranding, and now she was about to climb aboard it, Sativa certainly hoped it was as sound as Captain Ziemo's *Wydra*.

She glanced back, to see the *Wydra* still floating in its anchorage, though much higher in the water, thanks to the things the pirates had taken from her.

She'd heard that pirates sank ships, and killed all those aboard, after taking anything of value, of course. If they hadn't scuttled the *Wydra* and she and Nekane were still alive, perhaps these were not the sort of pirates she'd heard horrible tales about. Men of honour, maybe, who would take her to Reidar when she told them who she was.

"Take her to the captain's cabin," a voice said, carrying across the waves.

"No, no, please no…" Nekane pleaded as she was hoisted up onto the ship.

They were taking her to the best accommodations aboard, Sativa told herself. She would expect the same, once they knew she was a princess. Or even if she told them she was Lady Melitta.

"Up you go, boy," a man said, shoving her toward the ship.

Sativa stared up. This rope ladder stretched a lot higher than the one on the *Wydra*, but she would have to climb it, or be carried up like a sack of grain, as Nekane had. Judging by Nekane's protests, it wasn't a comfortable ride.

With one burly man above her on the ladder and another behind, at least she couldn't fall, Sativa told herself. Their weight kept the ladder from moving too much, too.

By the time Sativa hauled herself over the side of the ship and onto the deck, her arms were screaming a protest at having to work so hard. But none of the men complained, so she stayed silent.

Someone clapped her on the back so hard she nearly fell over.

Laughter erupted around her. "Boy's asleep on his feet. Wake up, boy. You'll get no rest until we get this cargo stowed."

Cargo? Oh, the things they'd stolen from the *Wydra*. Chests and casks she could not hope to lift. What had possessed her to tell them she'd be their cabin boy? Sativa should tell them the truth now.

"Captain's aboard!" The shout had all men bowing their heads as the hulking shadow stepped over the gunwale and onto the deck.

"Where's the boy?" the shadow growled.

Sativa was shoved forward again. "Here, Captain Zydrunas," someone behind her said.

A lantern was thrust toward her face, so close she feared it might burn her. Sativa cringed away.

"You ever sailed before, boy?" Captain Zydrunas demanded.

"N-no," Sativa stammered. "This was my first time."

"Can you lift a cask?"

Sativa wanted to say no, but some darkness in his tone gave her pause. Instead, she knelt and tried to lift the nearest barrel. She managed to tip it a little toward her, before she overbalanced and went down with the cask on top of her.

The laughter was louder this time as the crew took their time rescuing her from the heavy barrel.

"Take him below decks, and show him where he can sleep. Maybe he'll be more useful in the morning," Captain Zydrunas said.

Someone hustled Sativa down the steps below the deck, into a room that stretched from one side of the ship to the other. She had to duck her head to enter, and couldn't straighten once she was in, for the ceiling was too low. She bumped into something cold and hard, as high as her waist. Moonlight streamed through a gap in the wall, revealing the object to be a cannon, its mouth pointed through the hole. There was a whole row of cannons on each side, muzzles extended outward like gargoyles, or guard dogs ready to bite. Above them hung hammocks, stretched between the posts holding up the ceiling.

"That one's free, boy," a strange voice said. It sounded older than the others, and a whole lot friendlier. An arm extended from a hammock in the corner, pointing at the opposite corner. Sure enough, there was no sea chest below that one, like there were under the others.

"Thank you," she mumbled, picking her way

carefully over the clutter of cannonballs, chests and other assorted things she never knew lurked below decks. It took her a few tries to get herself into the hammock, but when she finally managed it, she found the hanging bed surprisingly comfortable. Better than a straw pallet like the sailors on the *Wydra* slept on, too, for it didn't make her sneeze.

Sativa closed her eyes and settled herself for sleep.

"NOOOOOOOO!"

A piecing scream tore the air above her.

Sativa thrashed, floundered, and fell out of her hammock onto the floor. "What in heaven's name is that?" she cried.

But the building dread in her heart whispered an answer she didn't want to believe.

The old man in the corner piped up, "The captain's new bedwarmer, I expect. They all scream like that until he's broken them in. Sometimes, when he's done with her, he lets the crew have a woman for a while. You ever had a woman, boy?"

Nekane's screams seemed to reach inside Sativa and slice through her heart. Right above her, the captain was raping that poor widow. A lady. And when he was finished, he'd give her to the crew. So that they might do the same. Like she was some sort of whore.

Sativa shivered. Part of her wanted to try to save the woman, but she knew it was no use. She wasn't strong enough to lift a barrel, let alone fight the whole crew of a pirate ship. And if they found out she was a woman…then what? If she couldn't save Nekane, Sativa would be next.

No. If Sativa lay with another man before she married Reidar, even unwillingly, there would be no wedding. Bile rose in her throat at the thought of her own cowardice as Sativa huddled in her hammock, wishing the screaming would stop.

"A smart woman would take her own life before letting herself be taken aboard a pirate ship, eh, boy?" the old man cackled. "But most women aren't smart. Too soft to take a dagger to their breast. But their softness is the best bit."

The screaming continued long into the night, as Sativa cried silent tears, cursing her own stupidity for landing her in such a situation. Then her thoughts turned to Nekane, and what the other woman must be suffering, and Sativa got no sleep at all.

Fifteen

By morning, Sativa's horror-filled mind had only one goal: to be the best, most convincing cabin boy she could be until the ship approached shore…and then she would escape as fast as her feet could sprint. She soon learned that the old man who'd helped her the previous night was the ship's cook, and his culinary skills made the food she'd eaten on the *Wydra* seem like ambrosia.

After this journey was over, she swore, she'd never take fruit or fresh-baked bread for granted again.

The best provisions the pirates had stolen from their victims belonged to the captain's table alone. Sativa thought of the horrible price Nekane had to pay to sup at that table, and shuddered. She could subsist on hardtack, dried fish and endless pickled cabbage for a little while, if it meant not having to share the captain's cabin.

After that first night, Nekane's screams had fallen silent, and Sativa hadn't heard her make a sound since. Not a sob, a complaint…nothing. The widow hadn't come out of the cabin, either, though she was certainly still there. In the absence of screaming, Sativa could hear the regular beat of the captain rutting in the bed above her hammock every night.

Some of the other men took this as a hint to pleasure themselves in their hammocks, a mentality that made Sativa feel even sicker. That one man could take pleasure in forcing an unwilling woman was one thing…but a whole crew who got excited at the mere idea of it? It was enough to keep her shuddering in her bunk for the rest of the voyage. Yet she could not stay below decks – as cabin boy, she had work to do.

Cook made her fetch and carry things up from the hold that he wanted. At first, it was just ordinary staples for the crew's meals, but then he started sending her down for the captain's special stores. Soon, she knew where everything was kept, and she began to plan. She set aside something each day – a skin of wine here, a dried sausage there – in a small cask behind the enormous tun of pickled cabbage.

As soon as they were within sight of shore, she'd wait until nightfall, load her supplies into a boat, and head for land. The one thing she hadn't found yet was coin – she'd need money to reach Reidar and she'd left all hers aboard the *Wydra*. Would it truly be stealing if she took coin from pirates who'd in all likelihood stolen hers when they took everything else?

Or perhaps she could call it fair payment. After all, cabin boys got paid, didn't they? She had no idea how much, but if she took more than she should, the pirates could come find her in Reidar's castle, and she would gladly pay her debt. Right after she saw Zydrunas punished for what he'd done to Nekane.

Nekane. She'd need to save her, if she could, too. Somehow smuggle her out of the captain's cabin and into the boat. Once they reached shore, if Nekane was too weak to travel, she would find someone willing to care for her until she could return. That would mean more coin, but Sativa didn't care. What Zydrunas owed Nekane was far more than money. No price was too high.

Sixteen

Another mug of ale, Reidar judged, and he'd have well and truly drowned out the pain in his arm. Today he'd met his first berserker, an experience he didn't want to repeat. The madman had run at him, screaming, then buried his axe so deep in Reidar's shield he'd cleaved the buckler in two, nearly breaking Reidar's arm in the process. Reidar's answering blow had sliced deep into the berserker's shoulder, at the base of his neck. The man had fallen to his knees, gurgling, before he died a noisy death at Reidar's feet. Reidar had only been dimly aware of it at the time, of course, because he'd had another foe to face, but now the battle was over, the man was once again on his mind.

The berserker had claimed to be the bastard son of either his father or his grandfather, Reidar wasn't sure, which he'd believed meant the throne Reidar occupied rightly belonged to him, and all of Viken's people would come to his way of thinking once Reidar was dead.

Except Reidar wasn't dead and the bastard's blood now fertilised the field, which didn't care whose son he was. Nor did Reidar care, not truly, for the man's claim died with him. What remained of his raiding party melted away across the border, either to join other armies or head home. Or to die of their injuries along the way, for his men had been particularly ruthless today. Perhaps it made a difference that instead of just fighting for their country, today they were also fighting for their king.

It was a heady thought. He'd fought

alongside these men for weeks now, weeks he'd fought as fiercely as any of them, knowing that he fought for them as much as the land they stood upon, but this was the first time he'd understood what that meant.

They would die for him, just as he would fight for them. He was their king, and they were his men. He owned the hearts and souls and bodies of free, fighting men. Reidar only hoped that one day he would truly deserve the honour they did him. Until then, he would draw his sword alongside them, to defend what was theirs.

Now he understood how his father had died on a battlefield. It was the duty of a king to live and die for his people.

Reidar tipped up his cup, but it was empty. Sighing, he headed for the barrel to get some more ale.

"I must see the king!" an insistent voice shouted. A voice Reidar didn't recognise.

The man rode into their circle, reining his horse in so close to the fire that its hooves kicked up sparks. He slid from his mount's back with practiced ease, then planted his feet before the fire like a man staking a claim.

Reidar edged closer, carrying his full cup. Most of the men present were deep in their cups, but they loosened swords and daggers in their sheaths, ready to take this new man down if their king commanded it.

"Where is the king?" the man demanded. "'Twas he who summoned me."

Reidar didn't remember summoning anyone. He squinted at the man. There was something familiar about him, but Reidar could not place him.

"Reidar!" the man cried, breaking into a smile. He strode across the trampled grass, heedless of the men who eyed him as he passed, and embraced Reidar. "Cousin, it is good to see you! Where is the king?"

Bursts of laughter exploded around the fire. Though Reidar still didn't recognise him, this could only be one man.

"Rudolf? I thought you'd sailed off the

western edge of the world!"

Rudolf grinned even more widely. "One day, maybe I will. But those islands…I can see why our people love them so much. Their men fight just as fiercely, but so differently! We'll never conquer them as long as they live. And the women…my God, the women…"

"It's hardly fair to speak of women in a war camp where the only women are in our dreams," Reidar reproached him, forcing back the unbidden image of Sativa that had come to mind.

Rudolf clapped his hands together. "That's right! I'm not the only man who missed out on a marriage. I got summoned back here before I could ask for her, and yours got handed over as the price for a dragon's head."

"What?"

Rudolf waved his hand airily. "That foreign princess you were betrothed to. When I left Portnahaven, every man who could lift a sword was talking about the dragon of Kasmirus, and how the king there had offered half his kingdom and one of his daughters as a bride to the man who could bring him the beast's head. Everyone thought I was leaving to do battle with the beast! They seemed quite disappointed when I said I was going home. Though after so long there, it feels like the Southern Isles are more a home to me than here. Has it always been this cold?"

Reidar's heart clenched in his chest at the thought of some other man marrying Sativa, but he banished that foolish notion. "Boreslas would not break off a betrothal with me without telling me so first. He has other daughters, I am sure. He would not break an agreement with the king of Viken. Even now, my envoy is at his court, to bring me my bride."

"King? So the rumours are true? Not just my father, but yours died, too?" Rudolf bowed his head. "I am sorry for your loss, cousin. Your father was a good king, and a wise one, too. Why else would he send me to the ends of the earth to learn warcraft from some foreign lord?" He laughed. "I can tell you tales of tactics their men use in battle that we would never think of. I would not have believed them, had I not seen it with my own eyes."

"Battle tactics? But Mother said – " Reidar clamped his mouth shut, but it was too late. Even he knew it was a sign of weakness for a king to rely so heavily on his mother.

"Is Aunt Regina still around? She will outlive us all, that battle axe will. I remember she caught me sitting on your father's throne once. She clouted me over the ear and gave me such a tongue lashing I couldn't open my mouth in her presence for a year. She said if she ever caught me sitting there again, she'd thrash my backside until I had nothing left to sit on!" Rudolf laughed as though it was all a joke to him.

It had been no joke to Regina, Reidar knew. For after Reidar himself, Rudolf had the best blood claim to the throne. Was Rudolf a danger to him?

Rudolf had been just a boy when he left,

and now he was a man grown. A man Reidar did not know. But he needed to know him.

If Rudolf was loyal and no risk, Reidar could leave an army in his capable hands to harry the border raiders, and finally win this war. If he wanted the throne…giving him an army would be tantamount to handing him the country and Reidar's own head in the bargain.

"Tomorrow, we ride west, to where there are reports of a foreign force waiting to ambush us. In three days' time, we shall go into battle. Will you join us, cousin?" Reidar asked.

"The Southern Isles may have softened me, but beneath it beats a Viken heart still!" Rudolf declared. "I will fight at your side like we did as boys."

As boys, they had been closer than brothers. Reidar hoped that would still be the case, but it would be three days before he knew for sure.

"Ale for my cousin! We must toast his return!" Reidar said. A cup was fetched and filled, which Reidar then presented to Rudolf.

Rudolf took it, then managed to drop to one knee without spilling his ale. "Nay, a toast to my cousin, the new king of Viken. May his reign be long and filled with so many victories the bards forget to sing of anyone else!"

The other men shouted and joined Rudolf's toast, before proceeding to offer him food and a place at the fire.

Reidar hung back, observing all that passed. The only person in his thoughts was Rudolf, and whether he would prove to be his staunchest ally or his greatest enemy. Only time would tell.

Seventeen

Cook shoved a covered bowl into Sativa's hands. "Here. Take the captain his dinner."

Sativa almost dropped it in surprise. "The captain?"

Cook made an exasperated sound. "Yes, Captain Zydrunas, the man who commands this ship and crew. He doesn't come and fetch his food like the rest of the men – we must take it to him. And tonight, we means you. I'm far too busy to wait on him."

"Where do I take it?" Sativa asked. The

captain was usually on deck, keeping his eye on everyone, but try as she might, Sativa could not remember ever seeing the man eat.

"His cabin, of course. Knock on the door, and if there is no answer, leave it outside the door. And be quick about it, for the captain prefers his food hot."

"Then if he does not answer, I should take it into his cabin, and leave it on the table," Sativa said thoughtfully. "For if he does not like his food cold, surely – "

"Do not enter the captain's cabin," Cook interrupted. "No matter what you hear, or what you think. Either he will open the door and take the food from you, or you leave it outside. You hear me?"

Sativa mumbled a resentful response. Even after weeks at sea, she still did not take orders gladly. Cook never seemed to care if she scowled, as long as she obeyed. The other men were not so happy about it, but the more she kept out of their way, the less they had to dislike.

So she carefully carried the bowl down the ladder, trying to ignore the rumbling of her belly as she inhaled the savoury smell of the captain's dinner. When she finally found her way ashore, she would spend the first week eating everything in sight, she was sure of it. She'd even settle for some of the stuff she'd eaten aboard the *Wydra*, for that was at least food, and not the swill Cook served to this crew.

But in the meantime, she made her way to the captain's cabin. This was where he kept Nekane. Perhaps she would answer the door and Sativa could tell her about her escape plan, so Nekane might be ready when the time came.

Cradling the bowl in her arms, Sativa knocked on the door, then waited. And waited.

Surely Nekane would come to the door. Where else could she be? Unless the captain had her pinned beneath him…Sativa swallowed. Last night she'd barely slept as the rhythmic pounding from the captain in this cabin above her hadn't stopped from dusk until dawn. Surely he couldn't be at it again now. Sativa might be a virgin, but even she knew men didn't last that long in bed. A man who could manage lovemaking for more than a few minutes was a miracle by most standards, and Captain Zydrunas did not seem the type to be blessed by angels. Sold his soul to the devil, more like.

She knocked again, louder this time. Perhaps the captain had not heard her over the noises he was making.

But she received no response this time, either.

Perhaps if she brought the man his dinner, he might leave Nekane alone for a little while, Sativa told herself. She could say she'd heard him tell her to enter.

She pushed against the door, but it didn't budge. She set her shoulder against it, and shoved harder. Still nothing. It wasn't until she looked down that she saw the bolt, fastening the door shut from the outside. Nekane couldn't answer the door because she couldn't get out, Sativa realised. No wonder she hadn't seen the other woman since they'd boarded the ship. She was a prisoner in the captain's cabin.

Sativa reached down to pull the bolt open.

"What in the devil's name are you doing, boy?" a voice roared.

Sativa jumped, barely managing to keep her grip on the bowl. "Bringing you your dinner, sir," she said, shrinking against the wall to put more space between her and the captain. In these close confines, he seemed bigger than ever.

He snatched the bowl out of her hands. "I'll take that. And you are never to enter my cabin, you understand? Never. It's forbidden."

"But what about the lady?" Sativa said before she could stop herself.

The captain's face loomed so close she could see the individual strands of his blue-black beard. "What about the lady, boy?" He spat the last word as though it was some sort of epithet.

Sativa swallowed. She had to say something. "Maybe she'd like a bit of company. It must be lonely in there by herself all day," she managed to say.

Captain Zydrunas snorted. "Never you mind about the lady, boy. She has all the company she'll ever need from me."

He unbolted the door, opened it just wide enough to let him through, and vanished into the cabin, slamming the door shut behind him.

Sativa craned her neck, straining to see, but there was nothing but darkness before the door closed the view off for good. But it also meant she was out of the captain's sight. She clenched her fists, swearing she would find a way off this ship. The captain could not always be near his cabin. One day, she'd find a way to sneak in and speak to Nekane. One day, they'd both be free.

Eighteen

Steel rang against steel as Reidar blocked another blow with his sword. And another, and another. Loath though he was to admit it, the slight man before him was too fast for him. His blows lacked Reidar's strength, or perhaps he was just holding back, hoping to tire Reidar enough to win. Reidar could not let that happen.

But not even a king is infallible, he realised as something stung his side. Reidar knew better than to look down to investigate the wound, for if it did not kill him, then the next blow would, if he did not block it. With a roared oath, he renewed his attack, praying his foe would fall before he did. The trickle of blood down his side told him time was of the essence now.

"Protect the king!" a voice bellowed.

Reidar lifted his shield to take the next blow, but the man's axe met steel instead. His eyes widened in surprise, meeting Reidar's gaze. So Reidar saw his eyes glaze over as the second sword withdrew from the man's throat, turning a live enemy into a dead one.

"Thank you," Reidar said shakily.

Rudolf lifted his bloody sword in salute. "Any time, my king." He turned away to fight another foe.

Hours or maybe minutes later, Reidar could not be sure, he called the end of the battle. There were few left alive from the raiding party, and his own men had wounds that needed tending.

The slice to his side had done little more

than scrape the skin, Reidar was happy to discover, so once his wound was washed and bandaged, he had time to walk around their camp and speak to his men. Rudolf's steel helm had been so dented in the battle it took two men to pull it off his head, only to find his face covered in blood from a broken nose.

While one of the men cleaned up Rudolf's face, amid a lot of swearing from the patient, Reidar approached him. He dismissed the healer and tended Rudolf himself so that he might speak with the man privately.

"Why did you do that? Call the men to me during the battle?" Reidar asked.

Rudolf shrugged, then swore as the movement pained him. "Because it's a man's duty to protect his king. We're yours to command. There's no doubt in anyone's mind that you can fight as well as any man here, and none of us question your right to rule. But if you fall in battle, I'll have to sit on your seat, and Aunt Regina will never forgive me."

"What, you don't want a crown, cousin?"

Reidar forced out a laugh to make the question sound more flippant than it was.

Rudolf smiled, or grimaced – it was hard to tell. "Right now, I want nothing on my head at all. My ears are still ringing from the blow to my helm. I would much rather a cup of ale than a crown."

Reidar wasn't sure if this was a jest or not. It certainly wasn't an answer. Nevertheless, he called for ale for his cousin.

Rudolf seized Reidar's arm and pulled him close so that no one might hear his words. "If you die without an heir, your crown falls to me anyway. We both know this. Go back to your castle, get yourself a bride, and put a boy in her belly. Several, if you can. Let me lead the army in your stead."

Reidar met Rudolf's blackened and bloodshot eyes. There was truth in them, he was sure of it. But something hidden, too. "To what end, cousin? You have a plan, I am sure of it."

"All men plan, but not all plans bear fruit.

Rest assured, mine do not need you to die here on a battlefield like my father and yours. I want this kingdom secure as much as you do. These raiders and would-be usurpers must die!" Rudolf shook his fist in the direction the surviving raiders had retreated.

Something in Rudolf's voice urged Reidar to trust him. Maybe not completely, but for now. Reidar nodded slowly. "Very well. Will the men follow you?"

Rudolf laughed. "They did today. They're loyal men who serve their king. Why would they not?"

Reidar had to admit his cousin was right. And, if his count was correct, his envoy should have brought Sativa to Viken by now. At this very moment, she could be waiting for him in the very tower he'd built for her.

"Tonight we toast our victory, and tomorrow I shall return," Reidar said.

Rudolf winked. "Share a drink with your wife at your wedding feast, cousin, for I doubt this war will be over by then, and I wouldn't want you to delay on my account. We'll drink your health when we hear of it."

"I'll send a cask of ale from my cellars. The very best," Reidar promised. And he would. When he had Sativa safely in his arms, he would want the whole kingdom to celebrate.

Nineteen

Sativa hugged the mast as she did the one part of her job she actually liked – keeping watch. Captain Zydrunas' *Barbe* had a sort of man-sized bucket built at the top of the mast for the lookout, and Sativa would stay there all day, if she could.

It also meant she'd be the first to spot...

"Land!" she cried, pointing. It looked like a just a shadow on the horizon, but it was growing larger, and she was sure...

"Check and see if the boy is right," Captain

Zydrunas ordered.

Sativa's face grew hot. Last time she'd thought she'd spotted land, it had been a bank of storm clouds. They'd steered well away from them, but the waves had been big enough for her to realise why the lookout had what the crew called a crow's nest: when the ship canted from one side to the other, it was easy for a lookout to fall into the sea and be lost, like the last cabin boy. Sativa had hung on with all her strength and stayed aboard. But today, she was sure she was right. And if she was, it would soon be time to go.

One of the younger men, barely older than Sativa herself, scaled the mast and peered in the direction she'd pointed. "The boy's right!" he shouted.

She was nameless to them, and she'd resolved they'd remain nameless to her, too. Pirate scum such as these did not deserve to be remembered. The moment she arrived on land, she would do her best to forget everything about them.

"That's the coast of Viken. You can see the Sea Tower on the cliff!"

Sativa stared across the sea, hungry for a glimpse of it. Was this the tower Reidar had promised to build for her?

But no matter how long she looked, she couldn't see it. Perhaps when they got closer.

The captain gave orders to make for Viken, and Sativa was ready to dance for joy. Perhaps she wouldn't need to steal a boat at all. Instead, she could simply walk ashore once they docked and vanish into the town. Once she was in Reidar's kingdom, surely his people would help her find him.

By the time the sun sank beneath the western waves, they were no closer to the shadowy land Sativa couldn't wait to call home, and she sank into her hammock distinctly dissatisfied.

Morning brought a renewal of hope, as she started to discern the shapes of trees and then buildings upon the shore.

"Search for somewhere we can go ashore

for water," the captain directed. "We're running low."

They weren't headed for a port after all, Sativa realised with a sinking heart. Then she would have to make a run for it when she found the opportunity. When they went ashore for water, perhaps, or at night, if no suitable stream was found.

All day they watched, sailing so close to shore Sativa could count the sheep and cows on the cliffs. Alas, the streams they did find were too hard to reach, and so they sailed on. More than once, she'd been tempted to dive from the bow and swim ashore, but she knew she would not succeed with everyone watching the shore so closely. So many men, bigger and stronger than she was, could surely swim faster, too, and they would haul her back to be punished.

She'd seen some of the punishments aboard the *Barbe* – men's backs whipped to jelly for drinking more than their share of ale, or stealing food from the captain's stores. If the captain knew how much she'd stashed away for her escape…Sativa shuddered. That was why she kept her supplies hidden, where no one could be certain who they belonged to.

Supplies she would need to retrieve tonight, before she left the ship forever.

When Cook sent her to the hold for dinner ingredients, she knew this would be her best chance to empty her cache. The dried sausages she stuck down her hose, where they'd be hidden under her tunic. She'd lost weight while working on the ship, so her tunic hung looser than it should. That would work in her favour tonight, though, for if she cinched her belt tight around her waist, she could tuck the wineskin down the front of her tunic and no one would be any the wiser. A small, cloth-wrapped cheese made up the rest of her supplies, which were already heavier than she was used to. Sativa was tempted to leave the wine, but unless she could replace it with coin, it might be the only thing of value she could trade when she got ashore. So, the wine stayed, curved against her belly as the leather warmed until it felt like part of her own skin.

She collected what Cook had asked for and lugged the lot up the ladder to the galley, where she could hear the captain roaring accusations at his crew.

He'd discovered the missing sausages, Sativa realised with a sinking heart. And he intended to keep haranguing them until the culprit came forward, when they'd all have to watch his punishment. Sativa muttered, "I shall be back. I think I dropped something," to Cook before she fled below decks.

Instinct told her to run and hide, but Sativa ignored it. She would run, yes, but not to somewhere aboard the *Barbe*. No, it was time to go, and now would be the best time to smuggle Nekane out of the captain's cabin, while he was busy.

Remembering the darkness last time, she took a lantern with her to the cabin. She set it on the floor as she worked the bolt open, then pushed open the door.

If the captain knew she was here…she didn't know what he would do. But by the time he found out, she and Nekane would be well away.

She stepped inside the room, holding her breath as she edged around the furnishings she could barely discern in the dim light filtering through the partially open door. "Nekane?" she whispered.

No answer.

What she really needed was the lantern that she'd left outside.

Swearing inwardly at her own stupidity, Sativa turned to retrieve it.

Just in time to see the door click shut, enveloping her in darkness.

Twenty

"Where is she? Spit it out, man!" Reidar said.

Sir Edwin ducked his head. "I cannot say, Your Majesty. Nor can King Boreslas, her father. I went to Kasmirus, as you commanded, and told him I was there to escort your bride home to you. For a week, he treated me as an honoured guest, holding feasts and hunting parties, while I waited for him to produce the girl. It wasn't he who told me, but some of his courtiers, that the girl was missing. She'd disappeared on the night of the huge celebration they held for the defeat of their dragon. The king sent men all over the kingdom, looking for her, but they've found nothing. She just disappeared." He looked like he wanted to continue, but closed his mouth.

Reidar was having none of it. "What are you not telling me, Edwin?"

Edwin seemed to struggle for a moment, before he relented. "There were tales, each more fantastical than the last. Some said they'd seen the princess marry the dragonslayer, some lord or other. But he's married to some lady from Queen Margareta's court, so that cannot be true. Others say her fairy godmother whisked her away, but no one has seen a fairy godmother in the city since the girl's christening. Some say she was kidnapped, but no one saw anything. The girl has lived all her life within the castle walls — sheltered, cared for, wanting for nothing. She had no reason to run away, and yet that is the excuse the king himself gave when he finally admitted she was gone. That or she was kidnapped."

The girl he'd known would not have run away from anything. Yet how could a girl be kidnapped from her own castle without anyone seeing it happen? "Someone must have seen something," Reidar growled. He leaped to his feet and prowled behind his seat, unable to sit still.

"Perhaps they did, Your Majesty, but you must understand..." Edwin coughed. "The whole city was drunk, sire. Celebrating. They had lived in terror of the dragon for years. It devoured all of the king's other daughters. Terrorised the countryside. And then a man brought the king the beast's head. Wine and ale ran like water that night. No one remembers what they did, let alone anyone else. They are not so different from us, truly. It was like one of our grandest victory feasts. The dragon could have come back to life and whisked away the princess, and no one would have noticed a thing!"

Reidar would like to think his men would have lifted their swords to defend the girl, no matter how much ale they'd consumed. "Someone has seen her, and someone must know where she is," he said, slowing his pacing. "Offer a reward for information about her whereabouts. More if they can bring her here safely. Unharmed."

Edwin raised despairing eyes to meet Reidar's gaze. "Her father already has. He has heard nothing. He fears she may be dead, like her sisters."

No. Reidar would not believe it. His bride was alive, and she would be found. "Find her, Edwin," he said finally. "Take what ships you need, and scour the coast. Bring her to me alive, and I will shower you in riches. And if she is not..." He swallowed, not wanting to allow the thought into his head. "If she no longer lives, bring me what remains of her body. I will still reward you, but it will be with a heavy heart."

"And if I cannot? What if the girl's body lies in the depths of the sea, or in the belly of some beast? Or what if she does not wish to be found?"

Reidar sighed, suddenly tired. "Just find her, Edwin." What sort of madness had infected the man? Of course she wanted to be found.

Twenty-One

Sativa's breath caught in her throat. Perhaps someone had seen the door open, and simply pushed it shut. She would have heard if someone had come in, because if anyone found her…

Light burst upon her, an unshuttered lantern that to her dark-adjusted eyes appeared brighter than the sun.

"They say there is a hell made for the inquisitive, and they surely have a place for you, girl," a male voice said.

Sativa blinked away her blindness, then wished she hadn't. Captain Zydrunas stood before the closed door, holding her lantern high.

"The door was open, and I went to close it, but it smelled musty in here, so I thought I might tidy the place a little..." Sativa began, then trailed off. There was an unpleasant smell in the cabin. Not musty so much as rotten. Like decaying meat.

"What part of forbidden do you not understand?" the captain asked.

Sativa reddened. "I heard a woman call for help, sir, and my father told me an honourable man should help a lady in need."

The captain laughed. "You are a terrible liar, but it does not matter."

Sativa refused to back down. "I did hear a woman call for help." Not tonight, but before. Why was Nekane so silent now?

"You did not, but before this night is over, you will," the captain said, his teeth gleaming in the lamplight.

Sativa's thoughts raced. If she could get the captain away from the door, then perhaps she could get out, run up the ladder, and dive over the side into the water. She could swim to shore. She just had to make it to the water. And get the captain to move. "Then let her speak now."

Sativa hoped he would cross the room and reveal where he'd hidden Nekane. She must be gagged or unconscious, to be so silent. Sativa wouldn't be silent if there was even a slim chance of there being help at hand.

"You mean the lady from your ship? She will never speak again." The captain extended his arm and pointed.

Sativa glanced at the bunk. For a moment, she did not understand what she saw in the grey shadows. Then she realised what she saw was no shadow, lying upon the red coverlet, but a corpse. Naked and bloated, Nekane's skin had turned grey.

Sativa fought the bile rising up in her throat. This was the source of the smell. She'd been dead for days. A week or more, surely. A week in which the captain had…had…

The bile won.

Twenty-Two

"Your mother still hates me," Rudolf announced as he strode into Reidar's solar.

Reidar set down his quill. "What are you doing here? Isn't there a war you're supposed to be fighting?"

Rudolf shrugged, then stretched out on the bench beneath the window, sitting in the only patch of sun. The cat whose seat he'd usurped hissed at him, then trotted off.

"It seems word has spread among your neighbours that your throne is not worth the price they will pay to get it. That, or they are running out of men to send against us. The last two war bands we encountered took to their heels and ran away. Like rabbits!" He laughed.

"That still doesn't answer my question. Why are you here?"

"Your men can chase rabbits for a few days without me. I came to find out why you didn't send the ale you promised. Did the wedding guests drink it all, or did you just forget about us?" Rudolf sat up and peered into the corners of the room. "And where is your lovely bride? Or has she locked herself in her room, terrified after spending her wedding night with your mighty cock?"

Bawdy jokes about Sativa sat ill with Reidar. "She has not yet arrived."

Rudolf only laughed harder. "So she's heard tales about your cock and fled in fear before you can stick it in her?"

Reidar reddened. "I do not know what she's heard. I haven't seen her since she was a child. Do not jest about my bride, cousin. I warn you." Doubt gnawed at him for the first time. Crudity aside, had she heard something about him that would make her not want the marriage any more? Not want him?

"Consider me warned. You used to like jokes, Reidar. Has kingship turned you so serious that you can no longer laugh?" Concern wrinkled Rudolf's brow, all traces of humour gone.

"Not about Sativa, no. She has disappeared from her father's court, and no one has seen her since. He's sent search parties. I've sent search parties. I've even offered a reward for her safe return. She has simply vanished, as though some foul sorcery is at work betwixt her kingdom and mine." Reidar released a weighty sigh. "And while I worry for her wellbeing, my mother reminds me hourly that I need an heir. I think she has paraded every highborn girl in the kingdom before me, and quite a few not so highborn, too. More than anything, she wants me to wed. The longer Sativa is missing, the more I begin to think she might be right. Maybe I need an heir more than an alliance with Boreslas."

"Kings break betrothals every day, and alliances, too. What is so special about this girl that you cannot?"

Reidar eyed his cousin. Would the man think him weak if he confessed the truth? No one else knew. Time to test his cousin's loyalty. "In truth, I do not know. I made promises as a child, and so did she. I am loath to break my word, for what honour is there in that? I might not have seen her in years, but I have dreamed of her more nights than I can count. Not the child I knew then, but as though I watched her. She learned to ride like she was born to the saddle, and hunted with her father's court before she could lift a bow. She never made a kill, but she loved the chase. She would teach her sisters, teaching them to write so they might manage kingdoms of their own, when they were queens in their own right. And lately, I have dreamed of her flying through the air at a great height. Ships below her, or sometimes the sea. She's not an angel, but...it's like nothing I can explain. I know she lives, and she is coming to me. For weeks I have known this, and still she is not here!"

Rudolf nodded slowly. "There is some magic at work, then. A bond between you that perhaps only death can break. Tell me, what does this girl of yours look like?"

"As fair as the sun," Reidar replied. "No matter how many other girls my mother places before me, the only face I see is hers. A face I do not know!"

"You have it bad, cousin. I hope she is worth the wait. And, in a similar vein, I have a confession to make, too."

Reidar raised an eyebrow. "Oh?"

Rudolf's smile was rueful. "Will you ever release me to return to the Southern Isles?"

"You don't want to be king?" Reidar blurted out.

Rudolf laughed softly. "I never said that. I asked if you would let me go home."

Reidar wasn't sure what to say. "But you are

my heir. Until I have a son, that is. And there is this war..."

"The war will never be over, but your neighbours will learn, and so will your own men. There are leaders among them, and they are loyal to you. There will come a time when you don't need me. You will choose a bride – whether your betrothed or some other girl – and there will be children to take your place. When that time comes, I ask you to let me return home."

There was no laughter in Rudolf's eyes now. Only pain.

"Why?" Reidar asked hoarsely.

"Like you, I dream of a girl. A woman, now. I made promises, which I intend to keep." Rudolf smiled sadly. "Oh, not like you. There is no betrothal between us. But yours is not the only war – and other kings have seen the richness of the Southern Isles, wishing to conquer them for their own. There are many lords of the islands, and some call themselves kings, but they recognise one man as their leader, and he has no sons. Only daughters."

Now Reidar understood. "You want to be king of the Southern Isles, and take one of the daughters for your queen." A king in his own right. "But the Southern Isles still belong to Viken."

"Not for long, if the other kings have their way. I mean to take a small force and together with the men of the isles, claim them for my own. I will still bend the knee to you, of course, but without someone to lead them, the isles will fall." Rudolf clenched his hands into fists. "I will not let that happen."

"What is there about these isles that inspires such passion?" Reidar asked.

Rudolf coughed. "My passion is not for the isles, but for the lady. The isles are her birthright."

Winning lands a world away for the love of a woman. Well. Reidar had never expected this.

"When my wife gives birth to a son, you are free to return," Reidar said. "I'm sure you will find men here willing to flock to your cause, if only for the adventure of a trip to the Southern Isles. But do not take too many, for I will not lose the war here so you can have your woman!"

Rudolf bowed low. "As Your Majesty commands."

"Is she fair, this lady?" Reidar asked, unable to resist.

"Her skin is fair, but her hair reminds me of a bonfire blaze. Portia is like no lady I have ever met." It was Rudolf's turn to sigh, as his eyes turned to the south-west.

Reidar laughed. "What a pair we are, mooning after girls who are not yet our wives. But, God willing, they will be. What will we do while we wait for the time to be right?"

Rudolf shrugged. "What men always do, I suppose. Make war. Make merry. Make our mothers despair of us ever growing up."

Reidar clapped his cousin on the back. "Sounds like a fine plan. I have another. We have not celebrated your return yet, and

Mother is always pestering me to hold another feast. She wants only to parade more maidens before me, of course, but what of it? It is many months since I have gone hunting, and the boars are fat this time of year. Let's put together a hunting party on the morrow, and on our return, there shall be a welcome feast in your honour."

"I have not tasted Viken boar since I left your shores, and the pigs in the Southern Isles cannot compare. Let us forget women and the worries of your kingdom for a few days, and enjoy the hunt!" Rudolf grinned. "Thank you, cousin. It is good to be back."

It was good to have him back, Reidar thought. Now all he needed was Sativa, and he could be happy.

Twenty-Three

Sativa wiped her mouth with the back of her hand. Her mother would despair if she knew, but Sativa had no handkerchief here.

"Why?" she whispered.

Captain Zydrunas shrugged. "Like most women, she was too noisy for her own good. Inquisitive. Complaining. And tears…ugh." He shuddered.

An arrow of remorse shot through Sativa's heart. She had disliked Nekane's constant tears and mourning, too, but she'd never wanted to kill her. She was a widow, and widows were allowed to weep.

"You are a monster," Sativa said. It was a calm statement of fact.

Why wouldn't he move away from the door? she raged inwardly.

"All men are monsters in their own way," he said loftily. He nodded at Nekane, and there was considerable pride in his voice as he added, "She said I was like a dragon."

"It was no compliment," Sativa shot back. "Dragons are mindless beasts, who don't know the difference between a sheep and a woman in wool. They burn and devour because they don't know any better. Men are more than that."

At least, the men in her father's court had been. Those aboard the *Wydra*. And Reidar.

"I would take a dragon over you any day," she added, more to bait him than anything else.

It worked. He moved away from the door, but only to approach her. "But you will take me, girl. She could not stop me, and nor will

you."

He would kill her, and defile her dead body. Horror made her jaw drop, but some other instinct told her to draw her dagger. She did.

Zydrunas set the lantern on the table, and drew his own knife. Easily thrice as long as hers, the steel blade seemed to drink the light instead of reflecting it. He thrust across the table, and Sativa barely managed to dodge the wicked point. Her arm seemed to have a life of its own, driving down to slice his hand.

Zydrunas swore. "Little bitch. I was going to cut your throat, nice and easy, but you'll have no quick death from me now. You shall suffer."

Faster than Sativa believed possible, he whipped his blade to the side, slashing it across her belly. Warm liquid gushed out, soaking her tunic, but the wound came with no pain. Sativa pressed her hands to her belly, and they came away red. She turned horrified eyes on the captain as she backed away.

He made no move to follow her now. He

knew as well as she did that she was as good as dead.

Instead, he crossed to the bed. He lifted Nekane's corpse in his arms, and she flopped like some obscene rag doll as he carried her over to the bench Sativa recognised as a privy. He kicked open the lid and forced the body in, feet first. He managed to get her halfway in, before she stuck, her torso sticking out of the privy like a giant glove puppet.

"She can watch you die, then," he said, forcing the corpse's eyes open. Gore dribbled down Nekane's bloated face — there was nothing recognisable about her eyes any more. The widow was with her husband, now.

Doubled over in the corner, one arm pressed to her belly, Sativa still pointed the knife at him, but for how long, she wasn't sure. "You deserve to die," she hissed.

He laughed. "Not today. Today, I get a new bride in my bed." He crossed to the door and yanked it open. "I will return when you are finished fighting, but still warm." And out he went, closing the door behind him. He drove the bolt home, a final nail in Sativa's coffin.

She collapsed on the floor, spent. What was there left to fight for, now? Not even she could fight death.

Twenty-Four

"There is a particularly fine beast I've seen in the southern woods, sire," one of the woodsmen said. "Powerful fierce, like he's possessed by some devilish spirit. We stay in the northern parts while he's about."

Reidar nodded. They couldn't have brought him better news. "Just the sort of challenge I'd like," he said, tossing a purse of coin at the man's feet. "Stay out of the forest for a few days, while we hunt. You will know when the beast is caught, for there will be a feast at the castle."

Both men bowed. "Thank you, sire. We will."

Reidar had given them enough money to feed two families for a week, or perhaps a little more. Surely that would be long enough. A week free of the cares of his kingdom, or worry for Sativa. Bliss, surely.

He called to his men, and the spearbearers, to follow him into the forest.

A quick fight, a bit of spilled blood, and victory to follow. Truly the sport of kings.

He kicked his horse into a gallop, and set off between the trees.

Twenty-Five

He'd left the lantern to taunt her, Sativa was sure of it. There was not even a window to look or squeeze out of – no exit but the bolted door. Her only escape was death, like poor Nekane.

Who was still stuck in the privy, poor woman.

Sativa's hands were sticky and red, and her tunic and hose were soaked. She hadn't known a body could lose this much blood and still live. And yet…still she felt no pain.

Did that mean she was near the end? The end where the devil of a captain would do things to her corpse?

Never.

There had to be a way out.

She glanced at Nekane. Perhaps the dead widow did hold the answer.

As Sativa approached her, the stench grew, until she had to haul her tunic over her nose to bear it. This was the smell of death, though, and not the privy beneath her. And if it was anything like the privy aboard the *Wydra*, it let out into the water.

Sativa swallowed, took hold of the corpse's shoulders, and shoved. No, the body was stuck. She studied it for a moment, then realised why. Gingerly, she pried the woman's arms out of the hole and lifted them. The body slid so fast it almost took her with it, but Sativa grabbed onto the lip of the privy in time to save herself.

Save herself from what? A watery death was better than what waited for her here.

Something tumbled from her tunic, and she instinctively reached to catch it before it fell. Too late, she realised she could be grasping for her own innards, and drew her hand back.

To her surprise, a slashed wineskin dropped into the privy, landing in the darkness with a splash.

A slashed…but the wineskin had been full. Sativa fumbled at her soaked tunic, trying to undo her belt to see the skin underneath, and the wound that should be there. The one that would kill her. The wound that…

…wasn't there.

The stupid captain had stabbed the wineskin instead. But he'd soon be back, to do horrible things to her still-warm corpse. More than ever, she needed to get out.

She eyed the privy. It was the only way.

Sativa perched on the edge, uttering a prayer that she might reach shore safely. And not get stuck.

She took a deep breath, and let go.

Twenty-Six

The day ended without anyone sighting the boar, but Reidar was content. There'd been signs of the beast, and they were certainly in its territory now.

He shared a cup of ale with Rudolf by the fire as servants pitched his pavilion and prepared their meal.

"You should have seen your face. You were so certain you'd found the beast in the bushes, and that it would be your kill, when all the rest of us said we were too far north. Standing there like some ancient colossus…and out popped…a squirrel!" Reidar roared with laughter.

Rudolf didn't seem to find it as funny, though he did laugh. "You always were the better hunter. I left before I was old enough to join your father's hunting parties. It sounded big enough to be a boar!"

"Rudolph the great squirrel slayer!" Reidar howled. He laughed until his belly ached. He had not felt this free in years.

"Tomorrow will be better," Rudolf said. "You may take the beast, and when you miss, then I'll take my shot."

Reidar spat out his ale. "I do not miss!"

Rudolf smiled. "We shall see, cousin. We shall see."

The evening was a merry one, with plenty of ale and even a little singing around the fire, until someone reminded them all that singing would only drive the beast away, not bring it within range of their spears. They quietened after that.

When they retired for the night, Reidar felt an inexplicable chill. No one else seemed to notice, so he merely called for some extra furs and told himself that would be an end to it.

The cold seemed to have settled in his bones, and it took some time to dispel, but eventually he forgot he was in the forest and may as well have been in his chamber at home, he was so warm.

Rudolf was right. Tomorrow would be better. A sense of wellbeing washed over him, like he'd been engulfed by one of the waves he could hear crashing on the not-too-distant shore, and he drifted off into a dream where Sativa sat at his side instead of his cousin, and after they shared a cup of ale, they shared a kiss. The kiss lasted until he carried her to his bedroll and their night together was bliss. Oh, what a dream.

If only it were true.

$$Twenty\text{-}Seven$$

Sativa gasped as the freezing water engulfed her, her last breath before the sea closed over her head. She kicked off the side of the ship, heading for the wavering light at what she thought was the surface. She burst into cold air and wished she hadn't, as the breeze turned out to be colder than the water.

Dusk had fallen, but there was enough light to see the darkness that was the shore. Praying that no one aboard the ship saw her, she set out for land.

Her hose and boots drank seawater like a drowning man, weighing her down. Determined not to drown when she was so close to her destination, Sativa stripped off the offending items. Only modesty made her keep her tunic. That and the camouflage it offered her pale skin as the moon rose.

An eternity passed, as she stroked for shore. Kicking, pulling with her arms, taking breath after breath and spitting out salt water as the waves taunted her, but the beach drew ever closer.

Then a wave picked her up and her arms windmilled wildly as she tried to paddle out of it, but to no avail. The wave broke, plunging her beneath the water until she grazed the sandy seabed. Gasping, Sativa kicked off the bottom, only to find that her head broke the surface before her feet had left the seafloor. She staggered ashore, barely believing she'd made it. She wanted to lie on the sand and sleep for a week, but she couldn't. Not while she was still so close to the ship. Still visible to them, perhaps.

Her legs felt like they carried their own ballast, they were so heavy, as she dragged herself up the beach and into the trees. A breath of wind was enough to send her teeth chattering as her bones turned to solid ice. Still she trudged on. There would be no wind once she was deep enough into the forest.

A few steps in, then a few more. Soon, she could no longer see the beach, but she could hear the waves. Still she walked. She would continue until she couldn't any more, and then she would lie down and sleep.

Moonlight was dim between the trees, so she stumbled often, but Sativa refused to stop. It looked like it was growing lighter ahead. Light could only mean people, and civilisation. Someone who could help her.

A large fire sat in the clearing, sending up a prayer of smoke into the sky. Sativa thanked whoever had lit it, and approached as close as she dared, holding out her hands to warm them. She had nothing left to trade but the small cheese, wrapped in its now salt-stained cloth, but she would offer it gladly if it meant getting warm and dry again.

"You kept me waiting," a grumpy voice greeted her. Oh, the voice was old and scratchy, too, but the elderly woman wanted her irritation known.

"Please forgive me," Sativa said politely. She had heard that old women who lived too long sometimes lost their wits, and she had been taught to be polite to her elders.

A hunched figure stepped out of the shadows and straightened. "Your father taught you well, Princess."

Sativa squinted at the woman. "Do I know you?"

The woman cackled, then coughed. "Perhaps, perhaps not. I am too old to be your fairy godmother, in truth, but as my daughter is still learning to take my place, I wanted to see you one last time. I am Dalia."

Though the hem of her tunic was too short to do it properly, Sativa attempted a respectful curtsey. "I am honoured, Godmother Dalia."

"Come, girl. My visions said you would be hungry, and in need of a fire's warmth. You are not out of the woods yet."

Sativa did as her godmother bade her. For the first time in she couldn't remember how long, she ate her fill, and the food was good. But the wine was too strong, and she began to wish that she had not drunk so much of it, for her eyes started to close of their own accord.

Sativa blinked back drowsiness, wanting to ask the question that burned in her mind before she surrendered to sleep. "Godmother Dalia, thank you for your hospitality. I am grateful but…I must know one thing."

Dalia grinned, her eyes seeming to glow in the firelight. "Yes?"

Sativa fought to find the words that wouldn't make her question sound like an accusation. "Why are you here now? Why not earlier, when I was kidnapped by pirates, or locked in that room, or earlier still, when my father tried to marry me to a shoemaker?"

Dalia nodded. "Do you know what my powers are?"

"You are a seer," Sativa said. "I do not know what else."

"I sometimes see the future, yes, as I foresaw your sisters would die because of a creature that came out of the darkness, as a different darkness would swallow you, too, in time. I have a talent for curses, or I did. It's been many years since I cast one."

"So you saw the pirates, and the shoemaker, and everything else?" Sativa asked impatiently.

Dalia nodded once more. "I saw the pirates, and much of your flight from your father's court. Yes. The shoemaker…ah, young George's fate has little to do with yours. He was always destined for Melitta. He's my daughter's godson, you know."

Sativa's head hurt. There was so much she didn't understand. "But why are you here?"

Dalia blinked. "Because you need me, of course! If I weren't here, you'd freeze your little titties off in the forest and never find your way to that handsome king of yours."

King? "Reidar is a prince, not a king."

"When his father died, your Prince Reidar became king. He's eager for a queen, though, so you mustn't delay. Tonight, you may rest, but in the morning, you must find him."

Sativa couldn't seem to stay upright any more. Too tired. Her head rested on the ground and it was too comfortable to resist. "Will you show me the way?" she mumbled.

"No, dear, I'm too old to be traipsing around the forest. My friend will show you the way. As long as you follow her, you won't get lost."

"Oh, good," Sativa tried to say but she wasn't sure if she managed to get the words out before she fell asleep.

Twenty Eight

A shaft of sunlight tickled Sativa's eyelids as it passed. She pulled her blankets more closely about her, wondering why her chamber was so cold. The fire must have gone out in the night, or someone had left the shutters open. Probably her sister Stella, who liked to look up at the stars.

No, Stella was dead, devoured by a dragon, like the rest of her sisters. And Sativa could not be in her chambers, for she slept aboard a pirate ship, pretending to be a boy until the ship came close enough to shore to swim to safety.

Ugh. Swimming. Fighting the waves until they grew tired of her feeble flailing and flung her on the shore.

Now she remembered the night that had been. Or had it been a dream? Nekane, the crazy captain, and her future-seeing fairy godmother?

Sativa blinked her eyes open.

Last night's great bonfire had burned down to coals, and her one thin blanket did little to keep out the early morning chill.

"Mrow?"

Sativa stared in surprise at the source of the sound. A cat the colour of smoke sat beside the fire, licking at a package Sativa recognised – the cheese she'd stolen from the *Barbe*. The only food she had.

Sativa scrambled to her feet and attempted to shoo the animal away, but it only turned to hiss at her before returning to what was left of its meal. Precious little, she found, when she ventured close enough to see. No point in wasting her time for a bite or two of drowned cheese.

When the cat was finished eating, it sat to wash its fluffy fur, taking its time in a grooming ritual that could have satisfied a palace lap-cat, instead of this forest-born beast. When the beast's bath was done, it crossed the clearing and stopped to look back at Sativa. "Mrow?"

She shook her head at the expectant beast. "No. Dalia said to wait here for her friend, who would guide me."

"Mrow." Was it possible for a cat to look exasperated, or was Sativa simply imagining the expression on the cat's face?

She regarded the cat for a long moment. "I don't suppose you're a female cat? Dalia did say her friend was female, though surely she would have told me if she was feline, too."

"Mrow."

Sativa sighed. Try as she might, she'd never understand the cat's meaning. Being able to talk to beasts would be a useful gift around about now. If she was wrong about this...

Reluctantly, she dropped her blanket on the ground, shaping it into an arrowhead that pointed in the cat's direction. The direction she would follow the beast, though it might be folly, and the way Dalia's friend would have to go in order to find her if the cat was not the promised guide.

Swearing roundly at all the sharp sticks on the forest floor and herself for losing her boots in the sea, Sativa set off behind the cat.

Twenty-Nine

Reidar sat by the rekindled fire, a crust of bread in one hand and a cup of ale in the other as he broke his fast, while the rest of the hunting party readied themselves for the day. His pavilion was already packed away, but others were not as used to travelling as he and several tents still stood in the clearing.

Einar strutted around without his tunic, pointing at the scars on his chest that were hard to see beneath all the white hair, and telling the tales of how he got them to any man who'd listen, and quite a few who didn't.

Dag had brought a hound that he swore could sniff out boars better than any beast alive, and he had a leash around its neck, letting it lead him around the clearing, sniffing for signs for their quarry. So far, it had found and frightened two squirrels, twice Rudolf's score from yesterday.

Rudolf emerged from the trees, straightening his tunic. Another man who had to piss away a lot of last night's ale.

Reidar nodded at Dag and his dog. "What do you say, cousin? Shall we let the beast lead the way today?"

Rudolf shrugged.

"He has a scent! Sire, we should follow it!" Dag shouted.

Others caught his excitement and headed for their horses.

Reidar rose. "Why not? Let's ride. I fancy roast pork for my dinner."

Rudolf was close behind him. "A wager, cousin? That you will take home your heart's desire today?"

Reidar turned to stare at Rudolf. Such a strange thing to say. Almost as though the man knew what he'd dreamed last night. "There is no wager to make. I smell victory in the air today."

Behind him, Rudolf's voice said softly, in a tone so low Reidar suspected he wasn't supposed to hear: "We shall see. Stranger things have happened to kings while hunting. I suspect victory will not be yours on this day."

A chill closed around Reidar's heart, but he shook it off. Rudolf's words could be traitorous or prophetic, or mere nonsense he'd spouted to make mischief. Whatever the truth, it would out itself today, for one thing was certain – there was something different in the air. An expectation, a promise...of change. And he would embrace it.

Reidar leaped onto his horse's back. "Time for the hunt to begin!" he shouted.

And so it began.

Thirty

The damned cat was like water – endlessly running, while Sativa struggled to keep up. When Sativa stopped to rest or take a drink before crossing yet another stream, the animal would sit and stare at her, occasionally uttering that same, superior, "Mrow," that seemed to be all it could say.

Her feet hurt. No, all of her body hurt, and her belly added an extra growled protest at the absence of breakfast. In the tales she'd heard as a child, there were berries and all sorts of things to eat in the forest. So far, she'd seen nothing except her stolen cheese. The one the cat had eaten. Idly, she wondered if cats were edible.

As though the beast had heard her, the cat stopped, then scrambled up a tree.

Annoyed, Sativa stumbled to the trunk and peered up. "I can climb, too, you know."

Something exploded out of the underbrush behind her, setting the squirrels chittering away in fear.

Sativa risked a glance over her shoulder and almost screamed at the biggest tusked pig she'd ever seen, mere yards from her.

The beast hadn't noticed her yet, but if it did, one of those tusks could end her as surely as Captain Zydrunas' blade, and she had no skin of wine to save her now.

Sativa leaped, reaching for the nearest branch as her feet scrabbled for purchase on the tree trunk. Her muscles screamed as she climbed, but she knew she'd scream louder if the pig got to her.

Her bare feet slipped, leaving her hanging in the air a few inches from the ground.

The pig turned, and its small eyes seemed to glow red as it spied Sativa. The beast charged.

Her arms ached from trying to support her whole weight, but Sativa did her best to swing her body to the side in one last, desperate hope that she might gain a foothold on the slippery tree.

She managed to get out of the way of the pig's charge, but then it crashed into the tree. Hard. She lost her grip and came tumbling down on top of the animal's bristled back.

Instinctively, she hung on, but the rampaging pig was no tree. Still, she knew if she fell, it would trample her to death if it didn't gore her first. Yet she stayed on, and it took her a moment to realise why.

When the pig had hit the tree, its tusks had gotten stuck. It seemed more concerned at getting free of the tree than bucking her off.

She could climb off and run, but where would she go? Could she climb a different tree before the beast fought itself free?

Hadn't the shoemaker told a tale of how he'd slayed a boar by getting it stuck in a tree?

Before she could answer her own questions, the cat intervened.

As nimble as any sailor, it ran down the tree trunk, jumped on the pig's head, then used it as a springboard to leap away into the forest.

And in so doing, freed the beast's tusks.

Summoning some vague memory from the shoemaker's tales, Sativa yanked out her knife and plunged it into the beast's throat. Once, twice, before the squealing animal threw her off.

Sativa landed heavily on her back, but she leaped to her feet, ready to run.

But the pig didn't seem to see her any more as it danced around in a frenzy, trying to dislodge the knife in its throat as its lifeblood flowed out onto the forest floor.

Finally, it collapsed in a heap, sides heaving, as it turned baleful eyes on Sativa once more.

Fury forced her to hold her ground. "After

surviving pirates, I'm not about to surrender to a pig," she said.

The beast seemed to understand. It took one last breath, and then stilled.

Sativa waited for a long moment before she dared approach. She nudged the animal with her foot, but it didn't move. Only then did she lean down to retrieve her knife. The handle was slick with blood, and it took her a few tries to pull it out. She succeeded on the fourth attempt, only to have a gush of blood spatter her with gore.

Sativa glanced down. Between the wine stains and the blood, she didn't think Melitta would want her torn tunic back.

Her belly growled in agreement.

Sativa wanted to laugh. How she could still be hungry while looking at the bloody pig, she wasn't sure, but it was a pig. Pigs meant pork and bacon and ham and all sorts of things that would make a lovely breakfast. She'd have to butcher it first and work out how to cook it, but just the thought of roast pork made her willing to try.

Hooves thudded behind her. Lots of them.

Fearing the pig's herd had come to seek their revenge, Sativa whirled, knife in one hand, and murder in her eyes.

<h1 style="text-align:center">Thirty-One</h1>

"This way!" Dag cried, urging his horse after the dog.

Reidar had long since come to believe there was no pig at all, a thought some of the others had muttered aloud, but he was loath to call off a chase when he was enjoying himself. So he followed Dag and the others followed after.

The dog went mad, almost dragging the leash out of Dag's hand. Dag's horse reared back, and the man had a good deal of trouble getting both beasts under control. In the confusion, Rudolf moved ahead.

"What's the beast found this time?" Reidar asked. "Another squirrel, perhaps?"

The others laughed. All but Rudolf.

Rudolf was strangely silent for a long moment, before he said, "The hound has found a pig, all right, and more besides."

"What do you mean?" Reidar said.

Rudolf beckoned, riding forward.

Reidar followed.

Not pigs, but men on horseback. Lots of them, armed and dressed like the warriors they were. They crowded into the clearing, and yet they held back, keeping their horses away from the pig carcass.

The girl she had been would have dropped the dagger and begged for help, but Sativa had not journeyed across the sea for nothing. She'd bury the blade in her own breast before letting any of these men touch her. So she brandished her knife and held her ground.

"There's your pig, cousin," one man said. "It seems the victor on the field is a girl today."

Laughter bubbled up from the other men.

"I'll thank you to keep your covetous hands off my pig," Sativa snapped. Her fury blazed bigger than the bonfire last night.

"This is the king's forest, his private hunting preserve, and he alone owns everything in it. Including that pig," the first man said calmly.

Sativa thought for a moment. She'd heard similar things at home, but there was more to it than that. "The beast charged at me. Tried to kill me. I vanquished my foe, which makes everything he owns forfeit to me. The pig might only have meat, but the meat is mine!"

Laughter died as the men surveyed the scene. The blood, the pig, the dagger in her hand. Lust began to smoulder in their eyes.

One man pushed forward, while the rest hung back. He stared hungrily at her chest.

Sativa glanced down. Her tunic left little to the imagination, and her necklace had fallen out. Carefully, she tucked the amber ring out of sight and tried to hold the worst rip together.

This only seemed to inflame the man further. "Back away, all of you," he said softly. "She is mine."

Sativa swallowed. "The first man to touch me will die like that pig." She jerked her knife at the carcass. "I belong to no man. Not even your king. Who owes me a bite of that beast, once his cooks are done with it."

<h1 style="text-align:center;">Thirty-Three</h1>

"Skadi," Rudolf breathed.

For a moment, Reidar saw what Rudolf did. The blood-spattered girl could have been a goddess from the old faith. Skadi, goddess of the hunt…but also the goddess of justice, vengeance and righteous anger.

"I belong to no man. Not even your king. Who owes me a bite of that beast, once his cooks are done with it."

Reidar laughed aloud at this girl's courage. Armed with a knife before a dozen mounted knights, she showed no fear whatsoever. But a girl who could take on a full-grown boar with nothing more than a dagger was a force to be reckoned with. A huntress indeed.

And yet...she seemed familiar somehow. Something about the proud set of her head, as she dropped neither bow nor curtsey as she met his gaze. Almost as though she considered herself his equal.

And there was that glimpse of gold, now hidden beneath her shift, that made him wonder all the more.

He slid down from his horse. "We will make camp here for the night," he announced. Reidar waited until he and the girl were alone before he added, "I will offer you a meal and a bed for the night, and on the morrow I will take you to the castle where the king lives. You can bring the pig, too, and I'll see that the castle kitchens prepare it properly. You can't ask for fairer than that."

She stared at him for a moment, as though reading his soul, then nodded. She crouched to wipe her blade on the grass before tucking it away. Only as she reached her full height once more did she fold her arms across her breasts, and Reidar realised that she must be freezing, wearing nothing but a shift.

He shrugged off his cloak and held it out. "Please take it. You must be cold."

Once again, she hesitated, before she accepted the cloak. "I thank you," she said.

He stood beside her in silence, though his curiosity burned fiercer than any fire. He had so many questions he wanted to ask that he wasn't sure which should be first.

When his servants seemed to take an inordinately long time setting up his pavilion, he decided to satisfy a tiny part of his curiosity.

"Show me what you wear around your neck," he said.

Her eyes seemed filled with fire. "What I wear around my neck is none of your business, sir."

So she did not know him, then. "What if I were to tell you that I am the king of these lands, and everything and everyone within my borders is my business?"

She sized him up. Finally, her shoulders seemed to relax and she said, "If what you say is true, then perhaps it is your business, after all." She drew a leather thong from beneath her shift, and held it up. Suspended from the cord was a silver ring with a yellow-gold stone.

A ring that would not fit on even Reidar's smallest finger, now, but he recognised it like it was yesterday.

"How did you come to have this?"

She tucked the necklace beneath her borrowed cloak. "If you are truly the king of these lands, then you already know the answer."

Sativa. Hope welled in his breast, but Reidar forced it back down. He couldn't be certain. Not yet. "This ring was given to a girl to whom I made a promise. Only she and I knew of it, though there was one other witness to my vow."

Her eyebrows rose. "There was?"

He almost laughed, but he managed to control himself. "One who is not likely to speak of it. He was the fattest pony I had ever beheld."

She laughed. "I'd forgotten about Philip. I gave him to my sisters soon after that, who spoiled him far more than I ever did. If horses ever receive a divine reward, then I hope he is reunited with them in heaven."

There was no doubt in Reidar's mind now. He'd found her, and he had no intention of letting her out of his sight until they were married.

"Sire, your tent is ready for you," a servant said, bowing low.

Reidar bowed to Sativa. "After you."

The servant looked surprised, but Reidar caught many startled glances aimed at the girl as they headed for his tent. For a moment, he saw what they did – a bedraggled girl in a torn shift, whose only protection was the king's cloak. They would look at her very differently when he crowned her as his queen. Reidar grinned.

Only Rudolf dared to put his thoughts into words. He bowed extravagantly in his cousin's direction. "I wish you a pleasurable night, Your Majesty, with such pleasant company. Your little goddess might be a beautiful woman under all the dirt." He eyed Sativa appreciatively.

"Put your eyes back in your head, man," Reidar snapped. "Don't you have a wife waiting for you on some island somewhere? This one's mine." He put a proprietary arm around Sativa and pushed her into his pavilion.

"If you are sure, cousin," Rudolf said, turning away. "My best wishes for your health and happiness, then."

Happiness. Yes. Reidar's smile returned, and he stepped into his tent.

Only to meet the point of Sativa's blade, aimed between his eyes.

"If you think I will allow you to kill me and rape my corpse, you are mistaken," she said fiercely.

Reidar's mouth dropped open. It was a long moment before he managed to say, "Honestly, neither of those things have ever crossed my mind. It sounds like you have endured quite an ordeal, Princess Sativa, since you left your father's castle. He's had men scouring the country for you, but it seems he underestimated you. Yet there is one thing I don't understand. Why are you here?"

"My father offered me as a prize to any man who could slay a dragon," Sativa said. "On the night he was to have me marry a shoemaker, I remembered a prior engagement."

Reidar laughed. "In that case, I offer you my protection, and my hospitality, for as long as you wish," Reidar replied. "Even my sword, to defend you against this shoemaker, should he come searching for you."

"He will not come searching for me. His heart lies elsewhere."

Reidar spread his arms wide. "Then what do you wish of me? If it is within my power, I will grant it, Princess."

For the second time, she tucked her knife away. Reidar hoped it would be the last, for this being threatened by women with weapons would take some getting used to.

"Years ago, you talked of a tower," she began cautiously.

Hope blossomed within him. "I promised a tower and a crown, to the woman who would become my queen," Reidar corrected.

For the first time, she smiled. "I'd settle for some water to wash with and a bed, then maybe a meal and something to wear that isn't covered in blood."

Reidar wanted to envelop her in his arms and swear to take care of her for the rest of her days. What had the girl been through to get here? Killing a boar with nothing but a knife. He couldn't have done it. Half foreign princess, half ancient goddess come to life, and every inch the woman of his dreams.

But her eyes were wary, as well they might be, for she did not know him yet.

"It will be as you command, Princess," he

said.

She lifted her chin. "I do."

Thirty-Four

As Sativa settled into the king's bed – without the king, for Reidar slept outside the tent, as he insisted her honour demanded – she let out a sigh of contentment. She'd washed away weeks' worth of salt and dirt as best she could with just a cloth and basin of water. She'd eaten a meal worth tasting for the first time in weeks. And she now wore a tunic without holes, as fine as Melitta's had once been before time and trouble had worn it to rags.

She was safe. Whatever happened next was

for Reidar to worry about, not her. No more pirates or perilous voyages or pea straw or pigs. Ever again.

She remembered the lust in his eyes, not unlike the look every man wore when he looked at a beautiful woman. What would it feel like to surrender to such a thing? Not the cruel hands of a man like Zydrunas, but the welcoming arms of Reidar. A king who could take what he wanted without asking, and yet he held back for honour's sake, or so he said.

He'd offered her his own cloak, his bed, his…everything. She'd crossed the seas to accept a man she barely knew, but she'd dreamed of for as long as she could remember. Could the dream match the reality?

His hands as he'd laid the cloak on her shoulders, wrapping its folds around her, still warm from his body. Strong and gentle, all at the same time. And reverent, too.

The look on his face as he'd brought her food. Not a servant – he'd carried the platter with his own hands, and shared it with her, for he'd brought enough for two. He'd pointed out the choicest morsels and insisted they were hers. The lust was gone, as though it had never been, replaced with tenderness. Did she imagine a little longing, too? Probably. But alone in her bed, nay, his bed, she let herself believe it. That Reidar longed for her the way she did for him.

Thoughts of him warmed her through the night, and in the cold morning, as well, as she mounted up behind Reidar for the ride back to the castle. At first, the heat of him between her thighs made her blush, but that was what she'd come for, hadn't she? To be his wife, to share his bed and his body and all that he could give her. So she held her head high, wrapped her arms around his hard torso, and hung on to the man who would be her husband.

All too soon, the forest gave way to farmland, and a castle appeared on the cliffs. Smaller than her father's, but above it loomed the most delightful sight of all — the Sea Tower, Reidar's promise.

"Thank you," she whispered, pressing her lips to his neck. "Thank you."

He reached back and cradled her head in his hand, as though he wanted to prolong the kiss. "I am a man of my word, Princess. I promise you that."

Not a princess for much longer. She had promised to be his queen, and Sativa would keep her word, as he'd kept his.

When they rode through the gate of her king's castle, Sativa couldn't suppress a smile as she surveyed her new home.

<h1 style="text-align:center">Thirty-Five</h1>

The warm woman at his back set him on fire. The grin on Reidar's face didn't fade for the whole ride home. Some of the other men winked knowingly, thinking they knew what had passed between him and Sativa. He let them believe what they liked. It was no dishonour for a Viken woman to take a lover, unless she had a husband. Sativa could have chosen any one of them to spend the night with, and Reidar would have had no right to complain. It would have sat ill with him, of course, especially if she decided she liked another man more than him...

Reidar shook his head. But she had chosen him, and no other man. He'd even offered her a horse of her own to ride, but she'd refused and insisted on riding with him. He couldn't tell her how thankful he was for that – the reassuring weight of her behind him, reminding him that everything was right in the world, now that she'd been found. When she was ready and fully recovered from her ordeal, she would name a date for their wedding, and the wedding night that would follow.

Then he would do things to her he'd only dreamed of – all of last night, in fact – as he worshipped her like the goddess she'd resembled. So what if it was sacrilegious? She would be his wife, the woman he'd vowed to honour and cherish. What was worship but an elevated mixture of the two?

All too soon, their ride ended as his castle loomed into view, with her tower standing sentinel above it. Reidar wondered what she would think of a castle so much smaller than her father's. Cold, grey stone instead of warm brick, perched on a clifftop over a turbulent sea, instead of sitting comfortably on a hilltop overlooking vast fields of prosperous farmland.

"I offer you the hospitality of my home, humble though it is," Reidar said. He held his breath, praying she would accept.

Sativa's arms tightened around him as her soft lips kissed his neck. "Thank you. Thank you."

Every bit of him wanted to turn around, take her in her arms and kiss her breathless. Kiss her until he was breathless, too. Reidar realised he had his hand on her face, and he'd half turned to do what he was dreaming about. Not yet, he told himself, forcing his hand to take the reins again.

"The king has returned! The king has returned!" someone shouted from the gate, and then they all took up the cry.

It wasn't a cry of triumph. Something was

wrong.

Hakon raced across the bailey and stopped, panting, as Reidar reined in his horse. "Raiders. A whole fleet of them, spotted from the Sea Tower this morning. Headed for the port. They should reach there soon after darkness, and if they do…"

Reidar understood. "With the army near the inland borders and our ships off helping King Boreslas with the search, they'll be defenceless. We'll go at once. Send any able bodied man you can spare after me."

"You're riding to war?" Sativa's voice asked near his ear.

Oh, by all that was holy, he'd forgotten her. But he didn't have time to explain.

"I must," he said, swinging her out of the saddle and onto the ground. "I will return when the battle is won, or the port is lost." He addressed Hakon. "Take her to the queen. Tell the queen to take care of her until my return." Reidar wheeled his horse around, ready to ride out of the gate.

Rudolf blocked his path. "You can't afford to lose the port," he said bluntly.

"I know that. I'm not a fool," Reidar snapped.

"The people of the Southern Isles have been defending against sea raids for centuries, sometimes successfully. They have an idea they came up with after watching some of our funerals," Rudolf said. He grinned. "Fire arrows. They set fire to the boats before the men can come ashore. Sometimes even ambush them where they know the boats will sink and the raiders will drown. You need fire arrows, and a narrow place they will be forced to sail through where they will be in range of our archers. How many archers can we have there in time?"

Hope blossomed in Reidar's breast. "More than we need. Every man and boy between here and the port can shoot a bow, because the lake is full of geese in the summertime, and any man who can shoot a bird may take it home for his table. Maybe we can save the port after all!"

He and Rudolf rode out, discussing likely ambush sites as they went.

Thirty-Six

Everything was wonderful…and then it wasn't, as Reidar dropped her on the ground like a sack of apples and rode off with his cousin to war, without even saying farewell. Not that she would have heard it if he had, for there was another word that burned in her brain with a ferocity she wasn't sure how to tame: queen.

As in: "Take her to the queen."

Wasn't she supposed to be his queen? His betrothed, his bride, the woman he would marry?

But if he already had a queen…it would explain why he hadn't even suggested sharing her bed. Why he hadn't mentioned marriage or their betrothal in the forest.

And why someone had seen the ships from the top of the tower – someone else already lived there.

Reidar's servant bade her to follow him and she did, but she paid little attention to her surroundings. For the first time, she wondered if she'd made a terrible mistake in coming here. If she wasn't wanted…

"Forgive me, Your Majesty, but the king said I must bring this girl to you." The look he shot Sativa was nothing short of a sneer.

Perhaps she deserved it – for how many girls would be as stupid as she had, to run away from her father's house across the sea to a man who no longer wanted her?

"What for?" a woman – presumably the queen – asked in annoyance

"I am not certain, Your Majesty, but he said something about wanting her here when he returned. Perhaps he wants you to find her a place to stay."

"Find her a room befitting her station, then," said the queen, dismissing him.

The man waited until the door was closed before he swore and turned to Sativa. "Follow me, you," he said curtly, setting off at a fast clip.

Sativa itched for a glimpse of the queen, the woman with the commanding voice that Reidar preferred over her, but she would probably see the woman at dinner. More important that she find her room first.

The man led her down several passageways, the aroma of cooking increasing in strength the further they went. Rooms above the kitchen would not be so bad, Sativa decided. She'd never miss a meal, for she'd smell it cooking.

The man stopped, then pointed through a doorway that had no door. "You'll sleep in there."

Curiously, Sativa stepped inside. At first, the

dimly lit room looked like another passageway, until her eyes adjusted and she saw that it was wider than that. Rows of straw pallets lined each side of the room, some with blankets or sacking coverlets, and others without. Pegs on the walls held an assortment of dresses and caps all made in a similar theme: practicality. If it weren't for the dresses, she'd have thought it a barracks hall, but the clothing marked it for what it was. The servants' quarters, where the castle maids slept.

On – Sativa sneezed – thrice-damned straw, the bane of her existence.

Sativa sneezed twice more before she turned on her heel and marched back the way she'd come. The man who'd guided her had disappeared, but no matter. Sativa would find her own way back to the queen's chamber, and confront the woman herself. She might be a queen, but Sativa was a princess, born with royal blood, and she would not endure such an insult.

After one wrong turning, she managed to

return to the queen's chamber, and Sativa did not bother to knock. Instead, she burst into the room.

"What is the meaning of this?" Sativa demanded in the tone she knew carried to the farthest reaches of her father's court.

"Who in heaven's name are you?" the queen countered.

For the first time, Sativa saw her, and was startled to see she recognised the woman. Oh, she was older, certainly, her fair hair almost completely white, but Regina's haughty expression had not changed a bit. This was the queen? Not Reidar's wife, but his mother?

Relief flooded through her, giving her all the authority she needed to snap, "I am Princess Sativa, daughter of King Boreslas in Kasmirus, betrothed to King Reidar of Viken, and when he returns, I will be the queen of this place. What do you think Reidar will say when he discovers you sent me to sleep with the servants?"

Regina's eyebrows rose so high, they

vanished into her hair. "Sativa? The dragon's prize girl? Impossible. She disappeared from her father's court months ago. The girl is dead."

"I am not a prize, and I am not dead," Sativa hissed through gritted teeth. "I will marry your son, and I demand the hospitality that was promised. With a bed befitting my station."

Regina managed to arrange her icy expression into a smile that held no warmth at all. "Very well, Princess. You may join me for dinner, by which time your bed will be prepared."

Sativa could afford to be gracious. "Thank you. I shall need some suitable clothing, too."

Regina eyed her tunic with the same distaste Sativa had once held for Melitta's clothing, once upon a time. "Yes, you will. My ladies will dress you."

Sativa was soon bundled into Regina's dressing room, a narrow chamber full of chests containing clothes from at least three generations of women, judging by the strange styles the ladies pulled out in their search for something suitable.

"This," one said, holding up a gown that glittered even in the dim light in the dressing room.

The gown was made of gold silk, and so richly embroidered it could probably stand up by itself. If that wasn't enough, someone had sewed dozens of jewels to it so that whoever wore it couldn't help but catch the light. It was a wedding dress, or one to be worn at a coronation. Not something for an ordinary dinner.

"It is too fine," Sativa said.

The second girl shook her head. "The queen said you must have the best. This is the richest gown in the wardrobe. If you don't wear it, the queen will punish us."

Visions of punishment aboard the *Barbe* flashed through Sativa's mind. Would Regina be so cruel as to have her ladies-in-waiting whipped? Sativa didn't want to find out.

She reached out to touch the silk. It had been so long since she'd worn anything half as pretty as this. She'd outshine everyone in the castle. Including Regina.

"Very well," Sativa said, and allowed the women to dress her.

When they were done, they guided her to the great hall, and left her with only Regina for company. Luckily, they were both at opposite ends of the great table, so she was spared the challenge of making conversation with a woman whose dislike could be felt from the other side of the room.

Sativa ate her fill of everything. It would take some time to replace the weight she'd lost aboard the *Barbe*, and she doubted Reidar wanted to introduce his people to a half-starved bride. She was a princess from a prosperous kingdom – she should look the part.

All too soon, she grew tired, and found she struggled to keep her eyes open. As Sativa tried to smother yet another yawn, Regina rose to her feet.

"My servants tell me your room is ready," Regina said. "Let me show you to your bed."

Sativa owned that it was a good idea, and followed the woman readily.

This time, the chamber wasn't far from the queen's own. A servant threw the door open and Regina peered inside. Her face lit with a genuine smile.

"Behold, Princess, a bed befitting your high station," Regina said, dropping a curtsey.

Finally. Sativa stepped into the room, expecting either another straw pallet or the sort of fine feather bed she had at home. Neither would have surprised her. What she did see made her jaw drop. It wasn't one fine feather bed, but at least a dozen, the mattresses stacked so high they nearly reached the ceiling. Sativa stopped to count them all. No, not a dozen. Twenty of the things, with a ladder beside them to help her climb to the top.

A calculated insult, or an over-the-top honour. Sativa was certain it was meant as the former, but she smiled sweetly as though it were the latter. "Why, thank you," she simpered. "Just like the one I had at home."

Regina's composure failed, and her true hatred shone through. "Liar," she spat. "You are no more a princess than the maids in the kitchen. No one sleeps in a bed like that. You will never marry my son, for he's too good for the likes of you." She slammed the door shut and Sativa heard the key turn in the lock.

Sativa was tempted to shout something after the woman, but someone had to show their better breeding, and it had best be her.

Besides, climbing a ladder into a bed that looked softer than a cloud seemed like luxury after climbing the mast every day and sleeping in a hammock on the *Barbe*.

Sativa scaled the ladder and climbed carefully onto the stacked mattresses. She sank so deep she suspected getting out might prove a challenge, but one she would tackle after a good night's sleep on what had to be the softest bed she'd ever encountered. Silently, she thanked Reidar and his mother, for this felt like pure bliss. Yes, she would show Regina, and marry Reidar just like she'd promised. And maybe, just maybe, she'd ask him for a slightly less decadent version of this bed. One that didn't require a ladder. Because she could definitely get used to comfort like this.

Until a growing tickle in her nose could not be ignored, and she sneezed. Not once, but six times in succession. And then again.

There was straw in this room. In the mattresses, she suspected, though she had no way to tell.

"Damn you, bitch," Sativa said softly, as her eyes teared up from the straw dust in the air. That was what caused it, not emotion or self-pity or any such thing.

She only had to endure it until Reidar returned, and then everything would be rosy.

Sativa sneezed. And swore. And sneezed again.

Damned rose fever.

She hoped he came home soon.

Thirty-Seven

"What are you still doing here?"

Rudolf's words jarred Reidar out of what had been a deep sleep. In a stable, judging by the smell.

"Because I distinctly recall telling you last night that we'd take care of the damage those two boats wrought when they made it through our hail of arrows. And we did, thank you. We only lost the roof of one house to fire." Rudolf glared at Reidar. "Why aren't you home with your bride, getting ready for your wedding, like you said you would?"

Reidar's mind started to work. Now he remembered coming into the stable, calling for a groom to saddle his horse, but all the men were off defending the town, so he'd had to do the job himself. And then he'd closed his eyes for just a moment…

…and woken up here, in daylight. Reidar cursed.

"I fell asleep," he admitted.

Rudolf snorted. "I can see that. You're lucky no one's come in yet. I'm not sure what the townsfolk would do if they found a snoring king in their stable."

"I do not snore," Reidar grumbled.

"One day, I will ask your lovely wife to tell me the truth. Now, get you gone and marry the girl before someone else beats you to it!" Rudolf said.

"No one commands the king," Reidar muttered as he reached for his horse's bridle.

"As the king's cousin and heir, I think I have the right to make strong suggestions that

I think the king should follow, if he's not to turn into a complete fool," Rudolf replied. "Who else will, if I do not?"

Reidar had to admit the man was right. But he didn't have to admit it aloud, though. "Mind your manners, or I will not invite you to the wedding feast," he said as he climbed atop his horse. He set off before Rudolf could reply.

"You'll have to ask the girl to marry you first!" Rudolf shouted after him.

Curse the man, but he was right.

Sativa was in his thoughts for most of the ride home. He'd have to tread carefully, for she'd evidently endured some terrible trials between her father's castle and his. A wedding would have to wait until she was willing to let him touch her without pulling out a knife to defend herself.

He'd like to find whoever had frightened her and force them to endure whatever they'd put her through. That was a cheering thought. Perhaps he'd offer to let Sativa help, or at least observe. She would want to ensure justice was served.

But that would have to wait, too. First, he wanted to see her, to ask her what had happened, and whether she was still willing to marry him. At least he knew she was safe under his roof.

He handed the reins to a groom and vaulted off his horse in the bailey, wanting nothing more than to see Sativa again when he arrived home.

"Where is the girl I brought here yesterday?" he asked a passing serving girl, but she did not know. Nor did anyone else he asked, it seemed.

How dare they mislay their future queen?

Incensed, Reidar headed for his mother's chambers. She would know where to find Sativa. Perhaps she could also explain why the girl was being kept a secret from his own servants. They would be her servants soon enough.

"Where is she?" he demanded as he strode into her apartment.

Regina set down her embroidery. "Where is who?"

"Princess Sativa." She would not hide her identity, he was certain of it. Not here.

Regina wet her lips. "You mean the girl pretending to be the dead princess."

Reidar fought to keep his temper. "No, I mean the very real, live princess I left in your care yesterday. The one who will soon be my wife." He prayed that this last part was true.

"You're a fool, my son, but most men are. Fooled by a pretty face and a tale of distress. That girl is no more highborn than any other maid in the castle. First, she had the gall to demand to wear the most valuable gown in the castle to dinner. Then she had the effrontery to demand the most outlandish bed, which she imagined was what a princess slept upon. I'll show you, if you like. Then you'll see she is playing you for a fool." Regina rose and swept out of the room.

No. His mother was wrong. Whatever she thought, he knew he'd brought the real Sativa here yesterday. No one else could know what she did.

Regina stopped outside one of the guest apartments and turned the key in the lock.

"You locked her in, like a prisoner?" Reidar demanded. He didn't want to lose his temper, but his mother was pushing him much too far.

"I could not have her wandering around the castle. Who knows what she might steal?" Regina said, then threw open the door with a flourish.

Sativa stood on the threshold, her red eyes and nose streaming. "If this is the hospitality you show to guests, I hope the devil shows you better in hell," she said. "I scarcely slept in that travesty of a bed. It was impossible, with that bloody…that bloody…pea – aachoo!" She sneezed twice more, then glared at Regina.

"But that's not possible," Regina spluttered. "No one's so refined, so sensitive, she could sense something like that through so many mattresses. Not even royalty. How could she detect such a thing through twenty mattresses?"

Pea straw, the stuff that made her sneeze, Sativa had meant to say, Reidar was certain. He peered into the room behind her and saw a strange sight. A stack of mattresses, including the straw one his father had slept on every day of his life, insisting it was far better than feathers. The old pallet had burst under the weight of the ones above, strewing straw all over the floor. It had been better for his father, perhaps. But not for Sativa.

Who had suffered even more, and it was his fault.

Reidar fell to his knees. "Forgive me, Princess. I promised to protect you, and I failed. I'd planned to ask you to marry me, and name the day of our wedding, but I find I must beg your forgiveness first, and pay a heavy penance, before I'd dare ask anything of you."

Sativa stared down at him. Once again, sizing up his soul. Reidar prayed he would not be found wanting. "A handkerchief," she said.

He felt through his pockets, and produced

one. "I'm sorry for the soot. We set fire to half a dozen ships last night."

"Thank you," she said, inclining her head. She wiped her eyes, then delicately blew her nose. "There. You asked for…things."

She swayed on her feet and Reidar caught her, rising to his feet when he realised she needed his support. She truly hadn't slept, and she was still weak from her ordeal.

"Tomorrow," she said. "Give me a bed without straw and a hot bath, and you shall have everything you ask for tomorrow."

Reidar didn't believe his ears. "What will I have tomorrow?"

Sativa slumped against him. Exhausted, poor girl. "Wedding. Forgiveness. Whatever. But I never want to see her again." She stabbed a finger at Regina.

"I will not stay here while she's polluting the place," Regina said hotly. "I shall go to live with one of your sisters until you come to your senses." She stormed off.

Reidar didn't intend to come to his senses

any time soon. Sativa drove him wild, and he had to admit he rather liked it. Reidar lifted Sativa in his arms. "Whatever you wish, my queen," he said softly.

She smiled. "A bed," she said before her eyes closed. "And don't go away this time."

He carried her limp form up to the tower room she should have been shown last night, and set her in the middle of the bed. He pulled the covers over her, not sure what else to do.

All he could do was wait and watch over her until she woke.

Which was what she wanted, so he did.

Thirty-Eight

When Sativa woke, the sun was high in the sky, but she felt well rested.

Reidar stepped out of the shadows. "I brought you breakfast, but I fear it is cold now. I will send for some more. I didn't want to wake you."

He was as chivalrous as she'd always dreamed he'd be. But the time for chivalry was done. She would marry this man – this king – and she would pledge herself to him so irrevocably that he would truly know she meant what she said. Reidar was everything she wanted in a man, and despite what she'd said in the forest, in her heart, she belonged to him and him alone. It was time he knew that.

"Come here," Sativa said, her voice a little shaky. She'd never seduced a man before, and she was sure her inexperience showed. When Reidar turned to face her, she pulled her shift over her head and threw it on the floor, so she sat naked on the bed.

His eyes raked her body before returning to her face. "Princess..." Lust smouldered, just as it had in the forest.

She patted the bed. "Here, Reidar. My name is Sativa, not Princess. You will need to remember that, when I am your wife."

He took one tentative step closer, then another. His eyes held something akin to awe. Another step. He stopped beside the bed, as though something held him back. "Sativa." It sounded like a prayer.

"Take your clothes off, too," she said, her voice shaking even more. "I wish to see the man who will be my husband."

To her delight, he shucked off his tunic. The hard muscles she'd held onto during their ride here were everything she'd imagined. Arms, chest, back…everything.

She rose up onto her knees, reaching out to touch.

He took a step back. "Don't," he begged. "If you touch me, I'm not sure I'll be able to restrain myself. I want you, the way a man wants his wife."

Looking down, Sativa saw that what he said was true. And she wanted him, too.

"Show me everything," she said, her voice breathless. "Take all your clothes off."

His eyes burned into hers as he did as she asked. Shoes, hose, until he stood as naked as she.

Then she rose from the bed, her steps as tentative as his had been before. She forced herself to stop when she was only a step away so she could gaze at his body before she said, "What a glorious husband you will make." She swallowed, then added, "I want you the way a woman wants a lover."

Then she pressed her body against his, softness moulding around hardness, and lifted her lips for a kiss. His arm was firm at her back as his other hand cupped her cheek. No more words were necessary for his eyes said it all as he kissed her, tenderly at first then with an urgency that rivalled her own. Long and deep and so delicious he made her dizzy.

"I have dreamed of this," she gasped.

"So have I," he said. "Tomorrow, after we are wed – "

"No," she interrupted. "I don't want to wait. I want you now." She reached down and wrapped her hand around his manhood. So hard, and yet so soft. What would it feel like inside her?

Gently, he pried her hand loose. "Sativa." Another prayer, as her fingers stroked his length before she let go.

Her eyes met his. "Show me how you will love your queen." Taking his hand, she led him to the bed, then lay down.

Something warred in his eyes. Sativa didn't care what, as long as she won.

"You said you would take me as your queen. So, take me."

He smiled. "As my queen commands." He climbed onto the bed beside her, his hands brushing lightly over her skin so that she shivered. His smile broadened, before he covered her body in kisses. She gasped and sighed under his caresses, until he said, "Sativa, have you ever taken a lover before?"

She sat up in surprise. "Of course not. I've been promised to you since I was six!"

He chuckled. "That never stopped the ladies of Viken from taking lovers if they liked. Marriage means being faithful to only the one. But if I am your first…then I must make sure you are prepared for me."

His caresses and kisses grew more fervent, making her gasp with delight as he drew pleasure from her body that she had not thought possible. After an eternity of foreplay, finally he declared that she was ready.

Sativa opened her mouth to say that she had been ready long before, but the sensation of him entering her took her breath away. She opened her legs wider, welcoming him inside. That first thrust seemed to take a glorious eternity, until she could take no more, for he had filled her completely.

She closed her eyes, relishing the pure pleasure she had never before imagined.

Reidar leaned forward, pushing deliciously deeper into her as he cupped her face in gentle hands. "Sativa, please tell me if I am too much for you. I will stop, I swear."

She opened her eyes, smiling in joy. "Don't stop, my king. Don't stop until we are both spent, and need to rest, before we can make love some more." At this, he moved within her and she moaned in pleasure. "Yes, more!"

Their bodies melded together in a union so perfect Sativa could not have dreamed it before this moment, and this moment was one she never wanted to end. A moment of unfathomable bliss between two shared souls. A promise joyfully fulfilled.

Much later, when the sunset light streamed through the window and kissed their naked bodies, lying side by side on the bed, Reidar turned to her and said, "Tomorrow is our wedding. After today, what will I have left to give you on our wedding night?"

Sativa laughed softly. "More of the same, I imagine, unless you have a different kind of lovemaking in mind. If we do this enough, we are sure to have a child. But until we do, give me the gift of your body, and your love, and I shall give you mine in return. Every day and every night, so that we may live happily ever after."

Blow:
Three Little Pigs Retold

DEMELZA CARLTON

A tale in the Romance a Medieval Fairy Tale series

One

Midsummer festival fever had caught them all in her heathen coils. The higher born boys fought with practice swords in the yard, their bouts descending into pitched battle with no guard or master at arms to break it up. Rudolf found himself stunned in the dust, unnoticed by the others as they pursued longer held grudges against boys they knew, and he scrambled to his feet. Retreating from the yard seemed the most chivalrous thing to do, for he had more training than most of them, though not enough to stop the fight like his cousin Reidar might have.

Outside the walls, pine had been piled up for the bonfires, huge as haystacks, that would be set alight after dark to feed some ancient, beastly god. Now, the fresh, life-giving scent of the pine lay sharp over the bed of long-dead peat from the bogs, reminding him of the inevitability of death, even in the bright summer sun.

His thick furs itched in the unaccustomed heat that was so little like home, but he did not dare take them off. They marked him for what he was, a Viken prince among these Islanders, who wore linen and leather that was surely more suitable for summer.

Peat smoke spiralled in a dark prayer to heaven as it roasted pork to what he hoped would be perfection. The rich smell took him back home, to his farewell feast and the roasted beast that had been Reidar's first kill. Oh, now that had been a feast. Could these foreigners match it?

The crack of what sounded like a spitting

cat forced his eyes open. No, it was just the beast's flesh spitting at the coals that roasted it, like its last act of courage before the old gods took it to Valhalla. Did pigs go to heaven, though, he wondered. The men of the new faith said no, but he didn't know enough about the old to be sure.

Hogs probably went up to the great feasting table in the sky, much like their bodies had here. Such was their fate, as this exile was his. At least he was not a pig, however much he roasted in his northern clothes.

He headed away from the clamour, toward the cliffs.

"Boy, boy!" an imperious, elderly voice called.

Rudolf turned. He'd learned the hard way not to ignore an old woman's commands. If he hadn't sat on that throne for a moment and Queen Regina hadn't caught him, then he wouldn't be here, exiled at the other end of the world. Better alive than dead, though, and alive, he could train more so that one day, he could better serve his king. The man whose backside belonged on that cursed throne.

If the approaching woman was Queen Regina, Rudolf would have run. As it was, he forced himself to hold his ground.

The woman everyone called Nurse limped up to him. "Have you seen them? Wee devils, they are. Their father insists they must attend the feast dressed in their best, and I cannot find them anywhere!"

The Lord Angus's daughters were missing? Rudolf's heart turned to ice, as he remembered the day he'd lost his little sister to the ice on the fjords.

But there was no ice here, and little water, either, for the burns that had flowed only yesterday were little more than mud now after days without rain. It truly was a different world to Viken.

If he had a choice, today he would be in the swimming hole the other boys had spoken of. A pool they said never dried up.

A place deep enough for a little girl to drown.

Panic gave his feet wings as he crested the rise, following the dried up burn. If he could get there in time, perhaps he could save them.

Perhaps…

A shrill scream stopped his heart, but not his feet. Still he ran. If a girl could scream, she could breathe, and he could still save her. By all the saints in heaven, please let him save her.

Low hanging branches sliced at his face, but still Rudolf ran on until he almost fell over the lip of the pool, or what had been the pool. Perhaps even this morning, it had still held water, but now…now it held three wriggling, shrieking girls as they played in liquid mud. Alive. Safe. All three. Portia, Lina and Arlie, so covered in mud he couldn't tell them apart – not that it was an easy matter anyway, given the girls looked identical.

Rudolf's heart dared to beat again and he took a deep breath. "Nurse!" he shouted. "I have found your three little pigs!"

Two

"You fought well today, and you have a knack for commanding men. I know several men owe you their lives after today, for it was your quick thinking in the heat of battle that saved them."

Rudolf's chest puffed at Angus's praise.

Angus continued, "You'll need new armour soon. You're not a boy any more, and your shoulders are too wide for that breastplate. Where there's gaps, an arrow will find them," Angus said, throwing the reins of his horse to a groom.

Rudolf did the same, but he lingered to stroke Hector's side as he was led off. He'd never owned a finer horse. Not back in Viken, or since he arrived here. How many years had it been now? At least six. Maybe seven.

"You like him, don't you? See, I told Lewis he couldn't sell him off the islands. Valuable breeding stock, he'll be, when you're not riding him."

Rudolf remembered his manners. "Thank you again, Lord Angus. He's a princely gift indeed."

Angus waved away his thanks. "No more than you deserve. My own father gave me my first warhorse when I reached manhood. My first ride, the bastard reared up and threw me on my arse. My brother laughed himself sick. You have a much better seat than did at your age. Better than Portia, though better not tell her I said that."

Rudolf laughed. "No, I won't, as long as you know that's what I'll be thinking about when I'm staring at her bottom next time we go riding."

"Man your age should be looking for a wife.

I know I was. Or will your father be sending one from Viken?"

Viken? Why would he send a girl after him? This was home. Rudolf would likely never see Viken again. "Viken girls choose their husbands, just like the ones here," Rudolf managed to say. "I left no sweetheart behind me, so no girl will be coming to find me."

An explosion of red blasted through the door to the longhouse. "There they are! I found them," Portia cried, tossing her hair off her face. She'd forgotten her shoes again, and with no Nurse to remind her any more, she'd probably been wearing holes in her stockings the whole time they'd been away.

"I brought you a gift," Rudolf said, pulling the feather from under his breastplate. He'd kept it in the pocket over his heart. "At the end of the battle, when those rank cowards were running away, a golden eagle circled the field and dropped it. Landed right at my feet. I thought you might like a new quill."

Portia dashed up to him and plucked the feather from his hand. Then she threw her arms around him and hugged him. Rudolf laughed as he returned her hug, conscious of Angus's thoughtful eyes on him.

Angus was planning something, to be sure.

"Can we go riding now?" Portia demanded. The woman-child had all the impatience of a child, while her body grew more and more into a woman's form.

Rudolf laughed again. "I have been riding all day, and Hector, too. I am starving. I hope you have a good dinner ordered."

Portia would not be put off. "Tomorrow, then? If we leave early, we might be able to make it up to Loch Findlugan, and search for its secret. While you were away, I went through Mother's things and found a scroll about the history of Isla. It said the standing stones – "

Angus interrupted, "Tomorrow, Rudolf needs to be measured for new armour. He's outgrown his."

Portia laughed. "Must be all the food he eats. And people call me and my sisters pigs!" This earned Rudolf a glare.

Rudolf hung his head. The tale of him finding the three little sisters, wallowing in the mud like pigs, had spread rapidly through the Southern Isles, as all good stories did. Even if seven years had passed since that day, Portia still had not forgiven him. She might never.

He glanced at Angus. "I'm sure I won't be needed all day for new armour. There will be time for a ride tomorrow. Perhaps not to Loch Findlugan, but we can take the horses for a ride on the beach."

Portia enveloped him in another hug, tighter and longer than the first. "I love you, Dolf!"

Rudolf patted her back awkwardly, his eyes offering an apology to Angus.

Angus nodded, unconcerned. "Enough talk of tomorrow. I'm famished. I fancy a fine leg of mutton for dinner, and I'm sure Rudolf does, too. Release your prisoner, Portia." He headed inside.

Portia let go, then tucked her hand into Rudolf's. "I'll release you on one condition. You must tell me all about the battle over dinner. How many men you killed, whether you were close enough to hear their last words…or did you shoot them with your bow?"

She was the same age as he'd been when he arrived on Isla, Rudolf realised, and just as bloodthirsty. "I did not use my bow this time. Angus had archers enough."

"I want my own bow. Viken women sometimes go to war with their men, you said. I could be one of the archers and kill those cowardly, thieving Albans before they could step ashore!"

Rudolf laughed. "Are you strong enough to draw a bow yet?"

Portia pouted. "No."

"When you are full grown, like me, you may practice with mine. If you can hit the target, I promise you I will see that you have your own bow."

Her eyes lit with the fire that seemed to burn without cease within her. "Really?"

Rudolf could refuse her nothing. He prayed that Angus would agree. "Really."

Three

Portia reacted to the king's demands the way she always did when something vexed her: she went shooting.

Her bow was a comforting weight in her hand as she marched to the practice field. The smooth wood was exactly the right size for someone of her stature – as Rudolf must have known, for he'd given it to her on her last name day. Much easier to shoot with than his own monster bow, easily taller than he was. It had taken her years before she'd had the strength to fire anything from his bow, but when a lucky shot clipped the target, Rudolf had made good on his promise – a bow of her own, and archery lessons to keep her from shooting him instead of the target.

Not that she'd meant to do that. The arrow had accidentally gone through his boot, and she'd told him so. She wasn't sure he believed her, though. She sighed and took aim.

She emptied her quiver in record speed, wishing the plain wood target had a picture of the king's face painted on it. She did not even know what the bastard looked like. She imagined King Donald as old and fat with thinning hair, a petulant fool who demanded things that were not his like the spoiled child he'd once been.

She fitted an arrow to the bowstring.

How dare he try to claim her lands. Her father's lands, truly, but hers, too, for she was his firstborn.

She drew the arrow back.

How dare he insist they pay him tribute. A man who had no right to their lands, or the fruit from it.

She sighted along the arrow, blowing out

her breath in a rush.

How dare he call their people foreigners. How dare he!

She released, and the arrow flew toward the target. It lodged in the side, so close to the edge that it only hung there for a moment before it fell to earth.

Earth that sorry excuse for a king had no claim on!

Portia stomped her foot for emphasis.

"Looking at the target, I wondered if Arlie had picked up a bow for her annual archery practice. But Arlie doesn't stamp her foot like that." Rudolf gestured at the target across the field. "Are you feeling sorry for the target, Portia? Trying not to hit it because hitting it would be cruel?"

Portia's face turned as red as her hair. Trust Rudolf to bring that up. No one else remembered something that happened ten years ago, except him. "I still think butchering pigs is cruel, but nothing I can say or do will stop it, for the rest of your will still eat it. So will I, and be properly thankful to the animal that gave its life so that we may eat its flesh."

She sounded like the priest at last Sunday's mass, and she knew it. Before Rudolf could tease her for that, too, she continued, "It won't matter if I miss my target, anyway. Men all bunch up in an army, so if I miss one man, I'm bound to hit the one beside him."

He laughed. "Since when are you riding to war? Your father is not so short of men he'll need you to fight." His gaze travelled from her feet up to her face. "Unless you plan on wearing a man's garb. There's many a man on the island who's dreamed of seeing you without your gown, but I'm sure none of them imagined you'd be wearing armour."

Just as her blush faded, it flamed into life once more. Only Rudolf could say these things with such brutal honesty, without apology. Not for the first time, she wondered if he'd been one of those dreaming men. Men who would soon be off to war, with no time to dream of anyone, she told herself sternly. "I have no need to ride to war. Raiders come in boats when they see fit, and if the menfolk are not at home, then it falls to us women to defend our homes."

Rudolf inclined his head. "So it does. Here in the south, right up to Viken in the north. But your father will never leave you here unprotected, and you will always have me." He drew a dagger from his belt and sent it flying toward the target. He hit the centre. "I will defend you with my life, Portia."

That serious look in his eyes heated her all over again, but not just her face this time. There was something about Rudolf that lit a fire inside her. The kind of fire she liked, but could never stoke. "I'm sure my father will be very grateful for your service," she said sweetly.

He opened his mouth, but no words came out. Then he shook his head, as if to rid it of ideas that had no place there, a feeling Portia understood well. Finally, he said, "But it would be lax of me to stop you from practising, when you so sorely need it."

"Why you – " Portia began, then stopped as Rudolf grinned. When he smiled, the man was charming enough to coax a honeycomb from an angry bear. Not even she was immune to him. Perhaps that's why she felt so hot inside.

"Help me retrieve my arrows, then."

Rudolf pulled the lucky few from the target while she hunted through the grass for the rest. When the quiver was more than half full once more, she marched back to where she'd left her bow. Rudolf with his longer strides got there first, lifting the weapon in readiness, though he didn't hand it to her.

"First, I must check your stance, Portia," he said. "Show me how you stand."

Never one to like being ordered about, Portia set her hand on her hip and waved an arrow. "You'd better hope I don't decide to make you my target instead."

"You wouldn't do that," he said easily. "You like me."

No matter how much he irritated her and make her feel other unwelcome feelings she had to ruthlessly suppress, Portia had to admit she did. Not aloud, though. "I might also like to see you hopping around with an arrow in your foot again."

"You have your dreams and I have mine. I like mine better. Now, do you wish to practise, or no?"

Portia relented and stepped up to the bow, angling herself so that she faced Rudolf and not the target. She fitted her arrow to the string. "There. Good enough for you?"

Rudolf inspected her, even going as far as to march right the way around her, before he nudged her foot with his. "Your stance needs to be a little wider, pointed to where you wish the arrow to go." His arms came around her, lifting the bow so that the arrow no longer pointed at the ground.

Portia wanted to relax into his embrace, and surrender to the promise of protection he offered. It would be so easy, and yet it was something she could never do. Rudolf was a foreigner, a ward sent from Viken to learn to fight in her father's house. One day, he would be summoned home to fight for whatever Viken lord his family owed fealty to. Portia was her father's eldest daughter, and heir to Isla. The man she married would follow her father as Lord of Isla, the largest and most powerful of the Southern Isles. She could never marry a mere household knight. It would take a lord at least, or a lord's son, to hold

Father's place in council. Rudolf knew this as well as she did, which was why he never took liberties, though he made it very clear he would like to. But that was an invitation she could never offer.

She straightened, paying more attention to the bow and arrow than the boy whose breath tickled the back of her neck. "Which foot do you like best, Dolf?" she asked.

"Your left one, because that's pointed at the target," he said, cupping her elbow in his hand. "Now draw, sight along the arrow..." His hand slammed into her gut, just below her breasts, forcing her to exhale. "Now I've made you breathless, you may shoot."

The arrow whistled across the field and thwacked into the target. Not in the centre, marked by the divot from Rudolf's knife, but nearer than any of her earlier attempts.

"There!"

Rudolf inclined his head. "Not bad. If you were aiming for a man's heart, you might have hit him in the throat. But we can improve on that."

With infinite patience Portia knew she

would never possess, Rudolf helped her empty her quiver – all into the target this time. Then he headed across the field with her to retrieve the arrows again.

When the quiver was full, he held it out and asked, "Are you still angry, or have you done enough shooting for one day?"

Until she hit the centre of the target every time, it would not be enough. She sighed. A landless knight like Rudolf would not understand. "One more time," she said, reaching for the quiver.

Rudolf caught her hand in his. "You're bleeding. I say you have done enough. We should get you inside, so one of your sisters can bandage these fingers. You can practise more on the morrow, but first, I must get you some pigs' ears."

"Pigs' ears are no use to anyone, except the pig itself," Portia said, snatching her hand back. Her fingers tingled where he'd touched them, a hint of magic that called for more. She refused to yield. Isla would not yield.

Rudolf chuckled. "Get you to your sisters. I'll return your things to the armoury, and find you inside." He shouldered both her quiver and her bow and headed across the yard.

Portia sucked on her bleeding fingers as she headed inside. Arlie would exclaim over the blood, fanning herself in case she fainted. Lina would be the one to clean and bandage her, like Nurse had taught her to before age and infirmity had called the old woman from this life.

As it would one day call them all.

But not yet, if Portia had any say in it.

Four

The moment Arlie spotted Rudolf, she cried, "Dolf will go to war to save us! Won't you, Dolf?"

Portia hushed her. She might only be a few minutes older than her sisters, but sometimes the difference felt like years.

"If you ladies need saving, I would be honoured to be of service," Rudolf said as he approached. He met Portia's eyes without a hint of laughter and bowed low. "From what must I save you? Is there another spider?"

Lina laughed. "No, only Portia screams at

spiders. This time, it's some pompous king, demanding tribute from all the island lords, which they will not pay."

"That's no way to talk about your liege," Rudolf said mildly. "I've never heard anyone call King Harald pompous before."

"That's because it's not him!" Arlie giggled. "It's some silly foreigner called Donald. He calls for tithes and men, to combat what he calls our foreign invaders, so that he might help us make the Southern Isles great again."

"Nay, he wants to make Alba great again, but he insists we are an important part of it," Lina corrected.

Portia frowned. "Important enough to attract his interest, because he thinks we might offer him men or money. No king has every offered us anything we didn't have to pay for. Not King Harald or this Donald. The lords of the isles know this, and they will refuse him, which will mean war."

"The lords are in the right of it. The isles are under Harald's protection, and they do not belong to some man called Donald. If he wants them, he will have to fight for them, and pay dearly," Rudolf declared.

Now Portia thought of it, he did sound like one of the lords. Somehow, over the years, Rudolf the boy had turned into a man, or at least something like one. A pity he would never be one of them. Because if he was…

"Perhaps this Donald should just ask to marry Portia. We all know no man on the islands is good enough for her, for she turns her nose up at all of them. Would a king suit you, Portia?" Arlie teased.

Rudolf's eyes were upon her, and Portia found she could not meet them. "Father knows as well as I do that I can only wed a man who can hold the islands. Hold them, and defend them, like he has. All this Donald has done is blow wind at us, and the isles have withstood greater gales than anything he's thrown at us thus far. I will wed when a strong enough man presents himself, and not before."

"See? Portia will never marry for love. Or she'd have picked Rudolf, long ago," Lina declared with a smile.

Arlie dissolved in a fit of giggles, falling back to kick her legs in the air.

Once again, Portia felt far too hot. She rose and marched out of the room, the sound of her sisters' laughter following her. And booted footsteps. Rudolf, of course.

"Portia," he began cautiously, as if wishing to warn her of his presence.

She turned and held up her hand to halt him before he said any more. "My sisters like to joke at my expense. And yours. I'm sorry if their levity sounds insulting to your ears. You are a strong and skilled warrior. Both my father and I know that. So do my sisters, I think. But when we hear whispered news of war…well, you see how we react. Lina will pick herbs to dry for every wound and ailment imaginable, and fill the cellars with all the food she can possibly preserve. Arlie…she will make light of everything, as she always does, for laughter is her way."

"And you shall shoot things, because even if every man on this island dies in battle, you will still defend it while you have breath left in your body," Rudolf finished for her. "Isla is your home, and the Southern Isles are your kingdom as much as Harald holds Viken, or

Donald does Alba."

Now it was Portia's turn to laugh. "No one understands me the way you do, Dolf. I swear it is as though you have some magical power to see into my head. I'm glad I didn't shoot you."

Rudolf laughed with her. "I'm glad you didn't shoot me, either. If it comes to war, I hope I am never on the opposing side to you and your father. I meant it when I said I would protect you." He held out his hand. "Here."

Portia glanced down and recoiled. "What in heaven's name do you intend to do with those?"

"Give me your hand."

Reluctantly, she did as he asked. He wrapped the pig's ear around her middle finger, the leather surprisingly warm and soft from being in his pocket. Next, he threaded a thin leather thong through the holes edging the ear, until he'd laced it like one of her gowns. He pulled the whole thing taut, then tied it at the bottom. "Now the others." Soon he'd shrouded all three of her middle fingers in pigs' ears. The leather was paler than boot leather, as though the pigs' ears were tanned differently. In fact, the pigskin was so close to the shade of her own skin that it looked like she wasn't wearing the finger guards at all. "Next time, wear these when you need to shoot out your frustration. Your arms will tire long before you make your fingers bleed. Pigs' ears are tough."

"Thank you, Dolf!" Portia threw her arms around his neck. Too late, she realised as her body moulded to his that she shouldn't do such things any more. Though he cared for her as much as any brother, Rudolf was most certainly not one of her siblings. Awkwardly, she peeled herself away from him, only now realising that he held his arms stiffly at his sides. Stopping himself from returning her embrace, or pushing her away? Oh, she was so stupid.

"It's my pleasure, Portia," he said. With a slight bow, he left her.

Portia sighed, only now realising she held her well-wrapped fingers over her heart. If only she was as free as her sisters. But the world didn't work the way she wanted to, for life was nothing like a fairytale.

Five

When Angus, Lord of Isla, slumped into his seat at dinner, no one dared ask what made him so weary, for they all knew. Lina gestured imperiously for servants to fill her father's plate, while Portia poured wine for him. He would share what he knew after dinner, and not before.

It wasn't until Angus dismissed the servants that Rudolf began to worry about what he might say. If he wanted to share secrets with his family alone, then Rudolf should retire and save the man from doing him the dishonour of dismissing him.

Rudolf rose. "I took Hector for a long ride today, and it occurs to me that he was limping a little toward the end. I should go check on him before it gets too dark to see."

Angus lifted his hand. "Stay, Rudolf. What I have to say concerns you, too. The horse can wait until morning."

Rudolf sat down. He could feel Portia's curious gaze upon him, but he forced himself to keep his own eyes on Lord Angus. Hope flared in his breast, but he forced it back behind his ribs.

Angus drained his cup and set it down with finality. "As you all know, King Donald of Alba has laid claim to the islands, and a list of the tribute that he believes is his due. Tribute we have failed to pay in the past, he says, which must be paid, too. He sent these demands by way of a messenger, who was commanded to read Donald's missive aloud to me, and all the other lords, to make sure we understood. For, apparently, we are an illiterate lot on the Southern Isles, or so he says."

This time, it was Lina who leaped to her

feet. "I suggest all the lords should pen him a message by their own hands, suggesting he shove his missive up his arse. No, that he instruct his messenger to do it for him, as he probably can't find his arse with both hands and a map." As quickly as she'd risen, she subsided again. Lina was both as calm and relentless as the sea. She'd make some man a good wife, one day, as long as he let her run his household without interfering.

Angus waved a hand in acknowledgement. "Our response to Donald is something all the lords of the isles will decide in council. I sent my own messenger with his, so they should start arriving soon, and I will be there to greet them when they do." He turned thoughtful eyes toward Rudolf. "I'd like you to come with me."

"So shall I!" Portia declared.

"No. You must stay here and protect your sisters," Angus said. "This may be a council of war, and no place for you. Your presence would complicate matters." He deliberately didn't look at her.

Portia looked ready to explode.

Rudolf placed a sympathetic hand on her wrist. "I would be honoured to attend a council. Then I will be able to carry a full account of the decisions back to the girls here if you are called away by other responsibilities."

Portia yanked her arm away. "You'd better," she said darkly.

She said little to him for the rest of the meal, and for the days before Rudolf departed with her father for Loch Findlugan. Her father received a fond farewell, but Rudolf merely earned a pointed look before she disappeared into the practice yard, where the thwack of arrows hitting the target could soon be heard.

He and Angus were barely out of sight along the road before the lord asked, "What do you think of her?"

"I think Portia is a lovely, strong-minded young woman," Rudolf said cautiously.

Angus laughed. "The stubbornest of my three little pigs, you mean. If it comes to war, as I fear it might, she would take up a sword to fight right alongside the rest of us. It would have been better for her if she'd been born a boy."

"I would not like her so much if she was," Rudolf said without thinking. He regretted the words the moment they left his lips, but it was too late to retrieve them.

Angus turned an appraising eye in his direction. "Yes, and she likes you, too. She doesn't think anyone notices, but sometimes she looks at you the way her mother used to regard me. She listens to you, too, though she won't listen to anyone else. Maybe you'll be able to control her."

Rudolf burst out laughing. "Control Portia? I pity the man who tries. She will huff and puff and blow his manhood away. She is your daughter, after all."

"And as my daughter, she is also my heir, as I'm sure you know." Angus paused, as if he wanted this to sink in. Finally, he continued, "The man who marries her will also inherit her claim to Isla, when I am gone, and perhaps even my place in council, if the other lords accept him. Birthright is not enough here on the Southern Isles, you understand. A man must also be a leader and a warrior worth following."

Rudolf nodded. His father had told him the same thing when he was a boy in Viken. Varg was the older brother, yet Harald had become king. "My people are much the same. This way, if a king dies while his sons are still young, another man may take the throne while the sons are brought up like any other highborn warriors. When the next king dies…his successor is chosen from among the men with suitable claims of birth, blood and marriage, but he must have the strength to lead the…I suppose you would call them chieftains, much like your lords."

"Here on the islands, every lord is a king within his borders, for an ocean separates him from the others. We have no kings."

This was less true than it appeared, as Rudolf well knew. "Ah, but there is King Harald, whose claim to these lands is responsible for the kind hospitality you have offered me for so many years. And this King Donald, a neighbour who covets what isn't his. And there is yourself, a lord among lords. If the islands had their own king, it would be

you."

Angus nodded in satisfaction, as though this was the answer he'd hoped for. "You've fought with us, as one of us."

"We both serve the same king. Protecting these lands is as much my responsibility as it is yours, though I do not command any men." Yet, Rudolf added silently. He'd distinguished himself in the battles and raiding parties he had fought in, to the point where he easily assumed command when circumstances required it. Lord Angus had taught him battle tactics and strategy were just as important as the strength of his army when battle was joined. But the men he commanded had always belonged to Lord Angus.

Unlike his father, who commanded all the armies of Viken, and the ships, too.

Lord Angus seemed to read his thoughts. "You fight well in the field, and the men follow you. That is no small thing in a land like this one. You understand battle tactics better than most, both on and off the field."

Rudolf was not accustomed to such high praise. "It is a while since I have had a worthy opponent. Perhaps you would agree to a chess match while we wait for the other lords to arrive?" He patted his saddle bag. "I brought mine."

Lord Angus shook his head. "I think your skills at that game surpassed mine a long time ago. But never let it be said that I turned down an offer for battle. We shall play on the shores of Loch Findlugan after the sun sets."

"I look forward to it."

They rode on in silence, lost in their own separate thoughts. As they always did, Rudolf's thoughts turned to Portia, and what she might be doing now without him.

Six

"You have a longer reach. You should be able to best him easily, Keith!" Lina called.

"Widald is so much stronger. Hit him harder, Widald, and you will surely win!" Arlie said.

Portia found her sisters watching a mock battle in the practice yard between two young men who were surprisingly evenly matched. She observed them for a few moments before she realised the men were not really battling at all. All that flexing of muscles, fighting without armour or even shirts, and blows that did not seem to land was a show to impress the two girls. A show that was working, judging by Arlie's gasps and Lina's white-knuckled hands as she clutched them to her chest.

"Your turn," Widald whispered. He hooked Keith's wooden practice sword out of his hand and sent it spinning across the yard, scattering chickens that squawked in protest.

"I yield," Keith said thickly. At some point, Widald must have landed a blow to Keith's nose, for it was still bleeding.

"You won!" Arlie dashed across the yard and wrapped her arms around Widald, who grinned at Keith over Arlie's head.

Lina beckoned to Keith. "Let me see to your wounds."

Keith winked back at Widald.

Portia pursed her lips and waited. When her sisters' ministrations culminated in an invitation to dinner that both men eagerly accepted, she knew the wait would soon be over. Sure enough, the men left the yard to put their weapons away.

"Does my father know you are trying to seduce my sisters?" Portia asked.

Keith and Widald exchanged glances, then bowed. "No, Lady Portia." Neither seemed to want to look at her.

"What do you think he will say when I tell him?" Portia said.

Widald lifted his head to meet her eyes. "When I ask for Lady Arlie, I would hope Lord Angus supports my suit."

"And mine for Lady Lina," added Keith.

Portia hesitated. They meant to marry her sisters, not simply seduce them? The girls were of an age for it, much like herself, but it had not occurred to her that they might marry so soon. Unlike the slavish daughters of other places, the women of Isla and the other Southern Isles were proud mistresses of their own destiny. They chose their own husbands, or at least most of them did. Even Portia's father could not force her to marry a man not of her choosing. Though the council might put pressure on him and hence her if they had a man in mind.

Perhaps that was why he had left her here — he wanted to discuss possible husbands for her with the council.

"We know how many suitors there are for your hand, Lady Portia. Lina and Arlie might not have the same claim as you, but they are no less beautiful," Keith continued.

Of course they were. The three girls were identical in appearance, if not disposition. Little wonder that people had called them the Three Little Pigs when they were children, for most people couldn't tell them apart.

Her sisters deserved to be happy with men who loved them. They could do much worse than these two. Portia herself might do worse, what with war coming and all. She would not let her choice place Isla in danger.

"I wish you good fortune," Portia said finally, "but not fertility. Not yet." With a sharp look at them, she marched off.

But in the back of her mind, a tiny seed of doubt took root: for the first time, she dreaded her father's return.

Seven

Lord Lewis was the first guest to arrive at Loch Findlugan. His companion was a messenger from King Harald who had much to say to the council. Lord Angus glanced at Rudolf, then took the messenger for a walk around the lakeshore, so that they might discuss weighty matters in private.

Rudolf burned with curiosity as he watched them go, so he jumped when Lord Lewis's arm landed heavily on his shoulder.

"Let them go, boy. We'll find out what they have to say in council, soon enough. Who are you? I don't remember Angus having a son. You look older than those girls of his."

Rudolf gave Lord Lewis his full attention. "I'm Rudolf, Lord Angus's foster son. From Viken."

Lord Lewis clapped him on the back so hard it would have tipped a lesser man over. "Thought so! My mother came from Viken, and insisted on marrying an Islander, for she declared she wanted a man who wasn't a blonde behemoth. She was a shieldmaiden on one of your dragon ships, but she was fonder of the shield than the ship, and she liked my father more than fighting, so when her brothers departed, she stayed."

"Viken women are as fierce as the women here on the islands," Rudolf agreed. "They have the same strong spirit. I'm sure that's why she stayed."

Lord Lewis winked. "Spirited island girls, hmm? Methinks you have one in particular in mind."

For a moment, Rudolf thought he might blush as brightly as Portia. Except no one could outdo Portia at that. He fought to keep his voice light as he said, "I have no bride yet, Lord Lewis. While I am dependent on the kindness of Lord Angus, so far from my family, I have little to offer a lady."

"Hmm." Lord Lewis made a great show of clearing his throat. It was clear he didn't believe Rudolf.

Best to change the topic. "Did your mother ever teach you Viken war games?" Rudolf asked. "I have a chess set I brought from home. Lord Angus and I sometimes play in the evenings. I'd be happy to give you a lesson in how to play, if you like."

Lord Lewis laughed. "I haven't played that in years! Fetch your set, and we'll see who teaches a lesson to who."

Despite his claim of not having played in a long time, Lord Lewis proved a formidable opponent, and Rudolf lost more games than he won. By the time the other lords arrived to occupy Lord Lewis's attention, Rudolf was more than happy to beat a strategic retreat.

Lord Angus caught him packing his chess set deep in the bottom of his saddle bag. "Don't feel too bad. Lord Lewis has such a passion for the game, I have yet to see him lose. If you wish for a fairer match, where you have a chance to win, perhaps you and I can play after the council meets."

Lord Angus was rarely wrong, but this was one occasion Rudolf was happy to tell him so. "Actually, I won several games. Almost half." Rudolf couldn't keep the smugness out of his tone.

Lord Angus laughed. "Then I had best watch out, lest Lewis try to steal you from my household."

"Nothing he has to offer could entice me to agree to that," Rudolf replied. There was no place for him in any household that didn't hold Portia.

Lord Harris hailed Angus, who clapped Rudolf on the shoulder with a vague, "Good man," before he headed off to join his newly arrived friend.

A fleet of fishing boats ferried the assembled lords across the lake to a tiny, bare island where two men were hastily erecting a sort of canopy to keep the rain off. Most of the lords' men had been left on shore with the servants, who busied themselves preparing food for the assembly. The firepit glowed to life and already a pig was turning on the spit, which would hopefully be ready by the time the council meeting was over.

Rudolf expected to be part of the shore party, but Angus had refused to board a boat until Rudolf was on it, so he sat in the bow, facing the green mound that didn't seem grand enough to be Council Island.

The grass grated under the fishing boat's hull. Automatically, Rudolf leaped out onto the waterlogged turf to help pull the craft further out of the water so that Lord Angus wouldn't get his feet wet. Of course, Angus didn't care, for he squelched down right beside Rudolf. "Good show," Angus whispered as he strode past to the top of the hill.

It took Rudolf a moment to realise what Angus meant. The other boats held off, waiting for Angus before they dared to set foot on the holy isle, which had been the place of council meetings for as long as anyone could remember. It was said that the druids and chieftains of a thousand years ago planned their campaigns against foreign armies on this spot.

And he'd been the first to step onto it, not Angus. Why hadn't Angus warned him? Unless he'd wanted Rudolf to precede him...

His suspicion grew stronger as each of the lords landed on the island and left their boats. Some merely glanced at him, while others openly stared. Lord Lewis grinned as though he was privy to Lord Angus's plans. Rudolf wished he'd thought to ask Angus to share his secret. Of course, he'd have had to know there was a secret...

"My friends, lords of the isles, honoured guest." A nod at Rudolf told him Angus meant him. "Welcome once again to Council Island. By now, you should have all received the message from King Donald of Alba..."

Muttering and grumblings erupted from the circle of men. No one liked King Donald, or his message.

Angus cleared his throat. "I, too, have heard it, and I share your discontent. However, for those who might not remember, he has asked for several things. First, that we recognise his claim to the Southern Isles, and acknowledge him as our king. Second, that we pay tribute to him – not just this year, but for every year of his reign. Third, that we provide him with men to fight the war he faces on his southern border."

The grumblings grew louder.

"In exchange, he offers us the opportunity to help him make Alba great again. He will send men to help us drive out the Viken people who have settled among us, and when they are all gone, the men will help us build walls to keep foreign invaders out." Angus held up his hand for silence. "And, he has offered one of his sons as husband for Lady Portia, who he insists must travel to Alba, where she will stay."

Rudolf jumped to his feet. "Portia will never agree to that!" he shouted.

But Angus never heard. Every lord was just as loud, so the cacophony of sound as the rulers vented their displeasure to the sky with shaken fists and colourful language drowned out individual voices. They were a rumble of thunder, heralding the storm to come.

But Angus was not the Lord of Isla for nothing. He waited patiently, letting the men rage until the volume subsided. Slowly, they sank back onto their benches.

All except for Lord Lewis, whose planted feet turned him into a mighty tree that would not be budged. "If you're going to throw out Vikens, then you may start with me," he roared.

Silence fell.

Most of the men looked shocked. Angus's expression never changed. They'd cooked this plan up between them, Angus and Lewis, Rudolf realised, impressed. This could only be the beginning. He settled down to watch what he knew would prove to be an intriguing show.

"My mother was a Viken."

"Mine, too."

"My grandfather came from Viken."

"My sister married one."

Around and around it went, until every man had declared his relationship to some Viken or other. Vikens had lived among the Southern Islanders for centuries, Rudolf knew, so over the last four hundred years, everyone on the islands had some Viken blood in them. It had been a long time since they'd been foreigners to him.

Angus broke the thoughtful silence. "This council made an agreement with the Viken king, an Erik who has long since gone to his heavenly reward. We would share the islands with his people, and they would defend us against invaders. We would stand together to defend our home." He stared around the circle, taking care to meet every set of eyes for a moment until he had them all. "King Harald sits on Erik's throne now, and we no longer share this soil with the council members who met on that fateful day. But we do stand with one of his descendants." Angus motioned for Rudolf to stand. "Prince Rudolf Vargssen is Harald's nephew. He came to my household as a boy, but he is now more than man enough to fight beside us as a member of my family, which he has. Often."

His interrogatory stare swept around the lords again. "King Harald is not here, but his nephew is. Prince Rudolf, what do you advise the council to do?"

He'd caught Rudolf unprepared, and Angus knew it. Rudolf wet his lips. "I would advise…the lords assembled here to honour your agreements. Oathbreakers are reviled on Viken as much as they are here. Is my uncle such a poor ruler that your oaths are worthless to you, and you will choose to buy another king of whom you know nothing? And not just with money and goods. You would buy him with the lives of your men, the virtue of your virgin daughters…for if he sets his sights on the Lady Portia, none of your daughters will be safe. What do we care for the greatness of our neighbours, who would drive a wedge between our combined peoples, and build walls for which there is no need? We do not need Donald or anything he has to offer, and I would advise you to tell him so."

Several men roared their agreement, but others remained silent. When the roars had died down, one man clambered to his feet, tugging his beard as though checking it was secured to his chin.

"You have something to say, Lord Calum?" Angus asked.

The bearded man nodded. "I do. It is clear the boy is Harald's man, however long he has lived under your roof, and of course his loyalty is to his king. To his family."

"I consider Lord Angus as much family as those I left behind in Viken," Rudolf said.

Angus waved him into silence. "Please continue, Lord Calum."

Calum nodded, then said, "I have no desire to be an oathbreaker, but I made no such oath to King Erik or Harald or whoever the Vikens have sitting on their throne. The council who made that long ago oath did so to ensure a lasting peace that we have known for generations. If a similar oath to King Donald now would bring a similar peace, while keeping to old agreements can only lead to war, should we not take the olive branch that is offered, and forge a new agreement?"

Another man rose.

"Lord Roe?" Angus prompted.

Lord Roe inclined his head in acknowledgement. "Donald isn't offering an olive branch. He's handing us a poisoned chalice. There's no promise of peace in his offer. He starts by wanting to make war on our own people, for Viken blood runs in all of our veins. Then he finishes with a demand for our men to fight his wars, which do not concern us. Donald is offering us war where we currently have peace. Harald does not ask for our daughters or our sons – he demands no hostages he can hold against us. I am with Lord Angus!" He sat down, smiling, as the other lords clapped.

All but Calum, whose expression had twisted into a sneer. "You're only kissing Angus's arse so he'll let your lackwit son marry his daughter!" He turned and lifted his tunic, baring his own hairy arse to emphasise his point.

It took several cries of, "Put it away!" and one "No one wants to kiss your hairy butt cheeks, you old walrus!" before Calum finally sat down.

Lord Harris, a giant of a man who didn't need to stand to be taller than the rest, cleared his throat. "Whether we choose Harald or Donald or declare some other poor fool king, I want one thing to be certain. Lady Portia must remain protected here on the Southern Isles, for as long as she lives."

Several men shouted their support, and a grateful Angus called for a vote. In the resulting hubbub, Lewis shuffled close enough to Rudolf to allow him to mutter, "Watch this well. Any man with an unmarried son will side with Angus. Those with none or too many daughters they wish to marry well will take Calum's side."

The lords divided and Lewis kept up his commentary: "Spinster daughter, daughters, doesn't like Vikens because his wife ran off with one, and Calum."

The other men argued loudly with one another, trying to persuade the others to cross to their side.

Rudolf lowered his voice. "Why does Calum hate Angus so much?"

Lewis glanced from one to the other. "Calum thinks he should be Lord of Isla, not his younger brother. But Catriona chose Angus, then died early in their marriage after giving birth to three girls, and Calum has never forgiven him. If Angus supports something,

Calum will oppose it."

Angus counted the men on each side. "The council votes to support Lord Harris's suggestion. My daughter will be protected here on the isles."

"How do you propose to do that?" Calum drawled. "Everyone knows the story of the Three Little Pigs. Locking that girl up is pointless, for she will only escape as soon as it suits her."

Rudolf had long regretted his flippant comment that had resulted in a nickname Portia and her sisters hated. Especially when the story that went with it was now being used so maliciously against her. By her own flesh and blood.

"Find the girl a husband! Then she'll be his responsibility."

Rudolf couldn't tell who had spoken, but he was soon drowned out by offers of sons, nephews, and, in the case of Lord Dand, the young lord himself. He wanted to shout at them all to be silent. Portia would have screamed it, and then delivered a scathing lecture on where they could stash their manhoods, if in fact they still had them when she was done.

Angus had been wise to leave her at home. Rudolf wished he didn't have to witness this.

Lord Lewis cupped his hands to his mouth. "Why not forge an alliance with Harald's family? The young prince here isn't married, so why not make him truly a member of Lord Angus's family by giving him to the girl?"

Rudolf had a sudden vision of himself wrapped in a giant red ribbon, being presented to Portia. At the very least, it would make her laugh.

Angus hushed them. "You have all offered many eligible bachelors for my daughter to consider. But the council has voted to protect her here in the isles, where a woman may choose her own husband. We should each choose our champion, to form a personal bodyguard for her, until that happens. In protecting Lady Portia, they will each have their chance to woo her, if that is their wish."

Now Rudolf wanted to laugh. Hard. Portia would not take the news well when she discovered she was to always be surrounded by a personal honour guard. He sobered when he realised he would be the one who'd have to tell her.

If there was a fate, she was the one laughing at him right now.

Eight

The council meeting dragged on in a series of debates, which ranged from stories the lords had heard about Donald to the difficulties of tithing their own people. This continued until the sun sank low on the horizon, and Rudolf could smell roasting meat from the fire pit on the shore. The fishing boats returned to ferry them across the loch, and Rudolf found himself in the same boat as Lord Ronin, one of the men who had stood beside Calum in the vote about Portia. At first, Rudolf wondered at the man's motive, but Ronin soon enlightened him. Just as Lewis had said, he was a man with many unmarried daughters, and an opportunity to sell them to an eligible bachelor like Rudolf was something Lord Ronin did not intend to miss.

Thankfully the boat trip was short, and Rudolf managed to avoid Ronin for the rest of the evening.

After talking all day, the lords still had plenty to say, though they spoke of more mundane matters. Daughters and wives, sons and servants, sheep and seals, cattle and crops. Rudolf had little to add to any of these subjects, so he simply listened.

Eventually, they all retired early, for they knew it would be another gruelling day on the morrow.

The second day started with less of a show than the first, for Rudolf knew to hang back and let Angus go first. The debate resumed, and Rudolf wished he hadn't come. Day after day, they droned on, seeming to get no closer to a plan of action than they were on the day they began. Yet there were useful suggestions amid the filibustering. Slowly but surely, each man realised what Portia had known instantly: that whatever action they took, it would lead to war.

Sometime on the fifth day, Rudolf was roused from his doze by an elbow administered to his ribs. He instantly regretted his late-night chess match with Lewis, whose sharp elbow was probably a dig at revenge for Rudolf's win last night. Feeling the entire council's eyes on him, Rudolf ventured, "Could you repeat that?"

Angus looked amused. "The council would like to know what kind of assistance King Harald will offer us in this matter. Can you tell us what kind of army he has at his disposal?"

Rudolf spread his arms wide and shrugged. "I have no idea. I was a boy when I left Viken, and I know more of your strengths than I do of my uncle's. Men have died in battle, old men who did not have retired. Boys have become men, and taken the places that belong to greybeards. To know my uncle's true strength, you would have to ask him."

Lord Harris said, "Never mind the numbers, then. Do you believe your uncle will offer men to help defend the isles against Donald?"

Angus stared at him hungrily, expectantly. Rudolf wished he knew what the man wanted him to say.

But he did not, so what Rudolf said was, "I would have to ask him."

Angus jumped in before any of the other lords could. "But a request from his nephew, his own blood, for warriors and weapons would be received far more favourably than anything from the rest of us. I propose that Rudolf make contact with his kinsman in order to enlist his support." Angus surveyed the circle. "Any man who doesn't agree, raise a hand."

Only Calum's hand waved like that of a drowning man for a moment before dropping limply into his lap, defeated. Angus produced a scroll and began to read from it. Amid all the waffling, Angus had paid attention to every word of their discussion. And from it, he had distilled a powerful liquor that would become their brave plan for the future.

Defences would be shored up, more weapons would be made, supplies of food and drink would be stored, and they would remain vigilant. There was no mention of Donald or even Harald.

In short, they would do nothing new. They would continue as they always had, preparing for an attack that might never come, but remaining in readiness for when it did.

The collected lords gave their assent to the plan, though Calum was predictably silent.

It was with considerable relief that Rudolf left the island for good, hoping never to return.

That night they feasted, celebrating their decision as much as the opportunity to see their friends again. For life held many uncertainties, especially with the threat of war, and who knew when they might share bread and meat again?

The ale flowed freely until Calum burst into a surprisingly familiar song. Even Rudolf joined in, though he did not know all the words. The song ended but the singing continued late into the night as all good feasts should. Rudolf grew brave enough to offer some songs from his homeland, though he found he had forgotten many of the words. By night's end, they all sang the same song, for at the bottom of a barrel of ale, all words sound the same anyway.

The next morning, Angus found Rudolf dunking his pounding head in the loch in the hope that the icy waters might wash away some of the cursed ale that still swam behind his eyes.

Rudolf rose and flicked the wet hair off his face. "Good morning, Lord Angus," he said. He glanced behind Angus to find a man he did not know. "And this is…?"

"Gustav Gustavssen, a messenger sent by the King of Viken. He came to summon you home." Angus looked as though the words pained him.

Rudolf did not believe it. "But I promised Portia…"

Angus sighed. "Portia will wait. More important is the help we seek from your uncle. I always knew this day would come, though Varg said it would not. Your King has need of you, and so do we. A message he might ignore, but you? He cannot. Tell him what we face.

Tell him that we are loyal. Tell him everything that took place during your time here. Tell him we were honoured to host you, and that we would be happy to host you again for as long as you wish to stay. You and any Viken men you bring with you." Only now did the worry show in Angus's eyes. "Please, Rudolf. If you have any loyalty or affection for me or my family, I beg you to do this for us."

The lump in Rudolf's throat made it hard to speak. Yet speak he must. "I will," he vowed. He squeezed his eyes shut, forcing out the words that cost him so much to say. "Protect Portia for me. That is all I ask. Protect Portia for me and I promise I will return with all the men I can muster."

Angus bowed his head. "I swear I will."

Rudolf said his farewells with the rest, smiling and nodding to hide the heavy heart within. By the time the sun was high in the sky, Rudolf was resigned. He would follow Gustav the stranger to his fate.

Nine

Portia met her father in the yard, barefoot and out of breath from running. "What happened? Will we be safe?" She peered around her father and her face fell. "Where is Dolf?"

"The council has decided to refuse Donald's demands. They have also sent a message to Harald, the Viken king, asking for reinforcements should Donald choose to invade." Angus sighed, a sound that sank beneath the weighty worries of all the world, or at least the Southern Isles. "Rudolf insisted on carrying the message to the king himself."

Portia didn't want to believe it. "He's gone to Viken? Why? And without saying goodbye?"

"Sailing takes time, and Donald could arrive at any moment. Or he might not arrive at all. Better to have King Harald's help sooner rather than later. Rudolf asked me to tell you goodbye, and to ask you to take care of his things until his return."

Her father might not know it, but his eyes wouldn't meet hers when he lied, just like now.

Portia took a deep, shuddering breath, forcing back the sobs that threatened to choke her.

Rudolf would not come back, and there would be war.

"What must we do to prepare Isla for the coming war?" Portia asked.

Father brightened. "During the council meeting, I made a list. Let's go through it together, shall we?"

He extracted a scroll from his saddlebag and Portia steeled herself for the storm to come.

Ten

The bustling harbour of Portnahaven seemed like another world after the strange solemnity that shrouded Council Island and Loch Findlugan. Rudolf almost wanted to turn back, to see if he could capture the spirit of the place to carry with him across the ocean. For the first time in many years, he felt afraid of what was to come.

He had so much he wanted to do with his life, and none of it involved a return to Viken right now. He burned to know why Harald had summoned him. He'd lived on Isla for so long, he thought they might have forgotten about him.

Yet Gustav was proof that they had not.

People stared at Rudolf and Gustav, as though they had never seen a Viken before. Which couldn't be the case, for two Viken longboats lay in the harbour.

A skinny boy called out from the mast of a merchant vessel, "Are you going to fight the dragon for the princess?"

Rudolf laughed at the thought that even cabin boys believed in fairytales. "No, there are no dragons left in the world, boy. Heroes have slayed them all."

"Not this one! He devours sheep and maidens and the king has offered half his kingdom and a whole princess to the man who brings him the dragon's head!"

A likely tale, though one that was widespread, for even the men on the longboats had heard of it. The details differed widely, but three things remained – the dragon, the half kingdom, and the whole princess.

Word had reached Viken, too, before their arrival. All people could talk about was this dragon. No one seemed to know or care about a looming war for the Southern Isles.

Rudolf paid far too high a price for a horse to carry him to the castle gates, where he drew to a halt, not willing to enter in case it was still Regina's realm. He was not afraid of many women, but Harald's queen had wanted to kill him as a child.

He addressed one of the guards: "Is the king at home? I carry an urgent message from the Southern Isles."

The guard shook his head. "No, he's up in the borderlands, dealing with some Opplanders. He rides at the head of his army – he shouldn't be hard to find."

Harald leading the army? "What about Varg?" Rudolf asked eagerly. Wherever the army was, he would find its commander – his father.

"Varg fell in battle not long ago. That's why the king commands the army now."

Dead? Rudolf received the news like a punch to the gut. He wanted to double over and howl in pain, but he knew he could not. So he straightened, stiffened, and said, "Thank

you."

He turned his horse away from the gate, and headed for the road to Oppland, and the borderlands in between. It wasn't until he was alone in the empty road that he felt the first tear fall.

He was all that was left of his family, and he would never see his father again. Never know if his father was proud of the man he'd become.

More than anything, he wished himself back on Isla, with Angus and Portia. Angus would know what to say to make him feel whole again, and Portia would be sure to hug him until the hole this loss left in his heart had healed over.

He would have settled for just Portia, feeling her soft body against his as their embrace became more intimate, her soft sigh as she yielded to him as she'd yielded to no one else and…

Rudolf cursed. Now he had a raging hard-on, a hole where his heart used to be, a horse which didn't want to do anything he told it to, and a king to find. Who might kill him on sight, to please his queen.

Oh, fate would be rolling around on the floor, she must be laughing to hard at him now.

Grimly, Rudolf rode on.

Eleven

"I caught them showing off for the girls in the practice yard, so I warned them, but Keith and Widald would not listen. I caught Keith kissing Lina in the stillroom several times and I lost count of the number of times Arlie came to dinner with bits of grass or hay stuck to her underdress. Both men said they had honourable intentions and talked of marriage, but I'm afraid – "

Father cut Portia off. "Afraid your sisters might be doing things only married women do? Well, you're all of an age for it. I shouldn't be so surprised. I like having you girls at home so much I admit I've waited longer than I should have to find husbands for you all, but perhaps I have waited long enough. Both Keith and Widald are worthy sons of loyal men. I take it your sisters are fond of them?"

Portia's mouth hung open. Her father wanted to reward them for seducing her sisters? "Y-yes," she stammered. "At least, I think so. Lina seemed happy about the kissing, but Arlie only blushed when I asked about the hay."

"Good, good," Father said. "I'll speak to the men myself. If your sisters agree, I will need your help planning the wedding. As soon as possible, I would imagine."

"Yes, Father." Portia struggled to moisten her dry mouth. "What about me? If I were to…find some man I liked kissing, would you be as happy for me to marry him as you are for Lina and Arlie?" She already knew the answer, but she prayed he might be more forthcoming about who he did want her to marry instead.

Angus sighed. "Portia. You know it is different for you. I would hope that you would stop at just kissing, and not let your feelings get in the way of what is best for you, and Isla. There is a lot riding on the man you choose to marry, and with war coming…we must wait and see. A marriage alliance to the right man at the right time might save us. You are too precious to waste. Instead, I must keep you safe. I have spoken to the other lords on the council, and they have agreed to send some of their best warriors to be your personal guard. They will arrive…"

Father kept talking, but Portia stopped listening.

Inwardly, she breathed a sigh of relief that she would not be asked to marry any man yet.

When the time came, she would do what was best for Isla and the rest of the Southern Isles, but was it too much to ask that she might be allowed to marry for love?

Twelve

Shouts and singing rang out across the valley, punctuated by calls for more ale. Rudolf was surely home, for that was the sound he remembered most. He'd had to sneak into the feasts he'd remembered, for he'd been too young to attend as a full man before he'd left Viken for the Southern Isles, but now he was a man he could take part in full measure.

Would they remember him? Accept him as the man he'd become, or think of him as the boy who'd been banished to the ends of the earth to keep him away from the throne that blood bound him to the same way it bound Reidar, his cousin, the man Regina insisted would be the king's heir?

They toasted the king's health and courage and long life, fearless roars echoing into the night. This was a victory feast, then, for they didn't fear an enemy hearing them.

A cheer rose up, then the bonfire flared as someone threw more fuel on top. Now he could see them – a band of men, mostly sitting, though some stood by, and a servant crouched beside a barrel to fill a cup of ale.

He'd not tasted Viken ale since he was a boy, and even those sips had been stolen, burning down his throat as he fought not to gag at the taste. Reidar had claimed to like it, but then he'd been older, bolder, closer to manhood.

Someone peered into the darkness, as though he knew someone watched them.

It was now or never.

He dug his knees into his horse's side, not wanting to be caught creeping. He was a Viken warrior as much as any of these men, growing up with the same songs they roared even now.

So why did this not feel like home?

He burst into their circle. "I must see the king!" he said, surveying the surprised faces, ale cups hanging halfway to gaping mouths.

He slid from his skittish horse. The foolish beast kicked up sparks with its hooves, frightening itself further. Not for the first time, Rudolf missed the palfrey Lord Angus had given him on Isla. Hector would have known how to make a proper entrance, though now he was in Portia's care, the horse would have no need to do so.

So Rudolf planted his feet as firmly as he'd tried to teach Portia, a memory that lent strength to his tone when he demanded, "Where is the king? 'Twas he who summoned me."

But King Harald was not here. These men were all strangers. Rudolf had been away too long. No sign of recognition on anyone's expression, as hands dropped to the dagger-hilts and axe handles. Then his eyes met the piercing gaze of the man by the ale barrel.

A man who stood straight and tall, no longer crouched like a servant fetching a drink.

"Reidar!" Rudolf cried in relief.

The boy had broadened, even aged a little, but there was no mistaking his cousin, or the way he lifted the cup of ale to his own lips. Reidar served no one; the heir to the throne had no need to kneel.

For a moment, Reidar could have been the Lord of Isla, pausing to take stock before delivering some weighty judgement. This was not the boy who'd hunted boar with careless courage so many years ago. This was a man who meant to be king.

And for the first time, Rudolf didn't care. Reidar could have his throne. Together with his horse, Rudolf had left his heart in Portia's safekeeping, on Isla. Though the girl did not know it yet.

"Cousin!" Rudolf cried, folding a resisting Reidar into his manly embrace. "It is good to see you. Where is the king?"

Loud laughter greeted him from all sides, and Rudolf realised his mistake. If Harald was not here and all those he'd spoken to swore the king rode at the head of this army, then the crown had passed to Reidar.

Uncertainty crossed Reidar's face for the first time – ah, there was a boy beneath the king still, though he tried to hide it. "Rudolf?" His grin of recognition was everything Rudolf could have hoped for. "I thought you'd sailed off the western edge of the world!"

The men around him relaxed, whispering to each other that he was Prince Varg's son, the other royal prince. Now the hostile eyes turned expectant.

Rudolf racked his brain for what they might expect of him. Gifts? Plunder? He had neither, for he hadn't gone raiding. It took him a moment to recollect that the people of Viken were no different to those of Isla when a traveller came to visit – they wanted to hear new tales.

So he kept his voice deliberately light as he spun a tale of paradise found at the Southern Isles. And the beauty of its women, though he didn't dare mention Portia by name.

Reidar's expression darkened at the mention of women.

Rudolf quickly changed topic to talk about the gossip in every port – the Kasmirus dragon that no man could slay.

Even that did not cheer Reidar.

Realising he was rapidly wearing out what little welcome Reidar offered, Rudolf bowed his head in memory of Harald. "I am sorry for your loss, cousin. Your father was a good king, and a wise one, too." After all, it had been King Harald's command that had sent him to the Southern Isles, even if he knew it had been his father's idea. Both men had seen how close the cousins were – like brothers, as far apart in age as Harald and Varg themselves. Yet Rudolf had faithfully promised his father that he would return to serve Reidar when his cousin became king.

Realisation dawned more suddenly than any sunrise. If Harald had died so recently, then he had been the one to summon Rudolf home, knowing Reidar would need him. Perhaps Harald had not had a chance to tell Reidar. With Regina pouring poison into Reidar's ear about Rudolf's desire for the throne, Reidar probably suspected Rudolf was here to make a claim for the kingship.

If Rudolf couldn't convince him of his

loyalty to the crowned king, Reidar could have him killed before he could return to Portia and fulfil his promise to her. Rudolf knew himself to be a capable fighter, but he was no match for an army. He was here to fight alongside his countrymen, not against them. Did Reidar know that? Or was he little more than Regina's puppet…and Rudolf would be forced to claim the crown he did not want?

"Why else would he send me to the ends of the earth to learn warcraft from some foreign lord?" Rudolf forced out a laugh to hide his pain at speaking so ill of Lord Angus. But needs must, if he was to win Reidar's trust. "I can tell you tales of tactics their men use in battle that we would never think of. I would not have believed them, had I not seen it with my own eyes."

"Battle tactics? But Mother said – "

"Is Aunt Regina still around? She will outlive us all, that battle axe will. I remember she caught me sitting on your father's throne once. She clouted me over the ear and gave me such a tongue lashing I couldn't open my mouth in her presence for a year. She said if she ever caught me sitting there again, she'd thrash my backside until I had nothing left to sit on!" Rudolf laughed as though it was all a joke to him, though it had not been to Regina. No, the queen would never forgive the slight to her son.

So Regina still lived. Pity. Her son would stand stronger without her. Even Rudolf knew that. But if he could pry Reidar away from her, perhaps he might still be a good king. He and Reidar had been like brothers, and the boy he'd known was no lapdog. The man before him might still be a stranger.

A stranger who doubted him.

Rudolf met Reidar's gaze steadily. Perhaps sending him away had made Rudolf the stronger man after all. The true king could not walk away from this meeting as the loser, though he did not need to win.

Almost as though Reidar could read his mind, the king gave a slight nod. It was decided – whatever it was.

Reidar cleared his throat, raising his voice so the assembled men might hear. "Tomorrow, we ride west, to where there are reports of a foreign force waiting to ambush us. In three days' time, we shall go into battle. Will you join us, cousin?"

A challenge, and a fight. Reidar knew what he was about. Even if he'd wanted to, Rudolf couldn't refuse. "The Southern Isles may have softened me, but beneath it beats a Viken heart still!" Rudolf declared. "I will fight at your side like we did as boys."

"Ale for my cousin! We must toast his return!" Reidar roared.

Another man filled the cup – not Reidar this time – but it was Reidar the man handed it to, and Reidar who then presented it to Rudolf. A masterful piece of theatre.

But Rudolf was better versed in such things. Regina would never have allowed her precious son to play-act, but Portia and her sisters had pulled him into their playing as often as they could.

Rudolf took the offered cup with both hands as though it held the blood of the saviour himself. He held it aloft as he knelt before Reidar, praying he wouldn't spill any. It wouldn't do to splash the king's shoes. He raised his voice to a shout that matched Reidar's for volume. "Nay, a toast to my cousin, the new King of Viken. May his reign be long and filled with so many victories the bards forget to sing of anyone else!"

Silence reigned for a long moment as the other men waited to see their king's reaction. Rudolf barely caught the tiny nod, but it was there. Reidar might not be perfectly comfortable in the role yet, but he was definitely their king.

The men shouted, raising their own cups to second Rudolf's toast.

Only then did they offer him a place at the fire. And Rudolf took it, pleased to be accepted back into the land of his ancestors.

A land that was no longer home.

Thirteen

If there was one good thing about the threat of war, it was that Portia's archery skills improved. The finger guards Rudolf had given her clung like a second skin even as they protected her, while she loosed arrow after arrow at a target so full of holes it resembled cork instead of wood.

"Portia."

Portia lowered her bow. "Yes, Father?"

"I have some men you must meet."

Sighing, she unstrung her bow, knowing she would have no more time for practice if they had guests.

Sure enough, the hall seemed full of men — young, loud and dressed in their best armour. Lords' sons, she guessed. Now, more than ever, she ached with loss at Rudolf's leaving. He would have greeted the men and deflected their acquisitive stares. Without him, she had the distinct impression they regarded her like a succulent leg of lamb. That desire to devour.

Portia shivered, then straightened. She was the lady of this hall, and her welcome must honour the ancient laws of hospitality that bound them all. "Good day, and welcome to my father's hall," she said.

The men stumbled all over each other to bow.

"We thank you, Lady Portia," said a man with hair as red as her own. "I certainly think I will enjoy my stay here." He made no effort to hide his approval as he looked her up and down.

Like he was buying a lamb for slaughter, Portia thought uneasily.

Angus edged into the hall beside her. "The council agreed that you deserved a guard of your own to protect you, now Rudolf has returned to Viken. Each of the lords offered one of their best fighting men to be your protector. With the prospect of war, I thought it prudent to accept their offers. All of them."

Best fighting men? Portia gave a breathy snort as she surveyed the newly puffed-out chests and proudly lifted heads. Finest fighters indeed. These were men who did not realise guard duty was nothing to be proud of. Men their lords would not miss. They were certainly no true replacement for Rudolf.

"Welcome to my father's household, then," she said, fighting to hide her fury. She turned to her father. "May I return to the practice field, please?"

With her father's permission, she marched back outside and across the field to the target. She ripped the arrows out, not caring if they took chunks of wood with them. She'd ask for a new target when she'd shot this one to pieces – next week, at this rate.

Her arms filled with arrows, she turned and found the band of men watching her from the edge of the field. Had they never seen a girl shoot before?

She let the arrows clatter to the sod at her feet, then strung her bow. If they wanted to watch, so be it. She would give them a show.

Notch, draw, aim, breathe, loose. It was Rudolf's voice whispering the words in her head.

Loose.

Loose.

Loose.

Unbidden, a smile warmed her lips. It was almost like having him here beside her once more.

"Lady Portia?"

This whisper was not Rudolf.

"Lady Portia, I just wanted to say that you have no need to defend yourself now, for I would be delighted to do it for you. My sword is always ready."

Portia followed his gaze to his sword hilt, raising her eyebrows at the tent his other sword had pitched beneath his tunic. "So I see," she said drily, turning away. Her next arrow skimmed across the top of the target.

As she notched another arrow, an arm

snaked around her waist. "Lady Portia, if you will permit me to assist you. I am a skilled archer, and I always hit my mark." His hand drifted higher, headed for her breast.

Portia stomped on the man's foot and twisted out of his embrace. "Not today, thank you." Not ever.

Her next arrow fell short of the target.

A heavy hand landed on her shoulder. "Lady Portia, if you but lift the bow a little higher – "

Portia whirled, drawing the bow back. The heavy handed one backed up so quickly he almost landed on his arse. She pointed her arrow at each man in turn, punctuating her words. "The next man who says my name or touches me is going to get an arrow through his manhood. And no matter how small that target might be, I will not miss."

When no one moved, she added, "Didn't your fathers warn you about me?"

Now they backed up a few steps. All but one man, who held his ground.

Portia aimed her arrow at the stubborn one.

He bowed deeply. "My father, Lord Lewis,

did indeed warn me about you. He said that one day soon, we would all be forced to fight for our homes, as foreign kings battle over who owns us. And not just us. King Donald offered his son to be your husband, and King Harald will undoubtedly do the same. As the Lady of Isla, you are at the very heart of our people, of our home. When you marry, the council will crown your husband not as Lord of Isla, but as our king. None of us deserves that honour. Not yet. We are here to defend your honour, because to lose you is to lose all the Southern Isles." Now he straightened and lifted his chin, so that he might meet her eyes. "Lady Portia, I will defend you with my life. And any man here who thinks he has the right to seduce you against your will, a lady who is courted by kings, will have to get through me." He marched across the no man's land and planted his feet firmly in the middle ground between Portia and her would-be suitors. He drew his sword, then threw it on the ground, followed by his dagger. "Go on. If you think you're man enough to be king, fight me!"

His first opponent was the biggest of them,

as broad and tall as Rudolf. He bunched one meaty fist and swung it at young Lewisson.

Lewisson dodged. His elbow swung behind him slightly before he jabbed his own fist into the giant's midsection. The man went down, with Lewisson on top of him.

They rolled on the ground, kicking and punching, until someone said thickly, "Yield!"

The two men broke apart. Only then could see Lewisson was the victor while the other man limped away, pressing a hand to his bleeding nose.

Lewisson's second opponent charged at him while his back was turned. Portia shouted a warning, but the stocky man bulled into Lewisson just as he turned to face him, too late to keep his balance. Lewisson grabbed him as he fell, so they both tumbled to the ground together. They wrestled for some time, each trying to break the other man's ribs as they rocked first one way, then the other.

"Enough!" Angus roared.

Lewisson rolled away from his opponent. He still had the presence of mind to place himself between the other men and Portia.

"You're here to protect the lady, not fight amongst yourselves. I have your oaths, boys. Break them, and I will send you home in disgrace."

Most of the men ducked the heads, shamefaced. Boys indeed.

All except Lewisson.

Portia held out her hand to help him up.

He laughed, waving away her offer of assistance as he clambered to his feet. He wiped away a trickle of blood from his split lip. "My father forgot to warn me about how beautiful you are, Lady Portia. Now I see why a war will be fought for you."

Portia shook her head. Her voice was chilly as she said, "Not for me. For my home."

He inclined his head. "As you say. We all fight for something. I will fight for your honour and mine, Lady, but I have more at stake than most. I am the youngest son of Lord Lewis, to be sure, but I was fostered at Rum Isle with Lord Ronin and his daughters. Lady Rhona and I have…an understanding, I suppose you would call it. Her father had no men to send to serve you, so he sent me. If I serve you well, Rhona and I will be allowed to marry when I go home."

Portia's expression softened into a smile. "I'm sure you will. I pray that Lady Rhona will have you home soon."

His answering smile was bleak. "If my father is right, as he usually is, this war will be long and bitter. You will have need of every man among us to defend you. But at the end, I hope to invite you and your husband to my wedding."

"Thank you." Portia remembered her manners. "What is your name?"

His eyes widened, and he bowed low. "Forgive my rudeness. Lady Portia, I am Grieve Lewisson, foster son to Lord Ronin." He straightened. "I should probably let you get back to your archery practice. You set an example we should all follow." Grieve turned and cupped his hands to his mouth. "Oi, you lot. You can't expect Lady Portia to shoot all the invaders herself. Get your bows and show the lady you can do more than stand around looking pretty and staring at her arse!" He reddened. "Sorry, my lady. Your bottom, I meant."

Portia waved away both the swearing and the apology. Instead, she watched in wonder as the other men hurried to obey Grieve.

They soon had a row of targets, bristling with arrows.

Grieve roared, "Cease fire!" He waited for the bows to lower before he pointed at the targets. "Right, retrieve!"

Portia marched across the field with the rest of them to refill her quiver. Out the corner of her eye, she watched Grieve as he walked the line of targets, offering advice to the others. Most of the men nodded in response.

So that was how you commanded men, she thought. Idly, she wondered if Rudolf would be as capable. He was no lord or lord's son, but there was something about him that made you want to follow him.

Grieve appeared at her side. "Do you need help with those, my lady?"

Too late, Portia realised she'd been so busy watching him, she'd forgotten about her arrows. Her face grew hot.

"No, but thank you," she said.

She might not have Rudolf, but Grieve might be a suitable substitute. At least for a while.

Fourteen

Rudolf had never liked the wait before a battle began. His armour hugged him like a protective parent, though he wished he'd forgone his helm for this battle. He wanted to see things clearly, and he was willing to risk his head to do so. Truth be told, he wanted to see how his cousin fought, and generalled the battle, but Reidar had placed him on one wing while the king himself stood in the other. Once the fighting began, he wouldn't be able to see across the Opplander army, for their men stood as tall as Vikens. Well, they must be kin, however distant, if they thought to claim Reidar's throne.

That, or fools who didn't care if they died.

Rudolf surveyed the Viken army. The Opplanders were fools indeed, no matter whose kin they were.

A roar rose up, commanding the Vikens to charge. As though they were one man, they did, Reidar with them.

Rudolf swore and took off at a run.

The king leading the charge? To hell with the Opplanders. Surely Reidar could not be such a fool as to believe he was like the great hero kings of old?

Rudolf blocked an attack that came in from the side, taking it on his shield as his sword slid below to gut the man before he could strike again. Rudolf pulled his sword free and kept running.

An axe came at him and he twisted away, but not before it took a chunk out of his shield. The man tried to raise his axe again for a better blow, but Rudolf was faster. The men of the Southern Isles sometimes fought barehanded, and when they did, they fought dirty. His boot caught the man in his midsection, folding him in half. He screamed as his axe bit into his own flesh, but Rudolf leaped over him and ran on.

Another axe clattered across his shield, badly thrown, followed by the arm of the unfortunate axeman. His corpse must be one of those littering the ground, a carpet of groaning, crawling dead, the like of which Rudolf had been told dwelled in hell. Something squashed and spurted beneath his foot, but Rudolf didn't care. His only care was his cousin, the king.

A giant of a man came at him, two hands clenched around his axe haft as he swung it in a deadly arc.

The blade took off the head of the Viken beside Rudolf, slowing for but a moment before coming to collect his.

Rudolf was faster. He ran at the giant and slashed upward with his dagger, aiming for the man's unprotected throat. Blood bubbled, but not before the axe finished its half-circle swing, for the weapon had a momentum of its own. Down went the giant, with Rudolf on top of him, pinned to the dying man by the axe handle across his back.

Rudolf stabbed again, determined to fight his way free. The giant screamed, gurgled, then stilled. Rudolf wiped the gelatinous globe that had once been the giant's eye off his blade before he rose.

He had a moment to see someone slice Reidar's side before another axe-wielding giant blocked his way. Rudolf hated giants.

"Protect the king!" Rudolf bellowed to the men around him as he lifted his sword to meet the down-swinging axe. Something squelched under his foot and a surprised Rudolf slid several feet before he stopped, now behind the giant who'd wanted to cleave him in two.

Now, there was nothing between him and Reidar, except the king's opponent, whose axe blade was red with Reidar's blood.

Rudolf broke into a run, lifting his sword to run the man through. Perhaps he should have slowed, for his blade went straight through the man's throat as he turned to avoid a sword wielded by another of the king's men. It mattered not. The king was alive, and his opponent was dead.

Reidar eyes were wide with a panic Rudolf shared. Yes, he had almost died. "Thank you," Reidar said.

Rudolf longed to tell him to leave the battlefield to his more than capable men, but Reidar would not welcome a command from his cousin, however well meant. So all he said was, "Any time, my king," before he turned away to take on another Opplander.

Out of the corner of his eye, Rudolf saw Reidar leave the field of his own volition, not as a coward, but as a general walking among his troops. The battle was almost won, anyway – only a few Opplanders remained.

Including one last giant, who charged up to Rudolf as though he was a human battering ram. "You killed my brothers!" he shouted.

Rudolf didn't see the man's axe strapped to his back until it came up in a deadly arc he was too slow to dodge, though he knew it would cleave through his head, helm and all. So he grabbed the giant's arm instead, and hung on with all his weight.

Then the axe blow landed, and the world

went black.

Fifteen

Father threw the scroll down on the table with a sigh. "Portia, do we have everything we need to put on a lavish feast? The sort we'd do for an important guest?"

Portia's heart leaped within her. "A guest?"

With her sisters married and gone to live with their husbands, that left just her and Father in the huge longhouse, and sometimes not even him, when another council meeting was called. Oh, she had her men, as Father called them, but they slept in the barracks across the yard. A barracks they'd built, to protect her honour, they said, though she suspected she had Grieve to thank for that.

He had this habit of asking her, oh so politely, every morning how she'd slept. After one particularly noisy night, she'd confessed that the men's snoring had kept her awake, and they'd started building the barracks that very afternoon.

They had settled down to do what they'd been sent here for - protecting her. Protecting her from what, Portia wasn't sure. Herself, maybe. Not that they had much to protect her from. The most dangerous thing to occur in all their time guarding her had happened yesterday, when her bowstring had snapped and sliced her arm. Rudolf would have seen the thinning string and told her to replace it long ago, she was sure of it, but he was still in Viken, and she was here with...her men.

Unless he was the guest.

Father sighed. He did far too much of that lately, and his smiles were more rare than summer snow. "Donald keeps sending more messages, and the council refuses to respond. In the last one, he said he would send envoys that we could not ignore. According to this missive, his envoy has arrived at Isla, and he invokes the ancient laws of hospitality for us to welcome the man."

Laws the Islanders obeyed, but would the foreigners? Portia wondered. Sharing bread and meat with someone under your roof gave them guest right, the right to your protection for as long as they stayed. Accepting this hospitality then gave the guest an obligation to honour the host. Neither could take up arms against one another while they dwelled under the same roof. Twenty years had passed, but people still spoke about the day Calum had struck her father at a feast. Portia had only been a baby at the time, and her father still grieving her mother's death, but she knew the details as though she'd been there.

Calum had arrived late, when everyone else was seated. He'd marched into her father's hall, and levelled him with one blow before accusing him of murdering Portia's mother. He'd remained in the hall only long enough to seize the remains of a ham which he swung by his side as he marched out, never to return.

When Nurse had told it, she'd added some fanciful embellishments of her own. Calum's eyes had glistened with tears, and his usually cleanshaven face had been shadowed with stubble. He'd never shaved since, Nurse said. Or that he'd called down a curse on Angus as he departed, swearing he would lose everyone he loved, a fitting fate for Catriona's killer. Then he'd choked on the ham and she'd had to save him.

Given how many times she'd had to save Arlie from choking on whatever food she tried to swallow whole in her eagerness to eat, Portia had believed it.

"Portia?"

Portia shook her head. "Mm?"

"I said he will be here by nightfall. Do we have sufficient supplies for a feast, or will we need to send for more?" Angus asked with a bite of impatience in his tone.

It was Portia's turn to sigh. Lina would know, if she were here. She would have enough on hand to feed every man on Isla. "I will ask the cook." She turned to go.

Father caught her arm, his grip gentle but

firm. "Keep your men near all the time now. I fear you will have need of them."

Her father was rarely wrong, and there was no point in arguing. "Yes, Father." At least she wouldn't be lonely.

She buried herself in preparations for the impromptu celebration that she had no heart for, so deeply that when she heard the clop of hooves on the road, she was surprised to find the sky fading into dusk.

It sat ill with her to set a place for Donald's man at her father's right hand, for that was Rudolf's place, though it had been years since he'd last sat there.

Would he ever return?

"My lady, are you well?" Grieve's voice cut through her grief.

Portia nodded and wiped her eyes. "Of course. A mote of dust in my eye, is all. Blown up from the road, as our guests approach. We should take our places in the hall before the dust in the yard gets worse with so many men and horses." She lifted her chin turned her gaze on the open doors to the hall.

Donald's envoy shuffled inside like a seal

walking on its tail flukes. A wide, grey column of a man, tapering only at his feet. A gold medallion suspended from a thick, gold chain was his only badge of office, distinguishing him from the other members of his small party.

When the envoy reached the dais that held the lord's table, Father rose, spreading his arms to offer a traditional welcome.

"You call this a hall?" the seal man complained. "I wouldn't keep pigs in this." He sniffed. "And where is the girl?"

Father hesitated for only a moment, but it was long enough for Portia to feel his anger build. Not that he let it show in his voice. "Sir, I welcome you to our humble home, where you will be offered every hospitality. I am Lord Angus of Isla, and this is the Lady Portia, of whose famed beauty I'm sure you have heard much."

And woe betide him if he hadn't, Portia added silently.

"That plain, freckled lass looks nothing like a lady, or a beauty. Prince Malcolm will be most disappointed. He'll have to bed her in the dark with his eyes closed. If she's the best you have, your women must all be uglier than this hall. I'm surprised King Donald thinks you are worthy allies at all. Savages like you people don't deserve to own land."

Portia rose, her blood heated to boiling within her. "And I am surprised you are fool enough to insult a man in his own hall, when his men outnumber you so. King Donald must be even more of a fool to send you as an envoy, unless he dislikes you so much he wants you to die."

The envoy paled, tugging at his collar as he licked his lips. "Tame your sow, Angus, and teach her to be silent, or Prince Malcolm will cut out her tongue."

"My lady," Grieve whispered. "Might I recommend – "

"No, you may not," Portia hissed. Only two men could tell her what to do. Rudolf, who was not here, and –

"Portia, please," Angus said.

Portia sat down, glaring at the envoy.

Angus continued, "Will you accept our offer of hospitality…ah, I do not believe I caught your name, sir."

"You may call me Lord Mason, for if a hall such as this makes you a lord, then I am surely one twice over, for I have a castle and my cousin is a captain in the king's guard," the pale-faced seal said with shaky grandeur.

A nobody, then, and Portia had guessed right. Donald did not care if this man lived or died.

Yet her father sat the nobody beside him in the place of honour and served him first.

Mason's complaints continued:

"This lamb is too tough."

"We only give such food to pigs."

"Why have you no music in this hall?"

Portia choked at the third one. Men sang when they were merry, and deep in their cups. Not when they waited for a word from their lord to avenge the insult done to him by his ungrateful guest.

Mason clapped his pudgy hands. The sound was moist, tasting of fear. "My men shall provide music for us."

The small band of men who'd followed him into the hall now clustered in front of the closed doors and pulled out various pipes and drums. To Portia's fascination, they began to play.

What came out couldn't be called music. No, it sounded like two tomcats fighting over a she-cat screaming in heat.

She wanted to laugh, or cover her ears as many of her father's men were doing, but she could not. No, she sat like the lady Mason said she was not, and presided over the meal with the composure of a queen. Pretending the caterwauling was as pleasant to her ears as it apparently was to Mason.

Food came and went from the kitchen, and Portia began to grow drowsy. Too much wine, she suspected, but it was too late to do anything about that now.

Mason rose to his unsteady feet. "Now, where is this bed you promised me? Little more than a straw pallet, I suspect, but King Donald will change all that in time!"

King Donald would change nothing at the islands, Portia swore, then rejoiced as the pipers finally finished. The silence was...heavenly.

Except that it wasn't silent. There was the clink of metal, the thump of boots, the…

Someone threw the doors open. "My lord!" the man gasped.

"What is it, man?" Angus asked.

"A…an army! Albans, by the look of them. The yard is full of them. Men and horses!"

Mason seemed smug. "You offered King Donald's envoy your hospitality, Angus. You didn't think I'd be fool enough to come alone, did you? The rest of the envoy waited for their horses to be brought ashore. Some of them may have to sleep in the fields, for now, until we can build barracks for them."

"Get into the barracks with your men. Now!" Angus hissed before he rose and forced a smile. "Of course, Lord Mason. I wish I had known how many guests you'd brought. I fear our paltry feast tonight will not feed so many."

Portia let Grieve hustle her through the kitchens to the barracks, her men falling in behind them. "You, get her things. You, clear mine out and find me a bed in the barracks hall. You and you, you're to stand watch until I tell you otherwise. No one enters the barracks unseen, you hear me?"

His men murmured their assent and divided to do Grieve's bidding.

Portia stared at the barracks hall, a smaller version of the longhouse with beds lined up along the walls. Fires at either end failed to keep away the chill tonight as Portia shivered.

"You will have your cloak soon, my lady," Grieve said. "You shall sleep in the loft, and pull the ladder up after you. Your men will sleep below to keep you from harm."

Portia couldn't seem to form words. Chaos swirled in her head, and she thought she might faint. She drew in a steadying breath, followed by another. "Grieve, tell me true. Is there an Alban army outside, one that outnumbers my father's men?"

Grieve looked into her eyes for a long moment. He had served her for long enough to know not to lie to her. "Are you sure you want to know?" he said finally.

"You could have just said yes," she grumbled. "I want to see them."

"Ascend to the loft. You will see all you need to, my lady."

She hauled her body up the ladder, and soon saw what Grieve meant. The roof that looked so solid from the outside had peepholes along its length, large enough to see through. Or shoot an arrow through, she thought idly.

Men milled around in the yard, and in the fields beyond. Small fires burned on all sides, silhouetting men like monsters from a nightmare.

King Donald had invaded, and she did not know if any of them would survive until morning.

Sixteen

Day dawned, and no one was dead. Except the dozen sheep they'd slaughtered to feed the Albans.

Portia dressed and made her way down the ladder.

"Wait, my lady. We must go with you."

Portia remembered just how many Albans were outside, and decided to do as Grieve said. Cowal and Damhan blocked the doors to the kitchen and outside, anyway. Or they did, until a nod from Grieve had them leading the way out into the yard.

Swallowing, Portia followed.

There were no horses here now, but that meant room for more men. Men who stared with longing and awe.

"That's the girl?"

"Prince Malcolm's bride?"

"Wish I had a wife so pretty."

"Beautiful, isn't she?"

"Wonder why the king doesn't want her himself."

Portia allowed herself a tiny smile at their admiration. It almost soothed away the sting of Mason's insults from last night. He might think her ugly, but he stood alone.

"Make way for milady!" Cowal bellowed, his hand on his sword.

He wasn't the only one. All of them were poised to draw their weapons in her defence. Portia prayed it would not be necessary.

As though they'd heard her silent prayer, the tide of yellow tunics parted, bowing with respect that did not appear feigned. She straightened her spine and marched proudly to the hall. When she reached the warmth it offered, she wanted to relax, but she knew she could not. Men crowded in here, too, as thickly as the yard.

"Good morning, Portia," Father said gravely.

"Good morning, Father," she said as she took her accustomed seat. A servant brought her bread and meat and fruit, and she thanked the girl profusely. When Mason curled his lip and made a disgusted sound, Portia turned to him and said, "Good morning, Lord Mason. I trust you slept well."

His response was a wordless glare.

"I wonder how long you will be willing to endure our humble hospitality?" Portia bit into her bread, not expecting an answer.

"Until something more suitable is built," Mason said. "I have sent men scouting for suitable locations already. I don't suppose there's a quarry on this island. Wood and straw, everywhere I look." He eyed the thatched roof as though it had insulted him.

Portia wouldn't have been surprised if it had. Mason definitely deserved it.

"I hope you find what you're looking for soon," she said sweetly.

"The sooner I have a house befitting my station, the sooner I can keep the prince's bride safe, where she will not be a distraction to my men. Angus, is there somewhere you can keep her in the meantime where she will stay out of trouble?" Mason asked.

Portia wanted to tell him that he was the one who'd brought trouble to her island, but her father's quelling glance kept her quiet. Mason wasn't worth wasting her breath.

"Portia, it might be best if you took your meals in your chambers from now on," Father said.

Her chambers? Or did he mean the loft in the barracks?

Grieve seized her plate. "Let me carry that for you, my lady." He motioned for Damhan to take her cup. With Dermot following close behind her, Portia found herself herded through the kitchen and back to the barracks.

By the time the door closed behind Dermot, Portia was so mad she could spit. "Do you mean to hold me prisoner here? Me?"

"Lady Portia, those are Albans out there. Our people honour you as you deserve but those men would carry you off whether you will or no. When they fight battles on their own soil, they expect their wives to follow after them, and collect the valuables off the corpses of those they've slain. If one of those men tries to take you…" Grieve trailed off.

He didn't need to continue. If someone tried to take her, her men would defend her. That would violate the tenuous truce between guests and host, and there would be war. Her men would die. Her father would die. And Portia herself…she swallowed. Whatever happened, she wouldn't like it.

Hiding in a loft was a small price to pay for her freedom, and her life. Even if her freedom was restricted to a smoky loft above a room where ten men slept and snored and occasionally forgot there was a lady listening.

"I will bring you anything you ask for, as long as you stay safe, my lady," Grieve pleaded. "As long as we have you, Donald cannot conquer Isla."

If only he could bring her Rudolf. She could endure anything, if he were here.

"If you swear to bring me news of

everything that goes on outside these walls..."
When she saw Grieve nod, Portia bowed her
head. "Then I surrender myself to your care,
Grieve."

Seventeen

Rudolf woke to someone trying to yank his head off.

"One, two, three, pull!"

No, make that two someones.

"Stop, you hellspawn whoresons! You'll pull my head clean off my shoulders!" he roared.

"Will you listen to that? He's not dead, after all. The king will be pleased."

Rudolf couldn't see through his helm any more, so he reached up to take it off. The steel wouldn't budge. A careful examination revealed a sizeable dent that ran from his eye to his mouth. If he hadn't worn a helm the blow would have killed him.

"Right, let's try this again. You pull, and I'll try to manoeuvre it so that it actually comes off without taking my head off, too," Rudolf said.

An eternity of tugging, face-pulling and swearing later, a third man joined in the fray, shoving down Rudolf's shoulders as the other two men pulled the helm up.

"Fucking…whoresons…rot in hell!" Rudolf shouted as the steel ripped off his nose, or at least that's what it felt like. When he dared to feel his face, he found his nose still attached, but badly broken. "Thank you. I hope you get your hats stuck on some day so that I might return the favour."

They all laughed, including Rudolf. Because that's what you did if you survived a battle against the odds.

Then a healer came over with a cloth he pressed to Rudolf's already tortured nose. "Fuck off!" Rudolf mumbled through the cloth, but the healer took no notice.

Reidar's wound was tended to, Rudolf

noticed with satisfaction as the king sat down beside him. Reidar still looked like something troubled him, though – something that made him send the healer away.

That got Rudolf's attention.

Reidar dropped his voice so low that only Rudolf would hear the words. "Why did you do that? Call the men to me during the battle?"

Because he needed the help and he was busy, Rudolf wanted to say, but that made Reidar sound weak. Angus would not have questioned it. Harald had been a fool for not teaching his son the most basic things about kingship. "By Lucifer's leathery balls, man! Because it's a man's duty to protect his king. We're yours to command. There's no doubt in anyone's mind that you can fight as well as any man here, and none of us question your right to rule." He tried to smile to lighten his words. "But if you fall in battle, I'll have to sit on your seat, and Aunt Regina will never forgive me."

"What, you don't want a crown, cousin?"

Rudolf's head throbbed at the thought. "Right now, I want nothing on my head at all. My ears are still ringing from the blow to my helm. I would much rather a cup of ale than a crown." And Portia's hands carrying the cup.

Reidar's face clouded, then he turned away from Rudolf as he called for ale.

It took a moment for Rudolf to realise what caused the cloud – suspicion. Regina's poison had truly taken hold in Reidar, and he would never be the king he needed to be while he clung to the lacings of his mother's gown. Reidar belonged on his fucking throne while Rudolf dealt with the borderlands, and it was time the man saw that. To damnation with suspicion and jealousy and playing politics. They spoke plain in the Southern Isles and Rudolf refused to dance around the truth any longer.

Rudolf seized Reidar's arm and pulled him close so that no one might hear his words. "If you die without an heir, your crown falls to me anyway. We both know this. Go back to your castle, get yourself a bride, and put a boy in her belly. Several, if you can. Let me lead the army in your stead."

Reidar raised hopeful eyes to meet Rudolf's. "To what end, cousin? You have a plan, I am sure of it."

Harald had needed Varg, as much as Reidar needed Rudolf now. Rudolf cursed inwardly. Portia would have to wait. "All men plan, but not all plans bear fruit. Rest assured, mine do not need you to die here on a battlefield like my father and yours. I want this kingdom secure as much as you do. These raiders and would-be usurpers must die!" Rudolf raised a fist and shook it, as much at the Opplanders as at the Albans keeping him from Portia.

Reidar regarded him for a long moment before he nodded slowly. "Very well. Will the men follow you?"

Rudolf laughed. "They did today. They're loyal men who serve their king. Why would they not?" Angus would not have doubted him. But then Angus knew him, as Reidar did not. The sooner Reidar left, the sooner he could take command of this army and scour the borders of men who thought the King of Viken was weak. The sooner he was victorious, the sooner he could ask to return to Isla with an army to drive Donald from her shores forever.

Eighteen

News trickled in slower than the rain leaked in through the thatch above Portia's bed. Oh, she'd moved the bed and set a pot beneath the leak, but it hadn't helped speed up the messengers bringing word to Angus about what had befallen the rest of the Southern Isles.

Befallen was the right word, all right. Most of the isles had fallen, much as Isla had. Islanders were hospitable folk, after all. There were exceptions, of course. Lord Calum had taken umbrage at his envoy's demand to hand over his daughter to be the man's bedwarmer, and slain the man on the spot. Dermot had lost two brothers in the ensuing brawl, but Lord Calum still lived, albeit under the heel of an Alban boot. They'd heard no word about his sister, Bedelia, except that she was being held hostage to Calum's good behaviour.

Much like Mason held her here, Portia thought but did not say. Her men knew better than to mention her captivity, and Dermot hastened to continue his report.

"Lord Lewis alone holds out against the invaders," he announced, with a nod to Grieve. "A contrary sea delayed the invaders' ship, so the rider Lord Harris sent from Orken Isle reached him in time to warn him of the treachery of Donald's envoy. Mahon met them with a storm of fire arrows, as though they were the Viken raiders they hate so much. Some still made it ashore, though, and now it is war on Myroy Isle. Lord Lewis has disappeared, leaving Mahon in his stead, intent on killing as many Albans as he can."

Mahon was promised to Bedelia, Portia remembered. She hadn't realised it was a love match until now, but there was naught she could do about it. War parted too many. Grieve and Rhona, Bedelia and Mahon, her and Rudolf…

"Is there any word from the Viken king?" she blurted out.

Surely Rudolf would return if there was.

"None, my lady. Or none that we have heard, anyway," Grieve said. "Mason has been absent much these last few months, though I hear he is still on Isla. Building somewhere suitable to keep a princess, or so he says. Any man with experience in working stone has been called to help with this edifice the man insists on building. He'd been bringing men from the other islands, too, which is why we have so much news to share now."

"Any news of Rum Isle?" Portia ventured.

Her men exchanged uneasy glances. There was news, but it was not good, Portia guessed.

Yet Grieve grinned. "Lord Ronin's longhouse was burned to the ground with no survivors, 'tis said, and the Albans have left the isle entirely, for there is little left on the barren rock." When the others stared at him, he added, "My Rhona is a witch, gifted with fire. Nothing burns on that isle that is not under her power. A blaze that could destroy her father's turf longhouse has to be her doing. My lady lives."

Portia wished she had his confidence about Rudolf. At least they had something to celebrate. "Fetch some wine, then. We shall toast the health and courage of Lady Rhona, Lord Lewis and all who still fight."

Wine was brought and poured. Portia raised a cup with the rest, not having to feign her smile, for any good news was worth celebrating.

"What good tidings have you heard that I have not?"

Her men scrambled to their feet, wine spilling as they remembered to bow to Lord Angus.

"We drink to the courage of Lords Ronin, Calum and Lewis, and their families," Portia said, her eyes daring him to object as she drained her cup.

Angus sighed. "Leave us, please. But do not go far."

Grieve did not hesitate. "Heber, Brian, Dermot – stand guard. The rest of you, archery practice."

"What does the winner get this time?" Berrach asked.

"The chance of victory against Lady Portia in a game of chess this evening." Grieve waited for Portia's nod before continuing, "And remember she can see you from the loft. Let's show her we can defend her even when she cannot practise with us!"

Portia gritted her teeth in what she hoped was an encouraging smile as the men left. Sometimes they set up a target for her in the barracks hall, but it wasn't the same as testing the breeze to see if it would speed or hinder an arrow toward its target. She couldn't remember the last time she'd felt rain on her face. Too long.

"You know if Mason hears you, there will be trouble," Angus began. "It is not politic to wish a guest's enemies well, while he still dwells under your roof."

"Turf him out, then, and tell him that he and his army are no longer welcome here,"

Portia challenged.

He sighed again. "You know I cannot."

That she did, though neither of them liked it.

"Portia, I must leave you for a little while. King Donald has commanded me to provide men to fight the Normans on his southern border, and I must obey." Angus's eyes refused to meet hers.

"Why, Father? What right has he to command you in anything? You are the High Lord of the Southern Isles!"

"If I do not, Mason will take you to Alba."

Portia began, "My men will not allow him to — "

"Your men will be slaughtered. He has an army, Portia, while you have only ten good men. Men who will die to protect you, and Mason will still win. To preserve their lives and yours, I must go."

Portia fought back the building tears. "But what will stop him from doing that if you are gone?"

"He has sworn an oath that he will hold you safe on Isla until my return. I have seen the fortress he is building, and if any edifice can be considered impregnable, it is that place. Please, Portia. Give him no reason to go back on his word. I know you do not like him – nor do I – but if you cross him, it is not just your life at stake. You hold all of Isla in your hands, and it is time you protect her as your mother did. A day may come when a man will rise to claim the isles as their king, and it will be up to you to judge if he is worthy. While the Albans are here, the council cannot convene, but you can make a choice. Whatever happens, you must survive, for while you live, your claim lives with you."

Tears streamed down Portia's face. She was helpless to stop them, or the tide of fate that washed over her with them. "What if I choose wrong?"

Angus's eyes were hard. "If you marry the wrong man, then your dagger must correct your mistake."

Portia swallowed. "You wish me to take my own life?"

"Heavens, no! Did I not just tell you that you must survive? Portia, if you take a husband who is not worthy of you or Isla, then you must bury the dagger in his breast, before he can do any more harm. That is why you must choose wisely, when the time comes." He bowed his head. "Even if I am not here, I trust you will make the right choice."

If she knew the answer to that, would she not have made a choice already? No such man existed, except her own father, and he still lived. For now. "Father…"

"You are the heart of Isla, my lady. Your father is right. When the time comes, you must have courage." Grieve stepped into the barracks. He bowed to Father. "Until then, I will protect her with my life, my lord."

Angus inclined his head. "I would expect no less of you. Your father would be proud, son. I hope you have the chance to tell him one day." He wrapped his arms around Portia and kissed the top of her head. "Farewell, Portia, and you keep that heart safe, you hear me?"

All too soon, the Lord of Isla was gone, and Portia fell to her knees, weeping as she had never done before.

"My lady," Grieve said hoarsely.

She wanted to throw her arms around someone, anyone, just so she wouldn't feel alone. But there was no one left here who could fill that emptiness inside. Rudolf, her father, even her sisters…all gone.

"Leave me," she choked out.

And then she was truly alone, with an unceasing downpour of tears mirrored by the sympathetic sky above. For Isla's heart was broken, and the pieces might never be whole again.

Nineteen

"We agreed on this. I told you war was coming."

Reidar didn't say anything, but he glared plenty.

"There's no excuse now," Rudolf continued. "Let me return home, with the men you promised. You have your heir. Two, even. And a queen who will no doubt give you more if you ask her."

It was the mention of Queen Sativa that did it. "You have a perverse obsession with my queen!" Reidar snapped.

"Send me away, then, as far from her as you can." Rudolf had told him many times he didn't care for Reidar's wife, but since that one flippant comment the day he met her, Reidar wouldn't believe him. Jealous fool.

"That's what she says, too."

This was new.

"Sativa says we must not concede territory we might need to divide among our sons. Even the islands at the edge of the world."

"She's quite astute, your queen. Did she tell you how many men to send with me, too?" Rudolf fought not to sound mocking, but he wasn't sure he succeeded.

"A large raiding party. Three ships."

Rudolf's eyebrows rose. He'd hoped for one. Three was…unexpected bounty. "Thank you."

"But you may only take volunteers. I won't order any man to die so far from home."

"You don't seem all that concerned about me dying," Rudolf said.

"I'm not ordering you anywhere. If you weren't such a stubborn bastard, I'd order you back to the borderlands, but you want to be a hero, to save these islands." Reidar eyed him. "If you can't, I order you to sail right back here so I can tell you I told you so."

"I will not fail," Rudolf said coldly. "I've fought more giants than I can count, protecting your borders. Albans will seem like mere children in comparison."

Reidar grinned. "If the Albans are so soft and tiny, there would be no need for you to go back, then, would there? The Southern Islanders would have defeated them already."

That was what worried Rudolf most. They should have. Unless the Albans had tried some trickery that the Islanders hadn't seen until it was too late. Surely Angus or Lewis…

"You did not see them. Like men who have been at sea too long, their arms and legs like sticks. Driven away from their own land. They weren't fighting men, Reidar. These were Vikens who'd settled on Isla to farm it. Fishermen, farmers, wives, children. Slaughtered, and their village burned to the ground. Those who made it to the boats and arrived here may as well have been ghosts." Rudolf shook his head, but the images would not leave him. "A foreign king has laid claim to our land, and killed our people. I will not endure it on our northern borders, and I will fight it in the southern reaches, too!"

"Like Sativa when we found her." Reidar bowed his head.

Only now did Rudolf realise why the king had refused to see the refugees, though he had not refused them anything else. Sativa had been captured by pirates on her way to marry Reidar, and Rudolf had seen her the day she arrived in Viken. With her torn, bloodied clothes barely covering her emaciated body, Sativa could have been one of the refugees on that fishing boat.

Rudolf had spoken to them all – every man, woman and child. In between slurps of stew from the king's own table, they'd told him what they knew of the situation on the Southern Isles.

The Albans had conquered them. How, they did not know. It seemed the lords had come to some sort of agreement with them almost overnight. Even Angus, though Rudolf did not want to believe it. Angus could not have known about the attack on their village, they'd said, for he was off fighting some foreign war on Alban soil.

"And Lady Portia?" he'd asked, not wanting to know the answer.

Vanished, he was told. No one had seen her since the Albans arrived. She'd last been seen at her father's longhouse, with the young lordlings who were never far from her. They were still at the longhouse – they hadn't gone to war with Angus, which was strange. They did archery training in the mornings, for all to see, Alban army or no. But there was no woman among them.

"Portia is still there on Isla. I know it," Rudolf said, more to himself than his king. "If it were Sativa, would you rest before you had rescued her?"

"I sent our ships out to find her. East, west, north, south…I searched everywhere. And if she had not come to me, I would be searching still," Reidar said. He seemed to see Rudolf clearly for the first time. "Will three ships be enough?"

"I do not know, and I will not until we get

there. Some said the Albans had conquered all of the islands, while others said some still held out. Myroy, Rum…I would have thought Isla, too, and if there is still fighting there, that is where I will go first. If the Islanders know I am there to help, that I come in your name, surely they will join with me to drive out the invaders." Rudolf could not allow himself to believe otherwise. Angus and Lewis were honourable men. They would not have sent him to Viken to beg for help from Harald and now Reidar if they'd meant to ally themselves with Alba.

"I still owe you a barrel of ale I promised you from my wedding," Reidar mused. "I'll send it for your wedding instead. Do you love the girl, Rudolf?"

Rudolf didn't hesitate. "Yes. I've thought of nothing else since I left. Every other woman I've seen only makes me think of her. Even the queen."

Reidar seemed to have forgotten his earlier jealousy. "Do they look so alike?"

Rudolf laughed. "Your queen is like a statue made of gold and ivory, a goddess our ancestors might have worshipped in the old faith. Portia…is a mighty blaze wrapped in lambs' wool. All that passion and power, trapped in a person as soft as goose down. If she were a man, she would be a warrior so mighty even I would fear her. But she is a woman, and all I want to do is stoke that blaze, feed it and protect it until she's willing to engulf me with that roaring passion."

Reidar looked faintly nauseated. "What you dream about in your bed at night is not the sort of thing you tell your king."

Rudolf shrugged. "You asked, my king." He rose. "May I go and recruit some volunteers? I have three ships to fill, and the sooner it is done, the sooner I can be back in my bed, dreaming about the girl I plan to marry."

"Away with you, then!" Reidar sounded stern, but his smile betrayed him. "And don't sail off the edge of the world with those ships, either. I want them back!" he called after Rudolf.

Rudolf made a rude hand gesture and kept going. Not even Reidar would stop him now.

Twenty

When Isla rose out of the mist, Rudolf let out a warcry from the bow of the *Sea Wolf*. His men took it up, echoed by those on the *Sea Dragon* and the *Sea Lion*. The sound had one purpose: to strike fear into the hearts of Viken's enemies. His enemies.

They veered around the cliffs, headed for Portnahaven, the harbour nearest Lord Angus's seat. Nearest Portia, Rudolf promised himself.

He waved at the watch tower on the headland, but no one waved back. He could feel the eyes on him, though. Angus was not fool enough to leave that tower empty.

The pale, rocky sand stretched out on either side, offering him a true Isla embrace to welcome him home.

This was home.

A strange glow appeared in the fog. A glow that spread along the beach like a trail of witchlights in the mist. But witchlights were white.

"Fire arrows!" Rudolf bellowed, but the warning came too late.

The first flaming missile took Sture in the chest, toppling him overboard. Yrian let out an impressive string of expletives, and his men started rowing the *Sea Lion* away from Isla instead of toward it.

A volley of arrows peppered the *Sea Dragon's* sail, scorching the wool that was fortunately too wet to burn.

Frey ordered the *Sea Wolf* to retreat, for Rudolf was too shocked to say anything. The men of Isla knew his warcry. They'd fought beside him often enough in the past. Had they all forgotten him? He hadn't been away that long.

When he'd managed to recollect his wits, Rudolf ordered his men to sail to two other landing spots on the island, but the fog had lifted by the time they reached Macherie, revealing the row of archers waiting for them to come into range. The third landing place was at Kildalton, where the Viken refugees had come from.

Where a thriving town had once stood, now there was nothing but scorched ground, surrounding the stone church and cross that the invaders hadn't been able to burn.

But behind the blackness was a sea of tents. An army camped here, and a shout from their man on watch soon had them lining up archers, ready to shoot Rudolf and his men.

Despair descended on Rudolf as it never had before. To be so close to Portia, and not even be able to land on Isla? Fate was a cruel bitch.

"My prince, what about Myroy?" Frey asked. "There were no archers there when we passed."

The man was right. Lord Lewis ruled

Myroy, or he had, and he had been a friend to Rudolf for the little time he'd known him. He might have news about Portia, and what awaited them on the other islands.

"Set a course for Myroy Isle," Rudolf said.

He'd return to Isla, and next time, he wouldn't leave until the whole island was his, Rudolf swore.

Twenty-One

While his men stayed offshore, Rudolf rowed a fishing boat he'd borrowed into Uig. Lord Lewis had waxed lyrical about the mead in the Uig tavern, and it seemed like the most logical place to ask for information on Myroy Isle.

No archers arrived to greet him. He'd changed from Viken furs to Isla wool, so no one gave him a second glance as he strode up the beach into the town. The tavern was right where Lewis had said it would be, though nowhere near as full. Only something terrible could keep men from drinking. And Rudolf was here to learn what.

He ordered a jug of mead, and paid with coin he hadn't used since he'd left Isla. For a moment, he wished Lewis was here to share the drink like he'd promised he one day would. One day would come, when the war was over, Rudolf swore.

"Is it always so quiet here?" Rudolf asked the tavern keeper.

The man jerked his chin at the jug. "Once you've tasted that, you'll be singing soon enough."

Rudolf hastened to pour himself a drink and compliment the man on it, though Rudolf never tasted a drop. "I mean, I heard word in port that something terrible had happened in the Southern Isles. Some said there was war."

"When there's war, things get burned and men die. Do you see any dying men here?" The tavern keeper peered into Rudolf's face. "I didn't catch your name."

"Rudolf," he offered, pouring a second cup of mead. "Lately come from – "

"Wulf, you're finally here! I thought you'd never come, and I'd die waiting!" an elderly voice cackled, as a heavy hand with the weight of the world behind it thumped down on Rudolf's shoulder. "Get my friend Wulf another jug, for he's promised me a battle!" The smell of strong spirits engulfed Rudolf as the oldtimer gave his cheek a sloppy kiss.

The man kept up a monologue that sounded more nonsense than words, never letting go of Rudolf, until he had the second jug of mead in his hand. His grip turned to steel as his words became clear. "Come, Wulf, I have your oath!" Surprisingly strong fingers dug into Rudolf's shoulder as he was all but dragged outside by the oldtimer.

"This way, Wulf!"

Back to the beach, then along the shore until the fishing boats retreated behind a tumble of rocks. Still the oldtimer led him on.

"Did you bring your chess set, Wulf?" Blue eyes seemed to see into his soul.

How did this oldtimer know? "I did," Rudolf admitted, extracting the board from the bag of belongings he'd brought along. A couple of spare tunics, and his chess set.

The oldtimer's hands set up the pieces with

an easy familiarity Rudolf recognised.

"Now, shall we play, boy?" the man demanded.

"Lord Lewis – " Rudolf began, not daring to believe he was right until the man confirmed it.

"Hush, Wulf. You're here to play, not tell tales about better men than you or me! The birds in the trees have ears, you know." He tried to tap his nose and missed. On purpose, Rudolf suspected.

Rudolf lost three games in quick succession before Lewis held his hand up. "They're gone, I think," he said. "And you have been wasting time in Viken, instead of practising strategy. I'm disappointed in you, Rudolf."

"I was busy fighting real battles for my king, instead of pretend ones where nobody dies, Lord Lewis."

Lewis shrugged. "Harald did fine without you for all these years. Why did he have such need of you now? Did you not tell him about the Albans?" He made the first move.

Rudolf shoved his own pawn forward. "Harald has need of no one any more. His son, my cousin, sits on the throne now, to the annoyance of all his neighbours, who feel his lands and crown belong to them instead." He studied Lewis's second move, and captured his pawn, setting the piece upon the rock beside the chessboard.

"So you have been practising, after all." Lewis regarded the board, and made his move. "Why are you here?"

"To play games with you, it would seem," Rudolf said bitterly, watching Lewis capture his first piece.

"Nay, the game is but the beginning. If you want to capture the queen, you must be ready not just to serve your king, but to become one." Lewis moved his queen into the middle of the board, a move which to an inexperienced eye looked reckless, but Rudolf knew it was anything but.

"Does she still live, Lewis?" He moved his knight to where he might tempt the queen.

"Angus believes so, or he would be home by now. Much like my son, who is one of the young men assigned as Portia's personal guard. If she's still on Isla, as I believe her to be, you'll need an army to free her. Do you have an army yet, son?"

Rudolf's knight claimed another pawn. "I have three ships full of men, but it is not enough," he admitted. "I need more than men, or ships."

"Aye, you're right. You need allies. Powerful ones." Lewis gleefully captured the knight. "Your king's in danger, son."

A rabbit exploded out of the underbrush, flew along the beach and scrambled under a rock, where it sat, quivering.

"Let's go for a walk, Wulf," Lewis said loudly, seizing Rudolf's arm with one hand and the full mead jug with the other. "My old legs get tired, sitting for so long."

Their listeners had returned, Rudolf guessed.

He feigned drunkenness alongside the suddenly unsteady old man, as they made their way along the water's edge. Lewis let out a few scraps of song, slurring the words, before changing to another tune that he murdered as well.

"Which is your boat?" Lewis whispered.

Rudolf led the way, and Lewis leaped

aboard. He shoved the boat into the water and was well out of bowshot before anyone could reach them.

"I hope you weren't lying about that ship, son," Lewis said. "You'll have allies aplenty if you can free them of the Alban curse. The Albans have guest right, and most of our lords are still honour bound to defend them."

So that's how they'd done it. Taking over the islands in a night would have required a lot of coordination. Perhaps Donald was not as stupid as they'd thought.

"Is there anyone I can ask?" Rudolf said.

"Well, there's me, but all I can give you are men, and supplies. If you want to win, what you need is a witch."

"I thought all the witches on the islands had died out," Rudolf said. From what he'd heard, it had been no loss. Some of them had enjoyed the evil they wrought.

Lewis laid a finger beside his nose. No missing it this time. "That's just what they want you to think."

The ships came into view, and Lewis's smile widened. "Oh, you've done well. This new king must like you. When I was a boy, I'd have said three Viken longships could conquer the world. When this is all over, I hope to be able to say it again."

Twenty-Two

The tiny rock island Rudolf rowed up to looked like nobody lived on it – let alone some powerful witch.

"Are you sure this is the place?" Rudolf grumbled, forcing his frustration into each stroke of his oars.

"Absolutely," Lewis replied, settling contentedly in his seat. Of course he was content. He didn't have to row.

"How do you intend to find your witch?"

"No need, son. She will find us. Unless I miss my guess, she already knows we are here.

The real challenge will be persuading her not to set fire to our boots. Or the boat." Lewis eyed the gunwales. "I hope you can swim."

Cursing Lewis for a fool, nevertheless Rudolf brought the boat up to shore and beached it. He waited for Lewis to climb out before dragging the coracle up beyond the high tide line. This time, his wet boots might work to his benefit, if the witch was as volatile as Lewis said.

Lewis led the way up the rocks and onto a rise. He cupped his hands to his mouth. "Lady Rhona, I have a proposition for you!" he shouted, turning to repeat his offer to the other three corners of the island.

"I'm already betrothed, and not to that beast of a man." The sharp female voice came from behind them.

Rudolf whirled. The diminutive girl stood on the sand with her hands on her hips.

Lewis gestured for Rudolf to say something.

"I am no beast, lady," Rudolf said gravely. "I am Rudolf Vargssen, Prince of Viken. I have come from my cousin, King Reidar, to cast the Albans out of the Southern Isles."

She sniffed. "Just you and old Lewis here? You have no chance, Prince of Viken. Not without an army that can match the Albans."

"I have three ships." Rudolf pointed.

"Is this the wolf we are waiting for?" Rhona demanded.

Lewis inclined his head. "He is."

She marched around Rudolf, looking him up and down. "What is your stake, Prince of Viken? What do you get out of saving the Southern Isles?"

Rudolf had never feared anyone so much as he did this dark-eyed imp right now. He opened his mouth, but no sound came out of his inexplicably parched throat.

"He wants Lady Portia," Lewis supplied.

Rhona's eyes narrowed. "Lady Portia is no prize, like the women of other lands. She is the Lady of Isla, and if she does not like you, may heaven help you, for no one else will."

Rudolf laughed. "Portia liked me well enough before I left. If she likes me still…well, I guess we shall see. As long as the lady is safe, I will be satisfied."

"She is safe enough. My betrothed guards

her with his life."

"My son has sent word?" Lewis asked eagerly.

Rhona eyed Rudolf, then answered, "When he can. His letters are carried in secret and left in a place only he and I know. The lady lives, and so does he."

"How goes the hiding, Lady Rhona? Are your sisters sick of fish yet?"

Rhona turned her glare on Lewis. "They complain constantly. The sooner this war ends, the better."

"Would you like to help with the war, Lady Rhona?" Rudolf ventured.

She pursed her lips. "My father will not approve."

Lewis laughed. "Old fool. He thinks my son should save you, for what man would follow a hero who got himself saved by a maiden?"

"Something of that sort."

Lewis jerked his head at Rudolf. "We can blame the victory on the Viken. I'm sure he won't mind."

Rudolf stiffened. "I prefer to fight my own battles, but I am not such a fool as to refuse the help of an ally. There are shieldmaidens among my people, Lord Lewis's late mother among them, who fight alongside their men. If you can assist my army…"

"Ha!" Rhona bit her lip, and the bush behind Lewis burst into flame.

He yelped and ran down to the water, but the fire followed him, blistering the very sands to glass until the sea steamed around him. "I told you! This witch can burn anything! With her on your side, you can't help but win!"

Rudolf fell to his knees. "Lady Rhona, I beg you to help me free the Southern Isles from the invaders. I will give you anything you ask."

She tilted her chin downward so that she might regard him. "I want all I've ever wanted. My husband. Free him from his oath to Portia, so that he can come home and marry me." With a wave of her hand, she extinguished the fire and a breeze came out of nowhere to blow away the smoke as though it had never been. "What would you have me burn first?" The fire burned in her eyes now, and it was a terrifying thing.

"Myroy Isle, and every other island where

Albans seek to hide," Lewis said, splashing out of the sea. He shrugged off Rudolf's and Rhona's stares. "What? I'm the Lord of Myroy. I can burn it if I want to." He fumbled around under his cloak and pulled out the jug of mead Rudolf thought he'd left on the shore at Myroy. Lewis uncorked the jug and lifted it in a toast: "To winning this damned war!" He drank deeply.

Rudolf held out his hand to Lady Rhona. "Do we have an accord?"

Her hand seemed so small in his, but the heat in her fingers reminded Rudolf that power came in many forms. "We do, Wolf Prince."

Twenty-Three

Rudolf rowed ashore under cover of darkness. Lewis snorted awake mid-snore as Lady Rhona leaped into the water to help Rudolf drag the boat beyond the waves.

"My lady…" Rudolf began.

"Shut it, Wolf," she snapped. "Your lady's not here. Lewis?"

"We check the houses. See if there's anyone left. Then I alert the tavern." Lewis smiled evilly.

The only lights in Uig were in the tavern, but Rudolf checked anyway. House after house was empty – people and their possessions gone. He met up with Lewis on the road to the beach. "No one left," Rudolf said.

"I found a few hiding, but they only came for supplies. They'll return to the caves tonight." Lewis squared his shoulders. "Are your men ready, do you think?"

Rudolf smiled. "Light the lamp, and you shall see."

Lewis unshuttered his lamp, and an answering light flared to life in the bay.

The sounds of a Viken drinking song floated across the water.

"Hey, I know that one," Lewis said. He seized Rudolf's hand and broke into a run.

"Vikens! In the bay! In ships!" he shouted, repeating his frantic call to arms all the way up the road to the tavern. He staggered through the door, breathlessly announcing, "Vikens in the harbour!" before he collapsed spectacularly on the floor.

Rudolf had to step over Lewis to enter the tavern. "I saw them too," he said. "Invaders!" He didn't need to pretend. Albans were enough to bring a genuine snarl to his face.

The men he'd taken for Islanders earlier in the day rose from their seats and headed outside with grim purpose.

"Vikens! To arms!" The shout from outside issued from more than one mouth.

The barman set out two cups and filled them, then pushed them toward Lewis. Lewis took one, and gestured for Rudolf to take the other.

"Fill one for yourself, man," Lewis commanded, and the barman obeyed. All three men lifted their cups before Lewis continued, "To victory!"

The barman drained his cup, then wiped his mouth on his sleeve. "So it is time, then?"

"Time to fight!" Lewis slammed his empty cup on the counter. "Come on, son. Drink up, or you'll miss it!"

Rudolf did not need to be told twice. Down went the mead, and it was with the memory of sweetness on his tongue that he said, "Leave town now, if you want no part in the battle."

The barman slapped a greatsword on the bar, followed by a bow and a clacking quiver of arrows. "I'm no coward. Lead the way, my lord."

Rudolf returned to the now deserted street. The Alban drinkers had run off for reinforcements and the unmistakeable march of booted feet in the distance heralded their arrival.

Rudolf cupped his hands round his mouth and let out his loudest warcry. A faint answer came from the boat in the bay. The rest of his men were in place, then.

The booted feet quickened their pace and for the first time, Rudolf saw them. As though every Alban he'd ever killed in his boyhood had come back to life, carrying torches as they raced to take their revenge. But not tonight. No, tonight they passed him by, headed for the beach.

The Albans formed up along the shore, lifting bows and nocking arrows. Runners made haste along the lines, carrying buckets of oil and torches to set the fire arrows alight.

In the bay, the *Sea Wolf*'s sodden crew struck up a tune again, louder this time. They paddled parallel to the shore, still singing.

"Fire!" someone shouted, and the arrows

flew. Arcing across the water to shoot the waves, sending up puffs of steam before they sank.

"Again!"

More arrows flew, but the boat was out of range.

Frey rose from his seat and bellowed, "The shore's that way, you fools! Turn this boat around!"

The singing men proceeded to row the boat in a circle, following the curve of the bay. Arrows rose and fell, but didn't hit their mark.

"Cease fire!" The Alban commander had seen sense. "Wait until they are in range!"

But Frey was not as drunk as he seemed, and every man aboard the *Sea Wolf* knew to keep their distance, however loudly they sang.

While Frey kept the Albans distracted, the rest of the Vikens crept out of the dunes. All of the raiders were veterans who'd fought the Opplanders under Rudolf's command – the enemy would not know they were there until they wanted them to. And then, it would be too late.

Rudolf silently signalled where he wanted

his men. When they were in place, he let out another warcry.

"Vikens in the town!" came the shout from the beach.

Arrows rained down on the houses, setting fire to roofs and walls alike. Vikens poured from the houses and into the street, running from the town as though fleeing from the fire.

The Albans gave chase, only to find the way blocked by a hay wagon that hadn't been there on their march in.

Rhona freed the horse from the wagon, gave it a slap on the rump to send it away, and stared at the wagon. The hay blazed into life.

The Alban soldiers turned to go back the way they'd come.

Only to find the way blocked by another wagon, driven by Lewis. Rhona cast some spell and set that alight, too.

Panicked soldiers turned to the houses, only to be met by a hail of arrows from both sides.

Rudolf climbed atop the tavern's roof – the only one not burning, for fire arrows didn't work on sod – and set his own bow to work. Beside him, the tavern keeper proved to be a surprisingly good shot.

In the flickering orange light, Rudolf glimpsed hell – dead and dying men, crawling and crying for help that would not come. Albans, all, as his men abandoned the burning houses to climb on the roof beside him.

Men still milled around on the beach – Albans who hadn't managed to get into the town before it went up in flames. Rudolf lifted his bow to finish the job.

A hand shot out and grabbed his bow. "Nay, let them run," Lewis said softly. "Rhona can speed them on their way. They have a tale to tell."

Ribbons of flame snaked across the sand, biting at the boots of the Albans who remained on the beach. "Run, ye cowards!" she screamed. "The Wolf Prince is coming for you, and all your kind! The Wolf Prince will burn out every Alban until the Southern Isles are free of you!"

The men swarmed over the fishing boats, launching a frightened flotilla into the bay as the *Sea Wolf* beached itself on shore.

"Shall we go after them, sir?" Frey shouted.

Rudolf shook his head. He watched the boats drift away, reminding himself that each battle brought him closer to Portia. To home.

"The war has begun," Rudolf said.

Lewis slapped him on the back. "And we'll need more mead before it's done. Padraig, get our Viken brothers a drink!"

"Yes, my lord," Padraig the barman said.

Twenty-Four

Portia watched the Albans pack their things onto their horses and head for Portnahaven, casting frightened looks around them as they went.

"Where are they going?" she asked.

"Some say to fight the Normans back in Alba, while others say they're being sent to fight the Wolf." Grieve shrugged and rubbed at a stubborn spot on his armour. "The lot of them pray that they might be sent home, for they've found a cold welcome here."

"I hope they're being sent to the Wolf, and

he kills the lot of them," Portia said.

Tales of the Viken prince had reached her even here, for with Mason gone, her men shared meals and news with the Albans. News they were only too happy to bring back to her.

"They are fighting men, no different from us, truly," Dermot piped up. "And I wouldn't wish the Wolf on any man. They say he moves like a ghost, taking a town before anyone knows he is there. And he burns places to the ground, with all the people inside, too. 'Tis a terrible death, to be burned alive."

Portia paled. "Towns? You mean the Viken prince can't tell the difference between our people and Albans?"

"Perhaps. It's not like the Wolf has lived among us, my lady," Grieve said. "Or mayhap he does not care. Our people gave the Albans shelter, invited them onto land the Viken king claims. While they dwell in our halls, we must defend them, too. If he sees us as Alban allies against him, you cannot blame a man for calling us all his enemies."

"I have not taken up arms against him! Neither have you." Portia smoothed her skirt to hide her consternation. "Surely he will not consider us his enemies."

"But we will take up arms against him, my lady. We are all honour bound to defend you. We swore an oath."

She remembered. How could she not? But the thought that these men, her only friends, would be forced to die for her, was one she was not willing to face.

"Why do they call him the Wolf?" she asked. "Surely the prince has a name."

"He has many names, lady," said Damhan. "The Wolf, or the Wolf Prince. Lately, the one I hear most from the Albans is the Big, Bad Wolf." He laughed. "He sounds like a villain from a children's tale, but he frightens grown men as well as children."

"Why?" Portia persisted.

"He's a Viken giant, as big as they come," Brian said. "Any man who burns whole villages cannot be good. They say he torched the port at Myroy when he first landed, and every town he's touched since. And he is as crafty as a wolf. The Albans who fled Myroy said they would see one Viken and hurry to attack, only to find themselves surrounded and outnumbered. He has a mighty army, all giants like him, and he will not stop until the Southern Isles are his."

A man so mighty, even the Albans fled from him. And all Portia had to protect her were ten good men. She shivered. "What does he do to the women he captures?"

"He's a Viken, so 'tis not hard to guess," Brian said. "Rapes 'em, takes the pretty ones to his ship to be whores back in Viken, and kills the rest."

"Brian!" Grieve roared. "Have you forgotten who you're speaking to?"

Brian shrugged his meaty shoulders. "Sorry if I offended, Lady Portia, but you did ask."

She had, though she wished she hadn't. Her people had allied with the Vikens to stop them from such things, but it was all for naught if this Big, Bad Wolf saw fit to ignore that and enslave them all instead.

"Set up my target for me. I wish to practise archery again, so that when I see this Wolf, I can shoot him," Portia said.

Cowal grinned and rose. "I shall do it, my

lady. If you shoot the Wolf, I want to watch."

Twenty-Five

Isla rose from the ocean, naked in the sun. Waiting for him. Rudolf's heart swelled within his chest.

No archers stood on the shore this time, and his three ships led a veritable flight of dragon boats from every inhabited island in the Southern Isles. They were filled with men from all the isles, too, not just those from Viken. Isla was ever the heart of the isles, and they would not be free of the Albans until they had been driven from Isla's shores.

Rudolf saluted the watch tower as they

passed, wondering if they had sent a runner with word to wherever the remaining Alban army lurked. It mattered not. He and his men knew every landing spot on Isla, and they would not be driven off this time. They would land, and they would fight, until they won. Isla would be his.

The sand crunched beneath his boots, and Rudolf almost wept. Home. He was home. Movement in the watch tower above caught his eye, and he turned to squint at the cliffs. A flash of red or orange, maybe, on the heights? If he looked closely at the window just beneath the thick straw thatch, he could almost see it.

He grabbed Frey, whose eyes were better than his. "Look at the watch tower, and tell me what you see," Rudolf commanded.

Frey shaded his eyes. "I see…an archer. Maybe more than one. Would you like me to take some men to flush them out, sir?"

Portia. His mind flew to her, though he knew it could not be. Portia would not be atop some tower, waiting to shoot men coming ashore. She would be with her men, who would protect her.

Unless this eyrie was the best place to keep her safe. Two archers could hold the cliff path for a long time.

"Pick two, and follow me," Rudolf said, setting off up that very path. He huffed and puffed a little, for it was steeper than he remembered. He knew when he was within bowshot, for he'd manned the tower himself for Lord Angus. Only then did he tug his helm down over his head and take his shield off his back. The familiar weight on his arm reminded him of the borderlands – the last place he'd needed it. He'd fought no open battles since he left Viken. On Isla, though, that would change. Everyone said this was where the Alban leader lived, and where else would his army have retreated to?

Peering over his shield, Rudolf definitely saw something orange at the top of the tower. Orange, and moving. He took a deep breath, followed by another, but there was no smoke in the air. Not fire, then.

Three strides up the path, he heard the whistle of an arrow. Up came his shield, but the missile fell short, slicing into the turf several yards ahead. He darted forward to retrieve it, then skipped back out of range before he dared to examine the arrow. An arrow from Isla, not Alba – he'd recognise the feathers in the fletching anywhere.

More arrows flew, bouncing off rocks and the path ahead.

"You'll not have Isla while I live and breathe, oathbreaker!" a female voice shrieked as a fist shook out of a window, high above.

Rudolf laughed.

"What would you have us do, sir?" Frey asked, bringing Alf and Erik up the path with him.

Rudolf blew out an exasperated breath and pointed at the tiny fist. "Fetch her down, and anyone hiding up there with her. Tell her if she doesn't come, I will bring the whole tower down around her."

Alf grinned. "Gladly, sir."

Rudolf held up his hands. "Without hurting her. She's to be brought to me, unharmed."

His men dashed inside. He waited, knowing they'd reached the top when shrieked curses cascaded down. He wasn't sure who was the whoreson or the walrus's…tail-warmer, but he filed the insults away for a later date. They would keep.

Slowly, the shrieking descended. The men let out cries of pain as the valiant lady fought back, and Rudolf almost regretted not allowing them to defend themselves. It was their own fault for not going into battle with full armour, he decided, feeling a smile lift his lips as the lady's boots came into view. Boots, and the most enormous belly he'd ever seen.

It took both Alf and Erik to hold her arms while Frey brought up the rear, keeping her upright so as not to damage the baby she carried.

Rudolf couldn't seem to close his mouth. Portia, heavily pregnant? To who?

"If you've torn my dress, you whoresons, I'll see you sew it back together yourselves!" she threatened. Her blazing eyes turned to Rudolf, who was glad his helm protected him from her wrath. "And you! A misbegotten wolf who has broken every oath the Vikens have sworn to us! Conquering your allies – your friends! You are no friend of mine, you…you…dog!" She even tried to spit at him, but Angus's daughters were too well-bred to manage such a feat.

Not Portia. He should have known from her poor aim. Arlie couldn't shoot a target a yard in front of her. Portia would have pinned the toes of his boots to the path before turning him into a pincushion.

Rudolf swallowed back his disappointment. Arlie would know where Portia was. Though not Portia herself, her sister was the next best thing. "Take her to Rhona," he said.

Not all of his men could be trusted around a pretty woman, even a pregnant one, but they kept a goodly distance from Rhona, and rightly so. She'd burned a few boots before they'd learned.

Erik and Alf left with the girl, but Frey remained.

"Was there anyone else?" Rudolf asked.

Frey shook his head. "Just her, and this." He held up the bow and quiver. A half-full quiver and a man's bow. What Arlie had been thinking, climbing to the top of the tower in such a state to shoot a bow she hadn't the strength to use, he did not know. But he could ask her that, too.

"Once the men have landed, find somewhere to make camp. Send out scouts, and have them report to me before sundown. Based on their information, we move out in the morning," Rudolf said.

"Yes, sir."

He supervised camp construction, breaking up more than a dozen fights that erupted before the men were settled. They might all oppose the same enemy, but they were an independent lot with grievances going back generations that none of them would forget. The men of Vatersay could not abide to be beside the men of Langroy, and the men of Eriska and Grimsay brawled if they so much as spoke to one another. Add those to the general complaints that one man had a better campsite than another, be it bog or rock or soft grass, and the men from Islay would defend their island with fists or weapons, if need be.

When evening fell, he was more exhausted than he'd believed possible. His shoulder ached from intercepting a punch meant for one of the Myroy men, delivered by an Eriskan with fists like hams. But as enticing scents started to waft from well-established cookfires, he knew his day was not over yet. He liberated a small pot of stew, three bowls and some bread, and headed for Rhona's tent. Where he would have to interrogate the prisoner.

Rhona met him outside, as if she knew he was coming. Magic, most like, but it still unnerved him. He'd seen the things she could do and he had to admit she terrified him just as much as she did his men, but he hoped he hid it better.

"I hope you know what you're doing," she greeted him. Rhona jerked her head at the tent. "My business is magic, not midwifery. If she births the babe in there, you'll be the one catching it, not me."

Arlie was in labour, and Rudolf would have to deliver the babe? He couldn't hide his horror. "I'll send someone for a midwife directly," he said, turning to find someone, anyone, he could ask.

Rhona laughed. "She doesn't need one yet. Some months to go, I understand." She eyed the food in his arms. "Did you bring any wine?

Ah, no matter. I heard the Eriskans brought plenty. I shall go and find some, for maybe that will loosen the lady's tongue. She had little to say to me that is not about the babe in her belly." She set off, and the men parted to allow her to pass.

Whoever her betrothed was, he was a lucky man. She paid the other men no heed, unless they became impertinent. Then the smell of burning leather boots would waft across the camp and a healer would be summoned to put salve on the burns.

Rudolf cleared his throat as he poked his hand through the tent flaps. "Are you in a fit state for visitors, my lady?"

Arlie's voice was just as he'd remembered it. "If you're looking for the witch woman, she's gone for dinner. If you're her lover, I suggest you find somewhere else to spend the night. I will not share a tiny tent with some rutting fool she will forget as soon as her true husband returns."

Rudolf stepped inside. "I'm not Lady Rhona's lover, I promise you, Arlie. I came to talk to you."

Arlie's eyes lit up. "Rudolf!" She tried to rise, but instead she just seemed to rock back and forth. "Damn this belly, I feel like a whale. You must come here and give me a kiss!" She held out her arms.

Rudolf kissed her cheek and sat beside her. "I brought dinner. It's not roast pork from your father's kitchens, but it's the best we have."

She took the offered food and ate with the appetite of a woman starving. Rudolf wordlessly handed her his portion as well, and began to worry there would be none left for Rhona.

"Maybe later," Arlie said, setting Rudolf's bowl down. "I am so hungry all the time, and yet if I eat too much, this baby of mine is like to kick a hole right through me. Very defensive of his territory, he is."

"Who is his father?" Rudolf asked. If some Alban had taken liberties with Lord Angus's daughter, he'd kill the man himself.

"Widald the whale hunter," Arlie said, her fond smile telling the tale of her love for her Islander husband. "He spotted a likely bull in the water yesterday, and left with promises to bring me back a whalebone cradle. How could I refuse such a man?"

"But why were you in the watch tower? And why was no one with you?" Rudolf pressed.

Arlie shrugged. "It is the best place to watch for whales, and for whale hunters coming home. The girls from the village come to visit every day, bringing food and word of what is happening. None have visited today, but when I saw this army sailing in, I sat at the window with Widald's old bow to defend my home, as any good Islander wife would when raiders come. The things this Wolf Prince has done..." She shook her head and muttered something about walruses under her breath. "What are you doing with this man and his rabble, Rudolf?"

Rudolf didn't know what to say. Telling her he was the leader of what she called rabble didn't seem like the best idea. Evidently she hadn't recognised him as the man she'd shot at, now he'd taken his armour off. Finally, he said, "They may seem disorganised, but they are united in a common purpose. Viken men and men of the Southern Isles fighting the Albans together, as our longstanding alliance says we will do."

She pursed her lips. "Not just fighting the Albans. I've heard the stories, even here. I bet Portia has, too. Whole villages burned, and everyone killed. How could you, Rudolf?" Tears sprang to her eyes. "Women. Children! How could you kill children?"

"I've never killed a child!" Rudolf protested, but he had hazy memories of Opplander boys wielding axes they could scarcely lift. Boys old enough to be at war, who were trying to kill him, however clumsily. He'd been the same age when he first went into battle, and he hadn't shied away from anyone who tried to kill him. As for women...like Vikens, Opplander women fought as fiercely as their men. He had several scars from wounds inflicted by women warriors. "This army has only fought Albans. Well, mostly Albans," he amended, thinking of the brawl he'd broken up only an hour before when a Viken had mistaken a Myroy man's drinking cup for his own. "They are good men, Arlie, I swear to you. They are here not to conquer Isla, but to free it."

"And this Wolf Prince? What sort of man is he?" she challenged. "Why do you follow him, Rudolf?"

She truly did not know he and the Wolf were one and the same, and Rudolf did not want to be the one to enlighten her. If he did, then he would have to tell her the truth – he hadn't come to free Isla, but to free Portia. What manner of man went to war over one woman? It sounded like madness, even to him. Madness that a whole army followed.

"I do not know," he muttered, rising to his feet. Before she could say another word, he'd left the tent to walk the camp perimeter with only his own dark thoughts for company.

Twenty-Six

When day dawned, Rudolf was resolute. He'd managed a second interview with Arlie, where she'd told him the last she'd heard, Portia was still in her father's house. No one had seen her for months, but her personal guard were there, and her men did not hide, so where they were, she would be, too.

It was strange to think of Portia as having multiple men, like she kept a harem of sorts. What did one call a stable of men? A barracks, or a company, perhaps – for they were a military unit, sworn to protect her, and not her lovers.

It took the men half the day to break camp, to Rudolf's bewilderment. If they did not move faster, it would take them three days to reach Angus's house, when it was less than a day's ride. But determination drove him – determination to free Portia and her lands from the enemy, and he needed the army at his back to ensure he did, this time.

Their slow progress gave him time to send out plenty of scouts, and mull thoughtfully on their reports. None of his men had seen a single Alban. In fact, they'd seen few men at all, though the villages on Isla were far from deserted. Women and children eyed the army warily as they passed, some unsheathing daggers they tried to hold in the folds of their skirts, ready to defend what was theirs.

His men knew better than to attack a village without an express command from Rudolf. These were their own people, not their enemies. He made sure to pay for any livestock they took, and the sight of coins loosened tongues that hadn't been free to speak for some time.

The Alban camp had been around Angus's house, though there were rumours of a second to the north, where Mason, the Alban commander, had a castle, or so it was said. Everyone seemed to know someone who had worked on the edifice, but none had seen it, or knew where it was. Somewhere hard to reach, they all agreed, before telling him it was on a clifftop, an island, or in the middle of a lake.

Rudolf found himself imagining an underwater castle, where basking sharks sat on thrones while mermaids serenaded them. Or would it be the other way around? He'd heard tales of a mermaid who married a king, and she now presided over his court, her long gowns hiding her tail and scales from all those who might know her for what she was.

"Sir, the men from Vatersay and Longroy are fighting again. It seems the only land left for them to pitch camp is a bog barely big enough for one of their groups, let alone both, and with no distance between them."

Rudolf swore. They were like brawling children. A pity he could not spank them all. "Send for Lady Rhona," he instructed. "Ask her to dry out the bog. Once she is done, I am sure there will be room for everyone. They will be bedfellows in the bog, or they may sail home."

Yrian grinned. "Yes, sir."

He liked the young witch, Rudolf was certain of it. He didn't seem to fear her as much as the rest, though he kept a healthy distance from her, too. If Rhona's betrothed died before she could marry the man, Rudolf had no doubt Yrian would offer himself in the man's stead.

Rudolf crested the rise and his breath caught in his throat. He knew they'd set up camp on the same site the Albans had deserted, but the sight of Angus's longhouse sent a wave of longing through his body that he wished would carry him to the door and happier times.

His scouts said the place was deserted, but Rudolf knew better. Even if Angus and the Albans had left, someone remained. The house and outbuildings had a watchfulness to them that Rudolf had learned not to ignore.

He wore a breastplate, but not his helm, and

he carried his bow and his quiver on his back. His sword bumped against his side with each step, but he would not need his shield today. Not for this.

The cookfire in the kitchen had burned down to coals, but there was no mistaking the fact that it had been used to prepare a meal today. A basket of apples lay on the table, their leaves not yet withered, as though they'd been picked only hours before. Someone was here. Someone who cooked, and took care to harvest the orchard.

A shrill scream that sounded like a distressed horse came from outside.

Rudolf picked up an apple and went outside to investigate.

The mare, a skittish beast that lifted her tail, threw back her ears and eyed him with menace before letting out a squeal, trotted away from him to rub herself against the fence. She stared him a while longer, as though daring him to try and ride her so that she might buck him off, before heading to the feeding trough to finish off her oats.

The second scream didn't come from her –

it came from the stables. Rudolf hurried to help.

The stables were as empty as the kitchen, except for the screaming horse, doing his best to kick down the door of his stall.

"Hector!" Rudolf lifted the bar to let the stallion out, then held out the apple. Would his horse still recognise him after all this time?

Hector ignored the apple and stepped on Rudolf's foot as he shoved past him to leave the stable.

Rudolf followed him, not willing to lose the beast.

Hector took off at a gallop, soaring over the fence, before landing in the mare's field. He moved purposefully toward her feeding trough.

Rudolf halted. The perverse beast had put himself where Rudolf would have taken him. Perhaps he knew better, and Rudolf should return to the buildings. Reuniting properly with his horse could wait.

He returned to the yard between the longhouse, the kitchen and the stables. Only now did he see the new building, its fresh cut timber splintering his memories of this place. The barracks hall had not been here when he left, and its newness meant it could only have been built by Albans, for who else would construct a wooden barracks where a sod-roofed longhouse would do? The only Islanders who preferred timber were the men of Myroy, who didn't have enough sod for roofs, though they had plenty of trees.

The barracks did not belong, and they would burn, he huffed to himself.

Rudolf reached for his quiver. He stabbed his arrow point into a block of the soft, white, waxy substance that made it burn whatever it touched. He marched into the kitchen and thrust the arrow into the ashes, but the stuff didn't catch. Swearing, he found some pine needles in the box of tinder and threw them among the coals.

A wisp of smoke rose up. Throwing his arrow on the flagstones behind him, Rudolf dropped to his knees and blew the tiniest puff of air at the smoking needles. He held his breath for a moment, watching, praying…and then they caught, flames licking up them as if they wanted to swallow the needles whole.

Again he stuck the arrow in the heart, and this time, the flames gratefully accepted his offering. Rudolf hurried out side with his blazing arrow, knowing he needed to fire the thing before the stuff melted and set fire to the kitchen.

Outside, the sun blinded him for a moment. He turned, glared at the barracks, and let his arrow fly. No need to aim when his target was as big as a house. His arrow arced up and hit the roof, then disappeared, as if by magic. Rudolf's mouth dropped open. What in heaven's name had happened to his arrow?

Smoke curled out of a hole he hadn't seen before. Several holes, actually – arrow slits in the roof, he realised.

"What do you think you're doing, you stupid beast?" a female voice yelled behind him.

Rudolf whirled in time to see a redheaded woman sprint past him, carrying a broom. He followed her around the stable to the field where Hector had…ah.

"Get off her, you randy bastard!" she shouted at Hector, who was too busy servicing the mare to care.

"You're too late, he's probably already got her with foal by now," Rudolf called, more to protect his horse than anything else. He would not want to be interrupted while making love to a lady, though he'd have chosen a more private place than Hector had.

"Did you let that menace out?" The woman rounded on him.

"He would have kicked the door down if I did not," Rudolf said.

She snorted. "You try telling Portia that. Mache is her mare."

"Lina?" he ventured.

"Of course, you fool. Portia would've whacked you with the broom, not the bloody horse. First for being away so long, and then for letting the horse out. Then I think she might've burst into tears." Lina smiled. "What kept you, Rudolf? She's missed you so much."

"I serve at my king's command," he said simply. What more could he say? "Where is she, Lina?"

"If you were here sooner, I could say the loft." Lina pointed at the barracks building.

Her eyes widened. "Why is there smoke?" She hurried toward it.

Rudolf grabbed her to pull her back. "Because it's on fire."

Lina wrenched out of his grasp. "Well, aren't you everybody's hero, then? First you let the horse out, and then you set fire to the barracks. What else have you done? If you bring the army down on this house, I will hit you with this broom."

Rudolf stared down at her eyes, as fierce as Portia's could be. He swallowed. "What if I told you the army is here to free Isla from the Albans?"

"So Keith was right." At Rudolf's blank look, Lina explained, "My husband. He's Father's steward, sending supplies to where he's fighting the Normans. He's seeing to a shipment of salt mutton, or he'd be here. Are you here to free Portia, too?"

From husbands to mutton to Portia, Rudolf wasn't sure if he could keep up. Especially with the barracks definitely on fire now — flames licked at the roof through holes that didn't seem so tiny any more.

"Where is Portia?" Rudolf asked again.

"He's taken her."

"Who?"

Lina sighed. "You've been away too long, Rudolf. Lord Mason, the Alban bastard who tricked Father and the other lords into hosting Donald's armies. He's an arrogant prick who pisses off anyone who hears him, but he works well with stone. He built himself a castle in the north, the sort of thing even the Normans would envy, or so 'tis said. You'll need an army to get in, and maybe not even then. That's where he's taken her."

"Where?"

Lina shrugged. "Some holy spot in the north, where the lords meet and drink so many barrels of ale they empty half our cellars."

"Council Island, on Loch Findlugan?" Rudolf asked, horrified. He didn't want to believe it. The Albans had built on the holiest site in the Southern Isles?

"That's the spot!" The fire crackled loudly behind her, seizing Lina's attention for the first time. "So you really are burning down Portia's barracks, are you? You're lucky she likes you.

Her men built that, and kept her safe in the loft while the army was here. They won't take kindly to you when they see you've destroyed all their hard work."

"Are they with her?" If he could not be with her, at least someone kept her safe until he could be.

"Of course. They are her sworn men. She – " Lina stared. "Who in heaven's name is that ruffian?"

A man staggered up the street, dressed in stained rags. He looked like he'd been buried in a bog and clawed his way out again. "You have to help me!" he shouted. He fell to his knees at Lina's feet. "Don't let the Vikens get me. Don't!" He caught sight of Rudolf and crumpled into a sobbing heap on the ground. He pawed at Lina's boots. "You must do as I say, you ugly whore!" His words ended in a scream as his clothes started to smoke.

Rudolf dragged Lina back from the flames a second time as the man turned into a human torch. Only one person could have done this.

"Rhona!" he shouted.

Rhona strode up the street, looking

supremely unconcerned. "He grabbed me, said some things that were not very complimentary, and tried to order me about. I set fire to his boots, and he ran off, so I thought that was the end of it. So when he did the same to this lady here, I figured he hadn't learned his lesson." She leaned over and spat on his smoking skeleton. "He was Alban, anyway. No loss. Oh, and he dropped this." She held up a large gold medallion, attached to a thick gold chain. "Probably stolen. Albans rob the dead on the battlefield. Keep it as a war trophy."

Rudolf wanted to say something, anything, but he couldn't seem to find the words. He'd killed many a man, but Rhona's cold-blooded slaughter seemed different, somehow. Despite the blaze behind him, he shivered.

Rhona regarded the burning building. "Ah, I'm not the only one who's been setting fires. Nice work, Rudolf. Perhaps you don't need me any more."

"I do," he blurted out. "The Albans have taken Portia to their castle in the north. On Loch Findlugan. The very heart of the isles. I need all the help I can get to free her from them."

Rhona gave him a long look. "I'll honour our agreement, if you'll do the same."

Rudolf bowed his head. "You know you have my word."

Twenty-Seven

Loud hammering startled Portia out of sleep. "What is it?" she mumbled sleepily.

"Stay aloft, my lady," came Grieve's quiet response from below.

She heard the scrape and thunk of someone unbarring the door. "What's amiss?" Berrach rumbled.

"'Tis the Wolf. He's landed on Isla, and she must be moved."

Fear trickled down Portia's spine. The Viken prince was here. The man who killed and burned everything in his way. Who would kill her men, burn this building like the woodpile it was, and when he got hold of her...Portia swallowed. Would he care about her claim, or see her as just another woman to rape?

"Seems to me there's more danger on the road than here," Grieve said.

"Perhaps, which is why we must move quickly, and under the cover of darkness. If we reach the castle by dawn, no one will be able to reach her. She will be safe behind my walls, I swear."

Mason. Their visitor was Mason, who sounded as frightened as Portia felt. Good. She hoped the Wolf raped him first, or at least ran him through so she could watch.

"My sister will be here tomorrow. We must wait for her. I cannot leave her for the Wolf," Portia called down.

Grieve tried to hush her, but Portia would not be silenced tonight. She shoved the ladder through the trapdoor and began to climb down. "You hush yourself, Lewisson. If I do not agree to go — "

"Then I will tie you to my saddle and carry you myself," Grieve finished for her. "I'm sorry, my lady, but your safety is more important than your wishes. Or your sister. We shall leave your things in the longhouse with a note for her to send them on. Pack only what you can carry, for if the Wolf is on Isla, then he is within a day's ride of here. We cannot defend you here with so few, but what I've heard of Mason's castle is such that it might be defended by ten men, for it is a formidable place. Dermot will wake the kitchen maids and the cook – they will come, too, for there will be no other women to keep you company otherwise."

Portia wanted to argue, but she knew he was right. So she glared at Grieve instead.

"You've been complaining for months about being a prisoner here, and how you never get to go riding. Don't you want to ride Mache?" Grieve coaxed.

"She's in heat. She'd bite anyone who tries to saddle her. I must leave a note for my sister, telling her not to let Mache get near any of the other horses until she settles. If she hurts Hector, Rudolf will never forgive me."

Grieve's shoulders relaxed. "Thank you, my

lady. It would try me sorely to have to tie you to the saddle like a prisoner."

She smiled grimly. "Sore is right. I'd bite or stab anything I could reach. I'll not be thrown over any man's saddle without a fight."

"Aye, I know."

"Have the men prepare the horses. All but Hector and Mache. They must stay." For a moment, she hesitated. What if the Wolf hurt Hector? If he did, she would tell Rudolf what his countryman had done.

"You pack your things. I will take care of all else," Grieve said.

Back up the ladder Portia went. She bundled up some spare clothes and pulled on some boots. Everything else she owned went into the chest of her mother's that her men had brought from the longhouse for her. She lifted her bow and quiver. "What will happen to the things I leave?" she called down.

"A groom will take the wagon, and follow behind us. Whatever you want him to bring should arrive late on the morrow," Grieve said.

She shouldn't need to shoot anyone between now and then. She'd be inside the castle before it was light enough to see her target, surely. She dropped the bow and quiver in the chest and slammed the lid shut. "I'm coming down. 'Twill just take a moment to pen a note for my sister, and I will be ready." She dropped her cloak and bundle on the barracks floor and launched herself after them.

"My lady!" Grieve lunged forward to catch her.

Portia landed neatly on her feet without falling over. She grinned, proud of herself. "I'm not a flagon of mead. I don't break that easily. Do you think I'll be able to run in this castle you're taking me to, or is there a special dungeon prepared for me that's smaller than this one?" She'd never seen a castle, but envisioned it as a sort of stone version of her father's longhouse. Or his hall, maybe. She could run the length of the hall, at least.

Heber laughed. "Lady Portia, this is a castle. It's huge. There's a practice yard inside the walls, or so my cousin says."

His cousin had helped build it, so Heber should know.

"So there'll be space where I can practice

shooting outside?" she asked hopefully.

"You shall see when you get there, my lady. Are you finished with your letter yet?" Grieve said.

Portia laid down her quill. "I am." She sent up a silent prayer for Lina's safety, and rose. "Let us go."

She fastened her cloak and took up her bundle as though this were an ordinary day, or night, but she couldn't stop the thrill she felt inside. She should be more frightened, but she was giddy at the thought of freedom.

In the harsh light of day, she could worry about the Wolf again and what he would do to her and Isla. Tonight, she intended to relish her first ride in longer than she liked to remember.

Her horse, a beast she did not know, sensed her excitement and pranced about like the animal had been locked up for too long, too.

"My lady, we must make haste!" Grieve said.

She grinned. "Haste, you say?" She squeezed the mare between her thighs and whispered a command, letting the horse have her head. The mare flew.

Startled shouts came from behind her as her men urged their horses to match her speed.

Portia laughed merrily. "I have not forgotten how to ride, boys. Have you? Let's see who reaches the castle first!"

Loch Findlugan was too far for a true race, but she held her own until she felt her horse growing tired and allowed her to slow. Her men caught up, muttering curses they normally would not voice. At least not around her.

"My lady…" Grieve began.

Portia turned innocent eyes on Grieve. "You did say we needed haste."

"That I did, but that's not something I need to remind you any more, I think. I wanted to show you that." Grieve seized her bridle and pointed.

From this height, she could see clear to Portnahaven…and what lay between. A sea of campfires, showing the sheer size of the Wolf's army. Thousands of men, surely. More than she'd ever seen, anywhere. Who could stand against an army like that?

"We do not stand a chance, do we? They will take what they want, and no one will stop them." Tears formed and fell. Tears for Isla, the precious island they would conquer.

They were already lost.

"Of course we do. We are the Southern Islanders, my lady. They may burn our homes, our harvest, our whole damn island, but our people will survive and rebuild. You will survive to lead them. I swear it." The same darkness that hid her tears concealed Grieve's expression, but Portia didn't need to see it to know.

"I don't want you to die for me, Grieve. Not you, not any of you."

His teeth glinted in the moonlight as he grinned. "Then you'd best pray the Wolf is a reasonable man who is willing to negotiate. After a week against Mason's walls, maybe he will be." He moved ahead to order their party into what he called a more defensible formation, before returning to her side.

The joy of the night-time ride began to pall sooner than Portia expected, but she did not complain. Anything to be out of her loft prison.

The sky was lightening as they approached

the loch. Portia had not been here since she was a child, and she'd read and reread her mother's scroll on the history of this place so many times in captivity that she knew every word by heart. Here was the seat of the original lords of this land. Her ancestors, through her mother's line. Her mother's people had carved those standing stones, weeping sweat and tears as they dragged them into place to honour deities long dead.

Or perhaps not, for there was a holiness to this place that hung over it like fog. Maybe the old gods had made their last stand here, and were buried in the mounds that ringed the loch round. Here, she and her men would make their last stand, too, before she was forced to surrender Isla and likely her maidenhead.

But not yet. The Wolf would have to breach other walls first, and mighty walls they were, too. Her breath caught in her throat as she took in the enormity of what Mason had built. The castle covered Council Island, so the waters of the loch lapped at the walls. Not all the way around, but then it had not rained for days. The water level would soon rise, and hide the island again.

She began to believe that maybe, just maybe, there was some hope left.

Two boats waited to take them to their island home, and Portia surrendered her horse to a man she didn't know, who swore he'd take care of the mare before sending her home. She glanced at Grieve, who was doing the same with his horse. Time to trust his judgement, she decided, for she was too tired to think any more.

Her boat drifted under a stone arch topped by a spiky metal gate. It was open to allow her entrance now, but the heavy chains holding it in place spoke of how quickly it could be lowered to keep the world out.

Dermot helped her out, and Portia found she needed his assistance, for her legs ached after the unaccustomed ride.

"Guard her," Grieve said, directing the rest of his men to search the place.

Dermot and Cowal stood by her side, staring up at the high walls as avidly as Portia did.

"It's huge," Cowal breathed. "You'd need a

dragon to get into this place."

Dermot laughed. "Didn't you hear? That dragon in Kasmirus is dead. Some knight slew it, and won himself a bride."

"As long as the Wolf doesn't have it. No one's sure how he manages to burn whole villages when it's pouring with rain. A dragon might do that."

"Someone would notice a honking great dragon in the isles by now!" Dermot scoffed. "If the Albans didn't see such a beast, then he doesn't have one. Maybe this Wolf is beast enough on his own."

Dermot and Cowal debated about how to beat wolves and dragons while Portia fought to stay awake.

"It's empty."

Portia blinked her eyes open. Damn, she'd fallen asleep on her feet. "Mm?"

"It's empty," Grieve repeated. "No one here but us. Now the servants are here, I shall shut the gate and you'll be safe, Lady Portia."

"Can I sleep?" she mumbled.

He laughed. "Yes, my lady. The men are preparing a pallet for you in the tower room.

Tonight, I'll have a bed brought up, but now you may rest."

"Where's the tower?" she slurred, looking around.

"With your permission, my lady."

Portia had her legs swept out from under her as Grieve lifted her in his arms. If she'd had the strength, she'd have shouted at him to put her down. But she did not, so she settled back and told herself she'd tell him off in the morning.

Behind her, the gates clanged shut, and darkness descended.

"You must let me in! You must!"

Shouted words woke her, and Portia struggled to rise. How long had she slept? It looked near noon, but it was hard to tell with so many clouds in the sky.

Loud clanging as someone rang the gates like they were a bell. "Let me in, damn you!"

Portia stuck her head out of the tower window.

Mason sat in a boat outside the gates, whacking at them with his oar. He shook his fist at her. "Let me in or I shall take a stick to you, like your father should have, you ugly whore!"

"Insulting my lady will not let you in, you great blubbery fool," Grieve shouted back from the walls above the gate. "In fact, I am honour bound to keep you out, for you threatened her, and I must keep her safe. Go back to your homeland, for you're not welcome here, or anywhere else on the Southern Isles."

"But there's an army on the way! An army of Vikens! The only safe place is inside those walls!" Mason insisted.

"Then I thank you for building them, as they will protect my lady. 'Tis a fitting parting gift you give her, after trespassing on her hospitality so long. Get you gone before they get here, man. For if they catch you outside the gates, they will squash you like the cockroach you are."

"What about your laws of hospitality?" Mason demanded.

"'Tis not my roof you lived under, nor my lady's. You may ask her father for shelter if you wish, but I've seen you shit upon guest right for too long to be stupid enough to offer it to the likes of you. Perhaps you should not have sent Lord Angus to fight so far away. Maybe if you hurry, you may reach his house before the Wolf's army do. Maybe he'll give you shelter if you offer to build him a castle such as this."

"I hope he gives that ugly whore you serve to his men, so that they may rape the bitch to death. She deserves no better," Mason shouted as he rowed back to shore.

Portia wanted to shout back in kind, but the barb in his words had hit home. Perhaps the man was right, and that would be her fate. She would rather take a dagger to her own breast first.

She slid down the wall to sit on the cold flagstone floor. Would she end her days in this prison?

"My lady, I will not let that happen." Grieve stepped into the tower room and closed the door behind him. He moved to the window and pulled the shutters closed, too, filling the room with shadows. "There is a reason why I chose this room for you instead of the lord's chamber, though the other is warmer. We have taken the room below you as our barracks, so anyone attacking the castle must fight their way through us before they can reach you. And if they do, then you must escape." He slid his fingers down the window frame, and pulled a section away from the wall. A dark void beckoned – a space within the walls Portia would never have guessed existed. "You must climb down, then follow the passage to the hidden door. There is a boat down there, so that you may row ashore. If the castle walls are breached, we will give you the time you need to get away." His eyes met hers, saying the words that he did not.

"I won't let you die for me, Grieve. None of you," Portia said.

He smiled faintly. "Lady Portia, you are the second most powerful lady I know, and not even you have the power to prevent that. I stand by my oath."

"And what of Lady Rhona?" Portia demanded.

"If nothing else, Rhona will avenge me. She has a temper that matches yours, my lady." He bowed. "Now, get some sleep, while it is still quiet. Or you'll wish you had, for there will be an end to peace once that army arrives."

She had to laugh at that. It was either that or cry.

Crying could wait until she had to make use of that secret passage, she promised herself. For if she descended into the darkness, all would be lost.

Twenty Eight

That blocky stone structure rising out of Loch Findlugan where Council Island should be was an abomination. The gods of the old faith would have struck it down with lightning, thunder and whatever else they had in their arsenal. He wished the new ones would do it instead, but he didn't think saints dealt in lightning. Pity. He'd happily hail it as a miracle if they did.

At least his army were getting better at setting up camp, though he had to admit the failing light hurried them along better than he could. No one wanted to be caught out in the rain without their tent up. Not when they'd marched in it all day.

Perhaps they were too tired to start any fights tonight, was all. Or awed by the place where they stood — for Loch Findlugan was the home of Council Island, a holy place where no Islander was allowed make war on another.

And he'd brought war to it.

Lord Angus would never forgive him for this. 'Twas a good thing he wasn't here to see it.

Rudolf would not have done this if it was an Islander who held Portia prisoner. No, he'd have called the man out and the battle would have been between just the two of them, as was proper. But the Albans had brought in their army and fortified Council Island itself. He had no choice. Better that it was a Viken leading this army and not an Islander, then, even if Islanders outnumbered the Vikens in his army.

He'd been considering possible attack strategies since the castle came into view, and he still had nothing. How did one attack a rock? Not even Rhona could burn stone. In all his years of fighting, ambushing and being ambushed in Viken and on the Southern Isles, he'd never come up against something like this. You couldn't climb those smooth walls the way you scaled a cliff. And the damn thing was in the middle of a lake, with no sign of the boat fleet that had carried him to the island last time. A tiny coracle was the only craft he could see – a one-man craft that might take two or even three, if they were slight and didn't mind the closeness. Children, maybe, or two women…

He would not need to attack if he offered them something they wanted. More than anything, he wanted an end to this war. If Portia was safe, he would be willing to trade almost anything.

Portia was the politician, as astute as her father, or Lord Lewis. Rudolf was a warrior and a strategist. She would know what to offer, when all he wanted was her.

A trade, perhaps. If he offered the Albans her sisters as hostages, perhaps they'd be willing to negotiate. Maybe even open the gates…

Lina settled Arlie in the boat, shoving a cushion between her sister's back and the gunwale. "If anything happens to her or the babe because of you, Wolf, I and my kin will hunt you to the ends of the earth to exact our vengeance."

Rudolf nodded. Coward that he was, he couldn't look her in the eye, so he'd worn his helm for this. Full battle dress, in fact, as he paced along the shore, letting those in the castle get a good look at him.

A young Eriskan lad had volunteered to row the ladies across the lake. He looked no bigger than Rudolf himself had been the day he arrived at the Southern Isles, but he had the same courage. And so Rudolf had agreed, letting the most vulnerable members of his army assault the castle. For they had a better chance of gaining entry than he.

His men lined the shore, and theirs lined the battlements, watching the coracle's progress as it rippled between them. Could two armies hold their breath? For it seemed the only sound he could hear was the plash of oars as the two flame-haired girls retreated from him.

A third flash of orange at the tower's top window stopped his heart. Portia!

He wanted to fly across the water and take her in his arms, but she was as far out of reach as heaven itself right now. Even her face was out of view – hidden by her hair as she faced the oncoming boat, not him. She'd seen her sisters, all right.

She turned her head further still, meeting the eyes of…was it one of the men on the battlements? She gestured imperiously, her meaning clear. She wanted them to let her sisters in.

One of the armoured men on the battlements let out a shout, waving his arms with as much energy as Portia.

Was he commanding his men to open the gates, or fire on the defenceless boat? Surely no man of honour would open fire. They couldn't…

The gate at the waterline began to rise.

Lina shouted and pointed, and the Eriskan boy headed for the opening gate.

The boat slid into the darkness before the

gate clanged shut once more. His army began to disperse, heading for their tents or whatever they wanted to do while they waited. Polish their armour, perhaps.

But Rudolf was rooted to the shore, his eyes fixed on the tower window that no longer held the flaming beauty who'd haunted his dreams for so long.

Gods help him, from the old faith and the new. He'd sacrificed a boy, two women and an unborn babe just for the hope of seeing her again.

He hoped Portia would forgive him if he failed.

Twenty-Nine

Despite all her talk of wanting to run and shoot and do all the things she hadn't done in the barracks hall, Portia found herself peering out the window just like she had when she lived in the loft. She could sit in the tower windows, if she'd wanted to, but the stone was too cold, so she hung back, not wanting to touch it. There was plenty to see.

The army came in an orderly column, creeping into the valley like ants until they grew into men and settled on the shore where her own men had left their horses. The beasts were gone now, back to her father's stables with a groom, for there were no stables here to house them. Most of the army marched on foot, with a few hooded or armoured figures on horseback.

The Wolf Prince could be no one other than the proud peacock who led them, probably insisting no one else could ride before him lest they kick up dust or mud that might foul the highly polished sheen of his armour. His poor horse had to bear the weight of not just him, but all his weapons, too, for the man had sword, shield, axe, bow…he carried an armoury on his back, as though he expected an attack at any time. And so he should. A Viken who attacked the Southern Isles was an oathbreaker of the worst kind, breaking an alliance that had stood for centuries.

She wanted to take up her bow and shoot him then and there, but she knew he was out of range. Even from this height, she was too far from shore to shoot anything not on the lake's surface. If he could be persuaded to board a boat, though…

The tiny coracle Mason had left in the mud

wouldn't stand up to more than a few well-placed arrows before the holes in the hide let in enough water to sink it. Wearing so much armour, the Wolf was sure to sink, and good riddance.

His army set up camp with alarming efficiency, which surprised her when she realised only the first few ranks of troops were Viken. The lines marching over the hill now were unmistakeably Islanders – so many men! She hadn't known there were that many men on all the Southern Isles, yet here they were.

Why?

Why would her own people follow a man who burned their homes and killed their families? No man of the Isles would throw away his own honour in such a way. He'd kill the Wolf with his own hands, for sure.

For the first time, she began to doubt the tales she'd heard. That the Albans feared him, she'd known. But her own people…they weren't stupid. They wouldn't stand by and watch their own people die.

Did they believe the Wolf was their ally? Big and vulpine, perhaps, but not so bad?

The vast army made themselves at home on the valley floor, while the Wolf paced the camp. He was a big man, bigger than most, and he'd pitched his own tent in the centre of the camp, bigger than the rest, of course. The cloaked riders favoured the second largest tent, on the far edge of camp, away from the water. Three of them. One waddled like he was as fat as Mason, but there was something about the way the figure walked that made her certain it wasn't him. Besides, an Alban among this army would be in chains, or tied to a stake. Not free to walk about the camp.

"Have you never seen an army before?"

Portia looked up to meet Grieve's raised eyebrows. "Not like this one."

"Me, neither. Now I know what Lord Angus faces in Alba. 'Tis a fearsome sight." He held out the covered bowl he'd carried up the stairs. "I brought your dinner. Seeing as you didn't come to the dining hall with the rest of us..."

She took the bowl. "Thank you. I suppose I have spent so long alone, I am not accustomed to...to..."

"Freedom?" Grieve supplied. "This is all new to me, too, my lady. There is what I know, and then there is…this." He waved at the view.

"What are they doing?" Portia leaned out of the window, to get a better look. "They're sending someone out in the boat."

Two of the cloaked figures. Witches? Priests? She couldn't be sure. They were accompanied by an Islander boy who rowed the boat like he'd been born to it. A fisherman's son, probably. But the cloaked riders…

The Wolf stood on shore, speaking to the riders. Together, they reached up and lowered their hoods.

Portia let out a shriek. "It's Lina and Arlie! My sisters! And Arlie…Arlie's pregnant!" She pointed at the girl's belly. "I'm going to be an aunt!"

Grieve swore and bolted down the stairs.

"If you don't let them in, I'll open the gates myself!" she called after him.

Soon after, he appeared on the battlements, gesticulating wildly as he argued with Brian. More than once, he stabbed a finger in her direction. Finally, Brian headed down to the gates.

Portia watched the boat sail beneath the castle, before it was her turn to race down the stairs. She was breathless by the time she reached the bottom, but she didn't slow. It had been too long since she'd seen her sisters.

They clambered up the steps, looking just as tired as she'd been when she first arrived. Of course, they'd been riding all day.

Portia issued orders for a feast to be prepared, and for water to be brought up to her room so that they might wash, for where else would they sleep? The enormous bed was more than big enough for three of them.

She wasn't sure who to hug first. Arlie, lest her baby decide to arrive this very moment, or Lina, who she'd only just missed?

Grieve stood beside them with a grave look on his face. "Tell them what you told me."

Arlie's face crumpled as she burst into tears, leaving Lina to say the words: "We are here as the Wolf's envoys. He offers everyone in the castle safe passage off Isla, if they open the gates and lay down their weapons."

Portia's mouth was dry. It was too easy. It must be a trick of some kind. Or..."What does the Wolf ask in return?"

"That King Donald gives up all claim to the Southern Isles and its people..."

Portia had expected that, and she would happily support it.

"...and that you surrender Portia to the Wolf."

Even Lina leaked a few tears as she said it, though she quickly wiped them away. "I'm sorry, Portia. That's what he wants."

"What does he want of me?" she asked.

"It doesn't matter. He shall not have her!" Grieve said.

The men on the walls rumbled their agreement.

"How long do I have?" Portia whispered.

"It does not matter. He will have to tear down the walls and kill every man among us before he can touch you!"

"He wants your answer by noon tomorrow," Lina said.

Portia nodded. She blinked back tears. Tomorrow, it would be time to end this.

"Then tonight we shall have a feast, to remind us of happier times, and tomorrow, he will have his answer," Portia said.

"His answer lies at the point of my sword!"

Portia linked arms with Arlie and Lina. "Come, I'll take you to my chamber where we may wash while the men make plans for the morrow."

It took some time to help Arlie up the stairs, and even longer to catch her breath. Being cooped up in that loft had not done her any good. She hoped the Wolf would let her see the sun a little, at least. What there was of it.

While Arlie collapsed on the bed, complaining about how her back hurt, Lina pulled Portia aside. "There's something else. I didn't want to say it in front of all those angry men out there, for they are beyond reason right now."

"What is it?"

"It's Rudolf."

Portia's mouth was dry once more, and she feared it might be a desert until the day she died now. "What news of Rudolf?"

Lina wet her lips. "He's down there. He

rides with them, Portia. This is the help he brought, at our father's command. Most of the men are our people, fighting to be free of the Albans. They fight with the Wolf, not against him."

"And Rudolf?"

"He has the Wolf's favour, I am certain of it. Because he was the one who took us prisoner, and it was nothing like I had heard. He has treated us as well as any of the men in that vast horde. Food, a place to sleep, a tent to keep the rain off…horses to ride, while the men march. None of the Vikens has laid a finger on us, and no man among them has even hinted at it. They fear the Wolf's wrath." Lina gripped her shoulder. "Portia, make your men see sense. When they surrender, you'll get to see Rudolf again. Isn't that worth it?"

She wanted to say that it was. A week ago, she might have given anything to see Rudolf again. But to see the man she'd loved for as long as she could remember as she surrendered herself to another man? A man who owned his allegiance, as he would own her, too?

Darkness lay on her heart, as never before.

This morning, she thought she could bear whatever the Wolf would do to her. But if Rudolf had to watch? It would break her heart.

She forced a smile for her sisters. "No more talk of war, or the morrow. Tonight we feast, and talk of the past. For I have missed much, it seems. I know Arlie was always a greedy guts, but when did she learn to eat melons whole?"

The talk turned to lighter things, but the darkness within remained. Later, she would surrender to it. Now…she had her last supper to enjoy.

Thirty

Portia waited until her sisters had fallen asleep before she crept over to the window. Despite their protestations about receiving kind treatment from the Wolf, their journey from their burned homes to here could not have been an easy one. They would sleep for some hours yet – so soundly, perhaps, that they wouldn't notice her absence at all.

Night air puffed through the window, chilling her bare arms. It was colder out here on the loch and the stone walls seemed to drink the chill, making the castle colder still.

Portia dressed quickly, trusting her long skirt and cloak to protect her from the biting breeze. Stockings and shoes would only slow her down tonight.

Her bow and quiver might come in useful, though. She slipped her finger into the quiver, questing until she found what she sought. She stashed the pouch in the pocket of her cloak before slinging the bow and quiver over her shoulder, leaving her hands free.

Placing both hands on the wintry stone, she climbed onto the windowsill. It was wide enough for her and her sisters to have used it for a bed, or for her to stand there while she opened the hinged section of the timber window frame to reveal the secret passage.

A whiff of the fish oil that she'd used to silence the hinges reached her nostrils, but it was better than a loud squeak rousing sound sleepers. She would endure far more discomfort before this evening was through.

A ladder led down into the darkness between the castle's inner and outer walls. A passage to freedom or, in this case, answers.

Portia twisted, trying to step from the sill to

the ladder, but something caught on the window frame, holding her back. Cursing quietly, she backed up. It was the bloody bow, of all things. Which wouldn't be much use if she ran into trouble – she was better at shooting enemies from a distance. Stabbing someone with an arrow was silly, especially when she already had a dagger. Portia considered for another moment, then unhooked the offending thing from her shoulder and dropped it on the floor. The quiver clattered down atop it, and Portia winced, wishing she hadn't been so loud.

Her gaze darted to the bed, where her sisters slept on.

She allowed herself to breathe again.

The ladder rungs were rough under her feet, making her wish she'd brought her boots, but she refused to return for them now. Instead, she pulled the window panel closed to hide her descent.

Darkness cloaked her, settling like a layer of wet wool. Or was that her dread at what waited for her? Not in the darkness, but across the loch.

If dread weighed her down, at least it gave her the push she needed to keep climbing down until her feet sank into sucking mud. Trying not to think of corpses sucking at her toes each time she took a step, corpses of the men who would die tomorrow if she failed, Portia made her way along the secret passage to its hidden entrance, or exit, in her case.

She stumbled over the boat Grieve had told her would be there, but she didn't take it. Not yet. She'd memorised her mother's scroll, and if it was correct, there was another, more ancient way across the loch that didn't require rowing.

She continued down the passage until she found what she sought.

A timber half door, covered in a thin layer of stone to conceal its true nature from the outside world, yielded to her touch. Its hinges were not so silent, but there was no one about to hear their squeaky protest.

Moonlight turned the loch into a mirror, for there was no breeze down here. No need, for the air was positively frigid. Portia scanned the shore, looking for the standing stones she knew had to be there. Stones that had seen the passage of so many people, yet they would still stand after this battle, sentinels of time.

One…and then she found the second, a finger pointing at the sky as if to remind her that she could only hide in darkness, so she only had until dawn to find her answers.

She edged around the castle walls, knowing she had to line the stones up properly to be certain she stood in the right place. Her ancestors had done this from time immemorial, or so her mother's history scroll had said. There was no need to be frightened of following in their footsteps.

But her ancestors had not faced a legend, a man who'd had so many stories spun about him that he seemed the very devil himself. And yet…her sisters' safety spoke of someone who understood chivalry and honour, who might save what others sought to destroy.

She wasn't sure what to believe any more. She dreaded, and yet she hoped.

Which was why she would face him alone.

Portia paused to squint at the stones again. Now she could only see one – perfectly aligned. She took a deep breath, and stepped into the loch.

Icy water swirled around her feet, and her breath huffed out in a startled cloud of condensation. Her boots would not save her from the loch, but she wished she'd worn them anyway, if only for an extra moment's warmth before they grew sodden and slowed her down.

She held her hem high to keep it from getting wet, until she realised that the water didn't even reach her ankles. She let the fabric fall, lifting her gaze to the stones to keep her on her course. The ancient causeway lay hidden beneath the surface of the loch and one wrong step would result in a ducking. Her nearly numb feet already found it hard to feel the stones, so she must maintain her vigilance.

The shore came closer and closer, and Portia dared to hope she might reach it before the numbness spread to her knees.

She was only a few yards away when a male voice demanded, "Halt!"

She blew out a breath she hadn't known she'd been holding.

Hope sank to the bottom of the loch, threatening to drown her courage with it.

722

Thirty-One

"I told you ghosts don't take orders!" one voice insisted.

"They might. She might have been a really obedient wife in life. How many spirits have you seen?" a second voice reasoned.

"It doesn't matter. She's walking on water. That makes her a ghost, or a witch."

"It's angels that walk on water, you fool! The devil's servants sink!"

"I heard a sailor at Beacon Isle tell the story of a woman who walked on water. She was a witch. She could see into men's souls to decide whether to sink your ship or save you, they said."

"There are good men and bad in every bunch, or on every ship. How'd she know which ships to sink if there were both kinds of men aboard?"

"I don't know – do I look like a witch?"

"You look like the idiot who just ordered a ghost to halt."

"Well, she did, didn't she? She even gave you a gift."

Rudolf listened to the exchange with amusement, but his curiosity got the better of him. This was his army camp, and no one got in or out without his knowledge. Not even a ghost.

"The gift's not for me. It's for the commander, she said. If she is a witch, maybe she's trying to curse him."

Rudolf poked his head out of his tent. "What is this cursed gift?"

The two men stopped, looking sideways at each other until one of them said, "It's like this, sir. There's a lady out on the lake who walks on water, who asked me to give you this." He set the small pouch on Rudolf's outstretched palm.

He weighed it for a moment, wondering if it was empty.

"I have heard of a woman who can walk on water. A witch so powerful that water obeys her. She used to live at Beacon Isle, but now she wears a crown. Queen Margareta, her name is, and her kingdom is not too far north of here," Rudolf said.

"Begging your pardon, sir, but what would a queen be doing out on yon lake so late at night?" the gift-bearer asked.

Rudolf emptied the pouch into his hand. "Handing out gifts, or so it would seem."

Both men recoiled and crossed themselves. "Dead virgins' fingers! That must be a powerful curse, sir. Throw them away before the magic takes hold!"

Rudolf prodded one of the pale fingers. It was hollow, as were its companions. When he turned them over, he found the lacings holding them together. The finger guards were so well-worn they still held the shape of their mistress's fingers. Portia would not abandon these on the eve of battle.

Unless she intended to stop the battle from taking place.

Rudolf tucked the finger guards safely back in their pouch. "Take me to this woman. I must see her for myself."

The two men hesitated, before the one who hadn't spoken yet ventured, "Sir, is that you issuing orders, or are you under the influence of the witch's curse?"

"Make me ask again, and you'll be on latrine duty until next year. Both of you," Rudolf stressed.

"Yes, sir!"

They trotted off, hunting hounds eagerly leading the way to his quarry.

Or so Rudolf hoped. If the lady had gone...

Yet as he reached the lake's edge, his breath caught in his throat. There was someone standing in the water, though she appeared to be floating on its surface. Now he understood why his men had mistaken her for a ghost.

Rudolf extended his hand. "Why don't you come ashore, my lady?" he asked.

She turned so that the hood's shadow hiding

her face pointed toward him. "Would you step ashore, knowing the land is occupied by an enemy's army?"

Rudolf pulled the finger guards from their pouch. "The lady who owns these will never be my enemy. I promised to protect her, and my promise still stands."

She lifted her hands to her hood, ready to lower it. "What can you tell me of the man they call the Wolf Prince?"

"A highborn Viken, cousin to the king, commander of this army and conqueror of the Southern Isles." It sounded quite impressive, laid out like that. Maybe it would impress her enough to make her forget how long he'd been away.

"Not this isle. Not yet," she said fiercely.

No, it was not enough to impress Portia.

Rudolf spread his arms wide. "Look again, Lady. This army has already taken Isla. The only holdout is that tiny fort on the lake, and it will not hold out for much longer."

"A week," she said softly, as though it pained her.

"You think it will take that long?" He

wanted to say that he could take it in a day, if she needed him to do so. For if this was truly Portia, he would scale the walls alone to save her. Yet here she stood, hardly a prisoner.

"We only have enough food for a week. I know the state of the castle store rooms, and how much we eat. Lina would not have made the same mistake, but I was not prepared for a siege with so many mouths to feed. I do not wish my people to die. I want to sue for peace."

"Name your terms."

Her head darted to the left and right. "First, take me to the Wolf's tent, where we might discuss this in private. Can you give me that?"

"Of course."

She nodded. "Do you swear to grant me safe passage into your camp?"

Into it, but not out. Interesting. "I do so solemnly swear."

"Then take me there, Dolf."

He held his hand out once more, more out of courtesy than any expectation that Portia would need it, until she stumbled. Courtesy be damned. He dived forward to catch her.

"Release me." It was a command.

He set her on her feet on the grass before he did as she asked.

She tugged her hood down. "Lead the way, Dolf."

It took all his willpower not to glance back over his shoulder as he took her to his tent. Now, he wished he'd accepted the hospitality of one of the nearby crofters so that he could offer her something better than this. Portia deserved better than this.

He straightened the coverlet on his pallet, as though he hadn't been roused from sleep by her arrival. The ancient laws of hospitality demanded that he offer her something to eat and drink, but he had nothing here. His tent was a place to sleep. Nothing more.

Rudolf stepped out of his tent and hailed the first man he saw. "Bring me a jug of mead," he said.

The jug was brought. Too late, Rudolf realised he should have asked for cups to go with it.

He re-entered his tent, and there she stood.

Her red hair glowed in the firelight of his

brazier, haloing her like the saint who had given Loch Findlugan its name.

"Portia," he breathed. It came out like a prayer to heaven. A prayer that after all he'd endured, this angel might become his.

"Dolf?" she asked uncertainly. "I have watched the Wolf striding around the camp in that armour all day. This is his tent. Tell me the truth now, for I must know. Who is he?"

Thirty-Two

Rudolf set the jug on the ground and bowed. "Prince Rudolf Vargssen, cousin to Reidar Haraldssen, King of Viken. Reidar's father and mine were brothers."

Oh, how she didn't want to believe it. But how could she not believe him? "So you are the Wolf. The man who has killed, raped and plundered his way across the Southern Isles to take my home from me."

Rudolf shook his head. "I swear to you, I am the Wolf, but I have done none of those things. I have never raped a woman, nor killed one since I set foot on the Southern Isles. Not even my aunt, who would not have been so kind to me. I have killed men, it is true, though they tried equally hard to kill me. As for plunder..." He waved at the unadorned interior of his tent. "Do you see anything of worth here? I have taken nothing from the islands that was not given to me freely. The lords of the isles are with me. All but your father, who I'd hoped to find here with you. As for your home..." He ducked his head. "I may have set fire to it. Just a little," he admitted.

"But Mason and his men said..."

"Is Mason your husband?" Rudolf demanded.

Portia had never seen such pain in his eyes. "Mason is Donald's man, sent here to secure the islands for Alba. And build high walls to keep people both out and in." Her gaze arrowed in the direction of the castle on Council Island.

"Is he your husband?"

Portia laughed bitterly. "Mason who thinks so much of himself? No. He believes I am beneath his notice. The fat pig of a man desires one of Donald's daughters, and he thinks subduing us will earn him that honour. He holds me safe from Viken raiders and other unscrupulous men, who might want to marry me for their own ends. More likely, he thinks to marry me off to whoever Donald sends to replace him. One of Donald's sons, he said."

"If you are a prisoner, how did you get out?"

She shook her head. "I cannot tell you that. The Dolf I once knew would not ask me to betray my sisters by letting the leader of an enemy army into the chamber where they sleep."

If anything, her words had hurt him even more.

"I have never been, and will never be your enemy, Portia."

For a long moment, she stared at him. Heaven help her, but she believed him.

All the fear and frustration and years of missing him and dreading the future bubbled up. She swallowed back a sob. She couldn't cry now. She had a peace agreement to broker with the Wolf, who was not the Dolf she'd known before the war. This man was harder, commanding armies and conquering islands. Conquering her island.

"What terms will you offer us, then, so that my people and yours are not enemies?" Portia said. Oh, but it hurt to call the other Islanders his people. This man was a foreigner to her, while she'd considered them friends. Once considered him a friend.

Rudolf shook his head. "That's not how it works. I have given the castellan my terms. I will let everyone in the castle go, unharmed, if they lay down their arms and release you."

"He cannot. Grieve swore an oath to my father, he and all his men, that they would protect me."

"But he does not have you now. I do. What will he do if you do not return?" Triumph glittered in Rudolf's eyes, something else she'd never seen there before.

Something died inside Portia. "Then Grieve and his men will come in search of me, even if it means attacking the camp. We both know they would die. Grieve is a good man, and so are those who serve under him. Good men, loyal to my father, and loyal to me. They don't deserve to die. Not yet."

"And what do I deserve? I have fought for years for this. For these islands. For your home."

She closed her eyes to stop the tears from falling. She should have sent Lina to negotiate on her behalf. Lina's knees would not have weakened at the longing in Rudolf's tone.

"You can have the islands. All of them. And my home. As long as you promise to spare them, too."

Rudolf shook his head. "They must lay down their arms, yet you say they will not. I once vowed to protect you, too, and I would fight as long as I had the breath left to shout a battle cry. If these men are as loyal as you say, they will fight to the death – theirs or ours."

"Or mine." It came out as a whisper, but Portia couldn't stop it.

"Never," Rudolf swore. He seized her shoulders. "There must be another way, Portia. I let go of you once, and I will not lose you now. Not to Donald or Mason or any man who dares to lay claim to you and your birthright." He dropped to his knees. "I will give you everything I've fought for. Every island, every rock, every fishing boat. For you."

Her breath caught in her throat. He couldn't mean...

"What would you ask in return?" she asked faintly, pressing her hand to her breast to hide her hammering heart.

"You. Other men may desire your dowry, but all I've ever wanted is you." He held out his hands in supplication. "Marry me, Portia."

All her adult life she'd wanted to hear those words, dreading the day she'd have to refuse him. Tonight, she'd come to offer herself to the Wolf, knowing it would cut her off from Rudolf forever. But now...

"If Grieve came in search of me, he could not break a marriage bond," Portia said thoughtfully. "My claim would pass to you, my husband. If I stand at your side as your wife, Grieve would open the castle gates to you."

She'd said something wrong. The shining love in Rudolf's eyes had gone. Had she imagined it?

Rudolf rose. "Of course. You think of your men. This Grieve must mean much to you." He sounded bitter.

"Until my father returns home, they are the last of his men. Just as they swore to protect me, I have a responsibility to them," Portia said. She had little choice, and it lightened her heart enough to see her way clearly for the first time. "Yes." Her father would understand. Rudolf had been her heart's choice, long ago, when she could not have him. As the Wolf Prince, she could. Hope blossomed. "But it must be tonight, before anyone notices I am gone. Or someone will die."

He eyed her. "A marriage is not valid without vows to be faithful, followed by a consummation. We must do that tonight, too."

She swallowed. Consummating a marriage was the hardest part. She'd never forget Lina's or Arlie's cries of pain on their wedding nights. Dolf might protect her, but he could not save her from himself. It was but a small price to pay to end a war. "It shall be as you say. We must wake the priest who serves Saint Findlugan's church, and ask him to marry us."

<h1 style="text-align:center">Thirty-Three</h1>

"I wish you both well. You may…you may use my house for the consummation. I shall return in the morning," Father Fintan said, ducking out the door and into the rain before Rudolf could stop him.

Rudolf and Portia stared at each other for a moment. His heart sank at the fear in her expression. He'd dreamed of this night for half his life, but never had he imagined his first night with her would be in a tiny, cold cottage with a straw pallet so thin and narrow they may as well be making love on the floor like animals. He'd imagined a roaring fire, a room so warm she'd want to take her clothes off, and a big, carved bed like the one he'd slept in in Viken.

"We don't have to do this if you do not wish to," Rudolf said.

She tossed her head. "We do. My father, Mason and this bloody king of his will dissolve a marriage that hasn't been consummated as quickly as salt in a stew pot." She hoisted her skirts up to her waist. "Where would you have me, husband?"

Husband. The word sounded so good on her lips, and yet…there was no love in the way she said it. Like his firebrand of a wife had died inside by marrying him.

Rudolf dismissed the priest's pallet, but that left him little more to choose from. He wanted to hold her close, to kiss her, to make her comfortable when he made love to her for the first time.

Reidar had made his bride scream for joy on their wedding night. They'd known each other for barely two days, and the whole castle had known just how much the queen loved her king. Rudolf had loved Portia for half his life, and he vowed he would show her that tonight.

Women enjoyed lovemaking more when they were on top, he'd heard, so Portia must mount him. That mean..."There," he said, pointing at a bench by the wall. He sat down on the broad seat, and patted his knees. "Sit here, my lady."

With some difficulty, owing to her bundled up skirts, Portia climbed into his lap. Gently, Rudolf guided her around to face him, so she straddled him.

"This is not how my sisters did it," she protested. "Their husbands made them lie down and..." She paled and didn't finish.

"When we have a bed worthy of you, I shall lay you down upon it, and show you every pleasure a man can give a woman," Rudolf promised. "But tonight, it is here or the floor, I'm afraid."

He could feel the heat of her, now, burning through his tunic. With her skirts so high, she was naked to the waist, and he longed to stroke her lovely legs right until he reached the apex where they met and then...

She squirmed in his lap. "Why are you so hard?"

His cock only hardened further in response. He freed it from the folds of his clothes and laid it beside her leg. "Because you are so beautiful," he said.

She didn't seem to hear him. Her alarmed gaze was fixed on his cock. "You're going to stick that huge thing into me?"

He wanted to laugh, but he feared that wouldn't help. He'd never seen his fearless Portia look so frightened. "Actually, the way we're sitting, you'll be in control of that. I'll just position it right, and all you have to do is sink down on it, as slowly as you like."

"Very well."

She rose. If she hadn't been wearing her clothes, Rudolf could have kissed her breasts. Next time they made love, he vowed, they'd be naked and he'd kiss them for twice as long to make up for it. Maybe even suck on her nipples a bit, too, if she liked that.

His cock was rock hard now, jutting toward her so eagerly it took all his willpower not to grab her hips and slam her down upon it. They had all night, he reminded himself. All night to take this as slowly as she needed.

Portia set her hands on his shoulders and glanced down. "It looks even bigger now. Are you sure it will fit?"

"Of course," he soothed, cupping one hand around her bottom to bring her closer. He wrapped his other hand around his shaft, positioning the head of his cock right against her sweet spot. One small push and the irresistible heat of her engulfed the tip. He sucked in a breath, fighting down the urge to thrust hard and deep into her. "Now, just sink down and I'll slide right in."

He closed his eyes, savouring the feel of her. Her nails dug into his shoulders as her molten heat embraced him, inch by inch, so tight he wanted to moan in bliss. He had to let her control this. He had to. Because if he did…in two or three thrusts he'd be done, she felt so incredibly good.

He cupped her bottom in both hands now, squeezing her soft flesh to stop himself from pushing her all the way down in one mighty shove.

And then, in one delicious eternity, she'd sheathed him completely, clenched down so hard on him that Rudolf feared his cock would blow then and there. He didn't dare move, she felt so exquisite. "God, Portia, that feels amazing."

She let out a sound that sounded like a sob.

Rudolf's eyes flew open.

Tears streamed down Portia's cheeks. "Please, finish this quickly, Dolf. It hurts so!"

He shifted and she cried out – definitely not in pleasure.

"Please," she begged.

He ripped his cock out of her as if he'd burned it, as well he might have. He tucked himself away, swearing at himself for being such a fool. Portia stumbled back, away from him, clutching her skirts to her face as she sobbed into them.

A thin trickle of blood ran down her thigh. Maiden's blood, for Portia was a maiden no more. He'd seen to that, and pretty damn clumsily, too.

Rudolf rose and sat Portia down on his seat. He found a bucket of water and a cloth, cleaning off the blood before she could see it. She cried out as he touched the cloth to her lower lips and Rudolf stopped. He'd dealt with most of the mess.

He dropped the cloth in the bucket and smoothed down Portia's skirts before he took her in his arms. "Shh, it's all right. It's over, it's over. Everything's put away, so you just hold onto me and cry as much as you need to."

God, she felt good in his arms, too. Not quite as good as she did with his cock buried balls deep in her, but nearly. Nearly. Maybe another night, when –

"Please don't make me do that again, Dolf. It hurt so much!" Portia begged.

Maybe never. Rudolf sighed. Who'd have thought he'd have such a clumsy cock? So much for giving his bride a blissful wedding night, or any night, for that matter.

"I'll never do anything to hurt you, Portia. I swear it." He swallowed. "And there's no need for more. The marriage is consummated. You did it. You and everyone on your island are safe. No one can dissolve our marriage now."

He held her as she cried herself out,

murmuring endearments aloud even as he silently cursed himself. He had what he wanted — the wife of his dreams, and all the Southern Isles. So why did victory feel as cold and miserable as stroking his own cock in the rain?

Because that's what he'd be doing, as soon as Portia fell asleep, he told himself, so he wouldn't frighten her with the sight of him again. But in the meantime, he could hold her close and love her, in whatever way she wanted. Because one thing was certain — Rudolf loved his wife, and he'd do anything for her.

Thirty-Four

Portia awoke cold and stiff, like she'd slept on the stone. And with ache between her legs that reminded her…

Rudolf. He'd returned, and she'd married him last night. She'd known he was too big, but she'd done it anyway. And now he was…

Not here.

But it couldn't have been a dream!

She wouldn't have dreamed such a terrible wedding night. Not with Rudolf. Heaven help her, she'd cried herself to sleep in his arms.

No wonder he was gone.

"Good morning, my lady. Do you wish to break your fast?"

Portia sat up. The middle aged priest who'd married them last night stood by the table with his head bowed, as if not daring to look at her.

"Or perhaps you would like to wash?"

Memories of Rudolf's hands on her thighs as he cleaned the most intimate parts of her made her blush. What must he think of her?

She turned suspicious eyes on the priest. "Do you know who I am?"

He smiled. "Of course, Lady Portia. Prince Rudolf was most adamant that I take good care of you until he returns to collect you. He even sent a man with breakfast, so that you might not go hungry. This is more than a poor priest usually sees unless he is invited to a feast." He waved at the table. "I look forward to the feast when they make him High Lord of the Isles, as is his due."

"What?" Her father was High Lord of the Isles, not Rudolf. Rudolf didn't hold lands here. He was a Viken prince. He probably owned an ice floe somewhere in Viken.

"I remember the first council meeting Lord

Angus brought him to. He was the first man ashore, at Lord Angus's behest. I knew it then, but it is even more clear now. Prince Rudolf will rule us well."

Rule? Rudolf? She'd married him, but...

The priest coughed. "Sorry, my lady. I forget that you are a new bride and perhaps have other things on your mind. Many new brides see their husband differently in the light of day after their wedding night. I often have to remind them that if they lay with their husband often enough, he will never stray, and may soon bless her with strong sons or beautiful daughters. I counsel – "

"Where is Rudolf now?" Portia interrupted. She had no need for a lecture on her marital duties from a man who knew little about them.

"I imagine he is with his army, preparing for battle."

"No!"

"I am sure he will return when it is all over. He asked that I keep you safe."

"To blazes with safe. There should be no battle. Good men will die if he continues with this stupidity." She smoothed her dress, retying her laces though she did not need to. "Do you possess a comb?" Heaven help her, but she would not turn up at an army camp with straw in her hair.

"Of course, my lady. No mirror, though, but sometimes I find the collection plate is shiny enough to see myself." He held up the bronze dish, and Portia peered at her reflection.

She cursed as she saw the straw in her hair. Combing the mess would be more painful than coupling with Rudolf last night, but she must. She made short work of it, then thanked the priest for his help.

"Eat, my lady." The priest pushed the bread toward her.

She did not have time, yet she must. Portia seized a piece of bread in one hand and a chunk of cheese in the other. She could eat on the way.

The priest helped her fasten her cloak, and she burst outside into the late morning sun. Nearly noon. She broke into a run.

Thirty-Five

Just before noon, the gate opened to let out a boat bigger than the coracle Rudolf had sent across the loch yesterday. With three armoured men aboard, it was no surprise. Two red heads watched from the tower window, but he knew neither belonged to Portia. No, she was safe with Father Fintan.

He'd ordered his men back from the lake shore, but they still stood to watch. Few wore weapons or armour as he did — this was supposed to be a peace negotiation. Yet the men in the boat looked ready for war.

As the three stepped ashore, one emerged as a definite leader. The castellan who'd ordered the gates open yesterday, Rudolf guessed. Was this Portia's man, Grieve, or someone else?

Rudolf removed his helm so that he might see them better. The men waited until they reached him before they did the same.

"Wolf," the castellan said, with the slightest nod. No, Rudolf did not know this man.

"Rudolf?" one of his companions said, nudging the third man. "We thought you'd buggered off back to Viken!"

"Damhan, Dermot," Rudolf greeted them after a moment's thought. "As you can see, I have returned."

Dermot grinned. "You never were one to run from a fight. I remember the day you arrived, I knocked you down once, but none of the other boys could touch you. You just got up and brushed it off. That's the day you found the Three Little Pigs!" His glee faded as quickly as it had come. "It seems we need your help again."

The castellan hushed him with a glare. "We are not here to ask for help. We are here to negotiate better terms than the ones you offered yesterday." He planted his feet firmly. "We will not hand over Lady Portia."

Won't, or can't? Rudolf wondered. Did they know she was missing?

"Did you ask Lady Portia?" he asked.

The three exchanged glances. Yes, they did, and yet they'd come to negotiate with him, knowing they had nothing he wanted. That took courage.

"What the lady wants is of no consequence. We have sworn an oath to protect her, and we will."

Rudolf snorted. He couldn't help it. "Have you even met Portia?"

This could not be Grieve. No man she spoke of so highly would try to peddle such nonsense.

He toyed with the idea of telling the man he was her husband. Then he'd have his answer, for no man who loved her could hide his pain at hearing that.

The castellan drew his sword. "Have you?"

A collective gasp rose from the men behind him. This was no way to conduct a peace negotiation.

"Sheath that thing, you bloody fool!"

The castellan's eyes widened and he nearly dropped his sword. "Rhona?"

"You lay one finger on this man, Wolf Prince, and our alliance is over!" Rhona said, striding to the man's side.

It seemed the alliance was over already.

Rudolf narrowed his eyes. "Who are you?"

The castellan opened his mouth, but it was Rhona who answered, "He's Grieve Lewisson, my betrothed, and the head of Lady Portia's personal guard." She turned on the man. "Why have the Albans sent you to negotiate?"

Damhan and Dermot burst out laughing. "What Albans? They've all fled, like the cowards they are. Even Mason, when we shut him out. Council Island and the castle belong to Lady Portia."

"No. It belongs to my husband." Portia's voice rang out over the water as she strode along the shore. She wore no shoes and her gown was muddied to the knees, but she walked like a queen. No sign of last night's downpour of tears. Now, she was the storm.

"Lady Portia! Thank the heavens!" Only now did Grieve sheathe his sword. "What happened to you? We thought...my lady, your boots!"

If his men hadn't noticed before, they did now.

But that's what he loved about Portia. Thousands of armed men watching, holding their collective breath, and she merely tossed her head and said, "I'm sure my husband will buy me new ones when he is done here." She laid a possessive hand on his arm, lining up beside him against Rhona and Grieve. She lifted her burning gaze to Rhona, something even Rudolf would have hesitated to do.

Should he warn her? he wondered, but there was no time.

"Lady Rhona," Portia said, offering the woman her cheek. "It is a pleasure. I have heard so much about you."

The two women kissed. A little stiffly, to be sure, for they were strangers, but the power play between them was palpable. The witch who terrified his men capitulated to Portia.

"I look forward to your wedding. You must

sit beside me at the feast to celebrate mine," Portia said. She shot a pointed look at Rudolf. "Of course, you and Grieve must sit with us at the high table. I insist."

"My lady," Grieve said weakly, looking from one woman to the other.

"I hope you mean Rhona, for I'm not yours any more. Protecting me is Prince Rudolf's job now." Her fingers squeezed his arm. "Isla is ours!"

Rudolf's men took up the cry until it echoed around the valley. He wanted to weep, but knew he could not.

The war was over, and Portia was safe. His to protect.

"But what will your father say?" Grieve asked.

Portia didn't flinch. "We will find out when he returns home. In the meantime, my husband will take his place in council."

And not a man among them dared argue. The Lady of Isla had spoken.

Thirty-Six

She smiled through her wedding feast and said all that needed to be said, but inside Portia felt empty. Rudolf would scarcely look at her, and every time she tried to get his attention, she'd find some lord or other already occupying it. He never even noticed when she bade him good night and headed up to her tower room, where she slept alone.

Her days were as dull as when she'd lived in the loft, for she saw so little of him, it was like she had no husband at all. At night, he did not come to her room, or summon her to his, as was his right. Why, she did not even know where he slept, or if he did. The lords never left him alone, and rumours circled, each wilder than the last.

Her men were hers no longer – they'd been pressed into doing things for their lordly fathers. Grieve had been sent to fetch Lord Lewis from Myroy, and there was talk of her father returning. Talk was all it was, until she saw the party riding over the ridge.

The men on lookout saw him, too. "Lord Angus! The banners of Isla!"

Preparations were made to turn the great hall into a council chamber, for there were important matters to be decided. Matters that could only be discussed here on Council Island.

Matters that she had no business being part of. So Portia sat alone in her tower, hoping her father might visit her when the meeting was over.

"There you are!" Lord Angus had other ideas, evidently. He'd aged, and he was now missing part of his ear. "Why are you not at Rudolf's side, in the thick of things, like you used to be?"

Portia managed a small smile. "Every time I see him, he has a lord on each arm, and a line of more men waiting to speak to him. He has no time for me. And there is talk of crowning him as King of the Southern Isles, an office we have never had. They wanted to do it right away, but Lord Lewis insisted we had to wait. For you, he said."

Angus nodded. "Aye, I've heard. It's been a long time coming, but it's for the best. Lord Lewis knew I would not want to miss the coronation of our first king."

"But you're the High Lord of the Isles! I thought he was your friend – why would he want you to answer such an insult in person?"

Angus laughed. "'Tis not an insult. He is a better man than me, and younger, too. I put him forward years ago, before Donald's army came to Isla. Rudolf will make a good king. Do you not think so?" He peered at her. "You chose the man, so surely you must."

"He will make an excellent king," Portia said warmly. She'd seen enough over the last few days to know that, if she did not already.

"But?"

She swallowed. "I thought he had feelings for me, instead of marrying me for my claim, like the others might have. But..."

Angus laughed so hard he nearly fell off the windowsill. "No feelings for you? Rudolf? That man's been in love with you since the day you donned a woman's gown. And I've seen the way you look at him, too. Why else do you think you got a personal guard while he was gone? It was not that he has the strength of ten men, though he is a mighty warrior. Nay, it was because I promised to keep you safe for him until he returned. He would never have left for Viken otherwise."

Portia couldn't seem to close my mouth. "But he has been so distant since we married. He hasn't..." She felt a blush burn her cheeks. "He hasn't summoned me to his chambers at all since our wedding night."

"Ah, he knows you too well, is all. Rudolf knows you are not the sort of woman he can order about. You'd punch him in the nose, or some more tender place, I'd wager, and he knows it. 'Tis up to you to come to him, I'm sure." It was his turn to blush. "Your mother came to me before we were married, and would not take no for an answer. She'd taken some fertility potion a witch had given her, and she wouldn't give herself to any man but me. I think we made you girls that night." He continued, too lost in reflection to realise that Portia had stopped listening.

Rudolf wanted her. Maybe even loved her. If her father could see it…

"Tonight," she said, so softly she didn't think her father heard. "Tonight, I shall bed the king.

Thirty-Seven

Rudolf stepped into the lord's chambers and slammed the door shut. Why in heaven's name had he agreed to be their king?

"Congratulations, my king." Portia stepped out of the shadows. The laces across her breasts had come untied, and her gown was in danger of slipping off her shoulders.

Rudolf's fingers itched to help, though whether to help her out of her gown or touch her breasts as he retied the laces for her, he wasn't sure. He knew now why he'd accepted the questionable honour of a crown. "I did it for you," he said simply. "As long as the Southern Isles are your home, this is where I shall be."

She frowned. "What will the Viken king say?"

"We will find out soon enough. His men sail home on the morrow, and they will tell him all." He waved away her worries. "I have no doubt Reidar wants to see me bend the knee with a crown on my head, so that he may laugh at me. But if he sees you, he will understand." Rudolf seized the crown and dropped it on top of a nearby chest. "Now I know how heavy the thing is, I remember why I never wanted one."

A tear slipped down Portia's cheek. "I don't understand."

Rudolf reached out to wipe it away. He never wanted to see her cry, much less make her do so. "My cousin, King Reidar, gave me leave to take a force across the sea to free the Southern Isles from Donald and his minions because I begged him to. I came for you, Portia. I took the Isles because they are your birthright, and your home, and I will not see anyone take them from you. Everything I have ever done is for you."

More tears fell, but this time Portia wiped them away herself. "Truly?"

"Truly."

She took a deep breath. "Then it is only fitting that I should do something for you, too. You must have an heir, and though it pains me to do it, I must give you one." Off slid the gown, with no help from Rudolf, puddling on the stones at her feet. She stepped out of it like a nymph out of a lake, lifting the hem of her shift.

Rudolf's breath caught in his throat as the filmy linen rose over her head before descending to join its fellow on the floor. "God, you're beautiful," he said hoarsely.

She toed off her stockings as she made her way to the bed. Naked as the day she was born, Portia spread her body across the covers, the greatest gift any woman ever gave a man.

"Please make haste, Dolf. It's cold, and I would prefer to get the painful part over with as quickly as possible." She shuddered, her nipples hardening until Rudolf could look at nothing else. "The pain was hard enough to bear the first time we did this."

Rudolf's brow furrowed. "But I thought it only hurt for a girl's first time. After that, there shouldn't be any pain." He'd never asked a girl about it, but he would never forget that first night Reidar spent with his queen. Her screams hadn't sounded pained.

"Are you sure? My sisters said their first few nights with their husbands were just as painful. It took them a full week before the act became bearable."

Rudolf had no idea – he had no experience with virgins. "You bled that first night. It takes time for a wound to heal, and perhaps that's why it took your sisters a week. It has been a week since we…since I…"

Portia wet her lips. "Can you check for a wound?" She parted her thighs wider.

Rudolf swallowed. He wanted nothing more to be inside her, loving her like Reidar did his queen. But if it meant hurting her… "Of course, I will check." He climbed onto the bed and knelt between her legs. He lifted his gaze to caress the soft skin of her inner thighs, remembering how glorious it had felt to plunge between them. Sliding between those wet lips, gleaming so tantalisingly before him now. Perfect, unbroken skin, with no wound to be seen. He wanted to reach out and stroke her, but he restrained himself. "You look perfect to me."

Portia rose onto her elbows, still frowning. "Did you check inside? It wasn't until you were inside me that I started hurting."

He lifted her legs over his shoulders, parting her lower lips with his fingers. Silky soft and so wet...his manhood grew rigid, but Rudolf fought to ignore it. Still he could not see anything but perfection. "I can't see inside you," he admitted. "But perhaps I can feel for it." He pushed a finger inside her slowly, stroking her inner walls.

She shuddered and clenched around his finger. "Dolf!"

"Did I hurt you?" He repeated the motion, more slowly this time.

She gasped. "No. You didn't hurt me. That feels...delightful."

The more he stroked, the hotter and wetter she became, until she cried out and clenched down hard on his finger as though she would keep it inside her forever.

"More," she sighed.

More…what? Rudolf slid a second finger into her, and started stroking harder. Watching her face this time, as her breathing grew shallow and her eyes closed, he sent her to her climax faster this time. God, what he would give to join her in reaching such a pleasurable peak together, he thought as she arched her back up off the bed and cried his name.

More than anything, he wanted to put more than his fingers inside her.

It would be different this time, he promised himself as he shucked off his clothes. At the slightest sign that he was hurting her, he'd stop, but he needed to be inside her. Now.

He lifted his manhood, poised to thrust deep into her.

"What are you doing?" she asked, fear darkening her eyes.

God help him, he couldn't. Couldn't hurt her again. It would kill him to see her cry and know he'd caused it.

Rudolf rolled onto his back so he lay on the

bed beside her. He ached to impale her. Soon, he promised himself.

"Just like the night we were wed," he said breathlessly. "You sit on top of me, so you can control how deep I go. There is no wound I can feel, inside or out. I won't hurt you, Portia, and this will feel better than my fingers, I promise." He prayed that this last part wouldn't be a lie. He'd never forgive himself.

"If you are sure…" Portia rose up onto her knees and shuffled until she straddled him, one leg on either side of his. "I'm afraid," she admitted.

"Don't be," he said, grabbing his cock in one hand as he rested his other hand on her hip. Gently, he guided the tip of his cock inside her, holding firmly to her hip when she reflexively flinched away. "Now, move down, Portia."

She bit her lip, nodded once, then lowered herself onto him. Inch by inch, he glided into her molten core. God, this woman was heaven. This time, he kept his eyes firmly on her face, alert for any sign of pain. He would not hurt her again while he was lost in his own pleasure.

Her mouth dropped open and her eyes widened, but still she descended, engulfing him so completely that her well-rounded backside rested against his balls.

"It doesn't hurt," she breathed. With agonising slowness, she rose up, and then down his length again. "That feels…good." She raised herself again.

If he left this all up to Portia, her next climax would take all night, so Rudolf took control. He fastened both hands around her hips and met her downward slide with a hard thrust.

She gasped, surprised, but then she smiled. "Again."

With Rudolf's help, she soon rode him in a rocking rhythm that felt every bit as good as he'd imagined it would. And when he felt her clenching around him in her third climax, Rudolf shouted her name as he found his own release.

"I love you, Portia," he gasped out, staring up at her.

Her breasts heaved as she fought to catch her breath, huffing and puffing as though she intended to blow the very castle down around them, but her brilliant smile was telling enough until she managed to say, "I love you, too, Dolf. Can we do that again?"

"Every night," Rudolf promised. "A good husband keeps his wife happy, and I intend to see you happy ever after."

She smiled mischieviously. "The tomorrow you shall take me for a ride, just the two of us, and when we reach a good place to stop, we shall make love all over again."

He stroked her leg, feeling his spirits rising once more. Portia was the only woman for him, now and forever. "Who said we must wait until tomorrow?"

Her eyes widened with alarm, before her expression softened to surprise, and she did some stroking of her own. "Don't make me wait, Dolf."

"Never again," he vowed, and when they came together again, it seemed the very air sang for joy.

About the Author

Demelza Carlton has always loved the ocean, but on her first snorkelling trip she found she was afraid of fish.

She has since swum with sea lions, sharks and sea cucumbers and stood on spray drenched cliffs over a seething sea as a seven-metre cyclonic swell surged in, shattering a shipwreck below.

Demelza now lives in Perth, Western Australia, the shark attack capital of the world.

The *Ocean's Gift* series was her first foray into fiction, followed by her suspense thriller *Nightmares* trilogy. She swears the *Mel Goes to Hell* series ambushed her on a crowded train and wouldn't leave her alone.

Want to know more? You can follow Demelza on Facebook, Twitter, YouTube or her website, Demelza Carlton's Place at:

www.demelzacarlton.com